STORMFLOWER

Keegan & Tristen Kozinski

More books by Keegan and Tristen Kozinski

CHRONICLES OF THE FAR DAWN
THE DARKNESS THE SLEPT

THE CITY OF LOCKED DOORS

SHORT STORIES
NEMESIS
DEATH'S BACKDOOR
A COMPANY OF TRAITORS

Published by Keegan and Tristen Kozinski.
Cover Illustration and Design by Keegan Kozinski
Edited by Tracy Wolf
Beta reader Shannon Doyle
Kozinskibooks.com
Copyright 2025 © Keegan and Tristen Kozinski

ISBN:978-0-9982440-8-2

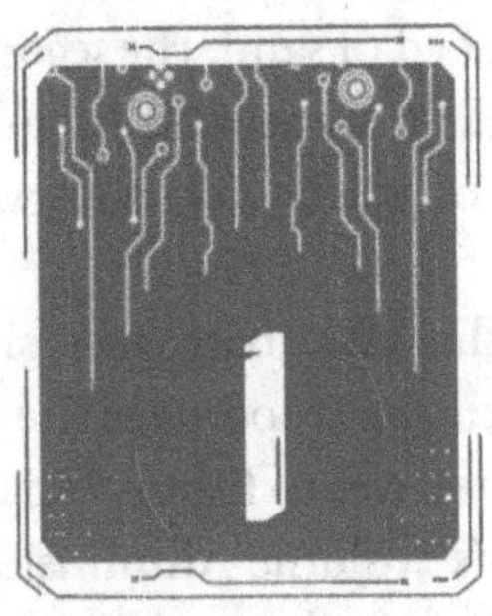

A Visitor from the Other Side of Existence

The sound of the rain surrounded her, thunderous in its deluge and soothing in its rhythm. She lay curled within her blankets, swaddled, warm, bleary in her fresh waking, and cuddling a stuffed fish. The air smelled of lavender, tempting her back to unconsciousness and the cotton candy colors of her dreams. She might have heeded it. Should have heeded it. But she knew her house, knew its silences and sounds and functions, knew it from the tiles underfoot to the floor above she never used.

She sat up, shivering as the blankets fell and the chill of night stung her face. She sat there briefly, legs folded beside her, aching head to foot, and heavy with familiar exhaustion. Then she carefully arranged the stuffed fish—one Sir Charles Henry the Fourth—on his perch atop the pillows and stood. A brush of her thumb across her wrist switched her adaptive suit's functions from sleeping to waking, exchanging the mild sedatives for energy stimulants and nutrients, and causing it to warm. Now fully lucid, she deactivated the ambient music and incense with a snap, the action simultaneously igniting lights along the walls and ceiling, which illuminated the disorganized mess of her room.

She searched for what had woken her but found nothing changed: discarded clothes littered the floor, the main door remained locked and bolted, and her brother's picture still stared at her from behind its black death-shroud. The two crystalline vases remained atop the mantle beside her brother's portrait, one housing a mottled scorpion on a bed of sand, the second a dwarf Stormflower with its roots immersed in water and its ruby leaves incandescent with constant streams of electricity. Nor were any of her alarms activated.

Jade stood from the bed, bare toes sinking into the plush carpets, and walked until she stood near the room's center—beside her settee—and closed her eyes to listen. "Apartment, activate sound dampeners." The rain's volume diminished, leaving only the atmosphere moderator's quiet hum. A second later, she heard it: a persistent muffled beep from her closet.

She strode to the right-hand wall and pressed her palm against it. The door slid into its alcove with a swish and her closet lights activated, revealing a jumble of open drawers, overstuffed containers, and discarded hangers. The beeping intensified, issuing from beneath the heaped junk.

"It can't be, not in a retirement district...." She burrowed into the mound, relocating boxes and ducking beneath what few clean shirts remained until she exposed the back shelves and sleek, grey crate buried there. She shucked the covering mound of faded sweaters and tapped the box's illuminated touch screen, activating first a retinal scan then a voice recognition test.

A few moments of sustained staring followed by a murmured command phrase satisfied the locks, opening the lid to an immediately louder beeping and a pulsing blue light. She rummaged inside, shirking various armaments that were technically illegal for her to possess, and retrieved a thin wristband device with a console screen: a military-grade environment tracker, also illegal. She closed the lid, waited until it resealed itself with a hum, and then stepped from the closet.

The wristband came alive in her hands, its screen displaying a grid of green lines, blue numbers, and a single red dot. She cursed under her breath and slumped onto her vanity chair. *"What the hell is a revenant doing in a retirement district? There's not enough people to attract it here."* She rubbed her eyes, ignoring the wristband's incessant alarm beeps.

The green lines represented the canals and buildings around her, the blue conveyed the water depth and—during storms—the strength of its currents. The red dot marked the revenant. *"Just ignore it,*" she told herself, "*the Purifiers will handle it.*" Except, the nearest patrolling Core would be miles away, minutes out at the soonest. Minutes might seem like a brief span, but a revenant could kill dozens in that span, leeching them of life to sustain and augment itself.

Activated by her prolonged proximity, the vanity mirror issued a prim female voice, "Would you like to change your appearance? It has been two thousand and ninety-six days since you last adjusted your hair color, two thousand and ninety–"

"Power down." The mirror dulled, the lines of text and symbols vanishing to leave only her reflection with her awful strip of pink hair. She raked her fingers through it and stood. Purifiers never patrolled the retirement districts because revenants never material-ized there, preferring the denser populated city-complexes. In a hundred and twenty years of tracking revenants, the governing corporations had recorded only two other instances of revenants venturing into retirement districts.

Her hair—mostly a lovely dark purple—fell back over her face, and she raked it back again. Memories broiled in the recesses of her mind, percolating up between her thoughts: indistinct, monstrous shapes prowling through a dirt-colored miasma, corpses shattered and gushing blood, others drained to husks and floating on a serene ocean, her brother screaming as they dragged— "*No, don't think about it!*" She repressed the memories with a grinding of teeth, and, unlocking the door, strode from her bedroom. "*Just act, it's only one revenant and you've killed hundreds. It's just one.*"

The rest of her apartment lights powered on as she navigated a short hallway cluttered with dusty boxes, illuminating a sparse kitchen, an attached living room of stone tiles flush with strewn pillows, and a slim, corner stair ascending to the second level. She crossed this space without a thought, unlocked and then opened the closet beside her front door. In contrast to her bedroom, this closet maintained strict military organization, with her shoes arranged along the bottom, and her gray military dress coats—emblazoned with the Purifiers' skull insignia—neatly arranged on hangers.

She snatched a small emergency protocols disk from the door organizer and pressed it against her chest. It spun awake with a whir and emerald lines projected through her adaptive suit, tracing the contours of her muscles and connecting to her nervous system. Additional, microscopic needles pricked into her skin all over her body, and the adaptive suit thickened, its exterior hardening into something like armor as new blocks of text appeared on her forearms, citing the suit's improved and added functions. She shoved her bare feet into a pair of advanced combat boots, capable of water skiing and magnetization as well as providing resistance to extreme environments. Only now did she hesitate, gaze falling on an old, faded, button-up coat of red leather, covered nearly head to toe in pockets of all shapes and sizes, some of which were locked. Some of these were locked by keys, others by fingerprint scans, a few by blood tests, and three were hidden. Finally, carefully, she donned it, sliding into the too-large sleeves and pressing her nose against the collar to inhale her brother's lingering scent. *"You can do this."* Then she grabbed a pair of training Siphons and attached them to the back of her adaptive suit. "Power up." The dull metal bars warmed against her back and a steady, if faint, white brilliance ignited within them. They were poor tools for fighting revenants, only ever intended to prepare Purifier recruits for true Siphons, but Jade's Siphon was hidden somewhere distant where it could neither be hunted nor found by accident. This thought stirred a different nightmare, but she quelled it before the memories could surface. Those memories were dangerous.

She stood there for a moment longer, breathing slow and deep to soothe her thundering heart, counting the pace of her breaths until the panic of her mind calmed. Then she steeled herself, spun on a heel and strode to her apartment's exterior wall. A patio door occupied most of the surface area, offering her a view of the storm outside. Rain assailed the canal outside her apartment in sheets, sometimes so thick it obscured the opposite complex. Jade opened the door with a press of her hand and emerged onto a patio enclosed in transparent duraglau walls, constructed high enough to be above the canal even during flood seasons. This was an uncommon luxury, ocean level housing was reserved almost entirely for retirement districts, which were built on the rare embankments or reefs that rose near enough to the surface to be considered shallow.

Ordinarily placid and knee-deep, the water rushed beneath her, so agitated by the rain and squalling winds it almost overflowed the complex's stilts. She yanked her hood up and retracted the patio's central door with another tap. Rain immediately besieged her, dousing her coat and the patio's interior before spiraling down the drain lines.

She swung out, clutching the support railing as she plunged into the frigid, waist-deep water with a stifled groan. Her adaptive suit warmed further in response, insulating her as she closed the patio door, which blinked once with internal light and turned opaque.

She wiped the water from her eyes with an unspoken curse at having forgotten her goggles and snapped her heels together. Her boots' water-skates activated with a jolt, heat spreading as their internal mechanisms worked, and propelled her from the water to its turbulent surface, stabilized by thrumming, green energy projectors.

She leaned into the wind and shoved off, skating over the ocean's surface between raised apartment complexes towards the revenant's last displayed location. The wristband beeped and sparked a signal against her right hand, directing her. She turned down the corresponding river-alley, ignoring the fluorescent one-way sign, and zipped two blocks before taking a left onto another main canal.

Hovering illumination-bots patrolled overhead, offering meager clarity to her surroundings. Beyond them, however, a golden radiance shone in the canal, almost blinding in the dark. She pushed her legs harder, streaking through parked skimmers and circumventing aquatic flora, their usually soaring stalks now lying flat on the ocean surface from the wind.

The radiance vanished abruptly, provoking a desperate curse and launching her into a full sprint over the last hundred feet.

An indistinct human shriek pierced the rain as she skidded to a halt outside the melted ruins of a patio, its walls still oozing and cherry red from the revenant's ingress. She hauled herself inside, steam sizzling off her suit's gloves as she scrambled into the attached apartment over steaming duraglau. The revenant's radiance blazed inside the living room, almost masking the shapes of a huddled man and the revenant itself: this one long-bodied and vaguely insectoid with a wide-eyed, expressionless, and pale human face.

It spun at her appearance, and the memories flashed across her mental eye: a thousand screaming horrors slashing, biting, and stabbing at her insubstantial body, crawling through and around her. She couldn't see where she was, she couldn't find the exit, where was her brother; he'd been screaming her name just a moment ago. She cast desperately about for him, but all was dark and the rain was drowning everywhere she looked. She tried to raise her HUD to pierce the dark and the deluge, but her fingers touched the bare skin of her face and jarred her from the memory. She'd almost always worn a helmet back then, even during the brief interludes between exterminations or hunts.

The revenant, a creature of radiant light wreathed in tattered fabric, blared a furious note and glided toward Jade, effortlessly surmounting an overturned table on a cavalcade of human hands and arms.

She retreated, luring it toward the canal and away from the elderly man cowering in the apartment. Activated by the revenant's proximity her earpiece clicked on, and a passionless, inhuman voice recited information into her ear, "Spirit-level seven, classified as a first-tier revenant. Low threat."

Jade forced a shuddering exhale and detached the training Siphons from her back. They buzzed in her hands and then punctured her skin with minute needles, linking their programming to the implants in her hands. The Siphons blazed alight and deconstructed entirely into gaseous energy, one orange and the other amber.

The revenant flared in response, issuing another furious musical note.

Jade retreated backward through the ruined patio and into the canal, her implanted lenses shading reactively to the creature's brilliance. It pursued, scuttling out onto the patio and then submerging up to its elbows in the canal. "That's it." She drifted further back. The Siphons' energies coalesced and solidified in her hands: one into a thin serrated blade of energy and the other into a tether with two attached stakes, both their respective energies' hue. This was a training Siphon's one advantage over a true Siphon, the ability to be transformed at will into near any weapon. Unfortunately, that necessitated the neural link, which in turn risked a vicious backlash should the training Siphon break while linked.

The revenant shot forward with a crude musical note, reaching for her with two of its many hands.

She leapt back, projecting herself into a bound with a burst of energy from her boots and twisting midair to land with her feet against the opposite building's patio walls. The force of her collision jarred her boots, provoking their reassessment protocols and instigating their conversion from water-skates to magnetized. They fastened onto the strips of metal buried in the duraglau, simultaneously activating the exoskeleton and force emitters in her adaptive suit to support her against the planet's gravity.

The revenant smashed against the wall just beneath her, and she lunged aside, skating along the metal strips to plant the first stake in the duraglau. The revenant pursued, half-crawling its sinuous body up the wall. She dove, ducked beneath its groping swipe, twisted up and dashed back across the building while impaling the revenant's hand with the serrated Siphon blade and leaving it there.

It shrieked a terrible note and reeled back, its vibrant essence bursting in the air and dissipating. The serrated Siphon brightened, converting from amber to gold as it drank the revenant's essence. A true Siphon would have consumed the energy, a training Siphon could only store and vent it.

The revenant shrieked again and leapt after her.

She launched into a dash up the patio front, yanked the string taught and vaulted, soaring over the pursuing revenant, to land back on the water and drag the cord down across its shoulders. Her water-skates snapped on with a disgruntled cough but kept her afloat. The revenant splashed down after her, and she sprinted past and around it, dragging the cord tight against its limbs. It flailed after her, hands and tail lashing wildly, and its mouth snapping.

She cut back across it, completing the first loop and wrapping the cord tighter as she vaulted from the water to the edifice and retraced her steps in another loop. Back and forth she leapt, from water to patio to water, ducking and diving through the revenant's arms and around its body. Her boots protested with every conversion, but she knew their tolerance and the exact amount she could push them.

Enraged by her ceaseless evasion, the revenant drew itself up and spat golden energy into her path. She cursed and veered up the adjacent building, hurling herself aside, but one of its many hands struck out and clipped her right boot as she leapt.

Pain tore through her foot, and the circuits in her boot failed, disconnecting from the wall and dumping her into the canal. She spun beneath the surface, dug her uninjured foot in the mud and propelled herself forward just before the revenant stabbed one of its multitudinous limbs into her previous location. She surfaced and yanked the tether Siphon taut while retracting the string. It snapped rigid, searing into the revenant's body and snaring it in the web she had woven. The revenant howled and lashed at her, but its brilliance was already dimming, guzzled by the web of the tether Siphon and expelled in streams of dense mist from the planted stake.

With the second stake still clutched in her hands, she shuffled sideways through the water, ginger on her injured foot, until she could plant the other stake in the wall.

The revenant began to sag, its once strident music becoming thin and stuttering. It still struggled feebly, but the tether Siphon held it fast.

She waded back toward the invaded apartment and hauled herself onto its patio. The elderly man still cowered in the wreckage of an olive-colored couch, his hands pressed against his ears as he whispered a frantic torrent of words, "... a revenant and a woman out of nowhere...."

Jade shuffled toward him and spoke slowly lest her voice quiver, "Hey, Mr."

He jerked and refocused on her. "Is it gone?"

"Yes. Is there anybody hurt? Anyone else here?"

He shook his head.

She nodded and sank into a nearby chair, letting her head fall back. Even as she closed her eyes to rest, however, a memory reared: someone's gore-stained hands tearing at her coat, the mouth—half melted away—open and shrieking as they struggled to stay afloat in the blood-stained water.

She sank deeper into the chair, wrapping herself in the coat and beginning to count her breaths. The man's petrified stare reverted to the outside and a sobbing whimper crawled from him. It should not have; the revenant would have withered in death. A tingling cold needled her spine, pulling her gaze up. "What is-" Her voice died mid-utterance, silenced by the spectacle of a new revenant crouched over and regarding the remnants of the first.

She surged to her feet, shoving the man toward the front door with a hiss, "Run!" And as he fled, she turned and crept along the wall toward the patio.

Outside, the new revenant towered, an immense shrouded mass swathed in black fabric and steaming in the rain, its two eyes radiant amidst the shadows.

She scanned her surroundings, desperate for a weapon of any sort, and found nothing. Her Siphons—left to finish draining the first revenant—either glowed beneath the water's surface or hung from the wall a short distance ahead, but she could not reach them without alerting the new revenant. She inhaled a deep breath, slipped into and beneath the water and kicked off the patio's stilts. A retired, and arguably senile, Purifier lived nearby. She knew the codes to his apartment from a previous disastrous party and knew he retained possession of his Siphon. She needed to hurry though. The new revenant had already consumed most of its predecessor's remaining essence.

Her earpiece hummed on as she submerged, "Spirit-level zero, classified as a tier-zero revenant."

She stopped mid-motion and surfaced. "Rescan."

"No spirit signature."

Jade tapped her earpiece where it clasped the top of her ear and hissed, "I saw its essence."

"No spirit signature."

She cursed under her breath and started to submerge again, then stopped with a low groan before standing to face the revenant.

It loomed over her in a crouch, a humanoid creature with red hair and streaked skin. Its head cocked to the side as she stared up at it. "Why are you afraid?"

She almost buckled in shock at the revenant's words. She tried to muster her voice, to discard her stupefaction and strike, or to at least answer the revenant but she couldn't. She saw a different image, that of her brother staring back at her, leering from a shroud of brown mists, laughing as he spoke. She reeled back, bile rising in her throat, and flailed at the memory; but it stayed leering at her, the lips moving as a twisted, broken hand reached for her. She fell and cold canal water crashed over her shoulders and head, shocking her from the memory.

The revenant settled back, pulling her gaze up with its eyes until she could see naught but the sky and its luminous, questioning gaze. She finally found her voice and spoke, struggling to shout over the storm, "Who are you?"

"I have yet to decide on a name." He continued to regard her, his eyes full of too much intelligence, too much life.

She shivered and moved back from the creature, teeth baring in a snarl as she stood again.

The creature straightened, rising to almost four times her height. "I see I distress you. I will leave." And so saying, it turned from her and glided away, soundless beneath the rain's volume. She watched it depart—watched until it disappeared—then collapsed to her knees and clutched her chest, panting. The current flowed past at chest height, pulling at her, but she could barely feel it, barely breathe. She fastened every thought she had on her breaths, slowing them, counting them.

Calm gradually returned to her, requiring several minutes before she roused herself and staggered back to her seat in the wrecked apartment. The waking nightmares began to fade from her mind, subdued by calming agents from her suit, allowing her to think and control her shudders. The Purifier Corporation hunted revenants, that's who the man would have called, and they would come. So she needed to wait because they needed to know what she had just encountered.

They announced their arrival with the thrum of hovercraft engines and a flood of blinding searchlight beams sweeping down the canal. She heard a thud on the apartment complex roof as another long, personnel aircraft landed on the opposite complex. Doors opened along its flank and unleashed a tide of officials and assistants in gray military uniforms. They immediately scattered, patrolling the site and searching for injured, while others cordoned off the area with walls of waist-high projected yellow light. As more floodlights activated along the canal, painting the whole of her view silver, residents began parting the curtains of their windows in confusion.

A Core of Purifiers—the typical four operatives—in colorless energy-plate armor dropped from a gunship and spread through the district in search of other revenants. One of them, the leader by the silver bars on her forearms, assessed the first creature's remnants for a short while before crossing the canal to intrude on the medic and clerk attending Jade.

"You the one who contacted us?" she asked, assessing Jade's bedraggled state with evident disdain. A green halo glowed on the iris of the woman's lenses, recording the interview and most likely transmitting it to the Purifier Corporation's database, where Jade's face would have initiated a sequence of alerts if higher authorities weren't already on their way.

"No"—Jade jabbed a thumb at the front door without lifting her head from the back of the chair or opening her eyes—"he went that way a couple minutes back."

The Purifier frowned. "Then what are you doing here?"

"Just passing through."

"At this hour?"

"Yep."

The Purifier stifled a low growl and her Siphon—a true Siphon—darkened in its holster at her side. "May I have your name please, miss?"

Jade cracked open an eye, regarded the woman, and then tapped the medic tending to her leg. "That's enough, you can go now."

"But, miss, I haven't finished applying the stimulants-"

"Don't worry about it. I'm fine."

The medic glanced from Jade to the Purifier, then left.

The Purifier seethed, her Siphon flashing a venomous red. "Will you answer me or-"

"That will suffice, Sergeant Mavis."

The Purifier snapped to attention and spun with a salute. "Yes, Prime March."

The new arrival circumvented the Purifier and indicated the patio. "Leave us, sergeant, and take the others with you."

"Yes, Prime March." She departed, rounding up the inspectors, clerks, and police officials as she went.

The man, a member of the Purifiers' Sovereign Cores, reverted his attention to Jade, assessing her as the apartment emptied. For her part, Jade disinterestedly regarded his pale helmet and stiff gray suit —deceptively soft-looking for the quality of armor it actually was—

then returned her head to its reclined position. She resumed her breathing exercises, trying to ignore that this man could return her to active Purifier duty with a word and a signature.

Prime March delayed until the last assistants vacated the premise before addressing her, "I thought you had retired?"

"I am; I just happened to be passing by."

"Well, at least you're consistent." A green halo brightened the lens in his right eye, likely playing back her brief interview with Sergeant Mavis or the medic. "You provided little to no information on the revenant and distanced yourself from the whole act, claiming to have been 'just passing by' when a vigilante killed the creature."

"And what? You don't believe me? I'm hurt." She dragged herself onto her aching leg with a groan. "The vigilante really was quite attractive too, had a nice scar across one of her eyes." She drew a line diagonally across her eye to illustrate, then stepped closer and softly added, "B.S. aside, there's something you should know, another revenant–"

Prime March spun abruptly about and moved to the patio, barking orders that catalyzed those assembled outside into frenzied action.

Jade rubbed her brow. "Prime March ... Prime March." He ignored her, too preoccupied with excising this new revenant to heed her steadily louder addresses. Finally, nerves frayed to razor's edge by the evening's ordeal, she barked, "Theeran, listen to me!"

His commands trailed off, "What is it, Jade?"

"The revenant spoke."

He froze, a single second of deathlike stillness as his mind recalibrated. "Are you certain?"

"Yes."

He tapped his earpiece. "Contact active Purifiers in the area." He waited, then spoke again, "You have new orders, return to the site of first contact immediately. Out." His eyes flicked back to her while his hand implemented a particular pattern on his earpiece. "Do you have a description?"

"Red hair, big, humanoid, and no spirit signature."

The last detail elicited a grimace but nothing more. "Thank you. Yes, Serras, rendezvous at my coordinates immediately. Yes, I know you have a date. No, the perfection of his physical appearance does not sway me. Just get over here; we have a speaking revenant. Good; red hair ..."

Jade trudged past him and dropped into the water. Someone offered her a ride on their skimmer, but she declined and clambered into one of the small rentals docked in a river-alley further along. The door slid shut behind her and the opaque roof cleared to bestow a view of clouded but now dry skies. She sank into the plush chair, which immediately warmed against her body, and brushed her wrist along the console.

"Welcome, please state or input your destination."

She typed her address into the console and then slowly stripped off her coat as the skimmer's low, angular body slipped out into the main canal. The coat's old fabric boasted enough scars, rips, and patches to bespeak several lifetimes. She turned it in her hands, every new scar a small prick in her heart. She could not fix it, there was no one to teach her how. It had been her brother's coat and their mother's before him and so on through generations of their family.

She flipped it front-wise and stroked the lovely gold buttons, each one emblazoned with a creature from myth. One, two, three.... She stopped and counted them again. One, two, three....

"God dammit!" Jade leaned over the coat, pressing her forehead against it.

She had lost a button.

She hugged the coat against her chest and brought her legs up. "I'm sorry," she whispered. "I'm trying, Ilin. I promise, I really am. Please, I'm sorry." But still, his eyes stared at her, full of pain and disappointment as she added one more failure to her monumental list. She hadn't saved him. She couldn't even protect his coat.

The Artificial Conception

Some Days before...

To experience death was to perceive the breadth of eternity in the confines of a single thought. To reawaken from this purity of being, to reemerge from the trackless current of death, was to fall from that existence and forget everything one had known and experienced while within it. Still, the soul willingly roused from death and relinquished eternity, waking to the world of Aeria and renewed life.

It spent a moment exploring itself, measuring the extent of its being, perusing the memories of its past half-lives and compiling all the knowledge that had awaited it upon birth. As it did so, *Aeria* gradually materialized to its perception, manifesting as a cracked, slender corridor of worked stone blanketed in the muddy brown mist called *La Neblina*. Partitions of aged, yellowing paper defined the corridor, stretched between slim wooden poles and painted with exquisite, impressionistic images in black that shifted as if alive.

All of this—everything it perceived—the *soul* should have recognized and known intimately for it had been traveling these corridors until the moment of its birth. Yet, it did not. The iconography on the partitions had changed, something only specific intent could achieve, and there were new scraps of tattered fabric littering the floor. These were not natural changes. For the *soul* to have no memories of these events, they would have had to occur while it emerged from death, but that was a lapse of minutes, too brief for something to have stumbled upon it, modified its environs on a whim, and then left.

No, its birth had been anticipated, mayhap even orchestrated. Something had a purpose for it. But why then weren't they here, waiting for it?

The *soul* completed its manifestation into the physical world, its consciousness materializing as wisps of transparent, drifting energy without nucleus or source: *luce*. These wisps the *soul* accumulated into a spherical shape before directing its attention, unconstrained by nonexistent sensory organs, to the altered partition and the stark images painted there.

These images began as a long-feathered crane streaking across the paper, spinning and shedding feathers in its wake. Where these feathers fell, they became pools of ink—like footsteps marking its passage. From these pools crawled a menagerie of miraculous beings, their forms staining the paper with rivulets of ink before transforming simultaneously into replicas of the same empyreal lion. All of these lions turned to look upon the *soul* in synchronized motion and, without breaking their stare, began to walk in place. The unpainted space beneath their feet became swelling waters over which they walked, ripples arching from their steps. Still walking in place, the lions stretched and changed, growing taller as they settled onto hind limbs, becoming men as varied as the lions were identical without once averting their eyes or ceasing to walk. Their steps carried them to an empty city upon the water, above which blazed a black sun. The men raised a hand, fingers becoming claws; and the sun scattered, unraveling into a deluge of black flame that fell to the cities and ignited their windows with light. There the iconography paused, the light dimming while the men stared at the *soul* in silent demand.

The *soul* slowly recoiled, recognizing its existence had been orchestrated for a purpose, and that purpose bespoke something terrible. Even so, it felt the urge to fulfill that intent, a sense of rightness and instinct compelling it forward, and yet it knew this sensation was aberrant. *Souls* were not born with instinct and compulsions; they were born with all the memories of their previous half-lives and a single ability unique to them, something shaped by their essential nature. Except, the *soul* could already feel a second ability coded into its essence, something roughly spliced into place and itching with discord because of it, a connection to read and manipulate the *luce* of other *souls*. It would need to transform and choose a physical shape to allay the itch. The alien instinct urged this as well, but in this instance the *soul* did not disagree. It needed a physical form to traverse *Aeria*; and if it did not move, those manipulating it would inevitably find it. So, it began shaping itself, condensing the raw energy of its essence into solid matter.

The *soul* breathed and formed lungs. A heart emerged in the center of its form and began to beat, pushing blood through veins and feeding muscles. It stretched taller, becoming humanoid and inhaling the damp air. Bones formed, followed by organs and nerves. It spread long fingers, tipped with retractable claws, and trailed them through *La Neblina,* feeling its chill. Skin streamed from its chest and across its arms and legs, followed by horizontal streaks of black and blue fur. It reared back a proud head, and a crimson mane sprouted from its skull.

The *soul* settled onto broad haunches, its shape undeniably inspired by the lion on the wall, but it was satisfied with the form because, compelled by instinct or not, it had found the lion's form appealing.

A soft flittering drew its attention to the tatters of black cloth that littered its surroundings, fluttering in stale drafts from cracks in the floor and ceiling. As it observed this fabric, the *soul* remembered the final moments of its half-life existences as *vestiges*. It recalled listlessly wandering the infinite catacombs of *Palacio*—the labyrinth of stone rooms it currently inhabited—of consuming *vestiges* before being consumed in turn. The memories of these insentient, emotionless existences encompassed a thousand different lives before culminating in the birth of a consciousness beyond base instinct: a *soul*. And yet, in all those lives there existed no memory of something interfering with it. But there was an inconsistency, a lifetime and energy it possessed but could not remember.

The *soul* robed itself in the tatters not because it felt shame in nudity, but because its memories always showed it being clothed. This done, it ventured along the corridor, gliding effortlessly over a crumbling floor choked with sprawling roots that felt warm to the touch. These roots were *Arbol*, a living organism that was vital to and pervaded all of *Aeria*, though they sprouted from no immense tree or plant. As the *soul* progressed—ever vigilant for signs of other life—a menagerie of painted creatures and flora trailed it along the partitions, animated and attracted by its *luce*, like moths to flame.

The *soul* ascended, sometimes vaulting through fissures in the ceiling, and other times scaling *Arbol's* bulkier roots up vacant shafts through dozens of floors. Small rooms and endless corridors transitioned to vast chambers, mausoleums, and vacant throne rooms. These in turn concluded at a wide stair leading to a final ceiling. The *soul* stilled on the first step, vibrant gold eyes drifting to the left-hand partition where all but one black silhouette stood motionless—a smoldering phoenix orbiting a circle of illuminated paper.

The *soul* dismounted the stair and navigated around it to an alcove behind a screen of *Arbol's* roots. Past those it discovered an archway into a secondary room inhabited solely by an ancient, lightless chandelier of pale stone. *La Neblina* swirled along the room's corners and alcoves but refused to trespass on the open space because there, hanging from the chandelier by a wispy green vine, dangled an orb of *luce*.

The *soul* crept into the *luce's* fiery luminescence and extended its senses, scouring the room for other *souls* without result. It relaxed muscles that had tensed against potential adversaries and approached the chandelier. Once there, it plucked the orb and swallowed it whole. Life flooded its being, deepening its reservoir of energy and strengthening its spirit. Overhead the green vine crumpled to dust, and *La Neblina*, no longer denied by the raw, unadulterated *luce*, billowed inward through the cracks and doorways.

The *soul* returned to the stairway and was greeted by a chill breeze sweeping away *Palacio's* dull warmth. The *soul* lengthened its stride, mounting one of *Arbol's* thicker roots to avoid the cracked stairs. Every step soothed its feet with warmth, but the air turned icy as the *soul* emerged into the exterior world, stepping into a vast openness beneath a trackless sky. There, the world transformed to a city of soaring stone edifices and waterways drowning in the drifting fathoms of *La Neblina*, all of it enwrapped in *Arbol's* roots. This was *Mar*, the surface of *Aeria* just as *Palacio* was the infinite labyrinth below.

The *soul* quickly bent low and began gathering scraps of drifting fabric from the cobbled street, wrapping them about its eyes to obscure the empyreal glow of its *luce* lest it attract a starving *soul*.

Satisfied with its precautions, the *soul* lowered itself to the cobbled road and crept through the city on all fours, navigating by scent and hearing. Grit scraped under its feet and desiccated leaves skittered past, tumbling through the open doors of towers and mansions as a stone merry-go-round creaked and slowly spun. It reached a crossroads in the city where the street had collapsed into *Palacio*, allowing a massive *Arbol* root to sprout skyward from the labyrinth below. The *soul* vaulted onto the pale, knotted bark, and scaled to its arching zenith, high above the street. There it crouched low and probed outward, blind from the cloth and *La Neblina* but infinitesimally aware of all that surrounded it. It expanded its consciousness, scrounging *Mar's* every crevice for a flicker of *luce*.

It waited for a span of days, motionless and unblinking, close enough to the place of its birth to notice if anything came searching, but far enough that it would likely go unremarked upon. *La Neblina* swirled around it with its inscrutable tides, sometimes rising miles high, and at others sinking until it barely covered the cobbles. *Oscuras*—little cloth dolls with heads of tiny, flameless lanterns—stumbled upon the *soul* and, their *luce* exhausted, huddled themselves against its feet and limbs. Their lights gradually rekindled as they clung to it, and then they trundled about their way, little metal heads bouncing and clinking cheerfully. They tended the natural *luce*—the life that *souls* depended upon—that accumulated in *Aeria*; and in turn, *souls* kindled them with *luce* they had absorbed and diluted, for raw *luce* would shatter their lanterns. Throughout all of this, the foreign instinct—the urge—persisted, gnawing at the *soul* to follow *La Neblina's* flow and find those who had made it. It could feel them somewhere out in the distance, a knot of entwined souls; or rather it knew they were there, like the phantom of a memory. But the lure was feeble and, though insistent, exerted no thrall for now.

Finally, a flash of warmth skittered through a corner of its senses: a *vestige*, an insensate fragment of life. The *soul* exploded forward, shucking the newly attached *Oscuras*, and crossed an expanse of miles in a beat of its heart, vacating the cityscape for a shattered plain of crags and roots.

The *vestige* sensed its approach but could only tighten its muscles to leap before the *soul* crashed into and pinned it against a jutting scarp. The *vestige* thrashed, not for fear of dying—for it lacked a true soul—but from simple instinct. Remorseless, the *soul* rent the *vestige's* form with a swift but detached cut, and consumed its *luce*. New memories suffused it in a rush, filling it with all the *vestige* had seen as well as a sensation of burgeoning as its own being expanded. With that burgeoning came satiation, a fullness of being that led to a perilous lethargy. It would need time to digest the new memories and reconcile them with the old, thus, the *soul* retired across *Mar's* cobbled and ruptured floor to recline beneath the eaves of a wide, arching root. Even as it did, however, a new consciousness intruded on its perception as if from nowhere, appearing alarmingly close for all the *soul's* constant vigil.

This new *soul* materialized from *La Neblina* moments later, slinking down the root's side with a susurration of indistinguishable speech. It dropped with a swish of fabric and scarce a thud, straightening to an easy, human posture, its eyes blazing with sufficient *luce* that *La Neblina* receded from its face and betrayed its power. That it was of small stature meant nothing, for *souls* could shape and alter themselves at will within *Aeria*. It could have just as easily arranged itself to the size of a mountain with the *luce* it possessed.

This new *soul* exhaled a slow breath of golden light, the particles lingering briefly—like the ejected embers of an open flame—on the cloth swaddling its beaked visage. "Greetings, newborn." It did not speak with words or sounds, or in any language divined by a living species. It conveyed pure meaning into the *soul's* mind, and in that meaning there was recognition: this *soul* knew it.

The *soul* responded in the same mental fashion, "What is your name?"

"I am Koin. Have you chosen a name?" Again, there was recognition, but also curiosity.

"I have not. What brought you here?"

"I sensed the presence of a *vestige,* but it appears you move quick for a newborn."

"Why do you linger?"

"Because you are a new *soul* and interest me."

"You do not interest me." The *soul* moved to depart, knowing this Koin was not one of its creators but concerned with its recognition and subtlety regardless.

"Wait."

The *soul* stalled. "Why?"

"Because I wish to offer you a place and a name...." Koin glided forward, effortlessly navigating the ruptured cobbles and roots on stilted carapace legs. "An infinite reservoir of *luce* and the protection of an *Extranjerra*." He swept around the *soul* and perched on a collection of roots, hands clicking as they undulated and swirled through *La Neblina*.

"I have no need of your name or the belonging you offer."

"I do not ask that you decide now, only that you accompany me and witness for yourself what I offer."

"Is the journey long?"

"No, just a sliver of time, and effortless."

The *soul* hesitated. It did not fear Koin as such, but it distrusted his intent because Koin's essence throbbed with unspoken avarice and a voracious hunger he concealed. Nonetheless, Koin possessed knowledge it wanted. "I will accompany you."

"Good." Koin lifted its beaked head and issued an echoing call, introducing first a moment of pregnant expectation, then receiving an answer in the dull, labored beat of cumbersome wings. The *soul* raised its gaze to the heavens and extended its consciousness. A leviathan swept into its perception with another wingbeat, causing *La Neblina* to coil and eddy around its body. The leviathan—a corporal, barely sentient denizen of *Aeria* that survived without *luce* —appeared from *La Neblina*, its dark undersides sleek and legless. It descended, circling until it hovered about a hundred feet over the two *souls*. It uttered a metallic call and lowered a sinuous tail for them.

Koin mounted it without hesitation and beckoned the *soul* to follow. They climbed to the leviathan's vast back and sat in the crook between its wings and shoulders, Koin in front and the *soul* behind. From atop the leviathan's head a *ralampa*, another of *Aeria's* natural denizens, glanced back at them. It was humanoid, with a body of hollow wire framing wrapped in faded cloth that squeaked when it moved. A dusky orb filled its midsection, the interior glowing dully with *luce* and swirling with captured mist. It wore a hard, funnel-like cap of metal upon its square head and concealed its face in layered wrappings that permitted only two beams of orange light to emerge. These beams skimmed over the *soul*, then returned to the front. The leviathan arched, and its wings swept down with a low groaning call that shuddered all through its length. It rose higher, *La Neblina* billowing away from it with every wingbeat to expose the ruptured ground far below. It groaned again and turned to follow *La Neblina's* tide.

The *soul* refocused on Koin. "Where do you take me?"

"To *Revenance*: a communion place for *souls* under the dominion of my *Extranjerra*."

"A city?"

"Of sorts." A flicker of deceit slithered through Koin's essence, igniting the *soul's* curiosity. The *soul* manipulated its own essence, consuming a spark of *luce* to project an illusion of wrath and lethal purpose within its own essence and direct it toward Koin. Koin demonstrated no reaction, either unperturbed by the *soul's* murderous intent or ignorant of it. The *soul* relinquished its deception, confident Koin could not read essences as it did, and focused on the emotions afflicting Koin's spirit: want, excitement, and fear. It attempted to parse meaning from their presence without success but persisted in this endeavor, heedless of the decaying edifices soaring skyward all around them.

Eventually, Koin disrupted the rustling quiet of *La Neblina* and the beat of the leviathan's wings, "Look, newborn, and see *Revenance*. We have arrived."

The *soul* shifted its focus at its companion's prompt and observed the resplendent false glory of *Revenance*. It occupied a sunken cavity in *Mar*, smothered with *Arbol's* roots beneath a sky choked by smaller leviathans, many burdened with itinerant *souls*, all of it aglow with hollow *luce*: a vivid, but lifeless brilliance bereft of everything but its basest physical attribute. *La Neblina* swirled around the pit's exterior in a soaring wall as if denied entrance, filling the air with a dull clatter as it struck and flowed through the surrounding edifice.

"Is it not beautiful?"

"No, it is not." The *soul* extended its senses, scouring *Revenance* for a flicker of the *Extranjerra* that presided over it.

The being's consciousness responded and ensnared the *soul's* mind in its cacophonous depths. "Who are—? You!" And again there was that same recognition, but now charged with fury and..., triumph? But also a multitude of lesser emotions, too many to count and many conflicting, as if it were a crowd of minds.

"None of your concern." The *soul* instantly extricated its consciousness, eluding the *Extranjerra's* grasping attempts to recapture it.

Koin shuddered and whirled on the *soul*, his essence and voice sharp with a frightened pitch. "What did you say?"

The *soul* straightened on the leviathan's back. Its consciousness still echoed with the *Extranjerra's* anger and, more prominently, its rapacious desire. Both the *Extranjerra* and Koin desired something of it, a desire they wished concealed, but neither were they its creators. The *soul* approached the leviathan's shoulder and, stripping the fold from its eyes, peered through *La Neblina* at *Revenance*.

Koin pursued it to the precipice. "Foolish newborn, why did you anger her?" His meaning echoed with rage, but his essence cowered with mounting desperation. He snatched a knot of the *soul's* wraps, but the *soul* brushed his arm aside. It still desired Koin's knowledge, but the *Extranjerra* was too overpowering a force to contend with and made the pursuit of that knowledge untenable. Even now, the vastness of the *Extranjerra's* consciousness swelled through all of *Revenance*, sending the native *Aerians*—in all their myriad, cloth-bound forms—into scattered flight from some unknown fear.

"I no longer possess any interest in your promises," the *soul* replied. "Do not follow me." It stepped off the leviathan and plummeted. Koin screamed a mental and physical howl, and plunged after it, *luce* billowing within its form as it transformed. Two great wings split from his back, spread wide and yanked his wild fall to a controlled descent.

The *soul* paid its pursuer no heed and simply twisted midair, landing in a concussive crouch atop one of *Arbol's* highest roots. It dug its fingers into the bark and scraped, exposing the sapphire liquid coursing within.

All around it, *Revenance* trembled, fissures splitting the ground in spiderweb cracks that blazed with the *Extranjerra's* radiance. She was emerging.

Koin landed, with a thud, opposite the *soul* and lunged to grasp its throat. "You will not leave this world. I will not allow it!" His essence seethed with fear and his grip tightened, burrowing his fingers into the *soul's* throat. *Luce* bled out, coating Koin's fingers before dissipating into the air.

The *soul* wrenched Koin's hands free and the *luce* ceased bleeding, its skin healing. "You cannot hold me."

Luce erupted from Koin as his form mutated anew, skin hardening to a substance like rock and nails lengthening into talons. "But I can delay you."

The *soul* knew he spoke truth; Koin possessed sufficient *luce* to combat and restrain the *soul* until the *Extranjerra* surfaced; whereupon the *soul* would be ensnared and either consumed or imprisoned to fulfill whatever these two desired of it.

Koin's terrified essence flashed across its consciousness again, cultivating a thought. The *soul* reached up, pressed a hand against Koin's midsection and inhaled, drinking the *luce* from Koin's essence.

Koin hissed and recoiled, clutching his midsection. "What did you do?"

"It seems I do not need to kill your mind before consuming your *luce*." The *soul* exhaled its breath and a thread of stolen *luce* escaped. Dropping its hand, the *soul* stepped into the sapphire current pulsing through *Arbol's* root. Its body flared and reverted to pure energy.

Koin howled and lunged for it, but the *soul* had already fled between worlds, from *Aeria* to the realms of the living. The last thing it saw was the *Extranjerra's luce* gushing through the fissures its emergence had caused, so vast in its form it would have inundated all of *Revenance*.

Dark Pudding and a Man Called Marsilias Wreign

The jovial notes of her doorbell disturbed Jade from the quiet of a warm doze. She protested the intrusion with a groan and, when the noise persisted, tapped the bedside console. "Tell whoever it is to drown themselves in the nearest puddle." Satisfied with her restraint, she returned beneath the covers and snuggled into the soothing darkness.

The console spoke, invading the blankets and warmth to rout her resuming slumber, "Marsilias Wreign requests entry, should I admit him?"

"No, tell him to go drown himself in the nearest lake."

"Very well."

Jade released a contented sigh and discarded all thoughts of her visitor. This contentment endured the brief minute it took her door to open and heavy treads to sound on her bedroom carpets.

"You do realize a condition of employment is to occasionally arrive on time?"

Resigned, Jade surfaced from the covers and blearily observed her guest. "I had a rough night."

Marsilias ambled through her bedroom with disconcerting grace for such a corpulent man and situated himself on the burgundy settee at its center, disregarding the dust this dirtied his expensive suit with. "So I heard; I thought you retired?"

She sat up, rubbing the sleep from her eyes and yawning. "I am, and how did you get in here anyway?" The adaptive suit warmed against her skin, its sable hue providing enough concealment that she was able to quell the discomfort her state of undress caused. That it was Marsilias as opposed to almost anyone else helped.

She had met him almost ten years ago at her first lecture in the Purifier Academy where he taught Social and Corporate Politics. A veteran of the Techcron War, and a full seventy years her senior, he remained one of the few individuals she bothered to call friend.

Marsilias doffed his hat—baring a head of tousled orange hair—and rested it on the armrest, causing the belt of gold medals about its crown to clink. "Oh, I convinced this complex's supervisor to give me the universal passcode a couple months ago. May have mentioned something about you being deathly ill."

"Huh, wonder when they realized I changed the code, or how they even knew to look? Never mind. Marsilias probably insinuated something. Gonna have to change it again now." "Isn't that illegal?"

"Yes, and so is supplying a smaller gross production value in a year than most individuals achieve in a month." He shot her a meaningful look, which she ignored, and resumed his original discourse, "You were scheduled to arrive five hours ago; it's already the break period."

She disentangled herself from the blankets, swung her legs off the bed, and stretched. "Is it? Oh well." Standing, Jade crossed to her closet and began sifting through the meager selection of clean clothes. She dressed herself in a loose, button-up beige shirt, a set of rough, but comfortable, labor pants, and a pair of soft house shoes. Without bothering to button the shirt or choose one of the numerous dress code ties, she exited her closet and retrieved the faded coat from where it draped the sofa. "You want coffee or something?" she asked through another yawn and wandered into the main living space.

"Quite the contrary, I've brought lunch." Emerging from her bedroom, he proceeded to the kitchen table where a dark container sat beeping. He unlatched the lid with a burst of steam and a hiss. He inhaled the aromas and set about unpacking its contents.

Jade dropped into a vacant seat at the table and propped her feet atop another. "Nothing for me, thank you."

"Are you sure? I have some lovely garlic cream cheese and a heavenly cherry jam for the bagels?" He presented this and she just looked at him from beneath half-lidded eyes. "How about some of this roasted rosemary swey fish? No? Suit yourself." He resumed emptying his container, though never once without offering her its riches. As he did so, Jade pulled the swey fish platter toward her and carefully cut the wide, staring eyes from its head and then exiled them to the trash. Marsilias made no remark on this, well accustomed to this particular oddity of hers.

Human technology, along with dramatically increasing life spans, had long resolved the need to eat; their adaptive suits provided all the required nutrients in addition to enhancing basic bodily functions, monitoring health, and attending to individual medical needs on a day-to-day basis. Thus, eating had evolved into a purely recreational act, one she partook of only in specific circumstances.

Marsilias deposited the last entrée, a side of lab-grown fowl garnished with a variety of spices and sauces that eluded her, onto the table and opened its sleek container with a touch. The heady, vaguely fruity, aromas poured out, and he waved the quail enticingly before her. When this elicited no reaction, he sighed, tapped the nearest chair's armrest so it expanded to compensate for his girth, and sat. "Speaking of last night: How are you doing?"

"Well enough, I suppose, only a little bruised."

He slopped a mixture of roasted vegetables and gravy onto the quail, thickening the aroma of spices. "Did you forget to activate the combat protocol again?"

She slid deeper into her chair and rested her head back. "It hardly does anything with civilian suits, might block a couple kilograms of pressure, and I didn't need it anyway."

"That's not what I heard."

She cracked an eye. "Whatever do you mean?"

"Oh, nothing much. Just a little of this and a little of that, speaking here and over there." His eyes flashed with something both mirthful and devious, then returned to the rapidly disappearing fowl. His free hand snuck to the traveling container, tapped a console on its side and a small compartment opened. Chilled mist billowed out, followed by a frosted glass cylinder of dark pudding and cream.

Jade perked up and leaned forward.

Marsilias uncapped the cylinder and the sharp aroma of coffee teased her nostrils. He lifted it and spun it slowly between his fingers. "I heard you talked with a revenant last night."

She paused, her arm halfway across the table. "Where'd you hear that?"

He wagged the coffee pudding in front of her. "No unnecessary questions now."

She considered him for a moment, measured the coffee pudding against her responsibilities as a retired Purifier and then snatched it. The cold glass chilled her fingers, but its contents melted blissfully on her tongue. She sighed and snuggled back into the heat of her chair cushions.

Marsilias retrieved a bagel from its container and proceeded to butter it with jam and cheese. "Returning to the broached subject; did it speak coherently or struggle to voice a few syllables?"

Jade brandished the spoon she had retrieved from a table drawer at him and held it for a second. "Don't go telling who you heard it from, 'cause Prime March won't be happy." He nodded, and she resumed, "It spoke a full sentence, and perfectly enunciated at that, like someone who learned from a textbook." She savored another bite of pudding.

"What did it say?"

"It asked me why I was afraid."

"What did you say?"

"Nothing at first, then I asked who it was. Very bravely, I might add."

"What did it say?"

"That it hadn't decided yet." She inspected a mouthful of pudding adorned with cream. "Then it left, and that is all I know on the subject." She concluded her observation of the bite and consumed it.

He examined her briefly, then quietly asked, "And how are you doing?"

Her consumption of the pudding slowed. "I didn't use the First Step, if that's what concerns you."

"Your suits' nourishment dispenser settings have been calibrated to permit the occasional use of a First Step and to ... help deal with the ensuing physical trauma, so no, that doesn't concern me; I'm talking about your mental state."

She stirred the pudding noncommittally. "I'm fine. It was just a small revenant, didn't even need a real Siphon to kill it."

"How long was the panic attack later?"

Her hand tightened on the pudding. "...About thirty minutes."

"Are you sure you're all right?"

"Yeah, I'm fine." And she mostly was; while shocking in the moment, in retrospect the revenant had posed little threat to her. Which made her rather embarrassed for herself in the moment of panic. Not that she'd ever tell him.

A little of Marsilias's tension eased, and he reclined, chewing musingly on a bit of the swey fish. "All right"—he swung to his feet—"I have decided." He faced her as she scraped at the dregs of her pudding. "We're going to search for this revenant."

Her mind spasmed then leapt frantically for an excuse. "Fat chance, I have work." She spooned the last bit of pudding into her mouth and tossed the container at the open trash bin, where it bounced ineffectively off the side. "Plus, I'm already late and you couldn't afford me anyway."

"Don't worry, I'll give you leave." Marsilias Wreign also happened to be the supervisor and security official of her work group.

"Nah, I'll pass." Jade stood and hastily began buttoning her shirt. "The Sovereign Cores probably have it quarantined anyway. So if we're caught, I'd have to explain how you knew all this classified intel, and I just don't have an excuse." She trudged into her bedroom, then stuck her head back out. "I'm surprised you don't know any of this, I really expected better from a professor."

"I do know it, just as I know there's a wonderful new confectioner near your revenant's point of arrival."

She stuck her head out. "Is there?"

"Yes, very expensive and very deluxe." She knew he was bribing her, but she also knew that Marsilias did not request favors lightly.

Jade fingered the final button. "All right, I'll do it, but you're paying and I'm only present for consultation. So, if some–"

"Some giant eldritch horror is eating me, the only thing you'll do is film and post it online. I know."

"Exactly."

Jade retired back into her bedroom, kicked off her house shoes and from there checked the contents of her coat: medical supplies, ammunition for canister weapons and charge batteries for pulse-arms, a variety of portable malware, a water purifier, supplementary adaptive suits, and the deconstructed pieces of several small armaments. She carried other materials and items in the pockets, but she did not need to check those, and she did not wish to risk Marsilias glimpsing some of their contents, particularly those of the inside pockets. After the last of these, she carefully reached inside and verified that each of her three hidden pockets remained concealed and locked, and that their contents remained untampered with, just as she always did after waking or the coat left her sight.

After completing her inventory, Jade returned to the primary living space and armed herself with a trio of training Siphons, an emergency protocols disk, and a pair of combat boots from her entrance closet.

Marsilias joined her at the front door, his hat once more seated atop his brow and a worn military coat draping his broad shoulders. A yellowed sash with gilt, silver lettering rested beneath the collar, crinkling when he moved. It was fashioned of a material the academics called paper and bestowed upon professors who attained tenure. Marsilias's hung to his knees on either side, each sequence of marks representing a subject and degree of expertise.

He tapped the door and it slid into its alcove, wider than customary so he could exit with relative ease. She trailed after him, the door whispering shut in her wake, and strolled down the corridor of paneled walls, giving no thought to bright digital displays of flowers or scenic ocean views. Apartment entrances lined the corridor on either side, some boasting similar—though more varied—designs, but each labeled with a number and the occupant's full name on muted consoles. Hers read, Jade Dieza: 314, and carried no design. As she walked along, Jade brushed a hand across the screens, connecting the implants in her fingers to nodes in the walls, linking her mind to the apartment complex's network and web of software. She needed only an instant to inspect the sprawling web of interconnected programs to verify that nothing new had been added, neither virus nor foreign devices, and that another hacker hadn't intruded on the software or made alterations or exploited the defense network to spy on her. She found none. Or rather, she found no viruses or foreign programs that weren't hers or Marsilias's. His amendments to her door were roughly implemented and recent, snuck in between her regular checks. Sometimes, he knew her too well. Sighing, she removed her hand, rubbing at her fingertips and the static that always followed a connection.

The panel beside them flickered on, and a man in a dark-green tweed suit with sleek blue hair appeared on the screen, super-imposing over a revolving artwork of assorted black and gold shellfish. The S.I.–Simulated Intelligence–program fell into step. "Good afternoon, Miss Dieza, may I ready a skimmer for your convenience?"

"Yes, thank you, Michael."

"Do you need a weather report, miss?" The walls changed into a scene of gentle rivers circumventing city edifices beneath a rare unclouded sky.

"Don't trouble yourself, Michael, we can manage." The corridor brought them to a modest reception room populated solely by another version of Michael at the desk and a variety of unoccupied couches. The apartment complex's transparent main doors opened preemptively as they entered this space, welcoming a flood of sunlight and a waft of ocean scent.

Michael followed them as they strolled outside, situating himself on the exterior wall. "Is there anything else I can do for you, miss?"

Jade waved without looking back—"No, thank you, Michael." —and continued along the gently rocking gangplank of her apartment complex's wet dock.

"Then I will take my leave and wish you a good day." He waved goodbye and faded from the screen, which reverted to an animated itinerary of events for the tenants: wine tasting, massages, and communal ballets, among other things.

Further along the dock, a series of wide, two-person skimmers idled with raised doors, the entrances barred by the projected names of whoever had reserved them. A collection of tenants and visitors milled along the line, most newly arrived but a few departing on some planned excursion. Jade slipped through the crowd until she reached the skimmer marked with her name, then slid down into the smooth, flat-bottomed craft and took the far seat as Marsilias squeezed in after her. He closed the door with a tap, and she retracted the windows and roof to bask in the rare sun, but left the sonic dampeners in place. He sank into his seat and swiveled toward her. "Can you describe this revenant's appearance in detail? I unearthed snippets from the files but few concrete details."

She brushed her wrist across the console and inserted their destination. "Huge with red hair, blue and black striped fur, and no spirit signature." The skimmer slipped into the main current, rocking gently as its engines energized with a barely audible hum and propelled them seamlessly forward. "Have you experienced anything like that in your workshop? I know they're closer to Afterlife than most of our sensors can detect."

"No, even we Magisters don't tread so close to death. Our workshops are in a ... between place, like standing upon the water without submerging. Is there anything else you can recall? Physical or otherwise?"

She considered. "Tusks, and yet"—she paused and gently tapped her fingers on the air—"some part of its aspect reminded me of a lion." She gestured about her face in attempt to characterize the fictional creature's mane.

"How large is it exactly? Are we talking ride to work, or piss ourselves and cower?"

"Piss ourselves and cower; big enough to lift most vehicles and throw them."

The skimmer turned into a thin one-way canal between apartment complexes a few blocks further on, passing beneath the arching bridges that connected their front walkways. Their skimmer halted just after clearing the bridge and autonomously popped its doors open. Jade vaulted up and out onto the service walkway affixed to the apartment on her side, boots scraping on the crusted salt. Marsilias mounted the opposing complex's walkway and followed it to the alley's end where the walkway abruptly concluded at a red holographic display of the words: NO PASSAGE.

Beyond it, the ruined patio from the previous night remained in shambles, with further warnings projected across the patios of both adjacent apartments and the three immediately above them. A quick glance revealed similar warnings projected across the complexes to either side of Marsilias and Jade, as well as the air above. A security matrix pulsed along the exterior of the quarantined area, barring all passage with a humming barrier and a platoon of automated vigilants.

Dropping from the walkway into the waist-deep current, Jade waded to the barrier and activated the small, silver console at its center. An automated vigilant immediately skimmed across the water and unfurled itself before her, transforming from an unassuming teal box into an elegant, humanoid silhouette. "Please choose an alternate route, miss, this is a restricted area–"

Jade tapped a series of keystrokes, swiped to a new screen, and pressed her palm onto the screen. The console beeped and the vigilant withdrew. "Welcome, Miss Dieza, is there any way I can assist you?"

"No, thank you. Also, you shall henceforth refer to yourself as Daisy Derringer." She inserted another command and the barrier opened across the alley. Then she plucked the console from the barrier and they entered the quarantined space, Marsilias following the walkway around as she waded forward.

Patios lined the complexes on either side of the canal, facing each other, their walls opaque for privacy and emblazoned with both the logo for the housing corporation and the subsidiary company they had awarded the contract for constructing and managing these complexes.

Marsilias cautiously scanned the quarantined area from behind the alleyway corner before venturing forward. "What did you do?"

"Nothing impressive, just activated a command code and virus I implanted into the system when I was still a Purifier. Oh, and gave it a name."

"You hacked the Purifier Corporation with a virus you devised years ago?"

She perused a list of files for recent activity by Prime March. "Yeah, a dormant one so they couldn't inadvertently discover it."

"Do I want to know what you named it?"

"Something awesome. Now get to work, minion."

"What are you looking for?"

"Information on the revenant and whatever Prime and Primess March have been involved in lately." She waded across the gentle currents, inserting a new series of commands into the console. A walkway ejected from the undamaged patio ahead of her and she heaved herself onto it in a sit, letting her feet dangle and swing over the edge. A school of swey fish gathered around Jade, their bright, warm-hued patterns glistening as they bobbed on delicate, wing-like fins in expectation of food. Jade obliged, delving into an unlocked pocket to retrieve and crumble a stale cookie. Then she rested her chin on a hand and watched them eat, humming quietly to herself and basking in the rare sunshine.

"You really aren't going to help me?"

A lazy glance showed Marsilias gesturing at their environs. "Nope. I'm retired, remember? And deathly ill. With a sugar addiction. You have to do the grunt work."

"Suit yourself." Marsilias obtained a marbled-sized sphere from his breast pocket and deposited it on the water. It floated for an instant then convulsed, unfurled into a miniature squid, and swam a wide circle around Marsilias. "There you go, now find me the lingering essence." It dove and Marsilias grinned as he activated another sphere, this one promptly converting into a robin that would scrounge the roofs and higher walls.

Jade refocused on the open file, a communication between Prime March and the Purifier Corporation's CEO. She skimmed through the initial paragraphs, discarding recognized and irrelevant information until she spied mention of the speaking revenant.

"Another speaking revenant appeared tonight."

"Under what circumstances and where?"

"Serenity, a privileged retirement district far to the west, secluded from any other district."

"This is the second appearance of a confirmed higher-intellect revenant in two years. Are they evolving, or are larger entities discovering the means of returning to the living world?"

"I do not know, sir. All attempts to access Afterlife have failed, even with the assistance of Magisters."

"Who discovered the speaking revenant?"

"Jade Dieza."

"I see; ensure she does not involve herself further."

"She's interacted with every speaking revenant we've encountered; she might know more, have some insight."

"That is immaterial, her judgment concerning the first revenant is highly suspect, as is her knowledge of Afterlife. Do not involve or allow her to participate in these matters any further."

The conversation progressed, transitioning to the Techcrons' increasingly frequent incursions into the Corporatocracy's airspace, as well as another ship lost in the Dywernen Straits—ships and communications were always going lost in the Dywernen Straits—but Jade barely registered either. She laid the console aside and leaned forward onto her arms. The words *first revenant* echoed in her head like a condemnation, and in their wake came a vision of violet eyes staring at her, hating her. She closed her own eyes against the vision, gritting her teeth until they hurt. The violet eyes faded from her mind, but the ache of loss stayed in her chest, sharp with failure and powerlessness, sapping all the day's warmth from her.

The water swished nearby, prompting her to open her eyes as Marsilias approached with a handful of dark fabric clenched in one hand and his devices perched on the other. "Has your snooping unearthed any interesting details?"

"Some, and your trespassing?"

"It's *our* trespassing as far as the law is concerned."

"They won't convict me of anything, so it's *your* trespassing."

"Either way, my endeavors have borne fruit." He presented her with the swey fish and the robin. "Observe: These have accumulated enough essence to discern a unique signature between the two. This one"—he raised the robin—"gathered the essence of the first revenant, which, for comparison, has a spirit-level of seven with a density of one, comparable to most first-tier revenants. Its counterpart has a density of twelve."

"What? The distinction is that extreme?"

"More so even, though we cannot properly quantify all the potential correlations between revenants and their essence. This could, however, be an indication of why some are capable of speech while the vast majority lack it."

"What's strange is that my reader couldn't even register it."

"Hmm, I wonder if the revenant was actively concealing itself? That has all kinds of unpleasant implications."

"What of the fabric?"

"I hope to encounter further dissimilarities between the two by examining their apparel. Now, what of you?"

"Nothing that'll help us here." Jade caught him with her eyes. "What are we doing here, Silias? What are you looking for?"

"I don't know, but I don't like revenants appearing in a retirement district. It doesn't make sense, and if something doesn't make sense it's because we can't see the reason. There has to be a cause for the revenant materializing here; it was either looking for something, or it was sent. Both are rather unsettling prospects. I need to figure out what I'm missing."

"Okay." She drew a slow, calming inhaling. "Okay, we can do that. Here." Jade pressed a thumb to the old, copper keyhole on one of her breast pockets. She felt a flash of heat and it clicked open, permitting her to extract a petite cylinder and toss it to him.

"What is this?"

"A sensor keyed to Afterlife's energy signatures; we can track a particular revenant if you have its signal." She nodded at the swey fish and robin and then clambered awkwardly to her feet, trying to keep the console off the wet walkway. "In this particular instance, it'll guide us to the nearest trace of the essence, likely their point of entry or return. Maybe there's something special about the speaking revenant's gate."

He pressed the mechanical swey fish against the sensor, spun the dial and a light bloomed in the cylinder's tip. "What now?"

"Return to the skimmer and let the sensor go, it'll guide us if there's a signature strong enough to follow. It's good stuff, Purifier prototype." Jade began restoring the quarantined area to its previous state, taking the opportunity to recolor its walls yellow with various smiling emoticons and daisies, as Marsilias returned to the skimmer and inserted the sensor into its guidance console. She added a final, decadent cake by way of signature and rejoined him, climbing directly into the skimmer from the canal and dropping into her seat with a wet squish. The seat warmed automatically, beginning the process of drying her damp clothes as she gave Marsilias a tiny nod. "Let's go."

The sensor directed their skimmer through the retirement district to its western edge, pursuing an unseen trail and marking their progress with incrementing beeps. Jade watched it throughout, timing the intervals between beeps and bouncing her leg on tempo with nervous energy. Internally, she turned Marsilias's arguments over and over, her nerves slowly tightening further. He was right, there was no reason for a revenant to appear in a retirement district, there weren't enough people, and the nearest city-complex was hundreds of miles of open ocean to the South. It hadn't been hunting; revenants, the non-speaking kind at least, weren't intelligent enough to avoid Purifiers, which meant this one had been sent.

Her bouncing leg quickened and she began chewing on her thumbnail. Marsilias had suggested the possibility as well, but he didn't know for certain and it wasn't safe for him to continue that speculation. She needed to divert him, to provide an answer to their current situation that would satisfy him before he delved too deep. There were secrets he shouldn't know.

She chewed harder on her nail, tearing off a sliver and spitting it out onto the skimmer floor, mind working feverishly. *I need to contact Connor and Ruon, ask them if they know anything. But that doesn't make sense; the Redeemers shouldn't be active.* Cold crept across her skin, and she almost dismissed it as building panic before realizing the cold wasn't coming from inside her. Her adaptive suit had deactivated, losing its passive warming functions. Her attention snapped outward, fixing first on the now dead sensor then on the skimmer as it shuddered and died. All thoughts of the Redeemers scattered and her gaze flicked outside, her hands slowly clenching to fists. Modern technology didn't work around Afterlife once the other world's energy levels reached a certain density, but that density couldn't be achieved just by the presence of revenants.

An old memory intruded in her mind, eclipsing all others with the view of a vast, fulminating tear in the fabric of the world, vomiting dirt-colored mist and a tide of horrors.

She looked at Marsilias, fighting to keep her breathing steady and her voice calm. "Marsilias, there's an open gate."

He was already on his feet, however, staring at the line of uninhabited apartment complexes before them, and between the edifices to the open ocean beyond. Without looking, he reached down and pressed the primary console, vainly trying to activate a distress signal. "Yeah, I've noticed. What I don't get is why there's no Purifiers, and why it's not quarantined."

Jade unclenched her fists, forcing the fingers to flex. "Because crossover points rarely persist longer than a few minutes, and revenants never cling to them. The Purifiers should have inspected this area as a formality then continued their pursuit. This gate shouldn't be still open." Why had the Purifiers missed it? But the why didn't really matter; all that mattered was that there was an open gate.

She sucked in a final trembling breath, unlatched the two training Siphons from her back, and vaulted the skimmer's edge, plunging into the cold water. The Siphons bit into her skin as she vaulted, igniting in brief flares of yellow and orange but remaining silver bars. Sliding her grip down, she found the button at the base of their hilts and pressed it, sending the alarm signal to the nearest Purifier station. The Siphons buzzed in her hand in response, functioning despite their proximity to the gate because the Purifier Corporation had developed some kind of code or device to shield their tech from the gates. Developed, patented, and restricted. No one else had access to it, or the Siphon technology. No one else even knew what it was.

Marsilias stood, attached a large black box to the small of his back and splashed into the calm, waist-deep water after her, hissing at the temperature.

They pressed forward, half-crouched with eyes fixed on the row of vacant buildings. The edifices, which had once blazed with signs, advertisements, itineraries, and global news were now silent. Abandonment clung to all of it like a shroud, visible in the lichen swallowing its foundations, the bird feces splattering its roof and gangway, and a long, empty dock.

Jade lengthened her stride to take point, barely listening as Marsilias continued to talk, "Do you think the gate's continued presence is because it came from a speaking revenant?"

She shook her head, then forced herself to speak, to concentrate on him. "Yes. Well, probably. Gates never change, Marsilias, they're uniform across all incursions in every recorded instance, their size and duration identical down to the second regardless of environment." Reaching the furthest pier, she propelled herself up and then crouched, dripping water on the gangway as he joined her. "But m-m-...my"—she clamped her teeth on the stutter, driving the words as quietly as she could—"my last gate, before my retirement, stayed open for days and the only similarity between that gate and this one, is a speaking revenant."

Marsilias settled beside her on the gangway and nodded, sending them creeping toward the complex's front door. She pushed on it without success, readjusted her grip on the emergency handle, braced herself against the frame, and pushed harder, but it refused to give. "Help me with this."

Marsilias grasped one of the emergency handles and easily dragged the narrow door into its pocket, eliciting a groaning protest in the process. Still holding the door, he flashed a grin.

"Showoff," she grumbled half-heartedly and peered inside. A lightless, sterile corridor greeted them. She took another breath and advanced, lifting the Siphons to illuminate the way.

Marsilias slipped in after her, accompanied by the click and thrum of a deploying and charging pulse-cannon: The black box he'd attached to his back, still functional despite the gate's influence because it operated with hardware rather than electric signals. Unfortunately, even that would fail if Afterlife's influence grew too dense.

Following the corridor further, they entered a lavish but dusty common room packed with tables for gambling and eating, chairs and sofas, serving carts, recreation consoles, a bar for gentler intoxicants, and recessed booths for privacy. Thick, intricate carpeting blanketed the floor, its soft colors just barely visible in the dull sunlight extending from the corridor. Above all of this, however, floated the gate. It breathed the chill of Afterlife with slow, unsteady exhales that never followed an inhale. Each breath carried a dull, filmy brown mist that eddied and sank to the floor.

Jade recoiled, pressing a hand against her lips and diving the other into her coat pocket. It emerged a second later with a clear pliant mask that she clamped over her mouth and spread to her nose. It conformed to her skin with a flare of gentle heat along its perimeter and expanded with a breath of sterilized air. Behind her, Marsilias snapped a hand-carried mask around his mouth and nose. It activated with the click of a button, circling around his neck, and scaling to cover his eyes as well.

He waited for a moment, testing the mask's functionality, then spoke, "Why is the miasma coming through? It should have faded long ago, even with the gate open."

Jade clenched the Siphons tighter and they activated fully, blooming into two pistols of surging orange and yellow energy. "The gate hasn't been open. This is a new one. A new revenant." But that wasn't right either. She *felt* it, the revenant from yesterday.

She looked up, up at where the towering beast crouched on the common room's second level, staring down at them.

The Monster and the Predators

Perched at the railing of a broad, encircling loft, the soul watched the two humans enter and shy from La Neblina. They failed to notice the soul at first, distracted by the apertura humming near the room's center, exhaling tides of silty brown mist. They crept inward, favoring the perimeter to avoid the sea of cloth-covered tables, chairs, desks, and other assorted clutter.

It recognized the woman, her perfect movements, the muted but distressed strains of her emotions, and the absence in her being where her soul—the fire of her life—should have blazed. She moved, conversed, and perceived like a living being, yet to its vision she appeared hollow. The *soul's* intellect and senses proclaimed her dead, yet it recognized this as a lie, both for the heat her form exuded and her emotions. This woman lived divorced from her soul, separated but connected.

The man differed, his soul blazed across the room's confines, rich with emotion, purpose, and necrotic energy. His bloated form spoke of affliction, but his mind occupied it serenely, comfortable with whichever, if any, disease plagued him. Despite the vibrancy of his life, something about him bespoke *Aeria*—a chill wound of discord in his essence's warmth, a vestige of death from which his power radiated.

The woman ceased her advance and raised her gaze, the strange devices she carried in either hand exploding with false *luce* and transforming. She directed them at the *soul* and the man followed her attention, leveling a substantially larger device on the *soul*. He charged it with the wrench of a horizontal handle and the weapon's barrel ignited with false *luce*.

The *soul* cocked its head, evincing confusion to mitigate their fearful tendencies. "Why do you react violently? Can you not see I have no intention of harming you?"

The woman inched back toward the corridor, her emotions stabilizing then tightening with purpose. "Why wouldn't we react like this? Your kind prey on us."

The man echoed her movements. "I don't know if speaking with it is wise, Jade." Her hand nearest the man twitched, silencing him.

The *soul* maintained its perch, recognizing that humans considered size and mass concerning when confronted with predators. Any movement it attempted could provoke a violent response, and it did not wish to kill these humans. "Yes, a number of my kind consume yours, but they are inferior creatures and incomplete."

The man slipped backward into the corridor they entered from and flattened himself along the wall, keeping his weapon pinned on the *soul* all the while. The woman circumvented the final table separating her from the corridor's entrance and kept retreating, boots squelching as they transferred from carpet to wet tiles. "So you're different from the others, the mute ones? You're sentient? Not a monster?"

"Are humans monsters for their carnivorous tendencies? For breeding and butchering animals by the millions? No, you act to survive, just as nascent *souls* act to survive." Her emotions flushed with a strain of hate so pure the *soul* abandoned its argument. "You loathe us." The hatred vanished, expelled from the canvas of her metaphysical being with an act of deliberate, inexorable control. Control a human should not have possessed.

She slipped through the room's doorway and urged the man backward with a jerk of her head. He obeyed and she leaned against the wall in his place. "Even if what you say is true, you cannot fault us for defending ourselves from revenants."

"I am not a revenant. By your definition a revenant is a dead thing returned to life, naming the creatures that cross over from *Aeria* to prey upon you; I was never dead. I am a *soul*. A renewed existence fabricated by the amalgamation of *luce* and living memories."

"Then what are the others? The revenants?"

"*Soul* fragments, pieces and remnants of a life: living memories, what we call *vestiges*. You confronted one recently, though it possessed but a spark of *luce*."

The man tugged the woman's arm. "Let's go, Jade. I can hear the Purifiers; they'll handle it from here."

"Wait." She refocused on the *soul* and although her voice had steadied her weapon remained leveled. "Why do they hunt us? And who are you?"

"They desire the *luce* in your essence. As for who I am, I am a *soul*, the culmination of a *vestige's* evolution. You may call me Chandris."

She stared for a final moment then fled, spurred by an unseen cue, and in their absence Chandris heard the thrum of approaching engines. He straightened and descended to the room's floor via a grand stair circling along its wall.

Chandris had no particular reason for choosing his name now, or even the name itself. The woman had asked a second time and he simply responded with a name that felt appropriate. Now that name suffused his being, and he could no more divest himself of it than he could expel his consciousness.

He perceived his hunters' arrival outside and subsided into a crouch. He sensed the humans sprinting through the complex's higher levels, boots crashing on texture-less tiles as they searched, and heard more breech the floor immediately above him. Others stormed through the various ground entrances and scattered through the corridors, close enough that their scents invaded his nostrils, mingling with the prevalent smell of ocean.

His *apertura* evaporated, allowing the warmth to brush against his skin—distinctly pleasant after *Aeria's* chill—but he disregarded it's absence. If the humans proved themselves truly capable of destroying him, he could easily restore the *apertura* to escape.

The first of his hunters emerged on the ground floor from a corridor behind Chandris and strolled to the right. The man did not move as the woman Jade had. He moved with indolent assurance, unassailable from a bastion of hubris. He wore a gray uniform with a suit of white, segmented energy panels thrummed over his person, defined by a series of pale, spiderweb veins glowing with false *luce*. Chandris addressed him with a glance and then focused on the slim rod he held, this one radiant with *luce* where those the woman possessed had merely glimmered. The device extended the length of his arm and physically seemed vacant but for a silver glow. The item throbbed in Chandris's consciousness, palpitating in unison with the man's heartbeat. Of greater interest to Chandris, however, was how the man reflected Jade, his soul likewise absent.

He noted other individuals, two men and a burly woman, appearing from alternative conduits into the room, each with an absent soul and a luminescent rod. The first man spun his rod and directed it at Chandris. "The rumors say you can speak, this true?"

"It is; does that knowledge stay your hand?"

"Sorry, but no. Orders are orders, bud."

A snarling crack of energy diverted Chandris's attention to a vortex of blue energy expanding about the woman's hands as she upended a table for cover. The rod she carried disintegrated, consumed by the vortex, and the energy mutated. It thickened and molded itself into the shape of a long-barreled weapon akin to what the man from before carried. She leveled the weapon on Chandris and braced herself. "Just kill the damn thing, Reese, we're not here to fraternize." She fired, her weapon unnaturally still despite the massive knot of sapphire energy it expelled.

Chandris leapt aside then erupted forward, passing the projectile mid-flight, and slammed into the woman, crushing her against the wall with his extended hand. The white energy coating her body flickered, spraying his hand with sparks that burned cold. He clenched his hand, meaning to crush her, but her armor flashed, the panels protecting her lower half deactivating and those warding her torso brightening, mitigating his grip.

She snarled and her weapon changed, shrinking to a third of its previous size and discharging.

Chandris recoiled, sapphire energy engulfing his front. Pain wracked his physical form, preceding the sensation of flesh tearing and bones snapping. He vaulted back and up, clearing the entire room and crashing through railings to land on the loft near his original perch. The other three hunters pursued as the woman, gasping, buckled from his assault, her weapon sparking in flares of silver, yellow, and vermillion.

The assailing hunters sprinted up the walls and across the underside of the loft, one directly below him and the other two on either side. The first vaulted the loft's railing to land in a crouch before Chandris, his weapon deconstructing into a vortex of teal energy manifesting into a twinning cord of radiant *luce*. He lashed and the cord snapped out, impaling Chandris's arm and then wrapping taut around him, burrowing into his skin to begin devouring his *luce*. Chandris yanked reflexively, intending to reel the hunter in, but the cord elongated. Before he could change tactics, the second and third hunters arrived, one armed with a pulse-cannon and the other with a serrated lance, both shaped of *luce*.

Chandris retreated, heedless of the cord gorging itself on his *luce*, and the hunters inched closer, weapons thrumming with power. It was here, in the pause between violence, that Chandris finally noticed their transformations: the hunters forms now swelled with the excited brilliance of souls, and nothing changed but the ignition of their weapons. *"Interesting...."* He coiled to strike.

The hunters recognized his intent and reacted, the one armed with a lance lunging forward as the other vaulted back while discharging his pulse-cannon.

Chandris, however, had already moved, slipping between the lance and the energy blast as the hunter with the cord leapt onto the railing and then off into open air. The panels on his chest flared white as those across his legs and back flashed out. Chandris—his talons burgeoning with golden brilliance—struck not for the man but for the cord connecting them. The energy cord initially stretched at the pressure from Chandris, then snapped. The hunter spasmed and all color fled his skin. The light of his armor winked out, and he plummeted onto a gambling table below.

Chandris landed beside him and spun, tail snaring a chair and flinging it at the pursuing hunters.

The lancer cleaved it with a slash and propelled himself forward with a burst of force from his armor. His companion slammed to the ground directly below the loft, braced his legs, and directed his pulse-cannon at Chandris. "Die, you bastard." The barrel of his weapon exploded with light and vomited a silver barrage.

Chandris leapt, streaking past the lancer, and smashed against the room's ceiling. He twisted, ground his feet against the white, glass-like material, and shoved off. The lancer hit the ground and frantically whirled upward just as Chandris arrived, crushing him to the floor with enough force to shatter his spine.

The third hunter never relented, his pulse-cannon sweeping wildly to keep pace with Chandris. In his desperation, he failed to notice Chandris's tail lashing from his left into his unprotected head. He slammed into the wall and slumped, leaving only the burly woman. Chandris crossed the intervening space and crushed her weapon, reverted to a silver bar, where it lay beside her. She spasmed and crumpled, life draining from her features as her consciousness faded.

He returned to the room's center and relaxed onto his haunches. Two other hunters occupied the vicinity, both now approaching while myriad other souls loitered throughout the structure and the environs beyond. He accessed his reservoir of essence and restored his body.

A man entered via the primary entrance, his gray apparel marking him as another hunter while the addition of a coat and skull helm differentiated him from his predecessors. "Hello, revenant, I am Prime March."

Chandris exhaled a slow breath. To all exterior senses, this man resembled his predecessors in demeanor and action. He moved with the same lethality, spoke with the same confidence, and breathed the same unruffled air. And yet, something in his mien distinguished him. His emotions ran in check, each vibrant in their diverse aspects but wholly controlled. Chandris concluded his exhale and spoke, "That is not your name."

The man cocked his head and his hand drifted to where the strange weapon of these hunters waited in a sheath. "In a way you are correct but not entirely. But, what of you? Have you selected your name?" He grasped the metallic rod, easing it free.

"You may call me Chandris."

A stream of *luce* bloomed in the man's being, restoring a sliver of his soul. It never bloomed fully, however: the man's soul either remained dormant, or he had chosen to access merely a drop of its potential. As with the first man's soul, the one who accompanied the first woman, a shred of *Aeria* inhabited Prime March's essence —just a drop in comparison—where the first man harbored a stream and thrummed to a different rhythm.

"Oh, so it does speak?" The final hunter advanced into the room, her weapon already in hand. As with Prime March, she exerted absolute control over her emotions and activated only a fragment of her soul to occupy her body. She also carried a drop of *Aeria* in her essence. "Hello, big fella, I'm Primess March. I love your hair, by the by."

Chandris glanced between them. "Who are you that you can shred your essence with such ease and suffer no ill effect?"

"We are executives of the Purifier Corporation," Prime March answered. "It is our task to excise you and your kin from our world." As he spoke, he drew a second weapon from the small of his back and activated it. The cylinder collapsed into a crackling orb of black *luce* and his being swelled with *luce* of the same color. Yet, it was not his soul that he manifested; the *luce,* for all its brilliance, was stagnant within him and to Chandris's eyes it felt misaligned. Even so, it eclipsed all others that Chandris had encountered.

"I have no quarrel with you or your kind, Prime March, and intend none of you harm–" His gaze darted to the ceiling. There, high above, a snarling coil of black energy materialized, originating from the direction of Primess March with a tendril beginning to extend toward Prime March. A snap before and behind him returned his gaze to where Prime and Primess March had plunged their hands into two crackling spheres of black *luce*, their forms now radiant with the power they borrowed. Lines shot from those spheres and pierced the walls, floor, and ceiling around Chandris, connecting into a web.

He punched the floor at his feet, intending to break through, but every line snapped shut, clamping on him like a box. Pain engulfed Chandris, followed by the utter failure of his muscles and prostration of his form. He could not turn his eyes to look, but he heard Prime March's approach and glimpsed a corner of his boot as the man paused by his head. "Do not worry, Chandris, we have no intention of killing you; there are better uses for you than that."

Chandris considered his words and then relinquished his half-formed *apertura*. He could abscond whenever he desired, but for now he wished to remain in this world. They hunted him in *Aeria*, and even his brief return there had brought dozens of *souls* in pursuit. Besides, the humans interested him. Especially the fragments and drops of *Aeria* inhabiting them like a disease.

Interjection 1

Miles below the ocean surface, Connor Drahma flowed with the crowd, shadowing the tall woman southward along a sidewalk of dark, reflective material. The soaring skyscrapers to his left and distant right admitted and disgorged an eclectic stream of customers, but the blazing lights of their advertisements and signs painted him and everyone else on the sidewalk with the same riot of colors and images. This permitted Connor to devote his attention almost entirely inward on the flow of his quarry's thoughts, perceptions, and emotions transmitted to him via a device on her adaptive suit.

~Tasairen Helio could feel the infection lodged in her soul, its presence a dull ache at odds with her native abilities as an Invoker. The superficial part of her mind demanded she excise the plague, but the logical part refuted the concept; they needed the affliction. It served a purpose, and that purpose subjugated her, forbidding disobedience of the PLAN.~

An omniveyor passed over their heads, attracting Tasairen's involuntary gaze by its proximity. The Adatra city-complex's simulated sky stared back, its hues rosy and vibrant with the waning day. The sun, or rather its simulated image, glowed on the far western edge, swaddled in clouds and veiled by the structures and immense support beams. Tasairen lowered her gaze and hastened, progressing through the maze of coarse synthetic-metal streets, skyscrapers, and mobile edifices that comprised the Adatra city-complex's first floor. Over a span of fifteen minutes, her trek conducted her and Connor to the metropolis's edge, where duraglau walls displayed the expanse of dark ocean. There were fewer people this far from the floor's center, and the structures here boasted more shadows, water stains, and flickering signs than actual lights.

Tasairen traveled the floor's perimeter for several blocks, ultimately approaching a modest, corner edifice smeared with graffiti and strewn with litter. She forewent the primary entrance, climbing an exterior catwalk to the second-floor entrance to a winehouse beneath an unpowered sign. Connor followed, disguising himself first with a vacillating electronic mask then an orange coat lined with black fur.

The winehouse doors opened automatically as he climbed the landing, admitting him into a dim, sweet-smelling foyer. Three manual sliding doors, all closed and intricately designed with scenery and beasts, lead from the foyer, the central and largest presumably, to the common room.

Seeing him, the maître d' wordlessly indicated the right-hand door, a construction of wood and paper emblazoned with three crimson apes chasing one another in a circle. Connor opened the portal just enough to slip through and proceeded down a paneled hallway lined with private rooms behind similar doors. He had no need of directions, he knew the destination from the woman's mind and even now saw as she saw. The view was superimposed over his left eye by his lens: a circular table spread with a burgundy cloth, furnished with expensive wines and, at its center, the statue of a doll carved entirely from wood.

~The assigned time neared and her superiors loathed delays. Compelling her limbs to move with casual ease, Tasairen retrieved an ornate card from her pocket. It sang inaudibly in her hand, vibrating with the music only she and other Invokers could sense. Answering its song with her own, though no sound escaped her lips, activated the card's power. The image it bore— that of a white tiled room—vanished, bleeding into the card's depths until only a gray slate remained. As the image disappeared, however, so did the world around Tasairen. It faded, replaced by an empty room of white electric tiles: the card's room.

No one waited for her, but Tasairen knew they would appear soon. She walked to the center, mind awash in the sensations of a lucid dream. None of this was real. She still sat in the reserved winehouse suite; this room, drawn from the card through her abilities as an Invoker, simply housed her mind, providing a secure environment for her superiors to convene covertly.~

Connor retraced Tasairen's steps, walking the creaking floor of faux-silver wood until he reached the corridor's third door, its black paper decorated with gold palm fronds. Here he paused and pressed his fingers lightly against the door's warm surface, feeling the illusory weight of it pressing against his hand ever so slightly, as if swollen in its frame. A chill crept through him, preceding realization and acceptance of what lingered inside.

Tasairen had spoken of an infection within her, an intentional disease whose purpose and origin were alien to him. That ignorance was dangerous, and he couldn't discern what he lacked from her thoughts alone. If it was a disease, lodged in her soul or not, it would affect the body and it would leave traces he could access via her adaptive suit.

Connor slid his fingers up into the handle notch and pulled the door easily aside. His eyes instantly fixed on Tasairen where she sat on a lush, emerald couch, her head fallen back and staring at the ceiling, but she did not stir. Exhaling softly, Connor entered and slid the door shut behind him, resisting the urge to inspect the table because now was not the time to lose himself in what it held. It called to him though, like a beautiful piece of art or an old vice.

He crossed to where Tasairen sat, waving at a thread of cinnamon-scented smoke that drifted from the central table to swirl around her head. She was dressed as he was, the same orange coat trimmed in rich, dark fur and the same electronic, black mask, its screen cycling rapidly through a stream of simplistic, pixelated images—faces, symbols, words, and animals—never persisting more than seconds and respecting no discernible pattern.

As he approached, Connor drew a simple knife from a sheath in his sleeve and laid it against her throat lest she woke. Then he gripped her bare hand and squeezed. She did not stir, earning a relieved sigh.

He proceeded to re-sheathe the knife and raise her sleeve to expose the connection-jack on her suit's wrist. Into this he plugged a slim, hard-cased flash drive from an interior pocket in his coat.

The device was archaic and limited, but also retrofitted to be compatible with modern technology and vitally, indispensably, isolated from the universal web.

The flash drive activated with an intermittent light at its base, commencing the download of her adaptive suit's medical data and leaving Connor with nothing else to distract him from the table's lure.

Carved of dark-cherry wood with a blanket of black silk wrapped about and concealing its pedestal, the statue was of a woman festooned in computer wires. She wore a wide-screened visor over her eyes and a glove on her left hand to which many of the wires connected. In her right hand, she raised a jagged piece of glass, which still dripped fresh blood from when Tasairen scored her hand upon it. Now the statue stared at Connor, and to him the woman appeared entrancingly beautiful, even as her benignly smiling lips seemed ravenous and expectant. Wordlessly, he submitted, kindling a spark from his adaptive suit with a snap of his fingers then touching the flame to one of the candles arrayed about the statue. The wick ignited into a green flame, joining the candle Tasairen had already lit, and Connor sank to a knee in reverence, pressing his brow to the table rim and murmuring words whose meaning he did not truly understand. The weight of expectation subsided, but the hunger endured, making his blood sing and heat. It felt good, and deep inside Connor wanted to press his hand against the statue's blade, wanted to fulfill the communion, but he knew the sickness that would follow, and the ache in his skull further warned against it. Jade had made sure he would never return. So, instead of giving his blood, Connor closed his eyes against the statue's call and turned away while rising.

He returned to Tasairen, grasped the arm of her couch for balance, and restored the brunt of his focus inward on the stream of her perceptions; he needed to know if the SECOND PLAN had begun, and if so, he had to hope her thoughts betrayed some hint of what it entailed. As he began to delve, however, his vision warped and darkened from the edges. A pressure enveloped his skull, crushing inward and suffocating his thoughts. Unable to stop himself, he twisted back toward the statue and felt it staring at him from the corners of its eyes. It didn't want him to see this. No, not it: She.

Clarity trickled through his reeling thoughts, fragments of knowledge She had erased before just as She would erase what he experienced now. He couldn't prevent it, not then, not now.

Connor staggered, shoving off the couch to brace on the central table, and focused on his reason for being here. He already couldn't remember the events of the morning, and he could feel Her erasing more, but he fastened onto the moments at hand, remembering what Jade had pounded into his skull years ago: 'She can't kill old memories, only new ones.' He dredged the memory, scrambling for what Jade had said: 'Don't trust the web, *never* trust the web.' He knew that already, it was why he used the flash drive, there had to be more but it was so hard to think—"Write. It. Down."

Connor lurched into motion, slamming an arm down on the table and sweeping it clean. The statue fell with a clatter of shattering glass, spilling wine and snuffing flames, but still it stared at him. He fumbled through his coat and yanked out a soft, leather-bound notebook full of messy, loose-leaf synthetic paper and, in its spine, a slim stylus.

He scrambled the book right-way onto the table and pressed his thumb into the blood test seal on its cover. The lock bit into flesh and gave with a click. He flipped the book open, sprinting through pages of blockish script until he came to one only half full, and pressed the stylus against it, causing the page to darken as if with ink, and wrote: WRITE EVERYTHING YOU SEE DOWN. YOU WERE FOLLOWING TASAIREN HELIO FOR INFORMATION ON THE SECOND PLAN. Then, he began to write what he saw.

~A step echoed off the floor, pulling Tasairen about to face two men, one small and unremarkable—the other—the tall, slouching Saccari Inuma: her superior and the Second's advocate. They were dressed, as she was, in the orange coats and vacillating masks of the Redeemers.

"Report, please, Helio." A synthesized voice emerged from Saccari's mask, stripped of identifying accents or dialects.

"The revenant we dispatched succeeded in attracting the *soul* and alerting the Purifiers to this *soul's* existence. It failed to kill Jade Dieza, however."

"Well, can't say I expected anything else." Saccari's mask

flickered, flashing through a sequence of images too fast to register before settling on an animated, revolving poker chip. "Doesn't make it less unfortunate, though. It'll wake her up and send her scrounging about for why. She won't be able to help herself. She never could. In the meantime, I'll speak with the Second, see if this attack was something he wrote, or the PLAN's doing. Regardless"—Saccari's attention shifted to his companion—"you supplied the promised revenant as requested: What do you want?"

"The new *soul* who entered this world recently and chose the name Chandris. You will deliver him, unharmed, into our custody. Consider him inviolate under threat of annihilation. He is everything to us."

"It will take a few days to infiltrate and supplant the Purifier Corporation enough to extricate him. Are you in a hurry?" Itai'ja stepped back, the colors and consistency of his form diluting like paint in rain. "You have seven days of grace, human. Failure to supply Chandris will result in punishment. As for the *soul* named 'Ilin', we renounce all obligation and claim to him. Do with him as you will." ~

Even reeling in a tempest of eroding memories and pressure, Ilin's name shocked Connor to stillness. Questions engulfed his mind, who was this *soul,* what objective did it serve, and why the hell was it named after Jade's brother? Then She swallowed that knowledge and Connor was left adrift. Bewildered, he fumbled for his purpose here, but his only response was a void of absent memories and a nauseating double vision. His eyes fell to the sheet of paper full of words and the command at its top: WRITE EVERYTHING YOU SEE. It sparked no memory, but he recognized his handwriting and older memories gradually resurfaced, recollection of near identical situations. The rooms differed, but the statue, the candles, and the book persevered, as did his reaction. As always before, he pressed the stylus to the page and obeyed.

~Saccari was facing Tasairen, one hand buried in a pocket, the other extended in command, "... on't share that with anyone."
"Why not?"

"Because the Fifth scribed a particular fate for Jade, and attacking her jeopardizes that." A whirlwind of associations flitted through Tasairen's mind at the mention of the Fifth Scribe: temple burner, traitor, murderously insane. His alias was Stormflower, because none could know who the Scribes were.

"Then what must we do with Jade Dieza?" Jade Dieza knew about the Scribes. Jade Dieza had betrayed the Redeemers, betrayed the FIRST PLAN and brought it to ruin. Jade Dieza couldn't be left to live, couldn't be trusted to preserve their secrets regardless of the Fifth's having written a special fate for her in the FIFTH PLAN.

Saccari shook his head. "Leave her; while she may interfere, Jade's not healthy and we can probably inflict enough emotional abuse to render her a nonentity. For now, return to your post and accelerate the infection rate; we have seven days to use this new *soul*, we need to maximize his effect...." ~

The rasp of a wooden door pulled Connor from the vision. He turned unsteadily, still braced upon the table and struggling to orient his thoughts through Her influence. Someone tall and slim entered, garbed in the vacillating mask and orange coat of the Redeemers. They slid the door shut and locked it with an audible click, then faced Connor, doffing the vacillating mask to reveal loose blond hair, freckles, and a quirked grin: Saccari. "Hey, Connor, long time no see."

Connor retreated, blinking and scrubbing his vision fruitlessly. His mind whirled for an excuse, rejecting the two Saccaris, but they were identical: voice, appearance, posture, even onto their mannerisms. It defied logic.

Saccari continued toward the table, fingers snapping to ignite a flame from his adaptive suit. "You know you don't have to eavesdrop to know what's going on, you could just show up for the meetings." Extending his hand to the right as if to ignite one of the candles where they lay on the floor, Saccari froze, his eyes alighting on the still open book.

Panic roared through Connor. "*No! He can't have it! Don't let him take it!*" Connor sprang forward, lunging across the table to snatch the book against his chest before backpedaling again.

Saccari finished igniting his candle. "That's clever. All our secrets in a place She can't reach. Explains a lot also." He doused the flame then spread the papers Connor's rough recovery had spilled from the book. "I don't want to kill you, Connor, but you're not leaving me much of a choice. I know you feel like you have to atone for the FIRST PLAN, but you really don't have to. You didn't know what you were doing, and even if you did, you couldn't have done anything; She wouldn't have let you. So there's no reason to feel compelled to help, don't be like Jade, think for yourself." Finishing his perusal, Saccari lifted the pages and held them to the candle flame until they caught. "You're probably terrified of what we're doing but, come on, give me a little credit. I'm not *that* awful of a person. It's not going to be as bad as you think, and it's still going to make the world better." He looked up, speaking softly while inoffensively catching Connor's eyes. "You can still get out, Connor, leave this room without having to fight. No one's going to pursue you, hunt you or your brother down for revenge or anything infantile like that. All you have to do is leave that book and walk away."

Connor shook his head, struggling to order his thoughts, to remember why he was here. It was something to do with...

Saccari's hand snapped out. A thin card as wide and long as his index finger shot from his sleeve, the image upon its surface rippling and burgeoning with light. Screaming, gale-force winds exploded from the card and tore through the room, flinging furniture, wine bottles, decorations, and Connor aside like toys, and snatching the book from his hands. He slammed into the wall, his skull smacking against the stone, and fell sprawling.

The wind subsided and, in its wake, he heard the fluttering of scattered papers. He struggled to raise his head and saw the air filled with his blockish writing, the book lying on the floor, still mostly intact thanks to its binding, and Saccari striding toward it. Connor pushed to his knees and pressed a red button—one of three—on the palm of his right hand. A card, long and slim, ejected from the canister up his sleeve, its song already swelling in his thoughts, violent and staccato. He answered with his own rhythm and the image painted upon the card's surface, that of a sleek, many-limbed, carbon-fiber android, came to life. The card's face throbbed, then drained of color and from its midst poured raw metal in a swirl of particles and fragments, forming the android in a crouch before Connor. The android straightened in a seamless, inhuman motion, its forearms deconstructing into a battery of pulse-weapons and unleashing a barrage of electric blasts on Saccari.

Saccari dove aside, dodging behind an upturned couch as his hands snapped to withdraw another card.

Connor scrambled to his feet, gasping a breathy, "stop him," and lunged for the book. He barely managed a step before a bullet whizzed past his head, hit the wall, and exploded. He dropped, hit the ground and rolled, frantically tracking the bullet's trajectory to see Tasairen swiveling with him, a canister-pistol in one hand and a card glowing in the other. The card's surface rippled, hue fading, and a multitude of thorny, winged insects began pulling themselves free, growing as large as his hand.

Connor kept moving, stumbling and pressing the blue button on his palm. Another card slipped into his fingers, its song slow and stately to which he answered with his own, expanding it to encapsulate both this new one and the android's rhythms. His mind expanded with the effort, swelling with internal pressure as he struggled to reconcile the discordant songs. In response, silver light poured from the card like mist and enshrined his body, painting all he saw in its color.

Tasairen's insects slammed into him in a wave, crashing and battering as their gold and black carapaces glistened. Their stingers reared and struck, feeling like barbed knives but failing to penetrate the hardening silver light. More collided with him, bludgeoning him into involuntary retreat through sheer force and number until his legs hit a fallen chair and he tumbled over.

Connor kept moving, scrambling over debris and scanning for the book. An explosion sounded to his right and his connection to the android severed. He twisted to look and saw it crumble to the floor, spasming, sparking, and crushed to scrap by a fist of electronic, white-plated tendrils from a crate on the floor. Saccari, eyes fixed on Connor, stepped around the crate, stuffing one card in his pocket and withdrawing a new one.

"*I can't win.*" Connor staggered upright, hunched against the besieging insects and desperately scanning for the book. "*Where is it? Where is it?*" A second bullet from Tasairen hammered his side and exploded, launching him across the room. There was a second of reprieve and then the insects assailed him again. Somewhere in the room Saccari began another invocation, but Connor couldn't see him, could barely see anything through the swarming insects. "*Where is it? I can't find it! I can't find it!*" He couldn't stay any longer. It didn't matter that he would forget about the disease and everything he'd heard. They would kill him.

Connor heaved himself up and into a run, pressing the red button and holding it. It triggered a second later, spitting out a card that sang a single booming note in his mind. He swelled his own rhythm to match and flung the card at the outside wall. There was a deafening crack and then a concussive force crashed into Connor, fracturing his silver armor and hurling him, along with everything else in the room, into the opposite wall.

He hit the door and crashed through with a spray of synthetic wood and glass to tumble in the corridor beyond. Furniture and glass lay all around him and his vision reeled, but he staggered up and scrambled back into the devastated wine room to gaze upon the gaping new cavity in the winehouse's wall.

Saccari and Tasairen lay sprawled against the wall, unconscious and bleeding for lack of armor, but he would only have moments before they stirred. He stumbled through an unsteady swivel, scanning desperately for his book. And saw it.

It lay close to Tasairen beneath the crushed remains of one of her insects. He could see pages scattered all throughout the room, but he didn't have time to gather them: Saccari was already stirring. He lurched forward and dropped to a knee, frantically scooping the pages into a heap on the open book. One of them contained something vital, a secret he couldn't remember. It would be on the latest page, the page he couldn't remember, but he didn't have the time to look for it.

Connor slammed the book shut on all the pages he'd collected and started running. Forgoing the door, he leapt out the yawning hole to the catwalk and then vaulted its railing to the street far below. Pain stabbed through his ankles, buckling his legs, but he didn't stop. He shoved himself upright and kept running, the book clutched to his chest.

Connor ran until his fear of losing the poorly contained pages outstripped his fear of pursuit. Slowing, he secreted himself away in an alley and sank to a panting sit. He spared himself only a few breaths, then opened the book and shakily adjusted the pages to sit evenly. Then he scanned through them once, and then twice, but every page he looked at he knew and remembered. There were dozens missing, pages with lists of names and locations, of meetings and interactions, pages full of minute details and conversations and secrets he couldn't find anywhere else. All of it gone. Including the newest page, the one that told him what he needed to do next.

Eavesdropping and Red Velvet Cake

Jade lay in the unruffled sheets of her mattress, counting the folds of her bed curtains. Ambient mist drifted through the environs, chilling her exposed face and teasing her nostrils with the scent of lavender. Memories of her brother plagued her, his easy smile and confidence, the lush violet of his eyes so much like a Stormflower, bright with the radiance of a fresh bloom. She remembered the low drawl of her brother's speech, an affectation that softened his austere persona. He had always been able to find friends, people who truly loved him, while effortlessly divesting himself of the sycophants and deceivers.

Her alarm beeped again, warning her for the umpteenth time that her shift neared. She dragged herself from the bed and pressed a finger to the button over her midsection. The adaptive suit peeled itself from her skin with a whisper and contracted into a hand-sized square of gray fabric. As it receded from her shoulders, it exposed the mass of purple and black bruising expanding across her chest and back from her lungs. It was old and faded with slow healing. She barely felt the constant ache of it anymore—only when she breathed too deep.

Jade peeled the gray square off her stomach and padded to her closet where a container of similar gray squares sat amidst the chaos. She deposited the depleted suit into the container and retrieved another—the last—from an open drawer in the wall. The warm fabric spilled out as she pressed it against her body, garbing her in a sheen of muted off-white mesh and ousting the chill already taking root. It contracted after a second, molding itself to her frame and inserting the minute needles necessary for her injections. The adaptive suit settled with a final purr and darkened to a modest tan. She reviewed the rest of her closet and sighed, realizing she had only a single clean pair of dress pants and shirt remaining, both the ugliest in her repertoire.

Resigning herself, Jade began dressing and tapped the wall with a toe. "Michael."

The projection appeared on the wall behind her. "Yes, Miss Dieza?"

"Have my room cleaned today please, excluding the second floor."

"As you wish. Is there anything else you need?"

She finished the last button on her shirt. "Yes, please order some nice, simple white shirts suitable for work. Black pants as well."

"Size small, correct?"

"Yeah."

"It will be done. Anything else?"

She hesitated. "Yeah, create a private line and connect me with Prime March." She emerged from her closet and dropped into the seat at her vanity. The screen powered on, but she flicked it off with a touch before perfunctorily dragging a brush through her hair.

The earpiece beeped and Prime March's voice sounded in her ear, "Hello, Jade, what can I do for you?"

"What happened with the revenant yesterday?"

"Oh, nothing much: we overpowered it with a polarity field and transported it to a secret facility designed for its kind."

"...Were there any casualties?"

Lord March considered his response, providing the only answer she needed, and then spoke with an audible shrug paired with careful nonchalance, "None."

Guilt swallowed her. *Damn it. I should have stayed to help.* Aloud, she said, "Don't lie to me, Theeran, or get better at it."

"Listen, Jade, they were paid professionals and knew the risks. They were also far better equipped than you or your politics-teaching friend."

"You don't have to remind me, I know that. *I know* that."

"Then put them from your mind and return to your retirement." Her earpiece clicked off.

"That's the problem, I can't." Her head thudded back, giving her a view of the boring, undecorated ceiling. The panels reflected a vague image of herself and the room, all distorted and sapped of hue. She could have altered the imagery at any time, selected a panorama of a forest or clear skies or even mountains, coded in dynamic progressions for stray clouds or migrating birds, even activated effects so she could feel the warmth and rays of sunlight. But that would have necessitated connecting her room to the complex's network, and that was connected to the universal web. It was safer like this. No one, and more importantly nothing, could come peeking in on her. It also ensured she alone, and those she trusted, had control over her living quarters.

"All right," Jade murmured to herself. "All right, let's go." She slapped her cheeks to waken fully and leapt to her feet. "Time for work." She collected her brother's faded coat from the entrance closet and exited into the apartment complex's hallway.

An elderly couple walked past her, whispering to one another as Michael shadowed their steps. The man waved at her. "Why hello, young miss, we don't see you out and about much. Do you have work?"

Jade's door sealed with a hiss and she managed a smile. "Yeah, I have a job at a subdivision of the Robotics Corporation: Data Management."

The woman sidled around her husband, beaming. "Oh, operations like that still exist?"

Her smile eased. "Yeah, just barely."

The man smiled and patted her shoulder. "Well, we wish you luck then, young miss. Knock 'em dead." They shuffled off, their staggered movements the result of a century spent in hard labor.

Jade proceeded the opposite way, her steps a little lighter as she performed her customary search of the complex's network. Nothing. Another Michael appeared beside her. "I have prepared a skimmer for your convenience, Miss Jade. It awaits you at the back entrance. Would you like to reserve a first-class berth at the regional station?"

"Yes, please." She yawned, the sleepless night beginning to exert itself as her mind calmed. "Upload it to my passcode when you finish."

"Very well. Is that all?"

"Yeah." She rounded the corner into the apartment complex's common room and plunged into a storm of sound: the clink of cutlery, the roar of conversation intermingled with laughter and shouts, the vibrant cacophony of various console entertainments, and the scraping retorts of moving furniture, all accented by the pervading ambient music.

She ignored all of these, merging into the crowd and traversing it with acclimated ease to the apartment complex's back entrance. The translucent doors opened at her approach, gliding effortlessly aside to reveal the drizzly morning and skimmer idling beside the walkway. Jade hunched against the drizzle and crossed the walkway, opening the skimmer with a touch and slipping into the seat. The vehicle woke as her weight settled, recognizing her from the implants in her hands and head, and would have begun transmitting information directly if she hadn't deactivated her implants automatic connection functions long ago. Still the opaque walls cleared autonomously, lights activated, and the door closed behind her. "Take me to Serenity's regional station." The skimmer's engines initiated with barely a hum, more tangible through the gentle vibrations beneath her feet than any noise they made. As it pulled out into the canal, Jade—already shivering—activated the heating and reclined her seat, wrapping herself in her coat and watching the rain trickle down the roof.

Her skimmer glided languidly through Serenity, circumventing huge, sealed domes that housed artificial environments, and navigating the meandering canals of water gardens, the catwalks elevated above them equally festooned with flowers and vegetation. The entire journey took only a few minutes before the canal opened into expanse of deeper water centered around a wide, desolate dock surrounded in branching piers. Her skimmer moored itself near the primary structure among several others of similar size, and she disembarked into the thickening rain, the coarse walkway scratching under her boots.

Raising her hood against the dropping temperature, Jade ascended toward the squat primary edifice on hurried steps. Thunder boomed, heralding a wave of northward-bound lightning. The water below her curved in accord, echoing the lightning's trajectory and causing the gangways to sway in concert. She rocked easily with the motion, disdaining the railing on either side, and passed between the automatic doors.

Inside, the building comprised of three descending tiers. The first, the entrance landing, spanned a dozen feet before concluding at a fence of cobalt light and a sequence of descending stairs. The second floor employed most of the available space and hosted a variety of chairs, restaurants, gaming parlors, and other recreational activities. The third floor housed the inner dock and boasted only a landing platform where passengers could access the regional station where it sat at the center of excavated trenches.

Every surface gleamed with the fastidious white of a professional corporation and flashed with an array of generated images or programs, mostly aesthetic but several informational or entertainment oriented. One of the attendant S.I. programs materialized on the floor panel beside Jade; her name tag read Catherine.

"Your seat has been reserved, Miss Dieza, please bypass the waiting line and proceed to the dock."

"Thanks, Cat." The S.I. program winked out, and Jade strolled to the dock, yawning. A slim, gray submersible surfaced as she approached and opened its hatch.

Catherine reappeared on the submersible's exterior. "As requested, a first-class and solitary berth. Is everything to your liking?"

Jade dropped in. "Yeah, you can go now, Cat."

Catherine materialized on the submersible's screen. "The Transport Corporation has several new–"

"Go away." Jade tapped a command key, one of the benefits for a first-class voyage, and Catherine vanished, leaving her stream of advertisements and sponsorships incomplete. Jade sank into one of the chairs and reclined it. "Take me to the Robotics Corporation, building one hundred and seventy-seven."

The submersible pulsed to life and submerged, its walls turning transparent and projecting light to illuminate the dark water. It continued diving, ferrying her along the trench until it reached the open ocean beyond, where a sequence of brilliant white lights gradually materialized into a corridor of massive, inverted metal arches running southward. Vessels, arranged by size and luxury, shot along the corridor in blurs of light, the wealthy segregated and the rest coming and going in parallel streams.

Her vessel idled briefly then dove, lurching gently as it entered the corridor of accelerated currents and a dull whooshing sound grew to fill the interior. They continued to dive, the currents accelerating to a roar before the sound and force dampeners activated, reducing the thunder of their noise back to a calming swish.

Jade relaxed into the cushioned seat, listening to the Deep Currents—these fabricated waterways—pass as her vessel reached it assigned depth. A news presenter appeared on a screen overhead and began a long drone of information, migrating through the latest unemployment rates to Techcron sightings near several city-complexes. The presenter's words faded into white noise somewhere during the transition between "estimated time to fully remove humans from the workforce" and "mounting crime rates," and Jade slipped fully into slumber.

```
01010111 01100001 01110010 00100000 01100111 01101111 01100101
01110011 00100000 01110000 01101111 01101111 01110010 01101100
01111001
```

The submersible hatch opened, rousing Jade with a beep and a patter of water. She yawned and stretched in the sterile illumination of electric lights from the ceiling high above. Drone music wafted through the open hatch, bearing with it the murmur of conversation, the dull buzz of a conditioned environment, and the prominent aroma of vanilla. The indicators on the console informed her that about an hour had elapsed in transit.

She exited the submersible onto the attending network of floating piers, wrapping her arms against the chill. Water sloshed over the textured floor, fluctuating with the surfacing and diving of submersibles but almost inaudible beneath the din of conversations.

Jade joined the flood of arriving and departing people, ignoring how the walkway flashed green beneath her feet, soundlessly scanning for unauthorized weapons or other paraphernalia. It dinged a second later and winked out, once again failing to pierce the folds of her coat to detect the training Siphons she always carried, or any other of her pockets numerous contraband.

The walkways climbed as she neared the main building complex, leading her toward an immense stair of solid, white metal that ran the docking room's entire length. A series of entrance terminals, scanners, and androids waited at the top, verifying all who entered. When her turn came, Jade presented them with her employment credentials and veered to the right after being admitted.

Inside, the facility boasted a plethora of decorative flowers and beautifully colored plants to enliven its spacious but otherwise spartan corridors, mostly regulated to pillars and corners but occasionally encompassing entire walls. Screens flashed on the ceilings and floors periodically, bombarding the passersby with regulations, news, advertisements, and a list of the Robotics Corporation's assorted projects.

Jade circumvented a group of arguing researchers and reached an unoccupied omniveyor. Entering the unoccupied chamber, she input her building number and slouched against the wall. The door closed and the omniveyor sped off, ferrying her several fathoms further down and three miles west to the Data Management structure, generally through open water but occasionally traversing other edifices, struts, and contained walkways.

The omniveyor arrived after a few minutes and opened to a partially lit foyer presided over by a bored looking attendant and several idling security androids. Jade meandered forward, yawning into her hand before swiping her wrist across the check-in console and allowing the attendant to scan her features.

"You finally decided to show up, eh, Jade? Run out of wine money?" His desk beeped and he scanned over the console screen to verify her authenticity. "We had a pot going for how long you'd be gone. I put in for three days, could've made a tidy sum if you actually showed up."

Jade shrugged. "How mortifyingly tragic. You should get back at me for it, report my absence to Marsilias."

He snorted "Eh, we're used to it by now. You check out, go on through." He nodded at the sealed doors behind him, opening them with the press of a button, and she passed through.

She entered a large, almost entirely dark room populated by rank upon rank of dully glowing desks and slumped people wreathed in thin, adherent wires. Jade navigated the neat, but crowded desks with the brusqueness of long acquaintance, circumventing the occasional far flung limb. Every time she brushed a desk, their surface screens erupted in a tide of numbers, words, diagrams, and graphs: the data streams her associates monitored, recorded, and most importantly, audited.

Escaping the final row, Jade mounted the stairs to a white door, the only generous source of light in the entire room. She opened it with a touch and entered.

Marsilias swiveled around in his chair and glowered over theatrically tented hands. "You never presented yourself for work yesterday, Miss Dieza. That's your third demerit this quarter."

She dropped into the waiting seat. "Yes, but hear me out: it lets you indulge in jokes you've beaten to death."

Marsilias dispelled the glower with a roll of his eyes. "Maybe, but I would still fire you if I could."

"You tried to fire me again? I compliment your persistence."

"Yeah; upper management rescinded the order before it hit payroll."

"I wonder if they're tired of your complaining yet."

"No doubt." He stood and circumvented his desk, footsteps soundless on the carpeted floor. "Anyway, I want you to concentrate on the Afterlife signatures today. Find where they're most common, and if either their frequency or strength increased of late."

She sighed, trying to ignore the sparking memories. "You're not still infatuated with that revenant ... *soul*, are you?"

"Aren't you? It's a talking revenant! And unlike its predecessors, I might actually have a chance to converse with it. Think of all we're going to learn concerning Afterlife?" Despite his enthusiasm, Marsilias's eyes remained serious.

"We're living people, Silias, best to leave Afterlife alone. You and I are close enough as it is."

"Nonsense." He tossed her a data file, a thumb-sized raised disc. "Plus, it may do you some good; gradual immersion so you can gradually learn to face this stuff. Don't worry, we'll start small. Now, cease your malingering and get to work. Reprobate."

"Oh, mark my words, one day you will rue this abuse. Mark. My.

Words." She rose and backed out of the room, finger waggling in condemnation.

Retiring to her desk, she connected the data file to her console, uploaded its contents, and attached the various wires to her adaptive suit and implants. A stream of information eased into her subconsciousness: names, dates, and events. Stripping off her coat despite the chill, Jade reclined and let her gaze drift to the obscured ceiling. She exhaled and slipped into the data stream.

Time passed without meaning for her, her mind inundated with the data to such an extent even recognition of her five senses faded.

Her delving ceased with a snap and a lurch as every light in the room flared. She instantly assessed her surroundings and straightened, hands grasping a training Siphon and a canister-pistol respectively. The cold air nagged at her perspiring skin while the brilliant lights stabbed her eyes, causing her to blink and shield them, a reaction most of the other reeling delvers shared.

Three individuals congested the entrance, the first two with girth and the third with presence, all dressed in dark purple uniforms and inscrutable. The first among them was a woman with emerald hair, sternly curtailed into a bun, and austere sable eyes. She wore a wide, metal-alloy belt on her waist, burdened with opaque, hard cases of varying size with a fingerprint scan sealing them. Two rows of ornamented buttons ran down her uniform's front, mirrored by the silver cufflinks on her wrists, buttons on her starched collar, and shining metallic fringe. On the lapels of her coat, she wore a silver circle pin with three needlelike lines projecting inward to a joint center. The third of these lines was copper colored, designating her as an Invoker Savant.

The men behind her, dressed likewise in violet but with distinguishing bronze adornments and lack of fringe, amounted to grunts. They were huge in the way of artificial or genetic augmentation, with unnaturally distended muscles, skin inflamed red from the strain of accommodating abrupt growth, and bloodshot eyes with shrunken pupils from the medications. They also wore pins on their lapels, except theirs had the second line colored copper, designating them as Specters rather than Invokers.

Jade dropped her head to the seat, feigning that all her interest in the strangers—Savant Corporation lackeys by the tri-tipped pins on their uniforms—had evaporated.

The woman sniffed at the clustered delvers and stalked around the perimeter, her heels rapping on the floor. Her brutes trailed after her, squeezing along the wall as assorted fish began congregating outside the duraglau, attracted by and reflecting the room's light in striking patterns. Without dithering for her guards, the woman ascended the stairs and entered Marsilias's office.

Jade immediately leaned over her desk and accessed the command screen. One command code later, courtesy of a virus, she connected the Data Management's mainframe to her ear and linked herself into Marsilias's office.

A moment passed and a steely voice barked in her earpiece, "Hello, Magister Wreign, we are here to retrieve the promised decks. I trust you have them prepared?"

"They're not finished." Marsilias responded calmly.

"You assured us of your ability to comply with our deadline, Magister Wreign, and you have already exhausted the allotted time." Her voice snapped, caustic with both vexation and the hard confidence of a bitter history.

Unperturbed, Marsilias responded, "They are not ready, Coleen, what would you have me do?"

The woman checked herself and then resumed in a calmer voice, "How much longer do you need?"

"I only have a few cards left, all of them requiring only minute adjustments and energizing."

"Finish your adjustments then. We will wait and handle the energizing ourselves."

"I am currently otherwise employed and am not free to do as you request."

"Stop creating issues; if you are truly apprehensive of your superior's ire, then we will compensate them for your time."

Marsilias's tone changed, reverting to simple, inoffensive, normalcy, "All right; but first, what's the rush?"

The woman hesitated. "We do not act out of desperation–"

Jade could almost hear Marsilias's eyes roll. "Then why are you conceding so much to expedite their delivery?"

The woman considered her words briefly. "The Purifiers extended a private contract with stipulations for prompt delivery. They require a reservoir of decks, enough to supply a hands-worth of Invokers for a year. They designated specific Magisters as well, one of which was you."

"Who is it for? The contract?"

"The Prime and Primess March."

"What's it for?"

"They wouldn't say, but the contracted Invokers mentioned something about containment."

A subtle smile of triumph infiltrated Marsilias's voice. "In that case, we'd best not keep them waiting; I'll finish your decks."

"Open your doorway then, I've brought a Specter."

Marsilias's chair creaked in relief. "No need, Coleen, I have a friend."

His muted footsteps sounded against the carpets, paused for his door to swish open, and then resumed louder as they struck the hard tiles outside. "Jade, would you mind helping me."

She roused her attention from her console, favoring him with a pointed, impassive stare, and tapped a combination into her desk without relinquishing her gaze. "Nope, I can't. Sorry. I'm busy. Very busy. All that work from my missed days to catch up on. Wouldn't want to get fired." A half-finished game of solitaire appeared on the screen before her with audible shuffling sound effects, the cards animated with various infant animals in adorable poses that cooed when played.

He bestowed upon her a sidelong glance, eyebrow rising in stifled humor, and assembled his features into a remonstrative glare. "Again, Miss Dieza? You really need to stop hacking my office. It is highly illegal in most corporations. Now get in here." He returned inside his office, leaving her to grumble and slink in pursuit, stalked every step by the attention of her associates.

Coleen fastened her with a stare the instant she entered, dark eyes briefly assessing and flashing with electronic light—likely accessing data storage—and then asked, "Who's this girl, Magister Wreign? She is absent from the Savant Corporation's records."

"I'm right here." Jade slumped into the unoccupied seat on the woman's right, draping a leg over the cushioned armrest. "And no, I'm not in your records; I'm more of a ... private, amazingly talented, freelancer."

"Fine, what's your name?"

Jade examined her chewed nails. "None of your beeswax."

Coleen railed her with condemning eyes and pursed lips. Unaffiliated Savants were both extremely rare, and deeply illegal. Savants, by law, belonged to the Savant Corporation. "I see. And why should the Savant Corporation trust your abilities? The cards you propose to retrieve are the product of years, a fortune potentially squandered by the slightest misstep. I am not of a mind to entrust it with a coarsely dressed girl of questionable taste." Her eyes scoured Jade's hair.

Jade rolled her head across her chair's back, meeting the woman's contempt with half-lidded eyes. "That's my problem like it's your choice: not at all. And you," she bestowed a look of reprimand upon Marsilias as he grappled with a smile, "shame on you; you knew she'd piss me off enough that I'd accept, and you didn't even have the decency to prepare chocolate."

He let his grin unfurl and rounded the desk. "I try, and concern yourself not with absent delicacies, you shall enjoy your tribute yet."

Jade swiveled with his progress toward the office's open center, his right thumb grinding into the palm of his left hand, twisting it like a man dousing his meal in sauce. He knelt, pressed his thumb into the ground, and straightened again. His thumb drew a line on the air, first rising, then crossing and descending again. Amethyst light bloomed in its wake and thickened as he finished the contours of a door.

Marsilias shook his hand as if to remove water and stepped back. Nothing transpired immediately, then violet mist boiled from the door's center, expanding against its confines in an opaque wall.

Orienting his back to Coleen, Marsilias offered Jade a private, reassuring grin, and crossed through the portal onto the waiting Bridge. He disappeared without sound or ripple, but with his passage the mist transmuted to dark, reflective glass.

Jade procrastinated, hand flexing minutely on one armrest, and her leg draped over and clamping the other. Her reflection stared back from the dark glass, delicately rigid with fear and condemnation, though she doubted the frittering Coleen would recognize them in her face.

"Well, are you going to move?"

"Yeah...." Jade physically hauled herself to her feet and crossed to the doorway, hand first clenching in the pocket of her coat, then emerging and extending to touch the glass. It burned cold against her skin, seeping into her bones until they ached and causing her breath to mist. She inhaled deeply and held it, the air filling her lungs with warmth. Then it vanished, and a familiar cold usurped its absence. The cold spread along her limbs and veins, sapping her of heat and desaturating her of color until she scarcely amounted to a phantasm. She had not died, merely entered an alternate space. Specters, those like her, called it the First Step, and it effectively made them intangible. Magisters, like Marsilias, used their bridges to access personal pocket dimensions—called workshops—on the edges of Afterlife, where they fashioned cards for Invokers. Invokers could materialize whatever was painted on these cards into reality, exhausting the card in the process. The cards would then be ground into a dust that, when consumed, allowed most Specters to access their abilities for a time. Specters using the First Step were required to ferry the card decks from a Magister's workshop. Due to ... events in her history, Jade did not require card-dust to activate her abilities.

Breathing normally now, as only specific intent would cause her to leave the First Step, Jade passed into and through the glass.

Every Magister's bridge differed, and Jade had traveled many. Marsilias's manifested as a circular tunnel of amethyst cloth that sagged beneath her steps, as if only air existed beneath. Silver bells dangled from the ceiling and walls, suspended on thin golden cords, but they never sang; and nothing she had attempted in all her crossings ever pried a single note from them. His bridge began with a stair of weathered, creaking wood and concluded in one of stone.

Jade stepped from the stairs and plunged into the wallowing fabric, clutching the walls for stability, but avoiding the bells, experience having taught her they burned hot to the touch. Thankfully, Marsilias's bridge enjoyed a comparatively short road that promptly delivered her to his doorstep.

She mounted the cracked stone stairs and hammered a fist on the waiting yellow door, provoking it to rattle on its hinges, jarringly discordant against his bridge's preternatural silence. The rusted latch squeaked, and the door swung inward.

She entered a spacious tent constructed of lush red, yellow, and turquoise cloth. The ceilings of the five rooms sagged, but the walls stood taut, and the black floor cloth rested on something solid that felt like sand. Wind blustered outside, jostling the fabric despite being, in of itself, entirely silent. Jade ventured further, ducking beneath one of the hanging lamps and through a silver curtain to enter the third of the four rooms branching from the foyer. This was the painting room, the others were the carving room, the leather room, and the one he'd added for her.

At her arrival, Marsilias turned from a cabinet stacked to the brim with leather wallets, excluding three slots near the top, and grinned. Arranged across the center of the room there was a pair of loveseats and a rectangular coffee table, its surface bedecked with brushes, cluttered paints in clay jars, numerous dried splatters, and three decks of Magister cards.

Marsilias brandished a long brush at her. "'Bout time you showed up."

Jade sank into one of the loveseats, commenting dryly, "What can I say, road conditions were terrible. I mean just god awful. You take the worst two things you can imagine and combine them." She leaned over the table while speaking, perusing its contents and brushing a hand over the first of the three decks, the soft wood delicately grooved beneath her fingers, as if unpolished and carved from a surface with rings. Their dark face depicted a rat on hind legs with tusks and horns, a cape thrust gallantly over one shoulder and a chalice in its paw. "These the decks?"

"Yeah."

She proceeded to the second deck, which depicted a cube of doors in striking red hues. One of the doors stood open, spewing a herd of elk, many of which bore a flock of sparrows on their antlers. She progressed to the third deck, this one painted in rustic blue, depicting an overturned table and spiraling in such a way that however you turned the card the image remained unchanged. Aside from their decorations, all three decks mirrored one another in size, height, and material, standing roughly four inches tall, with the width and length of Marsilias's hand.

"Marsilias, these decks are all complete...."

"Oh yes, I finished them a month ago."

"Then why say they weren't finished?"

He wagged his brush at her again. "If I had done that, they

wouldn't have revealed anything about this private contract."

"Which you already knew of, else you wouldn't have known to ask." She grabbed a leather wallet from the table and stored the first deck.

"Yes, but I didn't know all the details. Plus, I was fishing for something else." He squeezed between the table and loveseat opposite her and collected the third deck.

She started packaging the second. "Do I want to know what you were looking for?"

"Eh, you'll figure it out soon enough." He snapped the final deck shut and presented it to her. "Safe travels and try not to fall through; it's not going to like these decks. They have nasty cards."

She nodded and slipped the decks into her coat, locking their pockets with the key from another. "All right, see you on the other side."

Jade exited the painting room and crossed the foyer, absently digging her boots into whatever material existed beneath the cloth floor. Reaching the door, she hesitated, watching it shudder and blacken inward as if burnt. Some part of this world always knew when she intended to ferry a deck over, always knew and always resisted. This workshop might belong to Marsilias Wreign, but the power that sustained it derived from Afterlife, and Afterlife loathed relinquishing itself to the living world.

Jade braced herself, grasped the searing handle, though it did not char her flesh, twisted it, and leapt back as the door burst open. Scorching wind tore into and through Marsilias's workshop, launching it into a chaos of thrashing walls and flying implements. She bent into it, head ducking, and crossed beyond the workshop's threshold. A pull wrenched on her coat, clawing for the decks, but her pockets held. She slogged onward, dragging herself along the pathway as the heat thickened and the pull intensified. Despite this, the bells never sung.

Her heart beat faster, first racing then stuttering. Her breath faltered, lungs trying to expand but failing. She staggered, pain creeping into her chest, first as needles then as rasping knives.

Finally, her fumbling step struck wood, her toes scraping the face of a stair and pitching her forward onto the exit's wooden landing. She caught herself, then reached forward to dig her fingers into the violet glass and drag herself back into the living world.

The assailing heat vanished, leaving her with the numbing, breathless cold of the First Step. She opened her mouth and inhaled with conscious intent. Removed from the strain of carrying cards across borders, her lungs obeyed and warmth flooded her, followed by color and substance.

Jade buckled with a gasp, crashing to the floor and panting as the ice in her lungs sawed deeper. Her lungs screamed for air, her muscles for respite, and her stomach for nutrients. Her adaptive suit, constantly monitoring her physical state prickled against her skin and amplified the slow drip of her nutrients.

"Did you bring the decks?"

"What ... do you ... think?" her voice scraped out, breathy and inconsistent.

Coleen began to respond, but the sound of a step deterred her.

Marsilias emerged from the glass and with his passage it reverted to mist then dispelled. He saw Jade on the floor and strode over with a muttered profanity. Grasping her arms in featherlight hands, he guided her to a chair and settled her on it. "Sorry, Jade, I always forget the bridge affects you so much more than everybody else. Don't worry though, I have the perfect solution." He tapped a combination on his desk and a drawer ejected. His hand delved inside and returned with a generous slice of red velvet cake. "Eat up."

Coleen stalked closer, close enough to infringe on personal space, and coughed meaningfully. Marsilias answered her demand for attention with a raised eyebrow. "Yes?"

"What is the meaning of this? Your Specter could barely walk when she emerged from the Bridge. How was she the choice for carrying your decks? And what is wrong with her?"

"Jade suffers from extensive and chronic physical trauma due to previous extreme over-abuse of her Specter abilities. As for why her, I trust her, and she's never failed me before." As he spoke, Marsilias dug through Jade's coat, extracting first the small key then retrieving the three decks. "See?"

"All right, but are they functional? Did you provide a test card?" Coleen extended a gloved hand and Marsilias surrendered the first deck into her keeping.

Jade spoke through a mouthful, "Oh, they work; his pathway

wouldn't have protested as much if they didn't." She shoveled another bite between her lips, trying to ignore the ache in her lungs and the bruise across her chest. Occasional uses of the First Step typically caused her barely any pain, and only repeated abuse or accessing the higher steps deteriorated her condition, but ferrying decks across a bridge always exerted increased strain.

"Forgive me if I don't accept your word; I sincerely doubt you are capable of ascertaining a deck's effectiveness when other Specters are not." She passed the entrusted deck to the foremost of her lackeys. "Where is the test card, I wish to verify their effectiveness. Unless, that is, you wish to include a private Invoker?"

"Nah, it's the top card. I made one for all of them."

Coleen removed her left glove and snapped at her lackey, who delivered the top card. The card back flashed as she flipped it to reveal the image of a paper plane soaring over water. She raised the card to the ceiling light and a pulse rippled down her arm, into the card, then back. The card shuddered and its image eased into life. It started with the waves. The spray flecked the card's surface and then the water crashed forward. Finally, the airplane soared forward, up and out of the card into the room. It glided around them, circling the room before alighting on Coleen's expectant hand. In its wake, the card withered to lifeless gray.

"Quality work, Mr. Wreign; the Savant Corporation is satisfied with your labors. I suspect we'll have a new contract for you soon enough." Coleen snapped for her lackeys to collect the final decks, and departed.

Marsilias sat and waited for the office doors to close before addressing Jade, "Feeling better?"

Jade nodded, assiduously licking cake from her fork and scraping dregs of icing from the plate. "Another slice would increase my chances of survival."

"That's good, I'm expecting our announcement any moment now."

She froze, then slowly leveled a suspicious gaze on him. "What announcement?"

He grinned. "The announcement of our transfer, of course. I hear the Data Corporation's sending us to work with the Purifiers in some new operation or other."

"What did you do?"

"Oh nothing."

A buzz in her ear informed her of an incoming call. She acknowledged it with a tap. A man, probably a secretary, spoke into her ear, "Miss Dieza, please return to the Data Corporation's headquarters; you are being transferred."

The transmission ended and she refocused on Marsilias with a swallow. "Why?"

His smile saddened. "A couple reasons; you've been hiding from them for long enough, and it hasn't worked. Maybe a few drops here and there will help you actually start to heal mentally. Beyond that, something's happening, and I can't help solve it if I'm outside." His gaze fell to his hands. "And there's something else, a pressure, an urge I can't explain." He looked at her, his smile utterly gone. "I remember feeling like this before, two years ago."

Jade's head dropped back. *"God damn it."*

What Came Before

The rain screamed westward, pummeling their hovercraft until it trembled and veiling the world in gray. Lightning streaked past in waves, surfing the tumultuous clouds as peridons soared in pursuit, the fur of their vast wings erect and sparking with electricity. They craned long, sinuous necks whose veins glowed with harvested energy, and shrieked cries that sparked with internal lightning. The crests on their heads flared, turning from dull browns to luminescent, electric greens and blues, adding their own light to the storm.

Alone and seated atop a scavenged pillow, Jade observed all of it from the lounge's bottommost tier, her coat wrapped tight against a chill her adaptive suit just could not seem to mitigate. The lounge's two upper levels boasted spacious furnishings, warmed seats, video screens, consoles, and refreshments—everything required for a pleasant voyage—and the third level hosted telescopes capable of penetrating the storms. Her current floor delivered a view of the ocean, lightning, avian species, and torrential rain.

As she watched the outside world pass, her thoughts beat a staccato rhythm, whirling with inane fears and barking back at the stupidity of those fears. They weren't going to reinstate her into the Purifier Cores; they had no need or desire for barely functioning mental patients. *"Worst case scenario,"* she told herself, *"someone from one division or another comes back dead. Just stay away from everybody, don't get involved, make sure Marsilias gets out alive, and you'll be fine."* Images of Purifiers returning from a mission in screaming, mangled ruins filled her mind; men and women upon stretchers begging for help with crushed limbs or faces so charred she could only recognize them by their voices. Her throat constricted and she dropped her head forward to rest on her knees, groaning.

Jade pushed the images aside, concentrating on the other memories their destination roused: of the Purifier Academy; of being alone in small, cold rooms with android instructors, or of larger rooms where adults taught her how to kill and how to behave. She sighed and opened her eyes, focusing on the immediate surroundings before her memories inevitably shifted to her brother. A familiar pang of loss slipped through her, aching with the desire to hear him laugh again, to see him smiling at her, and the way his beautiful eyes sparked with mischief. Jade quelled her grief before it became something worse.

She watched the peridons until they escaped her vision then absently rose to tour the lounge's oval interior. The lightning swelled again, illuminating the floor an electric blue and skittering across the plane's underbelly. She quickly looked up, catching her shadow as it frolicked across the ceiling in the distorted light. Further above Marsilias sat locked to his seat in a web of belts.

He noticed her attention and beckoned her with a wan look and a wave. She chuckled but acceded, climbing the spiraling ramp to his empty tier and carefully masking her stress. He met her with a taut glance. "Tell me we're almost there, please."

She dropped into the seat opposite him, purring internally as it warmed, and snuggled deeper. "Almost. I still can't believe you're scared of flying, big bad former soldier that you are; must not have taught you how in training."

"As you well know, I was a combat medic, not a soldier, and I'm not scared of flying–" The plane lurched under a particularly onerous deluge, extorting a profanity. He swallowed. "It's not so much the flying as all the shaking and lightning. I dislike the former, all it takes is one mechanical failure for that lightning to fry all of us. Mostly, I just don't like not being in control of the plane personally."

"I can see if they'd let me fly." She batted her eyelashes innocently.

"That would be even worse."

She lounged back, bobbing a foot in rhythm with the skittering lightning. "I wouldn't resent the lightning; it's keeping us in the air. And it's beautiful." She reached down, tracing electric veins in the middle tier's floor as they coursed with borrowed energy.

"If it wasn't the lightning, it'd be something else powering us." He flinched at another shudder.

"Would you like me to ask how much longer?"

"Yes, please."

Sighing theatrically, she vacated her seat and crossed the lounge to where its crystalline walls merged into a shadowed corridor of metal. Polychrome energy lines sprawled over its walls, flashing in concert with the lightning and humming a constant soft resonance. Mild static electricity leapt onto her as she entered, weaving across her clothing and hair until the corridor opened into a low, but generous cockpit swamped with glowing consoles.

A Core of Purifiers glanced over from a round table cloistered in a plush alcove, the holographic game between them pausing. One, a young man no more than a few years graduated from the Purifier Academy, stepped out to greet her. "Do you need something, miss?" Impatience colored his tone, though none disturbed his features or posture.

"Yes, I was hoping for an ETA?" Jade absently inspected the weapons charging along the walls: an array of cannons and pistols in both electric and explosive canister varieties, clusters of shock charges—fist-sized discs containing energy equivalent to a lightning bolt—and stacks of pulse-knife bracers–thin rectangular boxes that attached to one's forearm and projected knifelike sidearms.

"We're about a minute out, miss. You can see the compound from here." The Purifier directed her gaze to the front windshield. There, obscured by torrential rain, racing lightning, and tenebrous clouds towered a protrusion of rock. It rose from the rampaging currents like a solitary spear and expanded at its tip, resembling a mushroom's cap.

She signaled her gratitude and rejoined Marsilias. "We're about a minute out, the compound's in sight."

"I don't know why we couldn't go by submersible; it'd be safer even in these waters."

"The Purifiers want to regulate access to their facility, so they omitted a wet-dock." She grabbed a reading pad from the side table and inattentively skimmed the available titles: tawdry romance mostly. "And there's big fish. Really big fish." She tossed the reading pad back to the table, rested her chin on her hand, and continued contemplating whether or not to steal one to 'accidentally forget' in a superior's desk drawer.

He issued a sigh of aggrievement at her logic as the hovercraft commenced its descent. "Did you and your brother stay here much?"

She shook her head, ignoring the pang of grief. "No, after the academy we never left the field, just proceeded from mission to mission. They never even recalled us for promotions or awards."

Decelerating, the hovercraft entered the stone cap's shadow and into view of the fleet clutching its underside like bats. Their hovercraft navigated the swarming schools of air traffic, circumventing both lugubrious transport vessels and sleek military vehicles of the smaller designations, until it located a vacancy and docked. Two Purifier capital ships idled near the ocean's surface, presumably Behemoth class due to their middling size.

"All right, we're here." Jade slapped Marsilias's shoulder in fabricated cheer and stood, armoring herself with a porcelain grin. He caught her hand as she moved to depart and squeezed, catching her attention to offer one last apologetic smile. She squeezed back. "It's alright, I understand." It wasn't, but she did understand, and she suspected he had little choice in the matter. Marsilias began unbuckling, and she continued toward the ascending ramp.

They climbed to the lounge's observatory, where a cluster of Purifiers waited at a circular lift encased in duraglau walls. A few acknowledged Jade and Marsilias as they entered, but most ignored them other than to provide space, their conversations fading, strangled by distrust and suspicions of inter-corporation intrigue.

The Purifiers represented a comparatively young corporation, having claimed governing influence and privileges mere decades prior when they seceded from the Defense Corporation's experimental division. Their nascence prompted conflicts and legal debates over boundaries, regulations, and authority concerning sibling corporations—debates that persisted even now, prolonged by the Purifier Corporation's naked ambition and vehement secrecy. As a result, the Defense Corporation nursed a particular loathing for them.

The lift ascended via a porthole in the rock into the Purifier Corporation's cavernous air-dock and delivered them onto a web of elevated walkways, the floor below reserved for the swarming vehicles, automatons, engineers, and clerks tending the fleet. Vast service ducts plunged from the ceiling, delivering crates of materials, equipment, and resources onto stacks in between the jutting portholes for the docking lifts. Purifier Cores populated the walkways, many returning from missions and burdened with injured or dead.

Marsilias advanced to the railing, draping his hands across it, and assessed the immense space, devoting scrupulous attention to the Purifier personnel. "Smaller than I expected, considering all the planes below ... lots of Savants also, more than the Defense Corporation employs."

"We're not fighting humans, and it's only one of six docks." Jade pointed to the ceiling where a command room surveyed proceedings. "Traffic is directed from there, as well as a sixth of the compound's energy supply." She redirected his attention to the tapered end of the room. "That's the entrance to the main building and–"

"The tour can wait." One of the Purifiers that had accompanied them on the flight abruptly stopped beside Jade. "Prime March said to bring you immediately. Please follow me." Gesturing sharply, the Purifier marched along the walkway, gracefully navigating the Cores of his fellows and the intermingled androids hauling equipment.

Jade followed at a stroll, leaning close enough to whisper to Marsilias, "Best beware, Master Wreign, rumor is it's all haunted." She oooohed spooky noises in his ear. "Of no natural substance is this complex made, and yet the only sign of life they ever found was a series of inexplicable dark pools interred far from the ocean, filled with skeletons and enormous idols of stone fish. Like blood, they say the water was, thick to the touch, cold as ice, and it stained the skin. Rumors also say it was the site of pagan sacrifice rituals, and the souls of the condemned still wander here."

He leaned closer, glancing about as if to ensure none overheard. "And what do you say?"

She drew back slightly, widening her eyes and lowering her tone to one of despair. "That I am a ghost."

He assumed a serious facade. "And why do you linger?"

"I search for that which was denied me in life."

"Which was?"

"Cookies."

"A worthy reason. I happened to have some. Would you like one?"

"Yes, thank you. I will forestall your haunting."

"I appreciate it."

Several Purifier groups further ahead, their guide glanced back to verify their progress, noted their absence and whirled about, scanning the massed people until he caught Marsilias overtly smuggling Jade a peanut butter cookie. His features contorted in disbelief then shifted to irritation. He stormed back to them. "Can you please move faster? Prime March expects us."

"Sorry"—Jade, munching on her cookie, indicated Marsilias's corpulence—"amble's the best I can get. I suppose we could push him in a trolley. He'd like that."

"I am growing rather old, and that flight turned my stomach, a ride could do me good."

The Purifier's finger stabbed Marsilias's chest. "You can move just fine, so stop it. You may not care, but we all have important missions to complete. And, a little advice, Prime March hates clowns." He stalked off, barking at a pair of lagging Purifier trainees and snapping to clear the way.

Marsilias rubbed his chin. "I wonder how he'd react if you fainted?"

"Probably with distrust; best not to torment him, we wouldn't want to be fired or cultivate a reputation for being unreliable. God, can you believe some people have the audacity to not arrive on time to their assigned employment? It turns my stomach." She shook her head in disbelief.

The air-dock's walkways converged at an extensive landing platform that functioned as both congregation point and routes into the complex proper, extending through a wide entrance and sensor-gates to an atrium of jagged rock veined with salt. Purifiers milled within, loitering, gathering for departures, accessing the numerous conveyor stations, or taking ramps to adjacent chambers or routes. Directory consoles flashed beside every station to instruct newly graduated Purifiers on the compound or brief outgoing Cores on their destination's intricacies.

Jade and Marsilias's guide delivered them to a private omniveyor isolated from the main atrium by an alcove and holographic lines. The doors parted preemptively, revealing Prime March at the omniveyor's center, the reinforced walls reflecting his masked visage. Jade flinched at the sight, the vestigial sense of ease scattering beneath the gaze of that imperious skull mask: a garish, but effective, affectation of the Sovereign Cores' lethality. Ilin had received a similar mask hours before he died.

Prime March assessed them perfunctorily, their disposition, the cookie crumbs on her jacket, and then dismissed the Purifier. "Come in."

Jade settled on the handrail opposite him, breathing in the stagnant, lemon-scented air. "Hello, Prime March."

"Hello, Jade, Professor Wreign."

Marsilias squeezed in. "Use Marsilias, I haven't been your professor in years, Theeran."

"No, you just happened to infiltrate my most clandestine operation within days of conceiving its possibility." He shot Jade a condemning look. "With a dying profession no less; this corporation's never even contracted Data Management before." He touched his thumb against a console, then inserted their destination when it beeped confirmation.

Marsilias grinned. "Peeved?"

"A little, but I suppose any man who can insert himself into my operations deserves a place there. I am curious as to how you convinced the board to hire you though. I queried, but they indicated that wasn't a welcome line of questioning." The omniveyor plummeted, humming down a shoot of dark stone punctuated by flashes of light from diverging routes and landings. The temperature declined with their descent, feeling almost like a tangible weight with the miles of black ocean and rock above them.

Jade wrapped her arms about herself, leaned back and forced herself to remember that the crushing weight and pressure of all that water was no burden to her. She could leave whenever she wished, simply float up through all those miles of ocean and feel nothing. "What are you doing here, Prime March? You weren't a man of research before."

"No, but I have more experience in the subject than any other Sovereign." The console dinged, its display indicating they had descended below the ocean floor. "We're researching revenants."

Jade snorted. "We're always researching revenants; there's nothing special about that–"

Marsilias interrupted, his attention riveted on Prime March but his tone more of confirmation than realization, "They're alive. You're researching live revenants."

"Yes, though the project's still young. Previously, we only had one inmate."

Jade shivered, violet eyes flashing in her mind and twisting her emotions taut. "... Oh."

Prime March nodded, grimace evident in his voice. "Yes. Anyway, this Chandris creature is our newest addition, and the current focus. Your jobs will be to record, evaluate, and filter any relevant information we receive. Adhering to strict codes of secrecy, of course."

The omniveyor halted and opened onto a vacant corridor of white-paneled walls. Prime March exited, metal-shod heels clicking. "The walls are outfitted with sensors, pulse-emitters, and electric barriers to sequester and destroy any escaped revenant." He turned a corner into a reception or common room of some sort. The carpeted floors here smelled of pine—which helped mask the burning odor infesting the compound—and an assortment of olive-green sofas, chairs, and beds occupied much of the floor space. A series of doors appeared to host a kitchen, showers, and a dormitory. The walls soared several floors high but boasted neither decorations nor any other features she could distinguish.

"This is extensive," Marsilias commented. "Your crew reside permanently?"

"Some choose to, but it is not a requirement, and their movements are unrestricted." Prime March summoned the lounging Purifiers. "Gather round, we have new assistants."

The Purifiers abandoned their games, drinks, reading, and dozing without a word, no more than a score all told–five Cores– and each bearing a Siphon.

Prime March clapped Jade's shoulder. "This is Jade Dieza, and that is Marsilias Wreign. Neither are combatants so protect them if anything goes sour. They are here to assist with our research and manage the data we collect, nothing more." He reverted his attention to Jade and Marsilias. "There's too many here to introduce properly, but you'll acquaint yourselves soon enough. You can be assigned quarters later if you so desire; but for now, let's continue."

He directed them to a narrow corridor opposite the primary entrance, where a crackling barrier of energy impeded their progress. "I apologize for this, but you'll have to request help from the other Purifiers to pass this point. Unless you've ... found your Siphon again, Jade?" She shook her head, prompting a shrug as he retrieved his Siphon and thrust it into the snarling electricity. It flared green and subsided. "We code this barrier so only Purifiers can pass, and they need their Siphons registered in its matrix beforehand." He proceeded down the passage and the electric barrier reactivated after them.

After a few turns and a brief upward jaunt, the corridor expanded to a room, though in truth it barely exceeded the corridor's width. Its walls soared upward, however, black and flickering with an intricate tapestry of silver and white lines. "This is our programming and information center; it's also where you'll do most of your work."

Marsilias spun slowly to examine the room. "You say information center, but where are the consoles? Our access hubs?"

"Every wall is a console and a connection point. Anyone can access the superficial layers of programming and information, but more delicate information and controls require passcodes. I'll entrust them to you when you begin. For now, I advise testing the data stream."

Jade knelt to press her fingers on the ground and a stream of data instantly slipped past her consciousness, causing her to look at Prime March. "We don't need connection wires?"

"No, the implants in your arms suffice to make a connection. Your earpieces as well if they made contact."

Marsilias laughed abruptly, his hand against the wall. "This isn't just the data for your operation, this connects to the Purifier Corporation's mainframe! Even the classified details from upper management."

"And I expect you to exercise restraint, Mr. Wreign. We linked our server to the mainframe on the off chance I needed information stored there, nothing else."

Marsilias disconnected, but his grin lingered. "Don't worry, I won't do anything."

Jade delved further and the network engulfed her mind, a literal ocean of information in files, programs, messages, and unattached phrases. A wall appeared before her, splitting the tides of information. It demanded the passcode, but she ignored it and submerged deeper.

She had always excelled at hacking and had nurtured that skill throughout her academy days. It still required a program, which she carried in her earpiece and arm implants, to access the firewalls but relied mostly on mental alacrity. Snare coding bombarded her, almost indiscernible from the regular data streams, followed by programs that assailed her and shuttered the routes deeper into the mainframe. And all the while, the net closed in on her, racing to capture her before she found its coding. All of this occurred simultaneously as she tapped a code into the floor. An instant passed and she found the firewall's coding. A quick amendment followed and the Purifier Corporation's defenses just drifted past her, unable to recognize her presence. This done she began to search.

It was the work of moments to find the code she sought, even in the sea of the Purifier Corporation's network, its location predetermined to her by experience. She found it attached to the surveillance web like a cancer in the bloodstream: a parasite of foreign programs and amended code to suppress, transfer, and collect information, and grant access; all of it invisible, unalterable even if they could have seen it, to any who were not among the anointed.

She carefully withdrew from the data stream and stood, schooling her features into a façade of calm lest Marsilias recognize her disquiet. He couldn't be allowed to explore where that code led, not when she knew what was waiting at the end of it. Internally she understood that the code's presence here made sense: the Purifiers were a young and powerful corporation, and would likely define the coming century. Normally, she would have left it at that, but there were forces compelling Marsilias to come here, and that made her hair stand on end.

Prime March addressed her, pulling her attention back to the immediate present, "You ready to continue?"

She nodded, discarding the revelation until she could properly devote the attention it required. They proceeded to the wall opposite the entrance, which Prime March opened with a touch. "This is our prison compound. It's designed as a maze, but every wall is a restricted access point to the mainframe, so don't worry about wandering lost. We call it the Labyrinth."

Jade peered through, grimacing at the stark white paneled hallways. One corridor ran horizontally past the door, another directly ahead, both identically bereft of distinction. "How do you observe the revenants?"

Prime March entered the corridor, gray apparel stark against the perpetual white. "The walls conceal the prisons and are capable of transparency on either one or both sides. Entrances are the same, only they open. There are no dead ends, and the revenants cannot access the data stream; so even if they escaped, they couldn't find their way out."

Marsilias peeked down the horizontal passage. "How many inmates?"

"Two speaking revenants, and fifty-seven normal of varying power."

Jade started. "Fifty-seven! How did you capture so many?"

"With a lot of work and several teams. It also involved a little help from our first inmate–"

"Prime March!" A voice intruded from the forward-running corridor.

"Yes, Major Vera?"

"Inmate One has requested to speak with someone named Jade Dieza."

Immediate, visceral horror welled within Jade, clamping on her throat and curling her shoulders inward to a huddle as a vision of gleeful violet eyes filled her mind. She felt a spectral hand on her cheek and saw it in her mind's eye, covered in gore and cold as the dead. It caressed her cheek, smearing her with blood and bits of bone and flesh, then clamped tight, digging broken nails into her skin until she bled.

"*Stop struggling,*" a phantom voice said, "*I promised I would never hurt you. Trust me, I love you.*" And then the voice started cackling, and the hand dug deeper as her brother grinned at her. She grit her teeth against the words, latching onto Prime March's voice as he continued speaking.

"What? He shouldn't even know she's here! How?"

"I don't know, sir. He–"

"Wait, never mind. It doesn't matter; deny him immediately. And sedate him while she's here."

"Sir, he's offered to permit physical testing."

Lord March froze, the internal debate obvious in his posture. Silence ensued, then his inscrutable features shifted toward her. "Jade, I hate to ask this, but ..."

Marsilias frowned. "Theeran, I'm not sure what this is, but I don't think you should be asking it. And, Jade, you don't have to accept."

"Actually, she does," his tone bitter, Prime March raked Marsilias with a look, "you returned her to our employ, and— unlike you at the Data Corporation—I can terminate that employ- ment. If she wants to stay here, she has to actually obey."

"You shouldn't ask her to do whatever this is then!"

"I have to! I still have a job to fulfill, and I am still subordinate to the Administration Board and other Sovereigns. Now, are you going to do your job or not?" He restored his attention to her, his posture like granite.

Jade clutched her coat tight, sick to her stomach but nodded all the same. "I'll do it." She didn't have a choice, not if she wanted to stay. She didn't want to be here, of course, but if the worst tran- spired, and Marsilias's words of yesterday, "... there's something else, a pressure, an urge I can't explain...." fulfilled what they implied, she needed to be here. "Show me where he is."

All protest died on Marsilias's lips, leaving him grim but resigned.

Prime March relaxed fractionally. "Thank you. This could be invaluable–"

"I don't care. Just get it over with."

He gave a stiff nod and entered the Labyrinth, barking orders and restrictions into his earpiece, summoning guards and researchers to accompany him. They trailed him through a dozen turns of unyielding white, their group inflating to thrice its original size with armored Purifiers, white-coated scientists, and clerks. He guided them to a featureless wall and pressed his hand against a smaller panel before glancing toward Jade for final confirmation.

She wordlessly stepped beside him, nodding stiffly with her hands buried in her coat.

The panel cleared.

A tall man glanced out, his gorgeous features illuminated with a smile, and his dusky hair highlighted by a streak of pink. He rose from the regulation cot, loose blue clothing fluttering from the unseen air vent. He stopped inches from the wall, perfectly opposite her, and gazed lovingly out with radiant violet eyes. "Hello, sister."

She flinched. Everything about him screamed that he was her brother, the way he moved, the way he talked, his mannerisms, even his expressions. Yet, she knew he was not. She remembered her brother dying in the mist, and she remembered something else stepping into his body. She remembered him trying to kill her, grinding her into the stone cobbles of a foreign world while laughing.

"What do you want?"

The smile never faded but it softened, as if with melancholy. "Just to say hi. It's been forever since we've seen each other. I miss you. I also wanted to show you something."

"Stop it," she growled unsteadily, trying and failing to conceal the turmoil of grief, fear, and pain inside her. "You're not him."

The feigned personality evaporated as naturally as breathing. "All right, suit yourself." He strolled back to his cot. "But I did want to show you something."

"What?"

"Just this." He grasped either side of her brother's head and twisted it one hundred and eighty degrees around, snapping bones with a gristly crunch and tearing flesh.

Jade shrieked involuntarily and recoiled. Then she screamed hatred at him and covered her eyes.

"You see, because your brother's dead I can mutilate this body in any way I want. There's still pain of course, but that's no issue." There was another crunch.

Jade yanked her hands away and screamed helplessly, "Stop that!"

"Why? I'm not your brother, so why should you care what I do with my body?"

She stalked to the barrier, stabbing it with a finger and growling. "It's not your body. Leave it alone!" Somebody, Marsilias probably, caught her arm and gently, but insistently, pulled her back.

The monster in the cell twisted its head back around and stepped back to the barrier. "Wait! Not yet. Just a few questions, and I promise I'll be good." A moment of tense silence ensued, then when Jade made no indication of leaving, Marsilias released her. The monster stepped carefully away, hands spread in a gesture of appeasement. "So, how long do you plan on staying?"

Jade met its gaze, powerlessly hating it with every fiber of her being. "I don't know. Long enough to finish the job."

He lay down. "I see you're still wearing my coat, but you seem to be missing some buttons; that's no way to treat it."

She flinched, hands instinctively twitching to finger the frayed buttonholes. "I'll find a way to fix it."

"I could tell you how, you know. It's all up here...." He tapped his forehead. "All his memories, all his knowledge, and so very much about you. You were both prodigies, graduated years before you should have even entered the academy. And yet–"

"If this is all you wanted, then I'm done."

She turned to leave, but he spoke again, "All right, but I get to ask a question first."

"I don't have to answer anything–"

"Only if you don't want your friends to have their experimentation period...."

"That's not the arrangement we agreed to," Prime March snapped.

"You never agreed to anything, you just brought her here and opened the wall." His eyes flicked from Jade to Prime March. "All I want is one question. It won't even be a dangerous question, and then you can have your fun with me."

Prime March began to berate him, but Jade raised a hand. "What is your question?" She forced the words through her lips, forced herself to confront his quirked grin.

He stood again and pressed his lips as close to the wall as he could without deforming his face. "Are you still a Purifier? Or did you run away from that too?"

"I resigned."

"That's a shame." He reached across his body and snapped one wrist all the way back.

Jade screamed and threw herself at the wall, both hands snatching training Siphons from her back. But the guard was already moving, catching her about the waist and locking his arms so that she could only scream. "I'll kill you! You hear me? I'll kill you if you hurt him again!"

The monster laughed. "But I thought you were retired?"

Her words came out in a growl, "I will make an exception."

"And they will stop you, because I'm more important than you are."

Prime March pulled her from the guard's arm before she could make a reply and shoved her down the corridor. "Go. Leave before you make a mistake I cannot tolerate."

She stumbled and whirled on him, teeth bared in a snarl. He met her gaze and calmly addressed an assistant off to the side. "Prepare the research team. Full hazmat gear, only androids in the room, and a full Core for protection." His gaze never wavered from her. "Miss Dieza, if you wish to remain in our employ you will leave. Now."

She obeyed, visions of her brother's mutilated corpse rapidly usurping the rage. She staggered and then fled at a stride, his agonized screams filling her mind, condemning her, hating her for letting that thing live in his skin.

Marsilias called after her, but she barely heard him over the clamor in her mind. She heard the monster though, hailing after her. "Oh, and call me Ilin.

Voluntary Incarceration

Chandris roused from the half-sleep of his wondering consciousness and inhaled. The cold, sterilized air bit into his lungs and then seeped further down. His eyes slid open, reassessing the paltry confines of his prison with its sterile white hue and shallow roof. Only a small, transparent mattress disturbed the cell's symmetry. That, and Chandris's own hunched form in a corner.

His eyes drifted closed again, and his mind roved. A scattered collection of trivial, foreign consciousnesses brushed his own, but he discarded these and quested further, testing for any familiar essence. He encountered one within moments: the woman's, her emotions a tangle of despair, misery, and rage. As before, however, there was something of *Aeria* within her, and he found himself intrigued. How did a living creature such as her harbor any amount of death?

Chandris returned his questing consciousness to his body and settled forward on his haunches. He could feel the false *luce* of electricity coursing through the walls, his wardens' frantic excitement as their emotions flared and their attention fastened upon something else. He ignored them, sinking instead into the vast well of his essence and untethering it. The golden energy billowed free, a source of light and heat swirling within the confines of his physical form. He marshaled that *luce*—his essence—to eddy behind his lips, and then exhaled it as diaphanous light.

Warmth bloomed on the air before him, prompting Chandris to open his eyes and inspect the drifting cloud of soft light. He raised his index and forefinger, brushing them along his hair and causing them to redden as if immersed in dye, then swept them through the essence. Color bled into their trail, saturating and defining the *luce.* In quick succession, Chandris extracted colors from his eyes, skin, and clothing, and poured them into the essence, sculpting it into a reflection of his physical form without mass. Lastly, he bound a thread of *Aeria* from within himself to the reflection, enough to harbor his consciousness and fragments of perception. Then he lay his physical body upon the tiles, curled up like a feline, and closed his eyes.

His consciousness traversed the connecting strand of *Aeria* permeating the reflection, took root in its center and opened its eyes. He gauged his surroundings and all seemed as previous, his wardens ignorant of his actions, so Chandris propelled his reflection forward, vacating his cell, unopposed by the walls or defense mechanisms. His departure provoked no reaction from his captors, their cameras unable to recognize *luce* of such low density and thus blind to his reflection. So Chandris walked, phasing through barriers and corridors in pursuit of the woman's consciousness, heedless of the *vestiges* imprisoned within the cells he passed.

She seemed to perceive his advance, for her whole body stilled with it, as if paralyzed. Then her emotions evaporated like a snuffed flame, and in their absence, her consciousness darkened with violence, the preparation as sharp as a bared knife. Chandris stilled in turn, not in fear for she could not harm his reflection, but in realization that he interacted with a lethal being, and that this woman had experienced *Aeria*, not glimpsed or learned of it from a distance, but touched it so wholly her being echoed with it.

He emerged into the otherwise deserted corridor and settled in front of her, diminishing himself as much as his reflected physical shape would permit.

Pressed against the opposing wall, she answered his appearance with stressed appraisal, tapping a silver rod against her thigh. "Aren't you supposed to be locked up?"

"There is no need to arm yourself against me, or for fear, Jade Dieza. I intend no harm."

"That's hard to believe when you're wandering about unchecked instead of imprisoned." Her fingers spasmed on the silver rod, clasping and unclasping involuntarily, smearing it with sweat, betraying stress.

Chandris responded gently, stripping his voice of force and reducing it to decibels barely above a whisper, softening every aspect of himself. "Your senses deceive you; I do not wander freely. This is a projection of myself and can touch nothing."

"If you can't touch anything, then why leave?"

"To converse with you."

Her wide, staring eyes finally blinked. "Why would you want to speak with me?"

"To ask how you have such an extensive connection with *Aeria* when all those around you are almost entirely ignorant of it?"

"*Aeria?*"

"My world."

"Oh.... How would you know that?" Her thoughts surged with the preparations for violence. "Were you there?"

"I know nothing of what you imply. I perceived *Aeria's* influence on your being, a pervasive echo of its existence upon you that I have encountered nowhere else, and wondered of it."

"Then don't move." Her free hand delved into an external pocket, unlatching a simple clasp to retrieve a disc of tarnished metal. Her fingers flicked, launching it through his reflection to ping against the opposite wall and clatter to the floor. She regarded it, then sagged against her wall, expelling a sigh. "Okay. I ... almost believe you." She raked her hair back, exposing a brow glistening with sweat. "You can stop whispering if you want; I'm not going to attack you unless you earn it."

"Will you answer my question?"

"I have ... more experience with your world than most." She readjusted her grip on the rod and restored it to the small of her back. "There has to be more, Chandris. You wouldn't leave your cell for a single question."

He cocked his head. "Why not?"

"Because it's gonna freak out whoever's watching you! They must be terrified and.... Where are the alarms? Your escape should have triggered alarms. You didn't kill your guards, did you?"

"No. This form does not register on your sensors, thus it triggers no alarms."

"I suppose that's good to know." She observed him for a long while, the tension gradually receding from her posture until her shoulders drooped. "Why are you here, Chandris? The ... *vestiges* hunt us for sustenance but you only seem to be here for the sake of it."

"This world interests me. I have known the vastness of existence and forgotten it. Only memories of *Aeria* endure, nothing of this world, nothing of this existence."

"Then why do it from a prison?"

"Because I do not know this place and find it as interesting as any other." He left unsaid that he was hunted in *Aeria* and had no desire to be a fugitive here as well.

"Well, there's not much to learn here; this place is all about studying your kind."

"You say that, but *Aeria* clings to you, and infects many of you: death fused with life. I consider the contradiction interesting."

She slid to the ground and laid back, the turmoil of her emotions ceding to encompassing exhaustion. "I smell of death, do I? I guess I won't be interesting for long then."

Chandris lay himself upon the tiled floor beside her, resting his head upon his forearms. "It is neither disease nor sickness, nor does it seem to exert an ill effect upon you. Death appears unlikely."

She chuckled. "I know. I'm what we call a Savant. We have ... connections to other places. No one's figured out why yet. I guess those connections run through your world. Maybe because your *vestiges* keep crossing over."

"Perhaps. Will you answer something else?"

"Maybe. What's on your mind?"

"There is another of my kind in these prisons—a full *soul*—and I am curious: How did he come here?"

She flinched and the subsiding emotions returned with violence. "Oh, found him already, did you? He tried invading us a couple years back and lost. We'd never met one of your kind that spoke before, so we imprisoned him to study."

"Have you learned anything?"

"Don't know, haven't been here, and I'm not particularly interested in the results."

"What is he to you, then? Why did he seek to torment you?"

Chandris continued placidly. "And why do your kin suffer his assaults?"

"I think he does it because suffering in general seems to amuse him. They let him because his compliance is more viable than mine."

"If he has no other purpose here why does he not leave?"

"I don't know, I've never been here before, didn't realize it was anything more than a concept before today. Maybe he can't leave, you'll have to ask him."

"I will."

Voices and footsteps began echoing from the way she came, forestalling further conversation, "... worrying. She'll find her way back when she's ready."

"I am not worried; I do not want her wandering the complex unattended until she understands it and is properly registered. She should have known better than to run away, even if she was distressed."

Jade sighed. "Here we go. You'd best start running, or just poof and disappear because they won't like you being out."

"They cannot hurt me; I have no physical form."

"In that case, have fun." She rested her head back, crossed one knee over the other, and draped an arm over her eyes.

The steps and voices materialized into Prime March preceding a contingent of Purifiers and others in white coats, including Jade's companion from their first meeting, the large man. The group rounded the corner and froze, dialogues dwindling as all gazed upon him, agog, before erupting into motion. Those in white coats scrambled back while the Purifiers lunged to the forefront and fanned out, brilliant arcs of energy in many hues exploding from the rods they all carried. Prime March pressed through them, his silver rod expanding into an emerald scythe. "How did you escape?"

"I have not. I am a reflection of myself projected from my prison so I might converse with her." Chandris tipped his head toward Jade. "I represent no peril to you, even if I desired to cause you harm."

Prime March circled to the side, arching his neck to see over Chandris's bulk. "Jade, you alright?"

Without uncovering her eyes, she raised her other hand and waved. "Leave me out of this, I'm dead."

Chandris shifted to face the contingent, diminishing his voice as before. "She has sustained no injury, if that is your concern, and I have effected no change on any system, inhabitant, or device within this compound." His assurances fell on deaf ears, achieving neither physical nor emotional change in his wardens. They crept closer, spreading about Prime March.

Recognizing reassurances as pointless, Chandris rose. "As my presence causes you discomfort, I shall return to my body and cell. If Jade Dieza is amenable, I would appreciate resuming our discussion there." He relinquished his reflection and opened his eyes once more to the confines of his cell.

All remained as before with an exception: the facing wall's transparency. Purifiers dithered outside in two pairs, three females and one male, their weapons clenched in nervous hands and emotions vacillating between one extreme and the other, excitement to fear. The opening of his eyes spurred them from the wall, lips parting in profanities as their silver rods expanded in a kaleidoscope of such vivid amber and gold, mahogany and red, it dimmed the corridor's illumination.

Chandris stretched, arching his back from all fours, and lay himself upon the ground, resting his head on his forepaws. "You may inform your superiors I am once more imprisoned." Then he reclosed his eyes and waited.

Moments trickled into minutes before slow footsteps sounded in the corridor, enticing his attention to the window as Jade slipped into view and slouched one shoulder against it. "So, what else did you want to discuss?" Her fingers waved absently, shooing the attendant Purifiers to depart.

Chandris rose to a sit, moderating his shoulders and posture to slouch and appear vulnerable, inoffensive. "Why does your kind fear me? It is not a result I desire."

"Stop hiding, Chandris. We know you're capable of killing, so lying about it achieves nothing." Her head dropped against the window. "As for your question, didn't we discuss that already? Your kind hunts us like a predator, and you killed four of us not too long ago. You also recently absconded your cell, something they believed would restrain you. Your continued incarceration notwithstanding. Right now they're wondering if they need to kill you."

"Those four initiated the violence against me and, aside from that, I have attempted to dissuade their fears at every opportunity to no effect. The continued assurances of my benign intent seems pointless."

"Why should they—we—believe you? That's even without taking your appearance into account."

"Would the diminishing, the humanization, of my appearance alleviate their fears?"

Tension shivered through her, manifesting into a penetrating stare. "No, though it would probably help...."

"Even if it is a lie?"

"Deceit is human nature. We lie to ourselves every day and ignore disturbing truths. We don't even recognize it mostly, it's just habit and nature. All you have to do is make it easier for us."

He stretched. "Very well, I will assume a more human appearance."

The tension remained in her features. "You can do that?"

"Were we not just discussing the subject?"

"I ... hoped you meant hypothetically. Can you change yourself however you wish?"

"No. I may diminish parts of myself and discard others, but I cannot increase or fundamentally alter the form I assumed without returning to *Aeria*."

She hesitated then faced him fully, unable to stifle a twinge of interest. "Can you show me?"

"As you wish." Chandris reached for the *luce* comprising his physical form. He took and drank it anew, absorbing it into the depths of his being. His mane thinned and his streaked fur diminished to stripes of color. His tusks shrank into nubs, his claws into nails and his body to that of an ursine man in his youth, bright with magnetic vigor.

He assessed himself briefly and then reverted his attention to her. "Is this acceptable? I am loathe to diminish myself further but will do so if required." He flexed his muscles and rotated his joints, accustoming himself to the constraints of his new form.

She inspected him clinically. "Your hair and beard might need some grooming, but otherwise the ladies should be fawning over you in no time." The ghost of a smirk colored her lips. "One woman in particular; Serras always had a thing for redheads...." She glanced aside, focusing on nothing. "Okay. Commander says that's all, that I'm 'endangering' corporate employees by sharing private information. Yes, I know I wasn't supposed to share that with him, it, them? What are you, Chandris?"

"My current form is masculine."

"He's a– … Alright, alright I'm going." Purifiers followed after her, most glancing at him in the process.

Prime March assumed her place, pressing a flashing strip on his helm's side. All the while, his eyes measured constantly, reassessing. "You are a dangerous creature, Chandris, aren't you?"

Chandris situated himself on the mattress, having modeled his reduced stature against its length. "The other *soul* in your possession, how long has he lingered here?"

"Would he possess your same abilities or does your … species differ per individual."

"Variations are as common as similarities. How long?"

"Two years."

"Have you spoken with him often?"

"No, but I have conversed on occasion. Do you possess other abilities?" His emotions flowed through his spirit, a subdued confluence of excitement, caution, and dislike.

"Some. You do not fear us as others of your species do?"

"I have seen you die and consumed the vastness of your essence. I have no need to fear you."

"You drink of us? We are more akin than you believe, Prime March."

Something flashed green in the man's ear, inducing a pause. "I am summoned elsewhere, but I trust we will speak again."

Chandris observed his departure and then reclined on the mattress with an exhale. *Luce* streamed from his lips and he painted, constructing a reflection of himself as he now lay. Moments passed, and Chandris exited his prison cell anew. He traversed the corridors and pathways as before, following the presence of *luce* until he found the other *soul*.

The *soul* lifted an unabashedly serpentine gaze at Chandris's entrance into his cell, violet irises flashing an instant of surprise. He remained seated on the bed, however, legs crossed beneath him and arms resting on his thighs.

They regarded one another without so much as a twitch to disturb their composure. Chandris sought the *soul's* emotions but uncovered nothing. The silence slunk onward, passing back and forth between them until the other *soul* finally intruded with a single word and a low voice. "Hello."

Chandris lowered himself to ground and sat in imitation of his counterpart. "Do you have a name?"

"They call me Ilin. You may as well."

"Is that name given or chosen?"

"Both."

Their eyes never blinked, their lungs never swelled, and their skin never broke into goosebumps despite the freezing air.

"I felt your presence when I first arrived, and now I wonder why you linger? The meager entertainment of tormenting a single human seems insufficient to prompt such an extended sojourn."

"I cannot leave. They have imprisoned me here through their stolen energies." As he spoke, the other *soul* exposed his midriff, revealing a card of electric blue energy. It pulsed with its own rhythm, a storm of furious lines extending from where its edge merged with the *soul's* flesh. "One of their Magisters made this for me, a man called Marsilias Wreign; though he remained ignorant until today. It confines my essence to this body."

"Why not destroy the prison? You should be capable of such even in this state."

"My essence is fettered to this form. I move its muscles, breath its air, and consume the nutrients they provide. Still, this body is dead. It persists only because I expend energy to maintain it. And yet, I cannot survive on *luce* alone. I subsist largely on the nutrients they provide through their body suits. The ramifications of my position elude me, I cannot discern if my existence is tied to this body's."

"Are you dying?"

"Yes. I absorb no *luce* from the sustenance this body consumes and cannot gather more without escaping my cell and draining the humans of theirs."

"Could you abscond if an occurrence or time compelled you?"

"No. I am hampered by the extent of this body's capabilities. I can exceed them at a cost but doing so inflicts permanent damage to the body that requires *luce* to repair. Some of its natural abilities are moderately enhanced, however. This is a result of their Siphons I believe, and exclusive to the humans labeled Purifiers. What of you? Why submit yourself to captivity?"

"Because I am hunted in *Aeria*, and this world holds no acrimony towards me. Also, a particular human interests me."

The other *soul* smirked. "Jade Dieza?"

"Yes. She smells and feels of *Aeria,* and perceived my reflection's advent before my arrival. Something you were ignorant of. She diverges from her kin, and I wish to understand."

"Have you glimpsed her soul?"

"No. Does it harbor the truth I desire?"

"Yes. It is an impressive thing to witness, and bares the full truth of her existence."

"What does it say?"

"I won't tell you. But ask her how many revenants she's extinguished if you want a hint."

"*Vestiges* are of no interest to me, however many she has snuffed."

"No, but her kind consigns significance to that number, and comprehending their society is a method to understand her."

Chandris rose. "I will depart for now, lest they notice my absence and turn quarrelsome. I may return to converse later."

"I have one last question for you."

Chandris paused. "Ask it."

"Are you the one they're all looking for on the other side?"

"Unlikely, my pursuers are limited in number and obey personal motivations. Is one of our kin widely sought."

"Oh yes, one of the *Extranjerras* is in a frenzy searching for one of us, a newborn that matches your description...." A smile flitted across the *soul's* face.

"I am ignorant of this newborn, and much time has passed since my own birth."

"Well, if you find him, they're promising a feast for his capture."

"How do you know this, trapped here as you are?"

"Not everyone here is as they seem. Dig deep enough, and you'll find secrets on this side of existence. Some of those secrets have their fingers in this particular organization and will occasionally converse with me. They're privy to all sorts of interesting information." No deceit manifested in the *soul's* spirit.

"Then it is unfortunate I am not in a position to search." Chandris departed without further response, leaving Ilin to stare after him in a long silence.

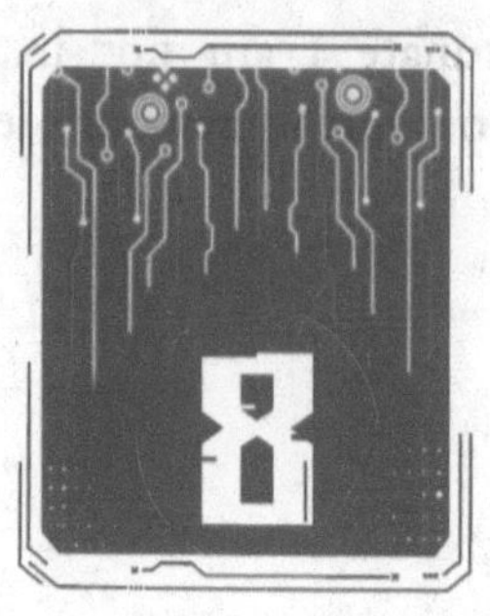

Index Case

The voice bobbed down through the haze of Jade's lucid dream, initially indiscernible from the murmuring dialogue filling her mind. Then it spoke, louder and out of sequence, intruding on another's dialogue, "–Jade!" She considered responding, the word hovering in her mind like a hook and bait as the dream continued to play around her, teasing her to surface and discover the purpose of its intrusion. Wearily, she accepted the hook, letting it extricate her from memories of mist and doors.

"Jade ... Jade...." The words snapped louder now, irritated by her lethargic response and emphasized by a hand jostling her shoulder. The insistence woke Jade fully and revealed a tall, muscular woman with one arm braced on her desk and the other currently badgering her shoulder.

"Who're you?"

The woman straightened, resting gloved hands on her hips with an affronted look. "Candice Yaal. We started at the academy together." She raked her blond hair back, catching it in a bunch. "I had short hair back then."

Another moment passed in uncertainty, then recollection gradually surfaced. "Oh, yeah. You ate a whole bucket of fire peppers on a dare, ended up sick in the infirmary for days." Jade stretched, extending her arms overhead with a satisfied moan, the embracing arms and sumptuous upholstery of her chair a cradle of warmth in the otherwise chilly information center. "Long time no see."

"I'll say, six years since you graduated?"

"Thereabouts. What are you doing here?"

"I graduated, dummy, Special Operations, and got assigned here on special request, don't know by who. Prime March wasn't pleased though. What about you? How long you been around?"

"About a week."

"And you're already sleeping on the job? That doesn't seem like you."

"I've changed."

Candice deflated. "Yeah, I suppose you would. I ... heard about Ilin, and your resignation from the Purifiers. They said it was a freak accident, something to do with a submersible?"

"Yeah ... something like that."

"At least they managed to salvage his coat. God, he loved that thing, would wear it all the time, said it was a family heirloom. Never understood how he didn't get hot, but he'd never answer any questions about it. I about died from curiosity."

Jade fingered one of the missing buttons, unable to quell a rise of shame. "Yeah. It's a Jysa heirloom, passed down from generation to generation. It was our mother's."

Candice sat on Jade's desk, grinning and crossing her arms. "So besides Ilin, what's been happening with you?" She leaned closer. "Any romantic interests I should know about?"

Jade started to respond, but Marsilias, happening to be passing by, dropped his weight on the back of her chair, causing it to dip perilously. "This woman? Hardly. She spends all her time sleeping. I honestly don't even know why she bothers with work if she's just going to sleep through it."

Jade slipped further down, snuggling into her chair's embrace and propping her feet on the desk. "I sleep better when there's something to do." Her eyes started to drift closed.

Marsilias tapped her nose. "None of that."

Currently regarding Marsilias with a slight frown, Candice blinked and leapt to her feet. "Professor Wreign! I didn't recognize you with the beard."

"There's no need for honorifics. I'm sure you were there when they discharged me."

Jade perked up. "You were discharged? I thought you left?"

Marsilias rocked his hand back and forth. "Eh, a little bit of both."

Candice grinned. "He got himself in a great big row with the entire Administration Board; they're still talking about it today. It might go down as an academy legend."

"What was this row about?"

"Nothing much; I disagreed with Principle Tarrison on some of her educating tactics, and she fired me."

"You called her a buzzard fish, among other things, and she never took well to contention in the first place."

Marsilias grinned. "You have to admit she does resemble one with those awful feathered cardigans."

"She does!" Jade exclaimed. "I never could figure out what she reminded me of. Ilin couldn't figure it out either. He always," Jade trailed off, and then leaned forward, freeing the chair from Marslias's weight and averting her face from Candice.

Candice coughed awkwardly and kept talking, "Anyway, I heard one of these new revenants has taken a liking to you?"

"*Souls*," Jade replied, "they're called *souls*. What we call revenants are partial, or vestigial, *souls*. And yeah, one seems to like me."

"Best not to get any ideas of going near it though. They're toxic to us."

Marsilias, his fingers gently rubbing Jade's back, froze. "Toxic? How?"

"They didn't tell you? That's– It doesn't matter. It's better shown anyway." She rose from Jade's desk, her previous conviviality fading to a grim intensity, and strode across the information center toward the Labyrinth, circumventing the scattered pillows and chairs Jade had smuggled in.

Marsilias followed her, unceremoniously kicking pillows aside. "Show us what?"

"Patient Zero." Candice opened the Labyrinth's entrance barrier then paused when Jade remained entrenched in her seat, scraping crumbs off her coat. "Jade, you really should see this too. You need to know what you're risking."

Jade rose and meandered to the other side of her desk, tension itching at the back of her skull. "I'm not a Purifier anymore, Candice. I'm here as an information specialist. It's your job to protect me, so I'll take full advantage of that and just cower in here."

"Jade–"

Marsilias touched Candice's arm, silencing her. "Jade, we should really know what this is about. It's ... not normal." His eyes and lips smiled softly, all apology and commiserations, but ultimately unyielding. This meant something and he knew it, like he always knew it when he brushed against something important.

Jade captured his eyes. *You sure?*

"Yeah."

"Okay, Silias." She rounded her desk, storing her hands in her pockets lest Candice see them shaking. *It's okay, you're here to research revenants and you're strong enough to handle it.* Barefoot, she stepped from pillow to pillow, squashing faces from various cartoons, popular bands, soap operas, and Prime March in several pink and indecent designs; because nothing bespoke the Purifiers' steel gray, killing extra-dimensional entities motif like the latest boy band. When pillows ran out, the tiles, warmed by their internal functions, thrummed invitingly beneath her bare feet, offering conduits into the data stream to the implants she carried in her body. She ignored these and reclaimed the fluffy self-warming slippers waiting for her beside the door. Extra fluffy edition. "All right, what happened with patient Zero? Why are the *souls* toxic to us?"

Candice continued into the Labyrinth. "I never saw it myself, and only saw him after I first arrived, but they told us about it a year ago in the academy. It began when they started experimenting on the first speaking revenant, this first *soul*. The chief examiner was a man named Thomas Yuer, and he often conversed with the first *soul*. There's weeks of dialogue between the two, ranging from conversations about this world to matters concerning the Afterlife. The first *soul* rarely contributed information freely, but Yuer managed to extract tidbits and accumulate information and names from Afterlife. Eventually, the *soul* struck a bargain with Yuer. It offered him the chance to experiment on it directly, promising not to harm him in return for a taste of our food. Eager to interact more closely, Yuer agreed.

"They experimented with and on the *soul* for two weeks, all according to scientific research guidelines of course, and discovered a wealth of information. Everything seemed to be progressing wonderfully until Yuer fell sick.

"He brushed it off as a cold at first and continued his research when the *soul* assured him no human virus could affect it. But Yuer's symptoms worsened, developing beyond coughing to cold sweats, hallucinations, and periods of blindness. His disease started to manifest external signs about this time. Black marks appeared around his face and fingertips. The assistant examiners forced him to take a hiatus and seek medical care. In his absence, they abandoned their research of the *soul*.

"He returned several weeks later in the peak of health and resumed his interactions with the *soul*. At first, everything proceeded as before, but after a couple days his symptoms resurfaced with doubled vigor. Yuer completely lost his eyesight, his skin mottled black, and his hallucinations evolved into periods of complete dementia.

"They immediately severed all contact with the *soul* and quarantined them both, but Yuer continued to deteriorate. He lasted another week before the disease consumed him. His caregivers and fellow researchers developed milder symptoms soon after the renewed outbreak and were quarantined as well. Thankfully, they recovered." Candice rounded a corner and pressed the wall. "They thoroughly inspected every afflicted team member but discovered no trace of any pathogen, virus, or even unknown substance. Besides the black spots, the infected appeared in perfect condition." The wall became transparent, revealing a prison cell and a naked man.

The man rocked back and forth on his feet in the center of the room. Transparent duraglau shackles bound his wrists and ankles. Drool dribbled from his muttering lips and feces littered the stained tiles around him.

"Most of the time he's catatonic, but other times he's viciously suicidal to the point of ramming himself into the walls repeatedly." She pointed to faded blood stains on the padded walls. "He's also utterly intolerant of other humans and will blindly attack anyone who enters. They have to subdue him every time they clean."

Marsilias peered through the observation wall. "How is he still alive?"

"They keep him permanently restrained and sustain his body

with nutrient gases."

"Why not just let him die?" Marsilias asked.

"Because they hope to find a cure or learn from him at least."

"What did the *soul* have to say about this?"

"That he had not anticipated Yuer's reaction, or the effect his mere presence would exert on us. I suppose it's to be expected though, with how we react to Afterlife's mist." She looked at Jade. "This is why you need to avoid your *soul* friend; he's poisonous to humans. Never go into the same room as him, and never allow physical contact. You'll be a danger to everybody else if you're infected; we don't need a pandemic on top of these things wandering around."

"Oh sure, of course. I'll be sure to cancel my afternoon tea with him. It'll be emotionally devastating, going without my inter-planar support monster, but I'll probably survive. About sixty percent chance, I'd say. Marsilias!"

"Yes?"

"If my math's off, you're in charge of my funeral. I want fireworks and cake. Lots of cake. That no one's allowed to eat. Bury it with me."

His eyes flicked back and forth as he copied her commands onto a digital notepad. "Lots of cake, got it. Everyone starves."

Jade nodded her satisfaction and grimly faced Candace. "My preparations are complete."

Candice observed her briefly then shrugged. "So long as you understand the danger, I'm sure there's nothing to worry over." She moved to depart then hesitated when they didn't follow. "You guys coming? We could get a few drinks, the selection here's actually really nice."

"Sorry, I am not a drinker." Jade shuddered. "Can't stand the taste and pass out after the first glass."

"She really can't hold it. We tried once a couple years back; she went from singing, to hysterical laughing, to hysterical crying between sips. I had to carry her out on my shoulder." Marsilias grinned.

"I would like to see that. You sure you won't come? I'll pay.... Okay, your loss. Do you guys need me to lead you back or let you out, or are you good?"

"We're good." Marsilias waved her away with a smile.

"Then I'm off, and I'm serious about hanging out sometime, Jade, just you and me. There's something we really should catch up on."

Marsilias waited until the retort of her steps disappeared before allowing his grin to die. "Jade?"

"Hmmm?"

He began stroking the lettering on his paper scarf. "I assume you've been plundering the Purifiers' suppressed information?"

"The incident about a man with black marks going berserk in an intoxicant den a couple days ago? Never heard of it."

"I don't know for certain if it's related...," He reached out and hammered the wall. Within the cell, Yuer erupted into shrieking frenzy. He thrashed, hurling himself back and forth with such violence both shoulders dislocated and then snapped back into place. "but don't you think we'd better check it out anyway?"

"I'm retired, Silias, and you are surrounded by special operations Purifiers. Find some other lackey. I'm just here to futz with information, annoy Theeran, and occasionally give you terrible advice."

"They're not as good as you."

"Yes, but they're paid to kill things, and I am firmly intractable on this subject. Resolute. Determined."

"Are you sure?"

"Indomitable. Like a duraglau fortress. With cannons."

Lips curling to an impish smile, Marsilias delved through a pocket and retrieved a metal thermos inscribed with some manner of poetry only he and a few other intellectuals could read. Marsilias unscrewed the lid and a wave of steam washed out, bearing the unmistakable scents of lemon, cream, and sugar. He waved it. "Fresh from the in-house confectioner, a new concoction they haven't debuted yet. A lemon syrup for dousing confections or drinking solo." He crept backward, still waving the aroma in her direction.

She sniffed after him, savoring the teasing steam, letting it distract her from the tumult within her thoughts. "You're shameless. And unscrupulous."

"Well, if you don't want it ..." He moved to close it, and she lurched a step after him with a muffled noise. He smiled, quirked an eyebrow and extended the container to her.

"Fine,"—Jade snatched it—"but I'm not sharing."

"I wouldn't dream of asking, which is why I brought two. Now come along, we have to visit someplace we're not supposed to."

"And I'm only tagging along for moral support. If a giant monster attacks us, I'm screaming like a little girl and leaving. Legit. I'll drop you so hard and fast there'll be a crater." Luxuriating in a final sniff of his offering, Jade drank the thick, heady mixture. Warmth and sweetness flooded her stomach and she released a blissful sigh. "Ooh, that's good, that's very good."

Intoxicants and Old Nightmares

Just over an hour later, the ivory whale-length aircraft, Damselfly class, alighted on the water with a purr of subsiding engines. The auto piloting program rumbled in the speakers, "We have arrived at our destination." Marsilias unbuckled himself from the center-most of six passenger seats and joined Jade at the entrance. She typed a quick combination, standard across Purifier vehicles, and the door opened onto the dock, which amounted to little more than a network of skeletal gangways without railings and a single entrance.

She vaulted from the Damselfly to the ridged walkway and regarded the fuming sky. "We have a couple hours before the rain starts again. If we're lucky, it won't be so thick the Damselfly becomes inadvisable."

"If that's the case, we'll take a submersible to the nearest major transit hub." Marsilias dropped to the walkway with a thud. "For now, let's find the intoxication compound. I think it's on the third floor."

She compulsively touched the Siphons at her back to verify their presence and crossed to the compound's nearest entrance.

Jutting from the gangway, the entrance's salt-crusted, gray door slid open at their approach, revealing a gilded stair ensconced in crystalline duraglau walls that descended into the ocean depths. They entered the complex's brilliant yellow illumination, steps soundless on the exquisite carpets as refrains of classical orchestra drifted through the chill air. A story below, the stairs expanded to a wide corridor illuminated by antique candelabras, the walls embellished with images and inscriptions of poetry, both shaped in sleek lines of stylized gold and silver. Elegant, cushioned chairs and tables occupied the floor at large intervals along the corridor's edges while attendant programs waited in the adjacent walls and ceiling.

A tall female attendant program blinked onto the wall beside Jade. "May I assist you, miss?"

Marsilias, a natural diplomat, stepped around her. "Yes, we were hoping to visit the third floor and speak with a moderator."

"Is there a particular moderator?"

"No, I don't think so. Not yet at least."

"Then please follow me." The attendant slipped onto the floor, her projection illuminating the dark ocean below. She glided along the corridor, the brilliant finery of her image melding perfectly with the entrance floor's exaggerated opulence. A few individuals occupied the chairs and tables. Most stared out into the water, waiting for their turn in one of the intoxicant floors below, but a few partook of milder drugs and lolled in their seats with dazed expressions. They ranged from grunt workmen with mismatched clothing and natural hair to managers with strictly uniformed apparel and a parade of hair colors.

Every so often side rooms interrupted the perfect, dark continuity of ornate walls. Their interiors were concealed behind partitions of purple velvet, but their purpose gleamed on the curtains as flowing red sigils, depicting an array of minor entertainments and comforts to pass the hours. They offered amusements varying from food and drink to games, massages, and simple sleeping quarters. All of these they passed without pause until the corridor concluded at a vast stair. Here the attendant paused and motioned them down. "The proprietor will meet you now."

Marsilias paused on the first step. "We asked to speak with a manager on the third floor, not the proprietor of this fine establishment."

"You are not the first person to express interest in the events of several days passed; the proprietor distrusts such extensive interest in an otherwise mundane occurrence. Please, continue. He awaits below."

Marsilias shifted minutely backward. "We never expressed our reason for visiting."

"You arrived in a Purifier vessel, but no revenants have ever appeared in our establishment, and then you inquired after the third floor, where the event occurred. My algorithms deduced the aforementioned incident as your most likely interest and I informed the proprietor as such, per his request."

Marsilias glanced at Jade, who shrugged, and then descended the stairs. An aromatic, deep-orange mist, rich with vanilla and other minor intoxicants, drifted up to meet them, coiling about their feet and impeding their sight of the floor.

Jade saw it and stiffened. There was mist everywhere. Mist and structures and monsters. The mist tasted like dirt. It filled her lungs: she was choking on it. She fumbled around but she couldn't see, didn't know where she was. There were monsters everywhere. She could hear them, but she didn't know what to do, where to go. Nowhere was safe, she couldn't make it safe, she couldn't be safe. Ilin. Where was Ilin? She couldn't find him. He needed her; they'd dragged him through, but she couldn't find him. He needed her. Where was he? She spun, searching for him. Where was he? Damn it, she couldn't see anything.

Then pressure, a touch on her arm and she nearly screamed, nearly struck at it with her knives, but a voice came with it. "Jade, you all right?"

She blinked, recognizing the voice as Marsilias's; but Marsilias shouldn't be here. She still followed his voice out, surfacing somewhat from the mists of her mind. "Yeah, I'm fine, just thought I saw something. It's nothing."

"You sure, you look a bit pale?"

She nodded and carefully focused her gaze up and away from the deep-orange mist, clutching her coat tight and fixating on the dark water outside. "Yeah, I'm sure. Hurry up, wouldn't want to be late!" She strode forward with false cheer as the mist continued to rise, flashing with lights further down the corridor, until it occupied the entire stairway. Jade, almost gagging with the suffocating aroma, activated her adaptive suit to project a mask around her face. Dry, sterilized air filled her mouth and she gasped at it until her bruised lungs ached. The ache spread across her chest and throat, sapping her body of heat. Shivering, Jade pulled her coat tighter and hastened her step.

The stairs ended at a tousled silk blanket and a room-wide red mattress in which their feet sank deep. Vague silhouettes of people wandered past, some murmuring indistinctly and others weakly grasping or striking at hallucinations. Jade slowed as she and Marsilias reached the threshold, then grit her teeth and forced herself onward. *"Shut up,"* she hissed internally. *"Get over yourself; you're not in Afterlife."*

They maneuvered over almost a hundred feet of blankets, red mattress, and prostrate or curled people in varying conditions of intoxication before arriving at a curved leather couch so long it disappeared into the mist on their left and right. A tall man sprawled across its central seat, legs flung wide and his head resting on a sumptuous pillow. Two gorgeous women slept to either side of him, their heads resting on his thighs and their veins glowing with whatever intoxicant they imbibed.

The man roused his head at their appearance and sucked from the pipe dangling in his left hand. "I hear you want to speak with my manager." Azure mist spilled from his lips and eddied down his form. "The first group I couldn't ask, the second I didn't want to, so you're going to tell me why?"

"Sorry," Marsilias replied, "we can't do that. We're with the Purifier Corporation on a subsequent investigation, searching for details we missed the first time."

The proprietor languidly spread both hands, the pipe suspended between his thumb and forefinger. "Then I can't help you."

"The Purifier Corporation—"

"Is not my employer. The Statutes of Corporation Conduct dictate that the Purifiers need the consent of my sovereign corporation to coerce my assistance. You have nothing without a stamp of approval from the Intoxicant Corporation." He pressed the pipe to his lips and inhaled. The corded muscles of his bare chest swelled, causing his skeletal tattoos to writhe. He wore no adaptive suit because adaptive suits automatically combated foreign intoxicants.

"None of that, please. There's no need to be obstinate; I'm sure we can devise an arrangement." Marsilias twisted his hand in a small gesture of invitation. "It's a private matter for a prominent member of our corporation, nothing that truly concerns you but which could be profitable with a little compliance."

"What do you have in mind?"

"How about a day's salary, three hundred marks?"

"I earn five hundred and keep whatever the patrons drop."

"Two hundred and an all-expenses paid trip to the environment of your choice?"

"I've tried them all. Try again."

"Is there something in particular you're fishing for?"

"A promotion."

"I don't know how you expect me to work tha–"

"I know who you are. You have a reputation, Mr. Wreign. I want to cash in on it." The proprietor leaned forward, shucking the two women, and beckoned into the mist.

Jade glanced over her shoulder as three masked thugs emerged from the haze. She faced them, a flush of stressed heat swelling in her center as her heart quickened, but it was a regular stress, a simple reaction to threat and peril. These were just men and women, people she didn't know. Jade could handle them. "Look what you've gotten us into now, Silias. You really are a magnet for trouble, and a bad influence to boot. Next thing I know, you'll have me committing crimes, like hacking a corporation or something."

Marsilias assessed the thugs. "Eh, they don't look that tough. You can take them." He readdressed the proprietor, "There's no need for barbarism; I'm perfectly happy negotiating your promotion. Would two levels suffice?"

"That would be grand, but it seems like a lofty price for a simple conversation."

"We'll just say you owe me a small favor."

"I can accept that. It's agreed then?"

"Yes, though your promotion only comes after we've spoken with the manager."

"Very well, there is a stair in the back that will take you down. Shayvien will meet you on the third floor." The proprietor slumped back onto the couch and sucked on his pipe.

Marsilias nodded at Jade, and together they rounded the long couch and navigated the room's second half. The proprietor's quarters ended at a metallic stair unadorned by the upper floor's embellishments. Jade emerged from the cloying smoke with a muted sigh and wiped at the perspiration gathering on her brow.

"Did you intend for it to result this way?"

"No, I had not intended this scenario, but was prepared for it in any case. Bad trade and all."

They descended two dozen poorly lit steps that ended at a wide corridor constructed of gray pillars and struts. The windows remained, but like the stairwell, all forms of embellishment had been omitted. A second stair continued the descent a few feet from where the first ended. Jade swung onto it as an attendant flickered into being beside them. "Greetings, Miss. Dieza and Mr. Wreign, I will be monitoring your discussion with Madame Shayvien."

"I assume that's her?" Marsilias indicated a stiff woman on the final step, her features painted vibrantly in a multitude of hues and her figure robed in a translucent over-gown of glistening yellow silk. Black iconography splattered her under-suit in dense configurations and impressionistic patterns, purposefully designed to conjure different images per viewer.

The attendant signaled confirmation.

"Wonderful. Hello, Madame Shayvien, I am Marsilias Wreign and this is Jade Dieza. We would like to ask you some questions."

The woman's eyes flicked from Marsilias to Jade, but she herself made no other movement. "I was apprised of your agreement with the proprietor of this establishment; I am willing to comply in any way that does not contradict this corporation's interest."

"Wonderful, can you describe the incident that occurred a couple days ago, the one involving a man covered in black marks? And any information about the subject in question would be helpful as well."

"I can't provide much clarity as I experienced only a passing acquaintance with him. He's an irregular customer with no previous displays of aggression; such conduct can result in the immediate expulsion from our property and the revocation of future business privileges."

"So what happened on that particular day? Anything atypical?"

"No, the man in question and every other patron acted to their wont. The man arrived for his appointment and I directed him to his seat. The distributor brought his beverage, and I heard no more of the man until the incident. I didn't personally witness the incident's beginning, but those who did say he simply erupted from his experience several hours before his dosage should have expired. He rampaged for several minutes and assailed anyone within reach. Our enforcers subdued him, but not without extraordinary effort and several injuries."

"Were the markings at all present before this incident?"

"No. Nor did the health scans notice any significant issues in his body or mental state."

"What did the markings look like?"

"Nothing in particular. Most resembled splashed ink, but others favored the look of scars. They covered his face entirely and most of his upper torso but faded completely before passing his elbows or first rib."

"You said it took an extraordinary effort to subdue him?"

"Yes, he struggled with uncharacteristic strength for any man, much less such a small one. He smashed several pieces of furniture with his bare hands."

"What happened after you subdued him?"

"The Defense Corporation assumed custody over him and removed him from the premise, though he had relapsed to a stupor at that point."

"Do you know where this individual currently is?"

"They did not inform us of his location, but he is liable for the damage he caused our establishment."

"Can you acquire that information? Or must we trouble the proprietor for it?"

"I may request the information from my superiors, but the proprietor is certain to know it."

"What of the other habitual patrons; have any of them displayed similar or unrecognized symptoms since the event? Similar markings perchance?"

"No. Was the man suffering from something?"

"That's what we're hoping to ascertain. Information is scarce, however, so if you can think or remember anything of importance it would help greatly."

"I am afraid not. As I said before, I paid little attention to the man."

"Thank you for your time. If you remember anything in future, please contact me."

They retraced their steps to the proprietor's couch, Marsilias making various calls to initiate the promised promotion.

The proprietor glanced over his shoulder as they arrived. "Did you get what you needed?"

"Yes, with the exception of the individual's current location."

"They advised me of his location when I expressed my intent to sue for damages. But first complete your end."

"It is already done; I sent the request during our return. The process takes several days of course, but I'm sure you can locate me if my efforts fail."

"All is well then. Your man languishes in the nearest Defense Corporation compound. I can't recall its name, though every console has the coordinates."

Marsilias nodded. "Goodbye."

"One last thing before you depart: Beware the warden down there. Rumors are she's a less than virtuous soldier."

The Third Victim

When they exited the building, they were met by a blustery searing wind and a world bathed in crimson radiance. The skies groaned, their once tenebrous clouds now lurid with the impending heat storm and warping with distortions. Jade scrunched her shoulders against the wind, pressing herself against the Damselfly's flank for what meager protection it provided.

Marsilias, perpetually averse to adaptive suits, paced several feet away, steeped in sweat and red faced as he fought a deteriorating connection to charter a submersible from the Transport Corporation. They needed passage to the nearest Defense Corporation penitentiary, but the heat storm made flight impossible, its above-water temperatures predicted to exceed two hundred degrees Fahrenheit, beyond even the most advanced aircraft's abilities to mitigate for long.

Jade tugged at her collar—the fabric sticking with perspiration from her exposed skin—and pushed off the Damselfly towards Marsilias, panting softly into her hydrating mask. Her optical lenses read the temperature at a hundred and seventeen degrees and climbing, hot enough that heat distortions rippled the air every-where she looked. Her adaptive suit sat lukewarm against her skin, its internal workings combining gases to create a cooling effect and pumping them through its veins. It helped, but could not counteract temperatures that would soon be reaching lethal heights.

A weak chirp sounded against the thickening air, causing Jade to glance about in confusion. Seeing nothing but the barren pier and turbulent water, she resumed her trek toward Marsilias, intent on harassing him for malingering. She'd barely managed another step before a second chirp sounded.

Raising a hand to shield her eyes, she performed a second, more exacting, survey but again without success until a third chirp guided her to the walkway's edge about a dozen feet further on. An infant seriat, its fur a dark red with heatstroke, clung feebly to the railing, either orphaned or abandoned, unable to dive or survive the cooler depths on its own. She crossed to it, keeping her arm raised against the ghastly wind, and knelt.

The seriat shrank away in the water, regarding her with large but dangerously dry eyes, and mewled faintly, terrified but too hot to flee. "Hello, cutie." She extended her fingers tentatively, but it continued shrinking away, whimpering. Jade wiped the perspiration from her brow, her suit failing to compete with the rising heat, and fumbled into a pocket for a package of sweet crackers from Marslias's last meal. She tore the silver wrapping, split one of the sapphire crackers down the middle, and dipped it toward the seriat. "I won't hurt you."

It sniffed her offering hesitantly and then licked it half-heartedly, its body temperature too high to eat. "Come here, you." She scooped the seriat up about the midsection before it could react and pulled it from the rapidly heating water. It squirmed in her arms, squeaking and hissing, as she undid the top button of her shirt and slid it down her front against the adaptive suit's soothing chill. The seriat, about two feet in length from head to rump, calmed then tentatively grasped her with its six hands and wrapped its long, flat tail about her waist. "Well aren't you just the sweetest thin–"

"All right, I ordered a submersible. We have to rendezvous with it at the aquatic dock below–" Marsilias, in the process of rejoining her, faltered at the seriat's head poking from her shirt. The seriat turned to inspect him and chirped.

"Jade ..."

"No! He's mine. You can't have him." Rising to her feet, she spun away, wrapping the seriat in an embrace. "Find your own." The seriat purred against her, its fur already returning to a healthier brown.

"Do you even know what they eat?"

"They're carnivores and are often kept as pets." She stroked its head. "I'm going to call him Cuddles."

"And here I thought you were a black-ops Purifier, a force of unmitigated destruction."

She turned her nose up at him, rewarding his sass with all the imperious disdain it deserved. "I'm retired, and he's adorable."

"Either way, come on, we have to cross the Deep Currents before visiting hours end." A message blinked onto her lenses a second later: a guide program through the intoxicant compound sent by Marsilias. She downloaded the guide and followed, raining praise on her new seriat's beautiful head.

They descended to the intoxicant compound's first floor again and continued along it, traversing the business and waiting centers until they concluded in a luxuriously upholstered and scented hallway of glowing advertisements, rule boards, and checkpoints. They followed the long hallway further down, descending until they reached the wide entrance to a wet-dock. Patrons crowded the interior, jockeying for position in the queues or for the attention of the attending S.I. programs, attempting to return home or to their occupations before the storm struck.

Jade parked herself just outside the entrance, cooing to Cuddles while Marsilias forged a path through the crowd towards the nearest managing S.I. program, which currently stood with its face projected in multiple directions to converse with a collection of customers. As a rule Jade disliked crowds, finding the pressing and constant unwanted contact stressful, as well as hating how they made it impossible to watch everyone in close proximity to her. It was another reason why she preferred solitary berths on aircraft and submersibles.

Marsilias returned promptly. "Subs waiting in one of the private docks; most of these people are trying to purchase berths on the commercial rides."

They re-entered the wet-dock hall, skirting the edges of the room and crowd as they navigated toward the signs marking the private docks, isolated from the main hall with the projected image of a red curtain. "Must have been expensive, due to private and storm rates."

"It was"

"Oof, you have my condolences."

"Condolences aren't necessary, I used your key code."

She replied with a squawk of outraged affront that he abjectly ignored—knowing the Purifier Corporation still covered most of her expenses—and then entered the private dock, phasing through the illusionary curtain without issue. Inside, they found a small, lavish submersible idling in the docking pool, an attendant program waiting beside the open door.

"Your submersible is prepared, madam and monsieur, is there anything else the Transport Corporation can provide to make your journey more enjoyable?"

"Nothing, thank you."

Jade and Marsilias stepped down into the submersible, the sleek black interior ringed in plush couches and soft lights. Jade sank into one of the seats, snuggling with and offering Cuddles another cracker, which, having cooled down, he delicately accepted.

Marsilias, having moved to the front to insert their destination into the dropdown console, glanced back. "So you truly intend to adopt it?"

Jade stroked Cuddles. "Yes." He purred against her, round tongue licking the cracker crumbs from his whiskers.

"Do you want me to order some kibble to your apartment for later?"

"Yes, please." She reclined in her seat, readjusting Cuddles to lie on her chest and kissing the top of his head before letting her own fall back and closing her eyes. "Wake me when we arrive."

"Will do."

01000011 01101111 01101100 01101111 01101110 01101001 01110011
01110100 00100000 01110011 01101000 01101001 01110000 00100000
01101001 01101110 01110100 01100101 01110010 01100011 01100101
01110000 01110100 01100101 01100100 00101100 00100000 01100101
01111000 01110000 01100101 01110010 01101001 01101101 01100101
01101110 01110100 00100000 01110010 01110101 01101001 01101110
01100101 01100100 00101110 00100000 01000101 01101110 01100100
00101110

A hand on her shoulder woke Jade from a dream of walking, of heat, and dry earth cracking underfoot. She cracked an eye open for Marsilias and then smiled at a likewise stirring Cuddles. "Hello, handsome. Did you sleep well too?" He licked her chin and she sat up. "Are we there?"

"Almost. We're leaving the Deep Current now, arriving just outside their wet-dock. I've already sent for permission to enter." Marsilias nodded at the console. "I expect a call any minute now."

Jade slowly stood, stretching and, now that she paid attention, recognizing the telltale signs of water pressure shifting against their hull. She tapped the console beside her, raising the command screen that governed the ceiling and changed its setting to transparent. The dark coloring faded away, revealing a vista of black ocean glimmering with the flashing green lights of marine repellants and, in the far distance, an immense bank of white lights "Would they have any reason to reject us?"

Marsilias joined her in appraising the compound, absentmindedly stroking his scarf. "Not logically, but what the intoxicant proprietor said concerns me. The Defense Corporation's codes of conduct are only as effective as any other law, and if what he implied is true, we could be dealing with anything from a spoilt brute given too much authority, to an official who's entirely corrupt."

The dropdown console activated, projecting the image of a man in a thick gray uniform with tin buttons to stand at the center of the submersible's floor. He wore a cap with the black sigil of the Defense Corporation pinned to the front: a cube standing upon one of its corners. "State your business and employers."

Marsilias stepped forward, smoothly straightening his posture and assuming a military stance. "We're contractors with the Purifier Corporation here to interrogate an inmate, as requested in advance. This is an unofficial visit."

The man's eyes flicked down, likely scanning the list of received requests, then returned to them. "Names."

"Marsilias Wreign and Jade Dieza."

"You may dock. A party will greet you inside, weapons are forbidden on the premises. This compound is Defense Corporation sovereign territory, any infractions here will be judged under Defense Corporation law. You have been warned." The projection winked off.

Marsilias nodded and removed his hat, beginning the process of swapping the central Education Corporation's gold badge, with a badge of the Defense Corporation. "Anything you want to grab before we disembark?"

She moved to the entrance. "No, I already got everything I need in case this goes sour." She slipped both arms out of their coat sleeves and nudged Cuddles. "C'mon you, on the back." He begrudgingly crawled his lithe body around to her back. "There, now aren't you just so much happier not being in the way?" He chirped and licked her ear, inciting a giggle.

The underside of an enormous, black metal structure gradually swept into view above them, blanketed in sweeping white flood lights, gun embankments, and pulsing sensors. The wet-dock's entrance waited about half a mile further on, enshrined in a dome of crystalline energy, projected between curving, rib-like segments. One of the segments deactivated as they neared, welcoming them in before resealing behind them as they began the process of venting water and rising.

They surfaced in an octagonal pool scarcely larger than their vehicle, the water's surface constricted by a series of metal valve-plates. Almost a hundred feet further on, the valve-plates merged with the elevated floor. Additional defensive embankments occupied the distant ceiling, bathed in the compound's painfully bright lighting. No windows afforded views into the ocean outside, engendering a mild claustrophobic sensation despite the wet-dock's immense size.

Their submersible's door gasped open with an expulsion of lingering pressure, revealing a cluster of soldiers in dark-blue Defense Corporation uniforms waiting atop the valve-plate just outside. A uniformed woman with spiked, fluorescent-green hair irritably acknowledged their arrival with a perfunctory glance up from a portable device, "I suppose you have an extraordinary reason for intruding after we already rebuffed your corporation?" She regarded them disdainfully, examining Marsilias first and then discarding him to land upon Jade. Something like a predatory recognition sparked in her gaze and immediately evaporated.

Jade recognized her as well, or rather the effect she had: a quickening of the blood as electricity sparked in the back of her mind then coursed through all her implants and devices. They were alike.

The woman's irritation mellowed, transforming to simple fatigue. "It's something personal, isn't it? A family member getting into trouble? Or something of the like? I can't promise to resolve anything, but I can probably let you see them."

Jade shivered, hackles rising as that same sensation passed through her mind and devices again. This was dangerous, more dangerous than they had bargained for, more dangerous than Marsilias realized, and she couldn't warn him. Jade stole a glance across the subordinates, fighting the urge to sink into a defensive crouch: none evoked the same electric response, but that was no guarantee they had not experienced Enlightenment.

Marsilias stepped fully from the submersible, causing it to bob visibly higher, and glided to the forefront, once again assuming his military posture. "May I ask who you are first?"

"Oh yes, of course. I'm Warden Shanra, overseer of all military affairs in this precinct, including the management, incarceration, rehabilitation, employment, and executions of prisoners etc. etc. Assuming your business is actually private, you're lucky I answered rather than my subordinate. He's a stickler, and too intelligent for his own good." Her attention returned to Jade. "And who're you?"

The hair on Jade's neck rose, her skin crawling at the woman's interest in her. Had she a choice, Jade would have left or dealt with the stick in the mud subordinate, but they needed access to that prisoner, so she grit her teeth and surrendered her name. "Jade Dieza. He's Marsilias Wreign."

Marsilias nodded and smoothly reassumed command of the conversation. "We hoped to interview a new inmate of yours, someone who'd have black markings somewhere on his body, maybe prevalent. We're concerned he has a disease, and if he does, that it's contagious–"

"Sssh! You shouldn't bandy words like that around, you'll scare people." Her attention snapped to the soldiers behind her. "None of you repeat a word of what you just heard to anyone, not your squad mates, not your families. Understood? Good." Her focus returned to Jade and Marsilias, now more calculating than anything else. Before either could say anything, the warden caught Jade's arm in a gloved hand. "We should discuss something like this in private." Beckoning Marsilias with her other hand, she escorted Jade across the largely vacant dock. "Weapons aren't permitted inside the facility proper, you'll have to divest yourselves of them and submit to scans. If you're worried about anything happening, don't be; you're entirely safe here." Her grip tightened, demanding compliance.

Climbing from the pool, they encountered a series of standing hexagonal terminals fashioned of humming, black metal. "You'll have to take off your coats as well, you can store all sorts of jamming devices in them. No exceptions." The woman released Jade's arm and passed through the terminals, activating all three as she went. "Just put your coats on the conveyor there and pick them up once you're through. Give your weapons to the guard; they'll watch them until you return."

Jade slowly stripped off her brother's coat, shivering as its comforting weight left her, and began folding it, using these actions to surreptitiously retrieve one of the training Siphons from her back and conceal it in an unlocked internal pocket. Then she did as commanded and walked through the terminal. Her coat slipped into the separate sensors and a buzz emitted from the enclosed conveyor, but it displayed empty on every scan and reached the opposite end with all its contents—weapons, explosives, specialized hacking equipment among other, less benign items—undiscovered.

The warden reclaimed Jade's coat and examined it as Jade crossed, turning it over in her hands. "This is a nice coat, strangely heavy for it being empty though. Where'd you get it from?"

Jade quickly finished crossing the checkpoint and reclaimed her coat, pulling it from the woman's still shifting hands before she could begin exploring any of the pockets. "It's not for sale, a family heirloom."

"It looks Jysa made?"

"It is, "Marsilias replied, finishing his own crossing and reclaiming his coat, "and it's something of a private subject, so I would suggest we move along."

"Of course. Just this way." The warden ushered them to a simple lift, pressed the keypad and settled on the railing facing Jade and Marsilias, forcing them to keep their backs to the rest of the dock—where her subordinates still watched them—or stand beside her. "Before we get started, is there anything I can get you? Tea? Hot chocolate?"

"No, thank you." Jade shook her head, turning about to face the immense wet-dock, trusting Marsilias to watch her back. As she did so, her actions concealed by her turned back, Jade covertly searched the interior of her coat, scrounging the open nooks until her fingers brushed against a small, square device that did not belong. She crushed it between her thumb and forefinger without bothering to ascertain its purpose.

The light was briefly obscured as the lift ascended through the floor of a transparent chamber overlooking the dock. Viewing screens on the walls displayed the Deep Currents, exterior of the penitentiary, and dozens of occupied cells. The two sentries waiting at the top straightened at their arrival and pressed fists together in salute. The warden indicated the door. "Please give us a moment. Wait outside until summoned." The sentries saluted again and filed past, recovering various personal items in transit.

"Please, make yourself at home." Gesturing vaguely toward the available seats, the warden accessed the nearest console and inserted a series of codes, sealing the observation room's doors and clouding its windows. "There, now we can speak without fear of interruption or our words getting out." She settled in the centermost seat and leaned forward, resting her arms upon her knees and her head upon her clasped hands. "What do you need from me and why? Leave nothing out." Her eyes fastened upon Jade again, the predatory light barely concealed.

Jade ignored her, too preoccupied with counting the defensive additions embedded throughout the walls, and remembering the sound of the doors sealing behind them. Her mind supplied the word she wanted: kill box.

Marsilias, no idiot and fully cognizant of their situation, interceded, stepping before the warden so he occupied the entirety of her vision. Jade slipped sideways in his wake, trailing her fingers along the ranks of consoles, testing their connection points and defenses while he spoke with the warden. "We need to speak with the inmate from the intoxicant compound. Or at the very least observe him. And he absolutely needs to be tested for a variety of signs."

"If he's actually infected by a pathogen, I can't permit contact; it would endanger other lives if you happened to catch it, and the backlash even for allowing it wouldn't just be a matter of demerits or my dismissal. I could be incarcerated. I need to know what we're dealing with, as much as you can tell me so I know how to proceed."

"We can't tell you everything, this disease is potentially linked to Purifier Corporation secrets. All we can tell you is what the report would have said."

"Look, I need to know what's happening if I'm going to help you all; I'm going out on a limb just as much as you are. Maybe more. Trust me, I'm not going to share what we talk about here with anyone. At least not unless it's as serious as you're thinking it is."

Marsilias exhaled slowly and rubbed his brow. "We can't do that; the Purifiers edited our implants to prevent sharing confidential information. We reveal anything classified to anyone outside the corporation, or of insufficient clearance, and our citizenship privileges get revoked." A lie, but not one the warden could challenge.

"Jesus," she muttered, leaning to the side to glance at Jade, "you serious?"

Jade confirmed with a nod, fingers pressed to the access point of a console, delving through the surface level information, and the programs governing this room.

The warden shifted her attention back to Marsilias. "Do you have a name at least? They refused to share it when they delivered him, said we should just refer to him by his number."

The return lie slithered a chill through Jade, almost drawing her teeth to an edge, but Marsilias only supplied the requested information, "Ceran Trawl."

The warden swiveled her seat and pressed a hand to the primary console, the implants illuminating beneath her skin like myriad delicate veins. "There are public records of him, and facial recognition matches, but all information from the last few months of his life has been redacted, sealed by the Purifier Corporation." She surfaced from the web, affixing her attention solely on Marsilias. "I can't get in, unless you're a Purifier...?"

The invitation was evident, and Jade's chill worsened. "*She wants my codes, but we said we were contractors; we wouldn't have codes. She wants Marsilias to sell me out first for some reason. No, that's not the issue. How does she know I'm a Purifier?*" Realization followed soon after. "*Someone told her, or she knows me from before*." Jade replied regardless, "I'm a retired Purifier, fairly high clearance; my code might still work."

"Will you use it?"

Jade nodded and slowly sat at the secondary console bank, shifting Cuddles to her front to avoid crushing him. Then she pressed her hand against the connection point and delved deeper. Information and defenses instantly bombarded her, initially fervent but eventually receding as the warden modulated the active programs and pathways to restrict her access. Jade ignored the warden's efforts and expanded her search, superficially rousing the information on Ceran Trawl while inserting her code but primarily inspecting the swarming subroutines and programs—all the engines the warden wished concealed from her. As the Ceran file declassified, Jade found the program recording her code for future use and another revising the audio and footage of their discussion so far.

Jade surfaced briefly, checking on the warden to find her and Marsilias engaged in further debate concerning the information she'd liberated and then delved anew, dismantling the compound's restrictions and alarms. Then she sought her name and a video played: the warden in a storage room talking with a man and woman in orange coats and vacillating electronic masks. One said her name, the voice toneless and warped by static as their masks displayed the white, cherubic image and tall ears of a bunny rabbit. That wasn't right, they shouldn't even have appeared on the screen.

Jade extricated herself from the dive, barely stifling a hiss as her previous chill became needles stabbing the back of her mind. She ignored them, forcing herself to breathe and think. *"How much does she know? No, doesn't matter. The bunny also—soft, weak creature, defenseless, representing me; they targeted her on me, told her I'm unstable, vulnerable. Dammit, Saccari, you knew I might come around."*

"Hey, are you all right?" The warden's words pulled Jade out of herself and snapped her gaze back across to the woman.

"I'm fine," she replied, "just a little stressed out. What did you learn?"

The warden offered an apologetic shrug. "Not much I'm afraid. Basic information on the event, which just confirms what we already knew, and restrictions forbidding anyone outside of the Purifiers from interacting with Ceran, even androids and medical machines. He's in utter isolation."

"You didn't know that?" Jade asked.

"No, the order completely bypassed me, came directly from upper management to this compound's automated section." An answer Jade knew for a lie; she'd seen the warden's signature authorizing Ceran's incarceration.

Marsilias hadn't seen that, however, and continued pressing towards their goal. "So can we see him? You know what's going on is big." Of course the warden knew, she'd always known. That wasn't the purpose of this discussion; the purpose had been to implicate Jade and Marsilias in something criminal for leverage while acquiring Jade's Purifier codes for the access they provided. It was about controlling Jade and Marsilias, and gaining power.

"I don't know. It depends on Jade's code because Ceran's quarantine will be Purifier enforced; if her access isn't high enough, we're stumped."

Marsilias leaned forward. "But you'll let us try?"

"Yeah, just as soon as you tell me why you're not leaving it to the Purifiers?" The warden leaned forward, the sympathy evaporating from her features without altering her eyes. "They're clearly handling this, so why are you two interfering? What do you know that they don't? Or is it the other way around?"

Marsilias coughed. "We didn't know they'd already discovered the issue; we thought we were researching something that might need their attention. That's clearly not the case, though." A blatant lie the warden didn't even need to challenge.

"It's still something important enough to send you out looking without permission. Just what exactly do I have in my basement?" She rested her hands on the holsters of two small firearms, tapping both with an unsteady touch.

"I already said we can't tell you."

The warden released one firearm and scratched the back of her other hand, lips twisting in the beginnings of a sneer. "What if I didn't believe you?"

Marsilias paused. "Are you ... threatening us?"

"Nothing of the sort." She scratched the other hand, the skin flaring red. "I just think you're lying to me, and that what you want from that man isn't in his, or the Purifier Corporation's, best interest. So now, I don't trust you, and I really hate that."

"You can abandon your accusations, warden, they won't work on her or me."

"Marsilias."

"Yeah?"

"Look at her hands."

The warden's hands were inflamed, the skin writhing with a tumult of black markings that extended beneath her sleeves.

Marsilias recoiled, a hand moving to the pulse-cannon he always carried strapped across his lower back only to freeze at its absence. "Tell me, warden, did you ever speak with the prisoner?"

Jade surreptitiously slipped a hand inside her coat against a reddish, circular lock on an interior pocket. A prick of pain against her finger and blood welled from her thumb, saturating the lock anew and deactivating it with a snick.

"I already told you, higher authorities forbid interactions with the prisoner." She crossed the room to a rack of gear, inserted a code and donned a pair of military gloves, their exterior riddled with power lines and minute batteries capable of materializing energy barriers. "Distracting me won't work, Mr. Wreign. Tell me what's really going on here and I might be able to help the both of you mitigate the consequences."

Marsilias carefully approached the warden as Jade rose and moved her concealed hand to the training Siphon she'd smuggled in. Marsilias extended his hands in a calming gesture. "Listen, warden, you might be infected with a cerebral disease. Your judgment's skewed and probably devolving toward violent psychosis at an exponential rate. That prisoner you acquired does have a disease, and we know it's infectious but not how. It's potentially airborne. You need to trust us."

"And why should I do that?" The warden shifted to face both of them, grasping the rack's frame with enough force to warp it. "You're just playing an angle. I'm mad you say, I'm violent, unhinged, in danger, and perilous to those around me. You say I'm the victim of an epidemic no one's ever heard of before; and all of this just when you're losing control over the negotiations." She twitched, a dark liquid seeping into the whites of her eyes. "You know what, I really don't like you, Mr. Wreign, and I think you need to leave. Now."

Marsilias advanced, retrieving his mask from a pocket as Jade activated her adaptive suit and earpieces to project hers. "We can't do that. You need to accompany us and quarantine yourself in the Purifier Compound."

"Well, I did warn you." She slammed the control panel behind her with a fist and the doors opened, admitting a trio of guards.

"Is there something you needed, sir?"

"Detain these two by any means necessary."

Marsilias didn't hesitate. He whirled, crossed the intervening space in the span the soldiers required to ignite their pulse-pistols, and slammed one with a blow to his sternum. The other guards lunged aside, mouths opening to shout warnings. Marsilias followed the woman on his right with smooth ease, shifting his weight back in the process, and bulled forward, ramming her against the wall. Jade pulled a taser from an external, non-locked, coat pocket and shot the third soldier before he could scream.

The warden cursed and ground her fist into the control panel. The com-link buzzed on, but Jade pressed her right hand into the secondary console beside her, connecting via the implants in her fingers, and dove into the data stream. The Defense Corporation's security systems reared before her: a barrage of firewalls, codes, poisoned data, and traps. She pierced them with a thought, discovered the nexus for the compound's network and locked it. The com-link buzzed off as the lights flickered and stabilized.

The warden snarled and spun toward her. "You little–"

Jade flung her Siphon across the room. It landed at the warden's feet and erupted, imprisoning the woman in four pulsing, transparent teal walls. "None of that, there's children present." She cooed at Cuddles, who chirped back, and readjusted him to her chest from where he'd slipped during the scuffle. Her free hand returned to the interior pocket, retrieved the miniature shock charge, and tossed it to Marsilias.

Marsilias caught it, activated it, and leveled it on the warden. "Jade, please discover who's second or first in command of this compound. We need to diffuse this situation and explain our actions before it escalates into a corporation war."

"Already done, I sent him a message requesting his appearance. He's her lieutenant."

"They'll never believe you." The warden slammed against the training Siphon's projected walls. "Release me immediately!"

"They don't need to believe us." Jade dipped into the data stream again and activated the holographic properties. A tide of images, words, and sound files erupted from the console into a screen of numbers. "This is the information you've illicitly brokered over the last three years, and my you do get around. There's a list of indiscretions here a mile long, more than enough to incarcerate you for life." The feeling of being in control again sent a bloom of relief through Jade, releasing the tension from her shoulders and mind.

The door to the observation room slid open and a tall, haggard man entered. He inspected the scene, his features twitching through a cascade of stifled emotions: surprise, realization, anger, realization again—with a glance toward Jade—concern, and ultimately acceptance. "I assume this is the disturbance you advised me of?" Jade nodded. "Then I trust you have an explanation for this assault on my superior?" Jade nodded again. "You might as well tell me your names."

"Jade Dieza"

"Marsilias Wreign."

"I am Lieutenant Huersan. Now, please explain the situation."

"Jade and I traveled here to interrogate and inspect one of your inmates for strains of a new pathogen. The warden initially acquiesced to our request but quickly grew volatile and contrary. We believe she's a victim of the pathogen that causes the skin to exhibit black markings, which are present on her hands."

The warden flung herself bodily against her prison walls and snarled. "Don't bother with them, lieutenant, just arrest them and be done with it. This was an act of childish temper, provoked by my unwillingness to capitulate to their demands."

"Warden, you will have the opportunity to speak when they have finished recounting events. Your behavior until then will be measured." He addressed Jade again, "You refer to the prisoner who went berserk at the intoxicant facility."

"Yeah, if you just compare their markings that should validate our concerns."

"You seem to have our network well in hand, so bring up an image of the inmate."

Jade projected the pale image of a small man kneeling in a cell across the rightmost bank of console screens. Thick white cuffs locked his arms and feet together and a mask covered his mouth. Beyond those, he wore only a pair of pants. This allowed them a clear view of the black markings covering his entire upper half.

"You can see by the advancement of his disease, that your warden is only newly infected. That is probably also the reason why she maintains a semblance of sanity."

The lieutenant disregarded his superior's continued raging. "I'm inclined to believe you; but if that's the case, we might all be infected as well. Do you know how it spreads?"

Marsilias shook his head. "We don't. We know next to nothing about whatever this is. We hoped to learn more here. We can't even guess how she contracted it. She said she never interacted with him, and I'm inclined to believe her. It's consistent with the Purifier Corporation's modus operandi."

The warden exploded into a rhetoric of vulgarities and insults directed at her subordinate. She threw herself against the barrier, hammering it with such violence her hands started visibly bruising.

Lieutenant Huersan grimaced as her volume multiplied and rubbed his eyes. "Someone incapacitate her please, it's impossible to think through the racket." One of his accompanying soldiers drew a taser and obeyed.

In the ensuing peace, Lieutenant Huersan selected the nearest soldier. "Instigate a compound-wide lockdown and recall all personnel who worked shifts since the prisoner arrived. Furthermore, distribute masks to all prisoners, and mandate all personnel to activate theirs, then initiate a compound-wide decontamination with all safety procedures and organize all the necessary requirements for the more aggressive treatments later. Physical contact is forbidden until this crisis is contained." He addressed the next soldier, "You, take over operations for the compound network and activate every member's tracking chips. Close all exits and drain all vehicles of energy. Then, when this facility is secure, contact the nearest general and inform him of the situation. When all this is done, investigate our prisoner's history for possible sources of this pathogen." He faced the final soldier. "You will assemble whatever researchers are deployed here and don full hazmat suits. Inspect our prisoner thoroughly, take whatever tests you can conceive of to define the extent and characteristics of this pathogen; we need to recognize it on a molecular level to ascertain which of us are infected."

Jade sidled to Marsilias. "He's not going to let us go for a while, or let us talk with anyone."

"And?"

"You stay here and give whatever assistance you can, I'll find the man who's been in charge of their prisoner. Jeck Harding."

"You know who he is?"

"Yeah, and I know where he is thanks to their tracking chips and network, and I can get to him a lot easier than you."

"All right, have fun."

"You too." She entrusted Cuddles to him and drifted back toward the rear wall with an exhale. The familiar cold flooded her lungs and veins, turning her blood to slush as she desaturated. Lieutenant Huersan glimpsed her actions from his periphery and spun. "Stop her!" But she was already sliding through the solid wall into the corridors beyond.

She quickly traversed the compound's spartan corridors, phasing through walls, floors and—where the structure ended— water until she reached the area marked by her quarry's tracking chip. She entered an isolated storage bunker floating in the lightless confines of a larger chamber entirely filled with toxic water, which served to insulate whatever the Defense Corporation stored in this particular bunker and as additional insurance against theft or escape.

Jade phased from the dark water through the bunker's metal ceiling and drifted to the floor through mountainous stacks of storage crates. She settled and inhaled, the inrush of overly hot air suffusing her body with heat before she stumbled and caught herself against an adjacent shelving unit. The pain followed moments later, creeping across her chest in the form of a dull ache. She straightened with a pained breath and cast about through the vast armory of weapons, prying little from the dim lighting other than she occupied a path of sorts through the stacks of crates. As she stood there in the dark, however, unease trickled up the back of her neck, tightening her jaw. She scanned her environs, trying to discern what was wrong. It took a moment before the right question occurred to her: Why was it dark? The automatic lights should have been activated by Jeck's presence.

"Mr. Jeck!" she called. "Are you still here?" No answer, and the unease worsened, her stomach squeezing taut. *There's too much dust for these boxes to have been touched or visited in years. What was he doing down here?"* She ventured cautiously forward, her lenses outlining the environment in green to help her navigate the dark.

A light activated overhead, triggered by her entering a subsection of the bunker, and revealed a matrix of locked cages, each containing mounds of leaner storage crates and the biohazard symbol emblazoned in red across the locks. She pressed forward, and the scent of something coppery tickled her nose. The tension in her stomach grew, driving her heartbeat faster; she knew that smell, had smelled it too often to forget it: new death.

She followed the scent with her gaze to a cage with its door ajar and hanging by one hinge. She crept forward—cautious to avoid the trail of black liquid dripping from a corner—and swung the door fully open and entered, flinching as the stench slapped her senses.

Private Jeck lay curled in the corner of the cell at an awful angle with his neck twisted while Ceran Trawl lay dead in the other, the veins of his arms and upper torso lacerated and oozing black fluid. She retreated from the corpses and sagged against the opposite cage as Jeck stared at her, eyes distended and black. She stared back, trying to make sense of it. They'd been alive just minutes ago. What had killed them? Did Ceran kill Jeck? Then who had killed Ceran? Himself?

Jade lifted a shuddering hand and touched her earpiece. "Marsilias?" She tried to speak calmly, but her voice quivered as the old panic mounted in her again. *"Please, not again. Not another calamity."*

Marsilias's voice broke into her head, "Yeah?"

"I found him."

"And."

"He's dead. They're both dead." *"I don't want this, please, I don't want this."* She slid to the ground, one hand pressing against her eyes as memories assailed her. She saw mist and monsters, and the faces of her dying Core.

"We're on our way."

"Just follow Jeck's tracker, and contact Prime March; there must be another *soul*." Ilin couldn't have caused this; he'd never interacted with anyone outside of the Purifiers, which meant there was another *soul* out there, spreading whatever this was. Causing people to kill each other and themselves.

The earpiece clicked off, leaving her alone with the dead man. She leaned forward, wrapping her hands over her head, and took a quivering breath. *"Please, not again."*

01110100 01110111 01101111 00100000 01101111 01110010 01110000
01101000 01100001 01101110 01110011 00100000 01101001 01101110
00100000 01101100 01101111 01110111 01100101 01110010 00100000
01100011 01101001 01110100 01111001 00101100 00100000 01100001
01110011 01101011 01101001 01101110 01100111 00100000 01100001
01100010 01101111 01110101 01110100 00100000 01100100 01110010
01100101 01100001 01101101 01100101 01110010 01110011

Jade huddled in a secluded corner of the warehouse, her head resting against the wall and her earpieces expanded to shield her ears as best they could. It was pointless. Noise surrounded her, voices the loudest of all, alternating between a constant suffocating murmur and strident exclamations. Footsteps and the crash of dropped objects accented the clamor, compounding the burden of noise until it became a sickening maelstrom. There was also someone, one of Lieutenant Huersan's corporals she thought, pestering her with questions about her discovery. She ignored him just as she tried to ignore all the other sounds besieging her, and focused inward.

She stared at the back of her eyelids, struggling to control the mounting fear. Memories flashed through her mind as phantom sounds echoed in her ears and her skin crawled with half-remembered sensations. She remembered the moment the gate opened, the instant of dawning horror as brown mist poured from a cavity into her world and spewed a hive of black-clothed monstrosities. She remembered the Syldra tree blackening beneath them, its bark rotting through in seconds. She remembered the water turning ashen as everything succumbed to the reek of mold. Then, in the seconds after this, the dawning realization in the moment that she had helped cause it.

A faint sound, though it boomed large to her, intruded on Jade's recollections and pulled her eyes open. There was no one immediately close to her, she would have known if there had been, so her attention immediately shifted across the clogged warehouse to the opening entrance. The door slid aside to reveal Prime March in the standard Purifier attire and a tall woman with natural auburn hair and a sleek violet and gold dress. They paused at the entrance, their eyes scanning the room once, noting where Marsilias conversed with Lieutenant Huersan, and ultimately finding Jade.

She stood as they approached, lifting Cuddles from where he lay curled in her lap, a small source of comfort from the panic pounding through her veins. She greeted them with a struggling voice, "Prime March. Primess March."

The woman tapped her left wrist and a web of blue lights swelled out to envelop them. "Hello, Jade, darling." Her wrist flashed again, generating another stream of blue light that settled beneath her in the guise of a chair. "You may speak freely; no one else can hear us." She reclined into the softly pulsing chair and crossed her legs, revealing dark leggings and high boots.

Prime March spared his compatriot a remonstrating glance for her absent decorum and addressed Jade. "What did you see?"

Jade shook her head, knowing where this would lead. "Why was the infected man even still here, Theeran? You knew he was dangerous."

"When we learned of the incident, the Purifier Corporation filed to claim him as an event related to Afterlife and thus under our jurisdiction. We then issued a quarantine mandate and requested extraction. The Defense Corporation rejected the extraction and demanded proof of our claims. We cited the corporation Confidentiality Agreement and they challenged. It's in the courts now and he's in limbo until they decide. Now, what did you see? And don't try deflecting us again."

"Nothing somebody else can't tell you. Talk to them and let me go." It was a weak plea, sounding cowardly even to her.

"We want to hear it from you, darling." Serras smiled, her teeth flashing white in a flawless face that still managed to be comforting.

Jade shifted Cuddles to her shoulder. "I came down here intending to question Mr. Jeck about the prisoner he'd been caring for and found him dead alongside his prisoner. He was covered in black markings that I assume came from some interaction with Afterlife. That's all. Can I go now?"

Prime March crossed his arms. "You're not telling us every-thing, Jade. What's going on here?"

She licked her lips, her hands tightening on Cuddles. "I. Am. Retired, Theeran. I don't want any part with gates, *souls*, or After-life."

"And yet, you seem to keep finding your way into matters that concern them, darling. One would almost think you couldn't help yourself."

Jade turned, pacing between the two Sovereigns and a pile of boxes. "I should never have listened to Marsilias. I knew this wouldn't lead anywhere else. Damnit!" She spun and kicked one of the nearby crates with enough force to shift it.

Prime March stepped forward, one hand extended. "Calm down, Jade. It's all right. You're fine."

She shuddered, clamping down on the waking nightmares and her racing thoughts. *"Just breathe,"* she repeated to herself, *"breathe through it, imagine the feather, keep it flying."* After a while, she faced Prime March again and spoke in as calm a voice as she could muster, "It doesn't add up. The first victim that alerted us to this is still alive and regularly displays mental instability. But the second victim, the one incarcerated here, is dead by apparent suicide and gave no indication of mental instability up to the very moment he went berserk in the intoxicant compound. What records we have show there's a marked period of decline before the mind fully loses control. Neither of these cases share any similarities besides the black markings. We have no idea how long any of these people were infected before their symptoms manifested. It can't be that ... thing in your basement because the two victims had no contact with each other, and share no significant genetic similarities to explain why the disease might have jumped between who knows how many carriers without raising symptoms."

Serras leaned forward, her smile fading. "Are you implying that this could already have reached a pandemic state? That thousands could already be infected?"

Jade stroked Cuddles, concentrating on the movement, making certain it stayed smooth. "Yes. We have no conception of how many people the second victim interacted with before his imprisonment, let alone the warden and Mr. Jeck. We have no barometer on how virulent this pathogen is, or the exact means by which it spreads." Her hand sped up.

Serras frowned and leaned back, her lenses igniting as she began surfing files. "Do you think this is a new *soul*, or merely the result of the first incident?"

"I think it's a new *soul*, but I don't know, and the only one I can think to ask is ..."

"Is who, darling?"

She stroked harder. "Chandris."

"That new *soul* that's so interested in you? I don't think bringing him out is wise. Especially if we think all of this is the work of a new *soul*."

Prime March's breath caught. "We wouldn't have to, depending on the range of his projection."

Jade nodded, speaking rapidly. "I could talk with him, see if he can sense other *souls* wandering about. He knew, knows, about ... Ilin. We wouldn't have to trust what he says, but I can probably verify it to some extent and he'll have insights we lack."

Serras nodded. "Very well, call the Purifier Compound, they'll patch you through to his cell."

Jade swallowed, forcing her hand to slow as Prime March spoke into his earpiece. He nodded a second later, and she tapped her earpiece. The device connected to the Purifier network and extended a thin wire along her cheeks to link with her lenses. A screen opened across her lenses a moment later, displaying Chandris's cell.

"Chandris?"

The *soul* looked up with slow deliberateness and faced her from his seat on the bed. "Jade."

"Can you sense other *souls*?"

"Within a certain distance."

"What is the distance, and can you sense any now?"

"Several dozen miles, and only one."

Relief flooded her. 'Thank God; it's just the old one.'

"Why do you ask?"

"*Souls* seem to have a poisonous effect on humans, and several have been showing symptoms of that poison. We feared that another *soul* was–"

"Untrue."

"What?"

"*Souls* are living creatures; we are not poisonous to humans. Not unless a certain aspect of our individual creation exhibited that effect."

Jade's blood ran cold. "But Ilin–"

"It is possible that lingering threads of *Aeria's* essence cling to us in the days following our appearance here, and they might have deleterious effects on humans. It is unlikely that those would be sufficiently potent to infect more than a few individuals; *Aeria's* essence is not parasitic."

Jade sank onto one of the crates and stared at the placid *soul*. "What are you saying?"

Theeran answered for him. "That the most likely source of this illness is another *soul* actively spreading the disease, or a continuous source of *Aeria's* energy, like an open gate of the sort Ilin used two years ago."

"Jade, Theeran, what is it? What did the *soul* say?"

"That there might be an open gate, Serras. Or another *soul*."

Jade wordlessly terminated her connection with the Purifier Compound, and then looked at Prime March as her earpiece contracted. "No...," she pleaded softly, her hand moving faster and faster.

"You have to, Jade. Even if we could trust them, it would take our sensors weeks to verify it, and this isn't something I want to trust the word of a *soul* on. You've been through that gate, you know what it felt like when it was open."

"Please...."

"I'm sorry, Jade, I have no choice."

She sagged against the wall and slid to the floor, just staring at him. They wanted her to go back. To revisit the first gate; the place where her Core died, where her brother died.

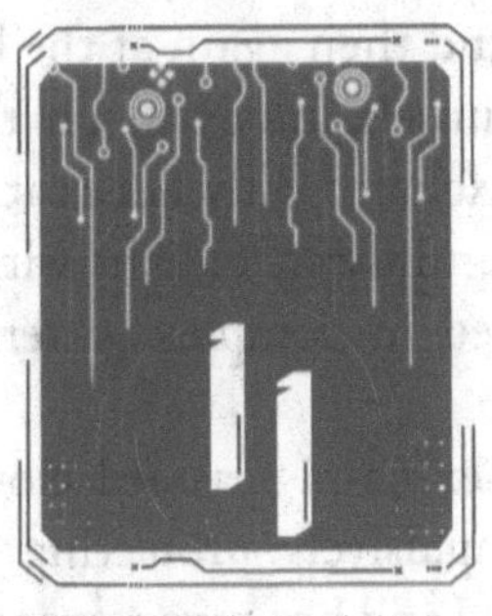

Where the Sky Split

Humans filled the aircraft around Chandris's reflection, loitering at its stairs and windows, most garbed as Purifiers and constantly verifying his position with furtive glances. Only two deviated from the group, the man called Marsilias and the woman called Jade. They sat apart, with Marsilias thoroughly belted to an expanded chair and her peering through the window she leaned against, her spirit a tormented knot of erratic emotions. These appeared to Chandris as a sheen of drifting colors within the surface of her form, a lush bloom of light centered upon the void of her soul.

Muted conversations graced the air, but all obeyed an unspoken solemnity, a grim unease about their destination. They refused to speak of it to Chandris, despite his gentle questions, and answered all his queries with silence or the quiet murmur of "a gate." If he asked what they meant by gate or about the purpose of his inclusion, they simply refused to respond entirely. Eventually he surrendered his attempts at conversation and joined Jade in the alcove she inhabited alone. Her gaze never rose from the churning water below, but the small amphibious creature draped across her shoulder chirped a greeting.

Chandris carefully settled himself upon a seat, crossing his reflection's legs and folding its hands in a decently human affectation. "What is it that causes your people such terror? They have seen *aperturas* before now and survived them without fear or ill effect."

She blinked and shifted toward him, startled from her reverie by his abrupt address and then again at the loose burgundy clothes he had painted for himself, modeled on the simplistic style she seemed to prefer. He excluded only her coat, for it was both inherently personal and magnificent, radiant with thousands of unique *luce* strands intertwined in complex patterns from thousands of minds.

In Jade's shock, her hand spasmed closed around something small and bronze, impulsively protecting it before recognition occurred. Then she eased and her gaze returned to the object, fingers parting to reveal a Purifier badge as her thumb gently polished it. "It's not the gate, at least not entirely. It's what came out of it that frightens them—us." She reversed the badge in her fingers, baring a name imprinted in the smooth metal: Lauran.

"What came from the *apertura*?"

Her hand spasmed again, panic swelling and suffocating her other emotions. For an instant, cracks sprawled through her, rigid with pain and jagged with fear. Then they faded and her other emotions spilled over them anew, masking but not entirely concealing the emotional scars. "One of you, I think: a *soul*. It didn't behave like the other revenants, didn't attack. Didn't matter though. He didn't come alone."

"He traveled beside another full *soul*?" This wouldn't surprise Chandris, there were a multitude of *souls* covertly inhabiting her world.

She replied in a small voice, "Yes. But that wasn't it. The gate, the gate never closed behind them." Her breath caught, eyes widening as her fingers clenched and the fear and pain returned. "It just stayed there. Open. And they kept coming out. Revenants and mist. And I just kept staring at it. Waiting for it to close. But it didn't. It stayed open." She shuddered and stowed the badge away in an inner pocket of her coat. Her hand emerged with a second, nearly identical badge: two sweeps of black cloth coiling around the golden Purifier mask. Only the names differed; this one said Naija.

"You were there?"

Jade gave a stiff nod. "Yes, from the beginning." Her hands jittered feverishly as she polished the badge. "It was like every other day, a routine check on an Afterlife reading, they were laughing and joking. Ilin was talking about some girl he'd met, saying she was pretty, that I'd like her." A fluttery, stressed giggle escaped her. "Then the air turned cold. It shouldn't have been cold; it was the middle of summer. In equator waters! We didn't know what was happening, everything was going haywire, we were crashing and then there was mist everywhere and I couldn't see–" The badge jerked from her fingers and clattered to the floor. She plunged after it, dropping to a knee, one hand stabbing forward to snatch it with a shocking slap. She stayed there for a minute, reduced to quivering breaths before gradually rising. "They didn't arrive all at once, but in ones and twos at first; all of them small revenants, disposable."

"Did you run?"

"No. How could we with those horrors crawling from the gate one after another." She stared at the badge for a long time and then slowly buried it back in her coat. "We couldn't run. We had to stop them, had to hope reinforcing Purifiers arrived in time." Her hand emerged again, carrying a third amulet in gentle fingers: Ilin. She stared at it for a long time, silent within the thrall of grief and guilt.

"How did you survive?"

"By killing them. We electrified them with lightning from the storm when they reached the water. We rigged our ship to explode and remotely crashed it into the gate as a new group arrived. We planted sonic emitters in the ocean and pulsed sound waves that drove the fish berserk. Ilin exhausted his magister decks with invocations; he bathed the ocean in fire, he turned the air to poison and rained meteors from the sky. Help started arriving also, dozens of Purifier Cores, and then they started dying. There was so much mist you could barely see, bodies everywhere, on the ice, in the water, islands of them floating and knotted up in black fabric. Naija got caught on a piece of ship and drowned, she was screaming for help but I couldn't find her, couldn't help her. We never found her body after. Lauran was eaten, bit in half and spat out like he tasted bad or something."

"And yet, you survived."

"Yes. Four days, I think. Don't know, lost count. My brother and I. Right up until the *soul* stepped through, all dark wings, sharp edges, and metal. Huge, like an aircraft, bigger than you, and screeching, always screeching." Her eyes never moved from the badge resting in her palm, and her voice, never higher than whisper, faded.

Chandris devoured the view of her, interested by the wealth of her emotions. Internally, however, concerns stirred; an *apertura* should not have remained open so long, and a *soul*, even several *souls*, could not have enthralled so many *vestiges*. More importantly, her recount roused a slivered memory, the recollection of a summons and his inability to answer, a recollection of being restrained, of being incarcerated? The memory, more impression than actual recollection, ended there, incomplete as if poorly erased. His concern endured, however, what use was there in restraining a *vestige* rather than simply consuming it? And why bother quelling the memories of said *vestige*? There was no answer in his present knowledge, nor any to be found from those around him, so Chandris pursued a question that could be answered, "Why do you mourn those who died? Your ... Core mates? Your brother?"

She finally looked at him, her eyes dry and unfocused. "Why?" Realization manifested in a blink and the emotions subsided from her periphery. "He was my brother, Chandris; I loved him."

"Why did you love him? Just because he lived with you? Just because he loved you?"

Jade tried to explain but failed. She tried to formulate a reason and failed. "I don't know ... I can't explain it. It just was," she trailed off, gaze falling to his name on the badge. "I loved him because he was always there, with me, for as long as I can remember. He made me feel safe, and he was kind, and he was funny, and I don't know! He never gave me a reason not to love him," she trailed off, attention fixating on the coil of white breath spilling from her lips despite the heated chamber. Her gaze lingered there for an instant, then shifted back to the window.

The rain had ceased, and in its place, the world reigned in stark clarity, flecked with particles of snow and the unimpeded vista of miles. Her focus descended to the frozen expanse far below. "We're here." She returned her brother's badge to her pocket and left the window. "Best ready yourself; I don't know if you feel cold as a projection, or in general, but the gate never warms, and that ice never melts." She walked off, navigating the crowded room to the opposite side where Marsilias had begun liberating himself.

Chandris observed her departure and then inspected the tundra below. A vast, cobalt dome appeared atop the ice in the distance, its peak crowned with the Purifiers' holographic sigil. He closed his eyes and extended his senses, scouring the white expanse for the promised *apertura*. He found nothing but a few scattered threads of *Aeria's* energy. He perceived the corpse of a *soul*, and recognized the lingering effects of a vast *apertura*, but nothing of *Aeria* that lived currently.

The aircraft dove, gliding toward the dome as tall red banners and forbidding energy walls activated across the ice. They flared and issued a piercing screech to warn all who approached to cease their advance.

Chandris watched the banners rush by in streams of red, the brilliance of their hues a stark contrast to the sheet of smooth, glistening ice. The aircraft slowed, granting individuality to the final rows of walls and banners before it landed outside the dome. As it did so, Chandris extended his senses to explore the edifice, attracted by a sensation of unfamiliarity, of alienness. Whatever comprised this structure, it was not a naturally occurring substance. It fascinated him, particularly because the humans displayed no particular interest in it.

The engines subsided with a final low purr, deactivating entirely as the primary doors retracted upward. Freezing wind swept inside, enveloping the already hunching Purifiers and eliciting a chorus of profanities paired with misted breaths.

Chandris thrust the grumbling Purifiers from his conscious thought and emerged onto the ice, his projected form impervious to the frigid environment. The Purifiers traipsed after him one by one and congregated outside the dome's modest entrance. A screen appeared on the door with a keypad and an eye sensor, followed by an attendant program. "Would the chief member of your party insert the necessary passcode."

Uninterested in the Purifiers' security methods, Chandris wandered further onto the ice, searching for remnants of life. He encountered nothing but the beings within the dome and its accompanying compound. The prevalent holographic banners deactivated around him, leaving nothing but the small, four-clawed projectors that covered the ice. He knelt and brushed his hand across the orb seated in the device's center, offering a question by way of greeting to the man following him, "So many warnings seem like excess; surely a single row would suffice?"

The soft rasp of Marsilias's boots ceased beside Chandris, drawing the *soul's* attention to his bearded face as he received his answer, "Not really, at least not if you consider their main purpose."

"They have another purpose?"

"They pump heat into the ice whenever they accrue enough power from the environment, try to melt it and fix whatever the gate's done to the water."

"Have they managed to decrease the ice?"

"Not in two years." Marsilias stamped a boot and shook himself. "Brr, this cold really bites into you, doesn't it?"

"I wouldn't know, I cannot feel it; and while *Aeria* is cold, it does not turn the water solid."

"That's oddly specific for a man who doesn't 'know'."

"I ... remember?" Chandris closed his eyes and followed the memory, the sensation it engendered until it ended with the darkness of the forgotten. "This is a strange place. I do not know why, but even my living memories begin to surface."

Marsilias cocked his head. "How many lives have you lived? Living or dead."

"Thousands, all of them perfect memories of *Aeria*, like a flash of light in the dark."

"How can you be anyone distinct if you have all those different memories, those divergent personalities, stored in your head?"

"I am not distinct. To experience eternity is not to know everything. It is to *be* everything. The fire and the wood, the bird and the beetle, the living and the dead. Living here, like this, is not different. I am not distinct. I am everything that I have seen and tasted."

"That must be difficult or confusing at least."

"For a race that can exist solely as a concept of 'I' then yes, it must be."

Marsilias scrutinized Chandris, wondering if the *soul* insulted him, and then shifted his focus across the ice. "You said this place was strange; what do you make of it?"

"I do not know, but it must concern this eternal *apertura*. Do you know the depth of this ice?"

"About a mile; why?"

"Does the clarity of atmosphere extend that high above the

surface level as well?"

"Yes, it has about a two-mile diameter. Does that mean something?"

"Not particularly." *The soul must have been desperate, starved almost to the brink of oblivion for it to possess such a small reach. If its apertura is still open, then why? Maintaining the apertura in life would have drained essence it could not spare, exhausted its luce and reduced it to a vestige. If the apertura is open, why does it exude no signature? And how did it instigate this freezing?"* Chandris turned back to the dome, which now stood open. "Let us return; we will find no more answers out here. The *apertura* holds the next truth."

They rejoined the Purifiers filing into the dome and navigated their group to where Jade and the chief Purifier conversed with a disheveled scientist. "... far as we know, nothing's changed. The gate produces no signature on any frequency or plane we can detect and displays no physical signs of life."

The chief Purifier frowned, her eyes darkening with skepticism. "Are you sure? All of our intel indicates that this gate should be alive and active."

The scientist shrugged. "I don't know what else to tell you, Captain Erda. The gate's dead. You can inspect it yourself and access our data reports." He raised a sleek, white cylinder and twisted a dial on its base until the device flashed green. Pressing the object to his lips, he inhaled and then exhaled a breath of scented smoke. The pipe returned to his pocket. "We have suits you can use to inspect the gate and containment chamber personally, or the revenant's corpse if you so wish."

Chandris glided forward, phasing through Captain Erda and Jade in the process. The scientist frowned at him, confusion blooming to dominate his emotions as he struggled to reconcile Chandris's incorporeality with his continued color. Chandris used the moment to verify what he had heard, "The *soul* left a corpse with its demise?"

The scientist glanced from him to Erda. "Who's this? He ain't no Purifier."

Captain Erda snarled under her breath. "He's a *soul*, an evolved form of revenant like the corpse you have below." She pointed down through the crystalline floor into a pit of ice. Far below them, on a sheet of cracked and darkened ice, stood an empty arch. Something large lay curled around the *apertura*, its form frozen.

"One of Prime March's pets then," the scientist mused to himself, briefly losing track of his conversation. He came back to himself with a blink. "Yeah, that revenant left a corpse. We don't know why, or if, it has anything to do with this blasted ice." He retrieved his pipe and sucked on it again. "So, can you explain that?"

Chandris shook his head in careful imitation of a human denial. "No. That is unnatural. *Souls* do not leave corpses."

The scientist frowned in return. "We assumed it lingering was a result of the specimen's drastically higher power density; you're saying it's not? That it's supposed to behave like a standard revenant?"

"Yes."

"Well, that's two years of theorizing wasted." The scientist sighed then proceeded, "Does your team want to go exploring?"

Erda faced Jade. "Can you tell if it's active from here?"

Pale and voiceless, Jade shook her head. Chandris said nothing either, his thoughts turned inward, dissecting the discrepancies and alienness of the area.

Erda continued, "We need a couple suits, four if Mr. Wreign decides to accompany us."

"Wouldn't miss it for the world."

"Very well. Take Miss Dieza, Mr. Wreign, and those two"—she signaled at two Purifiers—"and equip them to visit the gate. The rest of us will scour your data and speak with the others stationed here."

"Whatever you say, follow me."

The scientist flashed a brusque beckons at the four designated individuals and conducted them to a reinforced entrance. Chandris preceded them to the door and then phased through it as the scientist accessed a holographic console and commenced the insertion of an extensive passcode. Beyond the black door, presumably colored thus as a visual deterrent, waited a slim corridor and another door with an equally forbidding aspect. Chandris advanced, inspecting the energy patterns visible on either wall beneath the vaguely translucent surface. While he could not discern their exact attributes, he recognized an aggressive purpose in their dull red hue. *"La Neblina terrifies them, or the scientists believe the apertura is more active than they profess."*

The door retracted into the wall, and the scientist stormed in and futilely snatched Chandris's arm. Despite grasping only air, he continued in his efforts while snapping, "Don't do that! Do you realize how dangerous the miasma below us is? What if you had inadvertently released it? What if–"

"Even if the extermination of your facility had been my intent, I could no more affect a change on its infrastructure or state than you can grasp my arm. I have no physical form."

"Regardless"—the scientist slashed the air—"I don't want you out of my sight for an instant."

Chandris considered the man's emotions; fear eddied across the surface of his soul, but it was a superficial sentiment, an excuse for the emotion that actually defined his responses. "You loathe me."

The scientist flinched, unease flicking across both his features and spirit before his face contorted, abolishing any pretense of decorum. "Damn right I hate you. We all hate you; get used to it." He stormed forward, but his unease lingered long after.

Despite his evident misgivings, the scientist ushered them through three subsequent doors, each bedecked with increasing precautionary and defensive measures. The final door opened with a gasp of sterilized air and admitted them into a long, sleek room outfitted with two rows of shallow benches and opposing wall lockers.

The scientist removed himself from their direct path and gestured them forward. "You will discover all the necessary equipment in the lockers; hazmat gear for the most part but also some miasma specific sensors. Be forewarned, this is unlike any miasma you've encountered before; it's lethal within minutes of skin contact, and within seconds of inhalation."

The four designated people filed in, their features and spirits unperturbed by the scientist's claims. Only Jade betrayed signs of apprehension; she shifted constantly, stared without seeing and appeared almost divorced from her surroundings.

Chandris recalled what she had shared about her past and crossed the room, crouching atop the bench beside her. "What do you see when your mind wanders?"

She blinked awake from her wondering thoughts, the strange red coat folded over her arm. "What?"

"Your mind wanders, what is it you see?"

She shrugged, refocusing her attention on the arrangement of her coat, laying it on the bench between them and brushing out the wrinkles and folds. She did not speak at first, and Chandris did not press her, content to watch as she finished her preparations and then touch her suit's collar. A slim belt of corrugated, dark metal slid out, flowed along her jawline and expanded into a mask over her lower face, mouth, and nose. Only then did she speak, gazing upon him with grim eyes, "I see mist and ruins." Then she moved toward the omniveyor at the room's opposite extremity, breath issuing in a dense white cloud from the mask's gill-like slits.

One of the Purifiers scrambled to his feet as she passed, catching her arm, "Miss Dieza, your suit, you–"

"I don't need it." She gently extricated her arm and entered the omniveyor, slumping against the rear wall with a dull click from the Siphons strapped to her lower back. Marsilias followed her in, humming to himself as he explored the various sensors, gadgets, and weapons that accompanied his suit. The Purifiers raced to complete their preparations and scurried into the omniveyor.

Chandris joined them and the doors closed, preempting the scientist's image materializing on the omniveyor's wall. "I'm sending you down momentarily. There will be a second door in the main chamber that you will use to leave. It leads to sanitization chambers where you and your clothing will be sterilized before you can be permitted to depart. We have yet to discern whether or not miasma of this density is infectious." The omniveyor dropped with a whoosh, staggering the occupants with its abruptness, and concluded its descent heartbeats later, jolting them anew. The scientist's projection shrugged. "I guess all that's left is to wish you good luck." He saluted, and the omniveyor's door opened to a gust of frigid air.

The four humans flinched back, Jade with her arms raised to protect her eyes and the others muttering profanities. She lowered her arms after the initial gust dwindled and ventured out onto the ice. Chandris followed, absorbing the brilliant environment as he went. *La Neblina* coiled up about their waists, swirling as they advanced and rising in waves with their passage. The ice crunched beneath their footsteps, but that was the only sound to intrude on the chamber's stillness. Even *La Neblina* shifted exclusively at their movements, all else seemed in stasis.

Chandris matched his steps with Jade. "Why do you not fear *La Neblina*? Is it not deleterious to your kind, even in a diluted state?"

She looked at him, eyes suddenly crystal clear. "I have inhaled far worse things than this miasma. Besides, I have an advantage over regular men." Those lovely violet eyes hardened, devoid of the sleepy torpor that generally defined them. Her gaze swept away from Chandris to fasten on the *apertura* and the colossal cadaver encircling it. She marched forward, her body as rigid as the ice, and stopped only when the arch rose thirty feet above her and ten to either side. There she knelt, the corpse's many limbs surrounding her in walls of serrated armor and tattered black cloth, its actual form difficult to discern because of this.

Chandris followed her without attempting interruption, circumnavigating to the corpse's rear as he delved his consciousness into it. He discovered wrongness, a violent inversion of a *soul's* natural composition. Memories abided in the corpse's muscles, organs, and armor but fragmented by decomposition, too many to explore without hours to invest in the endeavor. Regardless, Chandris cycled through the strongest of its memories, reliving the violence and maddening hunger of its death, snatches of excited conversation with the *soul* now named Ilin alongside another *soul* Chandris did not know. He paused as a newer memory arose, that of the *soul*—now known to Chandris as Shafiras—addressing an *Extranjerra*. Much of the memories had degraded, sparing only impressions punctuated by flashes of clarity; Chandris heard a cacophony of voices—the *Extranjerra*—they were furious, they needed to destroy, kill, something, someone, a *soul*. The *soul* they needed to destroy didn't exist yet, hadn't been born, was being made. They needed to discover where. There was an impression of the *soul* they wished destroyed, and in it Chandris recognized himself. The memory failed entirely after that, leaving Chandris to surface from the corpse and ruminate upon the revelation.

The sound of crunching ice beside Chandris diverted his attention outward to Marsilias as the corpulent man meandered beside him and knelt.

The man extended a gloved hand and brushed it across the corpse's exterior, causing bits of gray carapace to flake off and expel tufts of brown mist. He glanced at Chandris. "What do you make of the body and the gate? Any insight?"

"Our bodies are manifested *luce*, light, energy ... pure life. We take that energy and concentrate it into muscles, flesh, and blood so that we might walk in your world. This *soul* is different. Its form is not *luce*. It is *Aeria*. What you humans call Afterlife or death."

"This *soul* was dead when it arrived?"

"No. Its shell was comprised of *Aeria*, like armor on your body, and entirely lifeless. That is the source of *La Neblina* here; as the cadaver decomposes, it releases *Aerian* essence."

"Is that what's causing the sickness?"

"Perhaps."

Marsilias frowned contemplatively. "That still doesn't explain how it's spreading. And there's another thing I don't understand: Why is it still here? If this body was derived from Afterlife energy, why has it not returned? Why does it linger?"

"Water merges with water, fire with fire, but the two do not mix. *Luce* would dissipate, merge with this world; but just as *luce* cannot merge or dissipate in *Aeria*, *Aeria* native energies cannot merge or dissipate here."

"So we're stuck with it."

"Yes, unless another *soul* opens and then closes an *apertura* in the near vicinity."

"Closes?"

"Yes, when an *apertura* closes, it reabsorbs all of *Aeria's* essence; this essence lingers because it only came into being after the *apertura* closed."

"Could you reopen that gate?"

"Were I here physically, yes, but that would only address the symptom. *Aeria's* essence would simply return unless you relocate the cadaver to *Aeria*. It is the body decaying that emits this essence." Discussing the subject reminded Chandris of how Jade had disdained the protective gear Marsilias and their other companions wore. "Why does Miss Jade not fear *La Neblina*? Does it not affect her?"

"Ah," Marsilias trailed off, observing Jade for a while. "That goes back to the invasion. I don't remember how long they fought for, but her whole Core died, leaving Jade, her brother, and whatever other Cores arrived to help. The two of them held everything together for hours, bought the time the Purifier Corporation needed to invent a means of destroying the gate. Finally, the Purifier Corporation found what it needed, a type of pulse-bomb that would sever the energy forcing the gate open; all they needed to do was plant it at the arch. They gave the bomb to Jade and Ilin, and dropped them at the gate with three other Cores, all of them Sovereigns."

"Sovereigns?"

"Sovereign Cores, a Purifier Core with a Prime and Primess of the corporation; our final aces. Normal Cores consist of four people, but it can vary for special cases and divisions."

"Prime March would be a sovereign."

"Yeah, and Primess March; they always come in pairs, one man and one woman." Marsilias offered Chandris a moment to voice further questions then resumed, "So they dropped Jade, Ilin, and the other Cores right at the gate. The Cores cleared a space, and Ilin started to plant the bomb, but something came from the gate and dragged both him and the bomb in. Jade followed them.

"I don't know how long it was for her, she won't say; but I know it wasn't a question of minutes. For us, it was a matter of seconds before she stepped back through the gate with her brother's corpse thrown over one shoulder and the bomb in hand. She set the bomb at the base and triggered it, disrupted the gate and saved countless lives. Only, her brother wasn't as dead as she thought; something came over with them."

"The *soul* who calls itself Ilin."

"Yeah, the rest of the story doesn't really matter, but they forced her to retire soon after with all expenses paid for life. Whatever she experienced on the other side stuck with her. Jade spent months recovering enough mentally to simply walk outside of therapy; most days it was incessant panic attacks mixed with hallucinations."

"I presume her foray into *Aeria* is why Prime March dispatched her on this mission; such an immersive contact would result in a permanent affinity."

"Yeah, and no one knows how she survived."

Jade finally stirred before the arch, and stood. The various expedition members congregated around her, wordlessly expectant.

She wrapped her arms about herself and slowly shook her head. "The gate's not open. Hasn't been for years."

Horror bloomed in Marsilias's and the Purifiers' essences, manifesting physically as an exchange of wide-eyed glances. The subordinate Purifier grimly spoke what they all feared. "So, there's another gate."

Jade nodded. "Yeah. Somewhere in the world."

The commanding Purifier grimaced. "We have to warn the Purifier Corporation immediately; travel needs to be shut down before this spreads beyond control, and we need to find this gate. Dieza–"

"No, "Jade said exhaustedly, "you have to. I am done. Maybe Chandris can find the other gate for you." Without another word, she staggered toward the far exit, her emotions a mass of guilt, shame, and grief.

Interjection 2

Connor climbed the stair of lavish black wood, separated from the dark by a halo of pale light from his upturned palm. His ascent delivered him through the silent, unheated environment to the mall's second story, where lush carpets of silver and blue quieted his footsteps. Here he paused, hand rising to illuminate storefronts of varnished wood and glass displays: diamond jewelers, masquerade boutiques, art galleries of every profession, and a bookstore with classic novels in luxurious leather and paper. None carried the name of his destination, so he continued on his way, ignoring the security cameras seated in every corner. Without fail they faltered at his passing, blind to anyone in the vacillating mask and orange coat of the Redeemers. Some would notice the discrepancy, but no record of who had trespassed would ever exist.

He slowed, the light from his glove flowing across the curtained windows and aesthetically worn sign of an antiques store. He cocked his ear briefly to listen, verifying no one had noticed him, and then knocked on the antique shop's lacquered door, causing the ancient wood to rattle in its frame. No lights illuminated the interior, and the sign detailing service hours indicated that the store had closed several hours prior, but Connor ignored these.

He knocked again, a muted urge thrumming through his chest like unspent energy: the PLAN striving to exert its hold upon him, to modify his actions to suit its needs. It had grown stronger of late, more insistent with fewer and shorter intervals of respite, and Connor had only a stretch of lost time to explain why.

The door finally swung inward, revealing a tired man in a suit carefully designed to appear stylishly faded. "We're closed, come back tomorrow...," the proprietor trailed off, noticing Connor's vacillating mask. "Who the hell are you? Some kind of psycho?"

Connor leaned close, fishing through an inside pocket to retrieve a miniature ornament comprised of wires and circuit boards fused in the shape of a Stormflower. "Jun Kol, I belong to the Fifth, and I need your help. The PLAN directs me."

Acknowledgement registered in Jun Kol's gaze and he stepped aside, his demeanor altering entirely. "Come in, it is safe to speak inside."

No one outside the Redeemers knew of the five, and no one within would have dared appropriate their symbol without permission. None except Connor.

Jun Kol stepped back into the antique shop's dark interior, beckoning Connor to follow and closing the door behind him. They ventured deeper, squeezing through weathered furniture and shelves cluttered with defunct tools, faded art, and sculptures until they reached the storage rooms in the back, where Jun Kol finally ignited a single dim light. From the obscurity appeared mountains of packing crates, most still sealed but a few open and displaying artifacts. Connor ignored them and faced Jun Kol. "I need to know who's above you. I need to speak with them. It's vital, the urge is strong."

Jun Kol hesitated, and with good reason for the Fifth had betrayed the Redeemers. Cautiously, he spoke, "... There are traitors amongst the Fifth's servants; I cannot speak unless I know who you are."

"What do you expect me to do?" Redeemers were not supposed to know one another in mass; anonymity was security; anonymity was power.

Disdaining an immediate response, Jun Kol crossed to a stack of two crates beside Connor and pressed his bare hand to the topmost's console. The dull, matte-black container opened, its faces projecting outward in an array of plates, wires, and screens before reassembling itself into a chair of hard, jutting edges, the arms of which blinked with teal dots: a connection hub to the universal web.

Jun Kol indicated the chair with a relaxed gesture. "Sit down."

Connor's heart stopped. Fear followed, cold in the blood, taut in the throat. She was in the universal web. She would know him for a traitor. But Jun Kol's hand remained pointed at the chair, silent and insistent, and to deny him would betray Connor as a traitor.

He sat, because there was nothing else he could do, and he prayed his mind went unseen amidst the billions inhabiting the web. Even Her reach suffered limits, and there existed no idols in the room to harbor Her presence.

Energy buzzed and the implants in his forearms linked with the chair nodes. The universal web filled the periphery of his consciousness, simultaneously white noise and a panorama of transparent images, webpages, links, and titles: breaking news, advertisements, suggestions based on his previous searches, and weather information. Despite the variety and noise, it remained detached, pending his active desire to immerse.

Repositioning before Connor, Jun Kol tapped his earpiece and held it there. His eye lenses activated, not blue, green—or any normal eye color—but vibrant orange. Redeemer lenses. She could see through those. She could *see* Connor. She could find him.

Connor erupted to his feet, his arm tearing from the connection hub to sever his link with the universal web.

Jun Kol frowned, confusion prompting the response more than suspicion. "What's wrong?"

"Energy surge."

"Ah, of course. Probably just left over energy from booting up. Go ahead and sit down again." Jun Kol's radiant orange eyes bored into Connor, reiterating his command: Sit Down.

Connor's mind raced. Why the hell did Jun Kol have Redeemer lenses for such a small role in the PLAN. Was there more here Connor couldn't see? Forget that. Not important. The chair demanded his return, a necessity if he wanted answers, but also something that might very well get him killed.

He reluctantly settled into the chair, right arm raised above the connection nodes as if wary of another surge. His other hand dropped beside the chair, surreptitiously concealing it behind protruding edges and wires. Then he touched thumb to pointer and middle finger in a silent snap, sparking his adaptive suit's flame function. Invisible to Jun Kol, small blue flames ignited upon his fingertips and burgeoned as his suit supplied the gas his needs required. The flames climbed, licking the internal machinery and spreading a light Connor prayed to God Jun Kol wouldn't see. Then he laid his other hand on the chair and began connecting nodes.

One after another, he linked his implants to the universal web, the ocean of information manifesting increasingly distinct in his conscious, and Her with it, fixed upon him: unseen, calculating, inhuman.

The chair flickered, almost pulling a gasp of relief from Connor as dark smoke trickled from below. It sparked, launching Connor to his feet with a real energy surge and thickening fumes. He retreated from it, waving a hand to bat the smoke from his eyes. "It seems defective."

Jun Kol grimaced and rubbed his chin, jaw working in frustrated contemplation.

"What now?" Connor asked.

Jun Kol said nothing.

"I still need help. Who's above you?"

Jun Kol's jaw flared in a tooth-grinding flex, then loosed in an exhale. "We belong to the Second."

"Not him, I don't need to know which PLAN. Who's directing you, explaining rolls, details?"

"Saccari Inuma directs us in the Second's name. For the PLAN to summon you personally is a sign of fated importance. Do you know your function?"

"No. That's why I need Saccari."

"I don't know his location; I was assigned here to wait and interact with the wealthy, nothing more. However, the PLAN is centered around the Jysa currently; he will not be far from them.

Relief breathed through Connor. "Thank you," he replied quietly, earnestly. "I ..." He fell silent again, a line of text scrolling across the lenses in his eyes: I'm here. Where are you? Connor dispelled the message with a blink and spoke to Jun Kol, "I need to go, the PLAN, something's happened."

Jun Kol tensed, concern effacing all else from his features. "I understand. There's a Warren entrance in the back; it runs all the way up the building to the next city floor. No cameras, no security, and tracking disruption; just don't stray from the Redeemer marked paths. They're not safe."

Connor was already moving, slipping between stacks of storage crates and swaddled antiques until he disappeared entirely in the storage room's shadows. He knew what to search for, a nook in the back wall, strangely clear despite the absence of available space and blanketed in dust. He knelt, running his fingers along the seam between floor and wall until they struck a sequence of five nodes impacted into the floor. He pressed his fingers into these and felt them link to the implants in his hand and arms. There was an instant of connection when the entrance affixed to whatever amendments She had made to his implants, and then the wall cracked open, just large enough to squeeze through.

The passage delivered him onto a slim ledge in a dark hollow between the walls, the space seemingly entirely comprised of blinking circuit boards. The tight confines should have been sweltering, instead he found them cold and silent. A ladder to his left offered the only feasible means of traversing the hollow space.

Connor swung onto the ladder and descended, leaving the entrance to close in his wake. It was not his first trek within a Warren. He knew the signs and therefore navigated it quickly, avoiding ancillary paths and ladders, and where the circuitry boards began transitioning to other material: wood and verdure, carved metal, bone and glass.

He bypassed several entrances across several stories-worth of distance, descending until he reached the exit he sought, its emergence point carefully annotated in brail upon the door's surface. Connor pressed his fingers into the attendant nodes and felt them connect. The door opened, depositing him into the steam-obscured confines of an alley. He hastily removed his Redeemer apparel and continued on his way, no one the wiser as to his origin.

New text scrolled across his vision, flashing subtly to ensure he saw it: You good? Safe?

Under his breath Connor said, "Command: Speech To Text.

Contact: Ruon Drahma." Then, still softly, he replied, "Fine. Couldn't speak. Can now. Where are you?"

Home. You?

"Secret meeting. Redeemers active again. Trying to figure out the PLAN. You disappeared again last night. What happened?"

Stop asking. Not safe. Better not knowing.

Connor emerged from the alleyway onto a white platform adjoining several skyscrapers. A glance toward the simulated sky revealed both an overcast midday hour, and that he had descended to the city-complex's subsequent floor. He began pathing toward the platform's edge, navigating the assorted synthetic trees and bushes, lunch stations, and crowd. Connor maintained the conversation all the while, "I don't like it, Ruon. I worry. You're always sick when you get back. And jumpy." He reached the platform's edge and settled upon the railing over the vast cityscape precipice, pressing the button to summon an omniveyor.

Ruon, his brother, had almost died just over two years ago, and would have except for Jade's intervention. She'd taken him some-where, somewhere Connor was forbidden to follow, and neither would speak of it. Whatever transpired, it left Ruon pathologically unwilling to speak, perpetually afflicted with nervous energy, and exiled him from the Redeemers; not exiled like Connor but entirely divorced, his implants and other Redeemer-enhanced electronics dead in his skin. Every so often he would disappear without trace and return two to three days later, quivering, fragile, and anemic.

Leave it alone. Not answering. What's up with Redeemers?

An empty omniveyor ascended the skyscraper's front to arrive before Connor and open. He entered, input his destination, then leaned back as it glided horizontally away, riding a rail system between two of the skyscrapers. No longer whispering, he responded, "They're doing something with the Jysa. Don't know what yet. PLAN'S in full flow, Saccari's in charge."

You heading there next?

"Yeah. You up to help?"

Yes. Jade?

"Not unless we need her."

Probably will. Redeemers too big for us alone.

"Yeah. But not yet." As they spoke, Connor pulled the book from inside his coat and began writing first what he had heard, then a recount of what had transpired. "First things first, figure out what the Jysa have to do with anything. They aren't part of the Corporatocracy, so why are the Redeemers involving them?"

Don't know. Gotta be careful, though. Redeemer or not, they will kill you—us—if PLAN gets close to finishing.

"I know. Still in?"

Always.

The Clan-Ship Imarah

Cuddles slumbered on Jade's shoulders as she dozed half-submerged in the Purifier Compound's main information server, waiting for something interesting to transpire. Her virus jack hummed beside her on the desk, surreptitiously sifting through, categorizing, and accumulating information. It had taken Jade a few hours to fashion the device, but now it artfully accomplished her job, which in turn allowed her all the time she could desire for lounging and snooping. She had already uncovered several secret Purifier operations, numerous classified projects, and a veritable library of illicit gossip material. Unfortunately, she had yet to hack the innermost layers of the Purifier information hub, so the juiciest secrets still exceeded her reach. No matter, she had plenty to occupy herself with rewriting codes, inserting phantom programs, and generally infiltrating every sector of the Purifier Corporation's network. Why? For amusement mostly, but also in case of potential need.

A program she recognized activated somewhere in the network: Prime March's seclusion system. "*And what are you up to?*" Jade inserted an override command and infiltrated his main console. She couldn't initiate audio and visual functions without alerting him, but she could process and decipher the information streams.

"Theeran Sule, I presume, unless you're his secretary again."

"You caught me at a good time, Mr. Darian, I have a few minutes to spare on you. I would appreciate the persistence and personal attention, but I doubt this is a social call. What have we done wrong now?"

"Get off it, Sule, you know what this is about and you've wasted enough of my time. Your corporation's negotiating a private contract with the Jysa; you're not supposed to be forming private contracts, you're employed by the Corporatocracy. We pay a fortune for your service and fund all the necessary supplies. You need to stop."

"The Jysa aren't part of the Corporatocracy, they're not covered by your fees; if they wish to contract us privately that's their prerogative, and you don't have authority to restrict us."

"Shut it, Sule. You're still a corporation and subject to corporation law. A defensive contract, even with an external culture, is a military contract and so subject to the Defense Corporation. By law you should have referred them to us, and by that same law you need to either desist now or transfer all proceeds to the Defense Corporation; failure to do so will incriminate you for racketeering. Have we made our position clear?"

"You know the Purifier Corporation won't pay."

"Then I guess you'd better cancel that contract."

"The Jysa need us, Darian. Revenants are actively hunting them."

"That's your moral quandary to resolve, Sule; we would love to help them, but we can't without an invitation. Maybe you should suggest that at your next meeting."

The conversation dwindled, a tense moment of relieving pressure before it resumed with Prime March, "Speaking privately, have there been any other ... incidents on your end, Darian?"

A hesitation, then, "Nothing, even from those who lived with that lunatic; you really think this has something to do with Afterlife?"

"Yes, and from one old friend to another, tell your board to watch out; the Purifier Corporation is about to become a lot more important and our CEO won't squander the opportunity to encroach."

"Yeah, and from one friend to another, best tell your CEO to back off. The Purifiers aren't as popular as you think." The data connection cut off.

Jade smoothly surfaced from the network, rose and crossed the information hub to the wall, startling Cuddles awake in the process. She accessed the door panel, securing the entrance to ensure privacy, and then returned to her desk to call Prime March. He answered promptly, appearing on the panel before her, his office and desk filling the space behind him.

"Hello, Jade, what do you need?"

"What incident were you talking about with Darian Pry?"

Confusion strangled his features for a split-second, then collapsed with a look of frustrated exasperation. "Did you hack my office again?"

"Try to concentrate on what's important. Was this another incident of the Afterlife disease?"

Prime March leaned back, crossing his arms. "It's none of your concern; and even if it was, I wouldn't tell you. It's not something you need to worry about, Jade, let us do our job and you do yours."

"Just tell me, Theeran, or I'll find the answer myself. What happened?"

His jaw worked silently, grinding the teeth together before ultimately relenting. "Fine, but if you end up causing yourself a panic attack because of this, remember you're the one that forced me." He settled onto his desk with a fatigued sigh. "Yes. There was another incident; the secretary of some middle-management director from the Defense Corporation went berserk. She displayed all the familiar signs. And no, she never met the first subject, or the second."

"Is there anything else you want to share?"

"No, not really. Plus, I thought you retired, and absolutely refused to work this job."

"That doesn't mean you can bury a potential epidemic! People need to know, the other corporations at the very least."

"Oh they know, and they run daily checks on all their personnel for signs of it; they've yet to find anything. The Savant Corporation has been supplying everyone with cards designed to expose whatever this is, but you know how hard those are to make and we're still hopelessly scrambling for a solution. We need more subjects."

"What are the other Sovereigns doing?"

"They have their own problems, not the least of which is a Techcron host-ship trespassing on our airspace."

"And you still think it's a good idea to antagonize the Defense Corporation?"

"Never let a good crisis go to waste; we need to eke ourselves a suitable position in the Corporatocracy or we'll never amount to more than a lackey corporation."

"What are you going to do about the Jysa?"

"Probably nothing; the board won't sanction anything that benefits the Defense Corporation and it's not a small enough job for us to just ask for volunteers. There's nothing I can do."

She dropped into her chair. "Whatever you say. Goodbye, Prime March." The panel deactivated and reverted to its original hue.

Jade slumped, resting her head on the back of her chair, and stared at the distant ceiling. "*Let it go, Jade. Just let it go.*" The blinking lights of passing information gawked back, a world of knowledge, secrets, and distractions if she immersed herself in them. Yet she could not dispel the dread gradually mounting inside her. "*Please, you don't want any part of this, it will only hurt.*" Her fingers tightened on the armrests. "*Think! You've done your part, you've given everything that mattered to you, even saved the world, maybe. The Jysa will be fine; Theeran will figure something out.*" Yet, the dread remained, slicing at her mind like a scalpel until she could only lean forward and clasp the back of her head with quivering fingers. "Damn It." Then she shoved to her feet, slashing one hand across the console just long enough to unfasten the doors.

Images of her brother, of the revenant that inhabited his body like a parasite, suffused her mind: his grin, his taunting voice, his smug, tormenting words all draped in his lies. He was the origin of all this, he had to know something more. "Just this one last thing, then you're done. You pull out for good, no matter what anyone says or you hear. Just this one last thing."

Cuddles licked her ear, trying to provide comfort. She stroked his head. "I'm all right." Ilin's eyes flashed before her, twisting her stomach into knots. "We're going to be all right." She stroked his head again and rounded the corner to Ilin's cell.

She walked to the access window and froze, paralyzed by what she knew waited behind it. The console flashed on her left, soundless and red in the white corridor. The window waited, obscured by white panels. She compelled herself to raise a hand and press the panel so it would open.

Her brother looked up from where he sat on the edge of his bed, playing with an infant seriat.

All the words building on Jade's tongue vanished, erased by shock. Fear and incomprehension followed soon after, twisting her stomach with nausea. Why did he have a seriat? Why did he even want one?

Her brother's body rose effortlessly to his feet, grinning and raising the seriat to display it. "Look, I got one too. Now we match." He lowered it slightly, turning the creature about to inspect it with a discerning eye. "I wanted it to look like yours, so it's not perfect, but it'll do."

"For what? And why?" She looked at the seriat again, the action almost involuntary, and couldn't help but notice how similar it was to Cuddles. They looked nearly identical, close enough that seeing the seriat in her brother's hands made her throat instinctively constrict.

"Why I wanted one? I heard you got one, and I thought if we both had one it might help us get closer. So I petitioned my chief researcher for one in exchange of some particularly invasive experiments. Isn't he cute?" He crooned into the seriat's ear, nuzzling and shaking it with a giggle. "You want to help name him? Has to be something cute."

She shook, hating his face, his voice, the way it made her want to curl up in some dark corner and weep. Jade, however, didn't have that luxury, so she grit her teeth and forced herself to match his stare. "You lied to us. Why?"

His stroking hand stilled on the back of the seriat's head, fingers partially wrapped around its neck and encasing its head. "Whatever do you mean?"

"The poison didn't come from you, it came from a gate—a second gate!"

His voice changed slightly, losing the playful familiarity of before for a tone of long-suffering tedium. "And how would I know that? I'm locked in here, in this prison, in this body. I see nothing of your world, know nothing of its laws; I am blind, restricted to the extent of my arms and the breadth of these walls."

"You have to know! You made the first one, but that's closed and new people are getting infected! You must know something! If you can't tell us where, then at least tell us how to find it?" She pressed her hand against the window, fingers splayed wide, and said the word she knew he wanted from her. "Please."

His demeanor remained unchanged. "There is no other gate, Jade. If there was, your world would already be inundated with *vestiges*, and you'd be out there slaughtering them with my Siphon and that awful thing you made your soul into. But you're not, so there is no other open gate. I don't know why you're so desperate to believe I am at fault, that I am involved, but I physically can't be, and your fixation on it is not the signs of a healthy mind; there is no conspiracy, no impending cataclysm or plot. This is just remnants of *Aeria* we don't understand yet, garbage the Purifier Corporation can manage on its own given time. They don't need you to save them, again. You just need to let them work, and not intervene."

She ground her fist against the window. "Stop. Talking. Like. That. You're not him."

"No, but I could be if you wanted. I have no particular affection for any one personality or life from the multitude that comprise me. I could ignore and erase everything else and just be your brother again. Would you like that? I'm genuinely curious."

"I. Hate. You."

"That was uncalled for." He retreated from the window, flipping the seriat over in the crook of an arm and stroking his fingers up and down its belly. As he settled back down on his bed, the curl of a tiny, expectant smile appeared on his lips. His fingers dug in deeper, raising in the seriat's fur and causing it to struggle in protest.

"What do you know? There has to be another gate; it's the only explanation."

"I know next to nothing, just what the people here tell me. How are your memories by the way, fallen silent yet?" His phantom smile resurfaced. "I wouldn't want you ... having a panic attack with all the recent excitement, breaking down, being forced to watch Lauran get devoured again. Or how about Naija screaming as she drowns? Must've been fun to hear her die."

Visions began filling her mind, summoned by his words, vivid with deepening colors and the cacophony of their screams. She squeezed her eyes against them, hunching away from him. "Stop," she whispered involuntarily, then cringed harder at her display of vulnerability, knowing it would just incentivize him to continue.

He leaned forward, eyes wide as he pinned the struggling seriat to his side under one arm. "I don't ever remember her voice going so high before–"

"Shut up. Shut up!" Jade snarled, more from desperation than anger, and shoved off the window, clenching her fist so hard her nails scoured her palm. The pain focused her, piercing the vision and grounding her in the physical. "You know about the gates; you opened the permanent one. Tell me how, and why hasn't it disappeared despite being closed."

"I'm afraid I can't help you, it's not my *apertura* spitting poison into your world. Maybe it's your friend's door. You know the other *soul* in custody? Although, now that I think about it, there is a strange urge within me, a pressure to leave and go south for some reason. Would you know anything about that?" He winked.

Panic bloomed in her, sharp and cold, twisting her thoughts into forced clarity. "Don't...," she warned, whispering soft enough that only he, and none of the surveillance equipment, would hear her.

His smile flashed wider, but he let the last comment die. In that silence, Jade's strength fled her and she sagged forward against the wall, dropping her head to rest against it. "Fine," she whispered, because that was the only thing she could say; he held the answers she needed, she knew he did, but she was powerless to compel or hurt him. She could exert no authority over him, and the Purifiers would oppose any threat she leveled. This whole endeavor had been an exercise of supplication, and he'd recognized it from the start.

She stepped back, preparing to leave to prevent him from tormenting her further, but then he stood and walked to the window. "Wait."

Jade obeyed, pausing with her hand once again pressed against the panel, braced for whatever awful thing he would say next. "What?"

He grinned, swung the seriat up, and snapped its neck.

Jade shrieked, lurched back, tripped, and crashed to the floor. Ilin flung the carcass at the window with a grisly thud, crowing laughter as he made snapping gesture after snapping gesture. She screamed hatred and pain at him, and then covered her face with her hands, trembling helplessly, hating that he had pried that reaction from her.

The shock dwindled after a moment, leaving dull misery in its wake as she stood to press the window panel closed. Then she sagged, head falling against the wall as her mind replayed the new nightmare incessantly, always replacing the image of Ilin's seriat with one of Cuddles.

She stayed like that for a long time, just trying to silence the cacophony inside herself, struggling to stay afloat over her memories and progressively grinding her head harder and harder against the panel until it hurt. The sensation of it helped, distracting her as she started rubbing her head across it, feeling and then numbering the minuscule cracks between panels. Slowly, she began to calm, the turmoil within replaced by a throbbing headache. Jade pushed herself off the wall, massaging her forehead with a whispered, "God damn it," and forced herself to return to the hub room and resume work.

She found Chandris seated on her desk with legs crossed. He began without preamble, his words inoffensively soft. "Why did you converse with the *soul*, Ilin?"

"What–" she caught herself mid-reply, delaying until her thoughts and emotions calmed. "What do you mean?"

"You detest the *soul* because he wears your brother's body and directly contributed to his death, but you also fear it because you cannot converse or look upon it without experiencing pain. Much here causes you pain. So why did you seek him out?"

She sat, lifting Cuddles into her lap and curling close to coo in his ears and stroke his soft warmth. "I ... thought Ilin had lied to us, that he knew the disease's source all along. It was stupid."

"What made you believe it was deceit instead of ignorance? No *soul* is omniscient."

"I know.... Well, I didn't know that specifically, but you get what I mean. Never mind. There's been another incident, this one in the Defense Corporation's primary regional compound."

"Does its location bear significance?"

"The compound is hundreds of miles away, and Yuer never had contact with anyone who worked there during either period of his sickness."

"Do you wish to explore the event?"

"No, I just ... they said it was resolved but I freaked out. I thought he had to be the source of this disease. He's where it began, but ... everything we've learned contradicts that. I already said it was stupid. I don't want to be involved, I hate it, but what kind of awful person would I be if I stood and let all of this happen? Who knows how many people could die because I can't get over stuff that doesn't matter and that happened years ago." She slid further down the chair, laying Cuddles to sprawl across her chest and kissing his head.

"What does Mr. Wreign think of the disease's reoccurrence?"

"I don't know, he hasn't been around today," Jade trailed off. An absent Marsilias usually indicated a Marsilias intent on trouble. Heart dropping, she scooted forward and dipped her bare foot to the floor, accessing the Purifier network and orienting the available information to Marsilias's recent activities. She scanned through various timestamps, meetings with officials, and settled on the latest occurrence: a flight plan.

Jade relinquished the network. Chandris twitched his head minutely in her direction. "Is Mr. Wreign available for a conference?"

"He's leaving the compound." She pressed the heels of her hands against her eyes.

"Why does this distress you?"

"Because his airship's fueling for a long flight. And Marsilias hates flying." She forced her hand to tap her earpiece. "Silias ..."

"Yeah?"

"Where are you going?"

"I discovered a message requesting a Purifier escort from a Jysa Clan; they've experienced a drastic escalation in revenant activity recently that appears to be following them. They've migrated three times in this month alone, to no effect, and revenant activity in their vacated region attenuates to normal immediately after their departure. This could be the gate!"

Jade clasped the back of her neck, face paling as she began to rock. "You can't go there alone. Requisition a security Core."

"The Purifiers sent one, but all of them somehow managed to get lost in an omniveyor, so I continued without them. I was just about to call you for help."

Her hands tightened. "You locked them in, didn't you?"

"I confess to nothing."

"Why, Silias? Why do I have to come with you?"

"I have a theory, Jade, but I'm not ready to share it, and not over an open channel. Just trust me, okay?"

She said nothing for a long while, just sat there clutching her head before finally whispering, "All right, I'll come. Meet me at the airship." She terminated the call and shakily unfurled.

Chandris watched from her desk, his position unchanged since her arrival. "Where are you going?"

"Marsilias needs my help."

"Why agree? His request causes you pain."

"Because I trust that he would not ask this without good reason," she slipped on her boots and met Chandris's eyes, "even if I never learn what it is."

Chandris's head pivoted, shadowing her journey across the hub room without responding until the door hissed open for her departure, then, "Before you depart, I would make a request of this corporation."

She paused on the threshold. "Yes?"

"An associate within the corporation spoke of scents he used within his home, discussing their varieties and effects with a colleague. I would like an assortment of the natural scents humans enjoy to be filtered into my cell in sequence. I wish to experience them."

"Was ... that your purpose in coming out?"

"Yes."

"I see no reason why not; I'll mention it to Prime March."

She waved goodbye and ascended to the air-docks in the Purifier Compound's uppermost level. There, she found Marsilias lounging on heaped crates with a medium-sized travel bag. He roused at her approach along the catwalk, hefting the bag over one shoulder and shifting so a Core of Purifiers could file past before greeting her, "Hey. You need to grab anything?"

"No. What are you bringing?"

"Clothes mostly, but also some personal hardware. Rumor is there's a Techcron Host-Ship in the area, so I requisitioned appropriate weapons." He patted the rugged travel bag, eliciting a clink from its contents and the dim power veins woven into its exterior.

"What's this about, Silias?"

He considered his words then spoke softly, "I don't trust the Purifiers."

"Why not?"

"Think about it, Jade, there's something off about this disease."

"Yes, and?"

"Who would benefit most, if anyone, from the outbreak of a disease born in Afterlife?"

"That's circumstantial at best; you can't mistrust the Purifiers on that basis alone."

"No, but people have been funneling rumors to me; the Purifier Corporation's been extremely active recently, excessively active: negotiating with other corporations, buying stocks, forcing their people into influential positions. They may just be riding the wave, but until they show their hand, I don't trust them."

"All right, then what do we do? You can't keep ditching your assigned guards."

"I have a couple things in mind, but for now I want to concentrate on the Jysa; hopefully they'll treat us more favorably due to your parents and actually share information."

"I don't know how much weight my word will have, Marsilias. I've never journeyed with a clan and never spoken with another." An old lie: That her mother and father had escaped the destruction of their Jysa clan when Jade and Ilin were still too young to know anyone, but an important one all the same. Jade's parents never escaped that ship.

Marsilias shrugged concession. "Still, you're better than a random Purifier and professor they share no history with. Also"— and here he bestowed a careful look upon her—"I thought you might be able to ask them about your coat, see if they can fix it?"

A sliver of hope fluttered awake at his suggestion, luring her eyes inevitably to the worn fabric. *"Maybe,"* she thought, brushing her fingers along a faded strip on one sleeve. Strange as it might seem, she had never honestly considered it a possibility, not the least because she hadn't thought of herself as a Jysa in years, hadn't thought she had any claim to them. She had been so young all those years ago, too young to remember much, and no one had contacted her or Ilin in the near two decades since. But still, it might not hurt to ask. "Maybe," she said aloud. "One can always hope."

"One certainly can." Smiling, he urged her along the catwalk toward a humming aircraft. "We'd better leave before someone ... liberates my wayward escorts. I locked them in an omniveyor, but it won't hold."

She snorted and started up the ramp. "You'll be in trouble when we return, and I won't be helping you get out of it. In fact, I intend to enjoy it; we're talking the works: snacks, drinks, video recording. I hope he docks your pay for a year."

The plane, a Damselfly class intended for swift transportation of small groups and recon, flickered on, the walls teeming with a myriad of sensors, maps, diagrams, and holograms detailing a book's-worth of information on their immediate surroundings.

Marsilias strapped himself into the pilot seat and activated the destination console. Jade dropped into the adjacent seat. "So where are we going?"

"A sky-city is about to descend from the Upper Storms to the west of us; the Jysa are submerged there, waiting for it."

She curled up. "Is there anything I should know before we leave?"

"I don't believe so. I anticipate no trouble from the weather or the route."

"Good. Wake me when we arrive."

01100010 01110010 01101001 01101110 01100111 00100000 01110100
01101000 01100101 01101101 00100000 01101001 01101110

Marsilias's hand on her shoulder woke Jade from dreaming of a delicious golden and sugar-encrusted parfait, an interruption that incurred an accusatory look.

He chuckled. "None of that, you asked me to wake you, and I can't read your mind to know when you're in-between delicacies."

"I don't only dream about sweets," Jade replied drowsily through a stretch.

"Yeah, sometimes you dream about eating sweets while you dream."

"That was only one time! And they had me on sleeping medication, so I can't be held accountable."

A groan of thunder shook their plane, preceding a tide of lightning overhead. Jade crawled from her seat and leaned past the dashboard for a clearer view of their destination but saw only tenebrous clouds and the irate ocean, both gray in the storm-strangled light. "Where are they?"

"Submerged. I already sent a message; their vessel, Imarah, should surface in a moment."

As if on cue, the sea bucked, disgorging a dark shape of lugubrious, overlapping, slate-gray metal. The Jysan vessel settled with a splash, two gorgeous silver and green dragonfly wings unfurling to drape the water, steadying it on the tempestuous surface.

The Jysa were nomads. They traveled the world in small clans, traversing both the ocean depths and open skies with impunity in their ancient vessels. They sought out the deep-cities, located in the uttermost depths of the ocean; and the sky-cities, which floated in the Upper-Storm regions where the lightning waves never dissipated.

The corporations had failed to devise a method of accessing the cities; whereas Jysa had been doing so for centuries, and traded the resources they discovered there with the corporations for what they could not provide for themselves.

Down on the ocean surface, a hatch retracted from the vessel's spine, exposing the air dock's shrouded interior as emerald guide lights activated along its frame. Marsilias inserted a sequence and maneuvered them downward, entering a long, shallow docking bay of old but untarnished metal illuminated by an abundance of warm yellow lights. Suspended on wooden beams, rope lines, and hooks, draping curtains masked the ceiling, favoring red and violet primarily but with accenting green and oranges. All of them glinted with the iconic, swirling Jysan script and glowed with inherent brilliance. Seeing them, Jade absently fingered her own faded coat, exploring the maze of Jysan words that filled its interior.

"Marsilias, you said they were experiencing an abnormally high number of revenants, correct?"

"Yeah."

"But revenants rarely manifest near Jysa clans, there's too few people; so how many are we talking about?"

He shrugged, likewise admiring the ceiling. "Three, in the last couple weeks."

They exchanged glances. "Silias, that's not normal; we don't get that many in the city-complexes."

"I know. That's why we're here. Let's just hope it doesn't go wrong and that we get out before any other revenants pay a visit." He squeezed her arm gently and rose to depart.

They exited the plane into ankle-deep water and scanned the landing bay before starting towards the nearest of several entrances, an old fashion door with a handle and hinges seemingly made of wood. It opened before they arrived and a diminutive man exited. He had blueish hair and layers of loose clothing, most notably a hair net of gold beads and a fraying purple shawl, both replete with the Jysan script. "Hello," he said, speaking with the strange, lilting Jysan accent that was as much pronunciation as rhythm, "are you the Purifiers we requested?"

"No, sorry. We're here about something different but related," Marsilias said.

"Ah, I see." The man retreated from the entrance. His fingers danced through a complicated series of gestures, as if playing an instrument: the Jysa rite of admittance. "Welcome to Imarah, my name is D'jira." His eyes fastened on Jade as she circumvented Marsilias, and gradually darkened as they perused her damaged coat. She flushed and hurried past, shunning his gaze. D'jira wordlessly assumed the lead.

They followed a wide corridor, likewise curtained on the ceiling, with wood-decorated walls and carpeted floors. Candle clusters in sealed containers swung from the ceiling on coral chains, exuding thin trails of incense. A groan toured the walls, trailed by a subtle arch in the floor as Imarah submerged.

D'jira's hand performed another series of hand movements, seeking permission for inquiry. "Why are you here?"

"We've come about the revenants and hope to speak with your doctors. Your A'sari?"

D'jira's hand danced again. "What do you hope to find?"

Marsilias hesitated. "There's a ... sickness afflicting the Corporatocracy; it derives from Afterlife."

"You believe a connection between your disease and our revenant issue exists?"

"Yes," Marsilias replied. "How do the revenants materialize

here?"

"They materialize directly in Imarah, despite the agony he causes them."

"What do you mean 'he causes'?"

"Imarah protects us with the gifts of our ancestors." D'jira extended his hand to the wall, trailing his fingers along the wood embellishments, elucidating the streams of Jysan script. "A thousand generations have added their names and will to his walls; no revenant ever dared to trespass on Imarah before."

Jade frowned. "Then what's changed? They've always preferred city-complexes and areas with dense population. Did you notice anything in their behavior? Anything anomalous?"

"Nothing. Whenever they materialized, the revenants immediately sought the Heart-Room."

"Heart-Room?" Marsilias asked.

"Imarah's center, where our people congregate; it's analogous to an engine room for your grander vessels."

"Is there anybody who studied them, tried to discern why this was happening?" Marsilias pressed.

"We all saw them. Well most of us did." As D'jira spoke, they reached a closed door. He touched its surface and the dark metal swelled over his fingers in a mass of grainy, sand-like particles. The door contracted briefly and then receded, molding in on itself entirely to permit entry. With its recess, a trickle of vibrant music slipped out. D'jira resumed his discourse, "Only Dama and Ch'luran have never seen the revenants."

"Why? Are they always sleeping on the job?" Jade asked, distinctly ignoring Marsilias's pointed glance.

"No, Dama is always protected, and Ch'luran has been sick of late, some kind of wasting disease our sensors can't identify."

Marsilias froze and Jade snatched D'jira's arm. "Is Ch'Luran covered in black markings? Or acting strangely? Suffering delusions or anything of the like."

"He has the black markings but seems wholly himself, if a little moody from being cooped in Imarah for so long."

"Is he quarantined?" Marsilias queried, the urgency in his tone belying the composure with which he extracted and donned his mask.

"Yes," D'jira responded, his features beginning to display concern as Jade also activated her mask. "Is something amiss? Do you know what Ch'luran suffers?"

"Let me ask you something else first," Marsilias replied. "Has anyone from one of the corporations visited you in recent months? Have any of your people conversed or met with ours?"

"Only during our last trade session, and for the monthly Purifier inspection." D'jira shifted his posture slightly and urged them forward, motions controlled but sharp. "But come, we've almost reached the Heart-Room. There will be others there better suited to your inquiries and, if what I fear is accurate, you should speak with Dama immediately. If you do, in fact, allude to a disease, tell me but speak softly; if real, we are all infected and the rest should not learn of that from an outsider." They continued, Jade and Marsilias quietly elaborating on all that had transpired at the Purifier Corporation to D'jira, who grimaced. "This is unsettling and critical. The Dama cannot afford further delay or a secondhand recount. You must accompany me; I respect that you have needs and a purpose as well, but they must wait." He lengthened his stride, rounding a corner into a cavernous room drowning in both electric and candlelight as well as sound and activity.

The room's eponymous heart churned at the center, its exterior oval, crystalline, and fused to the ceiling and floor via two bronze currents, and its contents a storm of coppery liquid. The Jysa sprawled, danced, and laughed around this heart, their voluminous clothing swirling expressively as they frolicked, played music and physical board games, ate, drank, and recited stories. They ranged across the room in a concert of colors and individuals, resembling an ancient fair more than a family clan.

D'jira effortlessly navigated this morass of people, his fingers flashing in an incessant litany of apologetic declines. Marsilias braced himself and pursued D'jira. Jade trailed in his wake, navigating the Jysa without disturbing them, though without elegance. Inside, she ached with old familiarity and loss. But it was old and easily ignored, hope long since abandoned.

D'jira ushered them to Imarah's heart, where a short, circular house constructed of wooden beams stood beneath a ceiling of mounded velvet. The Jysan script blanketed the structure and overflowed onto the floor in a spiraling web of linked words. Two Jysa, a man and a woman, guarded the entrance. They wore full suits, the only suits visible in the entire room, of Jysa-worked cloth and carried both an ancient metal spear and a collection of obsolete guns.

The Jysa possessed no Siphons, no Purifiers, or any natural Savants, but their alien script conveyed power into what it inscribed. They were a culture of inheritance, bequeathing everything from one generation to the subsequent, and every generation added script to what they inherited. Thus, through the centuries, their heirlooms became symbols of their families and storied relics rich with history. Jade doubted anything she saw boasted less than several centuries of life, which explained the defunct technology many of them exhibited. Even so, only foolishness or ignorance would lead someone to underestimate the effectiveness of a Jysa heirloom—their Mantles.

D'jira addressed the guards, "Is Dama currently occupied with anything important?" The sentries signaled the negative, and D'jira proceeded, gesturing for Jade and Marsilias to follow. They entered a room fashioned around a natural fire-pit with a floor dressed in a multihued carpet. An elderly woman in sinuous burgundy robes sat across the fire from them in a backless chair, her hairnet comprised of white beads and cloth.

D'jira advanced to her side, and the woman's eyes fastened first on D'jira then migrated to Marsilias and finally Jade, where they lingered on her coat.

"Dama," D'jira said, "this is Marsilias Wreign and Jade Dieza. They have information about Ch'luran's illness and more that, if accurate, is deeply pressing. Best to hear it from them."

Her sharp eyes relinquished their grip on Jade's coat and comfortably settled on both of them. "A Magister and Purifier come to speak with me of an illness that defies every means we have to quantify it, whether it be of science or magic. You believe it derives from Afterlife?" Jade nodded affirmative. "Do you have a cure?"

Marsilias shook his head. "I'm sorry but we don't; the corporations are still very much trying to resolve this issue themselves. We might be able to do more with a living subject whose infection has not attained maturity."

Sorrow tightened the woman's features. "It is going to worsen for Ch'Luran?"

"I'm afraid so."

"Then I see no reason to entrust him into your care."

"Please reconsider, Dama. We have no interest in removing him from his home, only observe him to learn more about his condition."

"About a disease that you cannot detect any more than we can? That is doubtful."

"Technology is not our only resource, we have other avenues–"

The woman raised a hand. "Mr. Wreign, we honestly appreciate your offer, but I have already contacted the Savant Corporation for assistance, and I doubt you can offer anything they cannot. Now"— the woman stood shakily and opened a cabinet recessed in the wall —"what truly brought you here? We told no one the specifics of Ch'luran's illness, so some other curiosity prompted this visit." She extracted a mesh net with four stakes, followed by a clear cylinder half-full of leaves and a teapot; all except the cylinder carried the Jysan script. She returned to the fire and knelt. "But first I should introduce myself properly, I am Dama Nhr'irena, mother of the Imarah clan; mother being an inherited title and not literal." Nhr'irena graced them with a smile as she assembled her tea set over the fire. "Will you sit with me?"

"Dama"—D'jira kneeled on the furs, his hand flashing in the symbol of apology—"there is no time for tea. There is more to Ch'luran's illness than you have surmised; according to our guests it is infectious."

"Then it is likely we are all already infected, and further actions would be unavailing; please inform the Savant Corporation's operatives of the risk when they arrive."

"As you say, Dama." He departed without further honorific or gesture.

Nhr'irena balanced the teapot on the net and urged Jade and Marsilias to sit. They complied wordlessly.

Nhr'Irena allowed the silence to linger, studying the length and scars of Jade's coat. Finally, she rested her hands in her lap and commenced, "Who are you that you wear a Mantle of our people, Miss Dieza?"

Jade flushed again and ineffectively smoothed the lapels. "I am a survivor of the Kaimur clan." An easy lie, invoking the name of a destroyed clan to shield the reality that her ancestor's name had been erased from all memory.

Sorrow and comprehension stirred in the Dama's eyes. "Ah, there is no need to feel ashamed of your heritage."

Jade's hand tightened on the coat. "I'm not, it's just ... this was never meant to be mine. It was ... my brother's before he died."

"May I see it?"

Jade hesitated, then removed the coat and offered it to Nhr'irena. "I'm sorry about the scratches and the missing buttons; I don't know how to fix it." A sudden hope flowered in her chest. "Can you? I know it's a lot to ask, and that I'm not part of the clan; but it was my mother's and then my brother's, and I don't want to lose it."

Nhr'irena mournfully rested the coat on her knees. "I am sorry, but I cannot. It is not of Imarah's heritage."

Jade slumped. "I see...."

"Nonetheless, this Mantle is yours, as it was your brother's and your mother's before him; it is the memories and hopes, the trials and achievements of your ancestors, the lives of centuries entrusted to you as a gift. It is a beautiful and powerful thing, but it is also incomplete. It needs your name. Take it to your mother's extended family; perhaps they can restore it for you." She returned the coat to Jade, who donned it again as the tea began to whistle. "Ah, it is ready; sugar or honey?"

"Neither, thank you," Marsilias replied.

"Both, please," Jade said.

Nhr'irena bestowed a quirked eyebrow upon Jade and surrendered both sweeteners into her keeping. After that, she poured tea into clay mugs warming beside the fire and distributed them; Jade proceeded to generously spoon sugar and honey into her cup while Nhr'irena waited for her to finish. Marsilias sipped in a futile effort to disguise his smile.

"Would you like cream with your sugar and tea?"

"No, thank you." Jade furtively added a final spoonful of sugar and returned the items.

Nhr'irena replaced the teapot over the fire and arranged the accompanying condiments on a flat stone. "I have taxed your patience sufficiently, Mr. Wreign. Why have you sought us out?"

"I wanted to ask about the increased revenant activity. Did they seem to have an objective? A destination?"

"The only concerted purpose I can deduce is hunger for our energy; they always targeted the Heart-Room, where our people congregate."

"And there is no other potential destination?"

"They did not materialize in one location, but in three distinct areas across Imarah."

"Was anyone able to inspect their gates?"

"Oh no, the gates collapsed immediately ensuing travel; they lasted seconds at the longest."

"Are you certain? Even the shortest enduring gates we've recorded have been several minutes, and those were the product of first-tier revenants."

"I am certain. We've chronicled every gate."

"May we see them?"

"Of course." Nhr'irena retracted her right hand's copious sleeve, unveiling a black console strapped to her forearm. She inserted a command sequence and a screen appeared on the wall opposite Marsilias. An image faded in, displaying a claustrophobic passage somewhere in Imarah. Nothing occupied the passage initially, then a trail of brown mist slithered from the open air, heralding a black fissure. Spindly arms pried free and dragged a sable-wreathed horror from its depths. The revenant clambered to the ground and the gate dissipated.

The image paused and Nhr'irena addressed Marsilias again, "The other incidents resemble this one almost identically, except for the first where the gate opened directly in the Heart-Room."

"I'd like to watch the others nonetheless."

"Of course." Nhr'irena accessed her console and the appropriate videos appeared in quick succession. They proceeded as she described, with only their locations varying. After the last recording, Marsilias rubbed his head with a frustrated sigh.

Jade nudged his shoulder. "Come on, Silias, what are you looking for? I can't help if I don't know."

"Something's going on, Jade, I just don't know what. None of what we learn clarifies anything or makes sense, and when nothing makes sense it means we're missing the primary piece."

"Maybe this and the disease aren't connected?"

"If that's the case, then we have a second problem. And we cannot ignore the disease being present in Ch'Luran."

"Do not worry on our account," Nhr'irena interjected, "we can control the revenants until the Purifier Corporation supplies the requested assistance, and leave the region if we must."

Something dinged in the back of Jade's mind. She twitched, eyes flicking about the room as Nhr'irena and Marsilias's conversation diminished. She heard and saw nothing at first, then felt it again: a chill crawling through her veins. She turned fully, rising to a crouch and closing her eyes. The sensation came again, this time accompanied by a familiar scent. She surged to her feet, vaguely aware of Marsilias querying her. She shoved him from her mind and zeroed in on the soft, persistent chill. It pulsed, gradually expanding from her fingertips, ears, and toes. It sparked, doubling in breadth through the duration of a single pulse.

Her eyes snapped open. "There's a gate opening somewhere." Then she exhaled and dove forward, phasing through the wall as her body lost its substance.

Panic tore through her mind, carried on a tide of frantic thoughts. *"I don't want this. I don't want this. I don't want this."*

The Ghosts Machine

"Don't think about it, don't think about it. Just act." Jade sprinted through Imarah's walls and corridors, the sensation of ice spreading through her body with increasing haste as she sought the burgeoning gate. She perceived it in the distance, not like a physical pressure, but like the mounting refrains of a mental song. She knew the music by heart but could not replicate or describe it if she had a lifetime for the attempt.

No one else could hear it; the Jysa wandered the various corridors, passageways, and rooms in blissful ignorance as she sprinted past, even the sentries with their amulets attuned to the emergence of Afterlife energy continued as if nothing was wrong. All the while, her memories screamed in the back of her mind, gradually accruing volume: visions of shattered corpses, dozens of people she knew dead or bleeding out as she stared helplessly at them.

Then she burst into a room with white medical tiles and a single bed. A young man kneeled at the room's center, his skin ruptured with inky black veins and his eyes rolled back. The bed lay in disarray behind his emaciated form, its sheets stained with the liquid seeping from his body's sores. Despite his body's horrific state, the young man moved with unflinching violence, his hands, arms, and fingers snapping through the air. Golden light trailed in the wake of his movements, forming symbols and images in the air similar to a Magister opening his workshop.

Jade inhaled and dropped to the ground, trying to ignore the strain already spreading through her lungs. "What are you doing?"

The man's eyes snapped into focus, his irises black and his pupils white with the inverse nature of Afterlife's energy. "The Master calls them...."

The training Siphon ignited with a flash of brass in her hand, the energy coiled and assembled into the shape of a pulse-pistol. She leveled the weapon on him. "Stop whatever you're doing, now." Training Siphons had minimal effect on humans and Techcrons, but the crackling energy could intimidate the uninitiated or timorous.

The man faced her, his body wrapped in swaths of thick white cloth replete with webs of Jysa script. "You cannot stop it now."

"Ch'Luran," Jade pleaded, praying it was the infected Jysa, "stop it, please. Close the gate." She ignited a second Siphon behind her back, molding this one into a shock charge.

Suddenly, the walls flashed and an alarm peeled through the vessel, "A gate is opening near the medical wing."

The man lunged for Jade, his arm extended as if to slash her. She vaulted back, hurling the shock charge at him. It struck and exploded in arching bolts of yellow energy, flinging the man to the floor, where he thrashed until the charge subsided.

Jade crept closer, deactivating her Siphon-pistol, and touched his neck to verify he lived. She sighed in relief and transferred her attention to the gate. It slithered open in cracks and fissures, like the roots of a tree growing on fast-forward. The lines sprawled out from a gestating center, pulsing wider with every second. A tendril of miasma trickled through the gap and drifted to the floor.

She needed to leave.

Jade grabbed the man and dragged him toward the door; she didn't know how the miasma—or the revenants that inevitably emerged from it—would affect him, and they couldn't spare the information he might possess. At the door, she clamped a portable air mask over his mouth and nose and then retrieved a small black package from her coat. She laid it against his midsection and then activated it with a push. The package exploded in a flood of dark material, enclosed the man, and sealed into an airtight bag. This done, she caught him about his midsection and heaved him onto her shoulder. The gate spread wider, the trickle of miasma thickening to obscure everything near it.

Jade staggered upright, pressed her fingers into the door's console, and delved into its network; she couldn't manually open the door as the man was quarantined and she didn't know the passcode. Information bombarded her, centuries of history files and coding—more than she had ever experienced—along with all of Imarah's technical workings. She dove through it, evading defensive programs and piercing barriers until she discovered the quarantined door. Latching onto it as the eradication programs—attracted by her trespassing—swarmed after her. She scrambled through the door's various programs and slammed the emergency release. The door slid open and she lunged out. It slammed shut behind her, the defensive programs initiating its lockdown sequence.

Jade struggled down the corridor, flailing at the watching Jysa. "Move! There's a gate opening in there! Didn't you hear the alarm? Mov–" Her legs buckled, almost displacing the man, but she barely felt it; the gate yawned fully open, and she could feel it like a tear in her mind. Jade couldn't feel the revenants enter her world, but she knew they did. A bottomless well of horror woke within her, clamping around her chest and squeezing. For a moment, she could see and hear nothing real. In that moment, she was back standing on the impossible ice sheet, staring up at a seeping black tear in the world tall as the sky.

Jade sucked her cheek between her teeth and bit hard. She tasted the copper of blood almost immediately, but she needed the pain to break the hallucination and anchor her in reality. Her pulse pounded in her veins, and her thoughts rampaged in panicked desperation, but she could mostly see what was in front of her.

A Jysa sank to the floor beside Jade, urgently shaking her shoulders. "Miss, miss, let me help you."

Jade shook her head, dispelling the remnants of the vision and found herself slumped on the ground, clutching the wall. "Take him!" she gasped, and unloaded Ch'Luran into the Jysa's expectant arms. "Take him to the Heart-Room, but leave him in the bag."

The Jysa, face pallid with stress, hefted the man onto his shoulder. "What about you?"

"I'll be fine, just go."

The Jysa fled, his strides confident despite the added burden. As he left, the wall behind Jade crunched and shuddered, warping out into the passage. She pulled herself to her feet and turned, crushing all the memories, all the panic down until all that remained was numb acceptance. The wall shook a second time and a new dent appeared beside the first, followed immediately by a third retort and a small depression. *"There's two of them,"* she realized. *"I have to stop them."*

Jade unhooked her third, and last, Siphon and exhaled. Cold slithered through her veins, spreading from her chest and seeding pain in its wake. She ignited both Siphons, shaping them into pulse-pistols, and phased through the wall.

She found three revenants inside, two small and humanoid, and the third a levitating sphere wreathed in miasma, but all three were formed of radiant *luce* and draped in tatters of black fabric. Her earpiece activated, "Three first-tier revenants, spirit-levels: six, six, twenty-four." The two humanoid revenants released a note of ethereal music and flung themselves bodily at the wall, distorting it further; the spherical revenant remained in the back. None of them acknowledged Jade, and with the gate already dispersing into flecks of light, there was no danger of more emerging or of either her equipment or Imarah deactivating.

She leveled her training Siphons and inhaled. Warmth blossomed inside her, restoring her to tangibility and gravity's hold. She dashed to the side and fired, raking the lesser revenants with spasming electric bolts. They recoiled—the trickles of *luce* from their wounds evaporating—and then crossed the distance to her in a split-second. Jade was already moving though, leaping back as she fired.

As she landed, she swirled aside, effortlessly slipping between the charging revenants and hammering their flanks with another barrage. The spherical revenant spun with her evasion, however, feelers coiling up and then lashing like a maelstrom of spears. Jade exhaled instantly, turning insubstantial so that its tendrils phased harmlessly through her. The feelers retracted and she inhaled back to the physical world, lunging back toward the lesser revenants and blasting the spherical revenant with electric bolts. It lurched, cringing and wailing, but still retaliated. Again she exhaled, and again the feelers phased through her, impaling the two lesser revenants behind her and pinning them to the wall amidst fountains of *luce*. The feelers retracted immediately, and Jade—sprinting—inhaled again, barraging the spherical revenant to little effect, the electric bolts barely singeing its skin.

The second humanoid revenant, only partially pinned, wriggled free of the wall and pounced. She ducked right, twisting and converting one of the Siphons into a long-bladed knife. The revenant landed and she glided past it, planting the knife in its lower back. The revenant bellowed a sharp, discordant note and flailed, slapping Jade as she retreated and launching her across the room. She exhaled and phased through the wall into the corridor outside, where she drifted to a halt, her side screaming.

She panted once, twice, and then leapt into the ceiling just as a dent distorted the wall she had just phased through. Diving forward through the internal machinery, Jade dropped back into the infirmary behind the humanoid revenant currently bludgeoning the wall. The revenant she had stabbed thrashed in place several feet behind her, the Siphon-knife brightening as it fed.

Without pause, Jade inhaled back to physicality and disassembled her remaining Siphon into crackling energy, shaping it into a spear. As the energy lengthened, it grew thin, erratic, and loud, struggling to maintain so large a shape. Its increased crackling brought the revenant whirling toward Jade as she hurled the spear, impaling it to the wall. The revenant howled and clawed at the Siphon, its skin boiling away to golden fumes wherever it made contact.

Jade exhaled and dashed forward, fingers contacting the Siphon's base in between the revenant's flailing strikes. She inhaled and activated the Siphon, converting it from a spear into a net. The energy collapsed to a nucleus, reformed and then spider-webbed outward, fettering the revenant into a bundle.

Jade swung around, scanning for the spherical revenant. She spied it hovering near the entrance, its various feelers and strips of black fabric swirling together to form a ball, *luce* streamed in rivulets along its many appendages to converge there.

Meanwhile, the knifed revenant spasmed with a baritone note and charged Jade, its skin livid with streams of energy. Jade exhaled, pressing a switch in her right palm. Unaffected by transitioning to the First Step, the pulse-knife affixed to her wrist snapped out into a foot-long blade and energized with a low hum. She phased through the charging revenant, spun, inhaled, and lacerated its back. It scrambled about without so much as a whisper of music—the wound, rendered with a physical weapon rather than a Siphon, already healing in flares of *luce*.

Ignoring the knifed revenant, she exhaled and rushed the spherical revenant at the entrance, the pulse-knife clicking in her hand to indicate its readiness. Consumed with its task, the spherical revenant disregarded her right up until she solidified beside it and stabbed the pulse-knife into its flank, pressing the switch. A lethal surge of electricity discharged from the pulse-knife, hurling the revenant to the ground and disrupting the *luce* orb it held, which promptly imploded. The resulting force flung Jade across the room and into the bed. She reflexively rolled to her feet and exhaled. A chill clamped on her lungs, stabbing pain into them and emanating outward, followed soon by a well of sickly, metallic taste in the back of her mouth. Jade hawked and spat a wad of pink saliva. She was transitioning too often too fast.

The spherical revenant righted itself with a long, vibrant note and, undiminished, flew back to the door. Its music increased, growing more complex as the light spilling from its body thickened and hastened. Across from it, the knifed revenant interposed between them and prowled toward Jade. She crouched, glancing at the Siphon planted in its body and saw that it was finally flashing: it could absorb no more *luce*.

Jade dashed toward the approaching revenant and leapt over it to grasp the Siphon. She inhaled, fingers solidifying, and discharged the Siphon's contained energy. It exploded, obliterating most of the revenant's upper body, destroyed the Siphon, and coursed harmlessly through Jade as she exhaled.

Jade tumbled into and half through the floor, coughing as the pain in her lungs worsened. She squeezed her eyes shut against the spinning ceiling and compelled her aching body to roll over. The last humanoid revenant remained fettered to the wall, but the spherical revenant held a renewed orb of *luce* at the entrance.

She groaned to her feet and pressed her right palm again to reactivate the pulse-knife. It elongated with a hum of expectant energy, the tip recharged from her adaptive suit's supply, and sparked. The revenant unleashed the orb before she could do anything else. It struck the door and exploded through and into the corridor beyond, upending Jade.

She staggered back to her feet and charged as the revenant floated out into the passage. Exhaling, she phased through the remainder of the wall into the corridor to cut it off. The revenant whirled toward her with a strident wail of two different notes. Golden light ignited across its body, coating it like a second skin, and it lashed out, feelers snapping like whips.

The revenant's feelers thrashed fruitlessly through Jade's insubstantial form, but behind that onslaught of blindingly incandescent limbs, she saw inner feelers coiling into a knot. She dove, phasing through its final assailing feelers, twisted midair, landed adjacent to the revenant, braced herself, and stabbed the pulse-knife forward without inhaling. Her strike inflicted no damage of course, but the revenant still reacted, uncoiling its knotted appendages and unleashing a storm of burning light.

Jade reeled, blinded and flailing. She saw the dark smudge of the revenant amidst the swamp of strobing colors and dove beneath the floor. She pushed sideways, propelling herself with the minimal resistance her body felt, stalled her momentum beneath where she estimated the revenant hovered, and surfaced. She saw the underside of a levitating mass surrounded in gold, inhaled and stabbed with the pulse-knife. It struck the encasing golden light and unleashed its charge. Arcs of electricity ripped through the revenant's body, throwing it toward the ceiling, and then dissipated without inflicting any real damage.

Still lying prone beneath the revenant, Jade rolled into a crouch and hurled herself backward as the revenant slammed itself down. She hit one of the walls, rebounded off, and dragged a foot beneath her, opening her mouth to exhale.

A voice screamed from down the corridor behind her, "Jade, duck!"

She dropped flat, and icy air swept over her back as something shot past. The revenant screamed an agonized note, followed by a thud as it struck the ground. Footsteps and people Jade didn't bother to look at rushed by.

Another pair of footsteps followed the others, but these stopped beside her. A hand nudged her. "Hey, you all right?" The voice was deep, fast, and warm, but neither rushed nor nervous.

She half-heartedly waved her hand without lifting her face from the ground. "I'm fine."

"You realize she'll just lay there until you turn her over," Marsilias said with a laugh, but the sound was tentative. She could feel his eyes on her, waiting to see if she would breakdown. They'd seen it before.

A pair of hands grabbed her shoulders and gently rolled her onto her back. A young man, only in his thirties or forties, with vibrant, natural red hair smiled down. "Hiya, Jade."

She marshaled a small smile, latching onto the warmth of his expression. "Hello, Connor. Where's Ruon?"

"Back with Dama Nhr'irena; unlike Marsilias here, he's not front-lines enthused." The bear of a man squatted, his thick hair and neatly trimmed muttonchops framing a broad, friendly visage. "So what brought you here?"

"Investigating, and you?"

"The Savant Corporation sent us to help the Imarah Clan, something about revenant assaults." As he spoke, Connor took a wide, green Magister's card and tore it down the center. He proceeded to retrieve a lighter from the breast pocket of his violet uniform and set the halves alight, preparing for its conversion into specter-dust. "I thought you retired?"

"I'm trying, but some individuals—who will not be mentioned —aren't letting me." She spoke weakly, the inhales and exhales necessary for speech scraping her lungs. Despite the coherence of her words, her mind ricocheted through mangled hallucinations and memories. Nausea clotted in her throat, as much a result of her unstable vision as the morass of relief, panic, terror, and fraught nerves.

"Ah, that does make sense." Connor stood. "Do you want help up? Or are you just going to lie there like a wet rag?"

"Seeing what I just went through, how about you carry me?" She raised her arms toward him, fingers waggling expectantly, hiding in the humor.

"Tell you what, how about we compromise and I drag you?"

"... Are there stairs?"

"A couple."

She groaned, arms falling theatrically over her face. "All right, help me up." They each took an arm and pulled her up, setting her vision to whirling. She staggered, stomach heaving, lungs spasming, and buckled.

They caught her before she hit the floor. "Are you sure you're all right?" Connor asked.

"Yeah, perfectly fine. Just practicing my dramatic collapse in case I ever land my dream role of damsel in distress." Still, they held her, neither moving until she squeezed their arms and slowly started down the corridor.

They stopped beside the contingent of Jysa inspecting the spherical revenant's corpse further along, prodding it with their spears while a secondary group filed into the infirmary. Three massive shards of smoking ice protruded from the revenant's body and continued burrowing deeper as she watched. Though less effective than true Purifier Siphons, Magister cards provided an adequate weapon against revenants, presumably because they were fashioned with Afterlife's energy—death energy—and revenants were born of *luce: life energy.*

"Ah," Marsilias said, remembering something, "here's your friend; you dropped him when you phased out." He scrounged briefly behind his back, then extended Cuddles to her.

She presented her arm to the seriat, and Cuddles immediately scampered up to snuggle around her neck and shoulder. "Hello, handsome, you doing all right?" she asked, stroking his head and burying her face in his fur. Cuddles chirped in response and wrapped around her, nuzzling and kissing aggressively. "Thank you for taking care of him, Silias."

"No problem."

"Did you get the man I sent?"

"The poor fellow you imprisoned in a packing bag after incapacitating him with a Siphon? Yes. One would almost think you a mafioso with such behavior." Connor grinned.

She whirled toward him then swayed for her efforts. "You didn't release him, did you?"

Marsilias hastily waved away her concern. "No, no no. We left him nice and snug as requested. Though I must admit curiosity almost overcame me."

Her hands tightened on Cuddles, but the seriat made no complaint, only snuggled closer. "He opened the gate, Silias."

Both men fell dead silent, Marsilias's expression darkening as Connor rocked back.

"That's ... not possible."

"No, not impossible, just unprecedented." Marsilias stroked his paper scarf, eyes flicking back and forth in a litany of thoughts and calculations. "We have never been able to discern how the revenants pry open gates into our world, or what the gates even are, but if someone—a human in this case—were privy to the knowledge we lack, they could conceivably open a gate."

"But the revenants are from Afterlife; wouldn't their power, I don't know, poison us?" Connor asked.

"No...," Jade said slowly, "revenants aren't comprised of Afterlife energy; they're made of *luce*, of life. We're the ones"—she gestured at the three of them as Savants—"who use Afterlife energy."

"Regardless," Marsilias said, "we need to speak with your captive and do so in a controlled environment where he can't infect anybody else."

"Okay," Connor agreed, "let's regroup with Ruon and Dama Nhr'irena. Jade, you up for that? Or do you ... need a moment?"

"I'm fine, let's just go and get it over with." She smiled and started down the corridor only to pause, realizing she didn't know how to get back. "Uh ... come on slow pokes, gotta save the world again!" She awkwardly gestured for them to get a move on.

Marsilias and Connor exchanged amused glances and took the lead, the redhead nudging her in passing. "Nice save."

They returned to the Heart-Room and pressed through the gathered clan of anxious Jysa to the wooden house, where a quartet of solemn guards admitted them. Inside, Dama Nhr'irena sat before the fire with the packaged man lying beside her, untouched, and a second man bouncing between the heels and balls of his feet.

Ruon, the second man, wordlessly flashed her the ghost of a smile and winked. As tall as but much slimmer than his brother, Ruon moved with constant nervous energy and wore an extensive tool belt about his waist, the pockets and loops thick with compacted tools and machines. His oil-smudged red hair was a snarled mass pulled roughly back with a worn hairband, highlighting fine-boned features that might have been beautiful were it not for the rough scruff of an untended beard.

Slipping in behind her, Connor tapped Jade's shoulder. "Ruon says hi, and asks how you've been?"

"I'm good." She offered the second brother what she knew was an overly bright smile and tapped her chest. "All here in one piece." Crossing the room as she spoke, Jade dropped into Dama Nhr'irena's unoccupied chair and draped her arms over the sides.

She had met the brothers, known as the Redheads to almost everyone in the Purifier and Savant Corporation, years ago, even before the Purifier Corporation adopted her and Ilin.

Unperturbed by the confiscation of her seat, Nhr'irena addressed Jade, "I hope you have a reason for packaging one of my people?" Despite her placid tone, her fingers flashed in the Jysa sign of challenge.

"He opened the gate."

"Did you see him do it?"

"Yes."

"How is this possible?"

"We don't know," Marsilias said as he began collecting the tea implements and passing them to Jade. "This will have to do for now, but I know some wonderful delicatessens we can visit on our return." He gave her shoulder a gentle squeeze. She gave a tight nod and proceeded to shovel sugar and honey into the cup.

Marsilias assumed a place beside the fire. "That's why we need to interrogate him, learn who or what taught him this. My hunch is that him contracting the disease and opening gates are related; we know the disease messes with a person's mind."

"Oh and another thing—"Jade brandished the spoon with a spray of tea droplets—"he spoke to me, said something about 'the master calling them'."

"He spoke coherently?" Marsilias asked sharply.

"Yeah." She resumed stirring. "That's all he said though."

Dama Nhr'irena stood. "We need a quarantined room to question him in, and something to restrain him should he become possessed again. I will arrange everything." She made a gesture of farewell and exited.

Slouching further into her seat, Jade set the spoon aside and gulped the tea. Ruon approached her and leaned on Nhr'irena's chair, bouncing his weight on and off it. Connor observed him briefly, then translated, "Ruon's asking what you guys know. If you can share it that is; he realizes the Purifier Corporation can be a bit tightlipped at times."

Marsilias provided an abbreviated recount of their findings and experiences, culminating with Jade's abrupt departure. "... and that's about when you two walked in."

Connor processed the information before responding, "This disease is acting abnormally; normally a virus has a fairly stagnant incubation period, a set amount of time before it manifests. Your victims are displaying distinct symptoms and affliction periods. This disease doesn't feel natural, it feels engineered."

"And that's my fear," Marsilias replied. "The question is: By whom?"

The door opened, admitting a trio of Jysa entirely wrapped in multihued cloth, the folds gleaming with sapphire script. Only their eyes, concealed behind delicate, half-buried goggles differed. Moving in concert, they grasped the packaged man and toted him outside.

Jade groaned and heaved herself from the chair. "Well let's go." Leaving a ravaged sugar container and empty tea mug, she trailed after the Jysa and the others followed.

The Jysa guided them to a claustrophobic room empty besides the ubiquitous Jysa script. It contained a single duraglau chair with hairline electric wires and restraining bands. Dama Nhr'irena, already situated in the room, wordlessly directed the Jysa to situate the man in the chair. This accomplished, they hastened to depart.

"Best put on your masks," Marsilias advised Connor and Ruon, before advancing to the chair, inspecting it briefly, and then pressing a button on its side. A hum of electricity slid through the chair and the body snapped rigid in the package with the exception of the head which flopped back. The package contracted into its previous minute square at a touch from Marsilias. He tossed the package to Jade, along with her Siphon, and gave the man a tentative slap. The man remained unresponsive. "Do I have permission to rouse him, Dama Nhr'irena?"

"Yes."

Marsilias dug through his rucksack and retrieved a hand-sized canister. Snapping it open, he extracted a thimble-like vial. "This is a chemical intended to increase brain function for a short period of time and suppress exhaustion. It's harmless unless used for extended periods, in which instances the accumulated exhaustion can prove deleterious. In this situation, it should jar him awake; is this chemical acceptable?"

"Yes."

Closing the canister, Marsilias positioned the vial beneath the man's nose and uncapped it. A thin trail of green mist coiled up into the man's nostrils. A second elapsed, and he lurched awake with a gasp, though his movements remained constrained to his head. He scanned the room frantically and fixed on Nhr'Irena. "Dama, you shouldn't be in here! I might–"

"Please, hold your silence, Ch'luran. We know what you have done."

What color inhabited Ch'luran's features died at her miserable tone. "Dama, I don't understand….Why am I bound to this chair? Who are these outsiders?"

Marsilias snapped his fingers in Ch'luran's ear, pulling the man's attention to him. "You opened a gate in Imarah, inviting three revenants into your own home."

Ch'Luran swung his attention back. "No, I didn't! Dama, I swear. I would never hurt the clan; I don't even know how to open a gate! Please, believe me!"

"Wait," Connor interjected, "this is futile unless we can verify the truth of what he tells us."

Ruon, pacing back and forth along the entrance wall, paused beside him. Something passed between the brothers and Connor resumed, "Ruon has a card that will compel him to speak the truth. He says it shouldn't cause him any harm."

Dama Nhr'irena hesitated, but Ch'luran did not. He stretched to look around Marsilias again. "Yes, Dama, please. Use their card, I swear I did nothing."

Nhr'irena looked away, visibly shuddering beneath the force of his pleas. "Someone saw you open it, *Chiho*." She nodded at Connor. "Do it."

Ruon stopped mid-step and strode back to Connor, delving

into his pants pocket to reveal a medium-sized, yellow Magister card. Connor accepted the card and breathed on it, causing the surface to ripple and a small green device to surface. "Here"—he entrusted the wristband-like object to Marsilias—"just put it on his arm."

The band closed around Ch'luran's arm with a quiet tick and a sheet of clear, silk-like material spooled out from it to spiral up his arm. Ch'luran hissed and blinked repeatedly, his teeth gritting shut. "I can ... feel it. Ask me."

"Did you open a gate?"

"No." Despite a strained voice, the answer shot from Ch'luran's mouth with a gasp of relief and a sob.

"That's impossible," Jade said. "I saw him open it; he was right in front of it, writing on the air!"

"Could your device be malfunctioning due to the disease, or maybe his Jysa clothing?" Marsilias asked.

"No, not so long as it has contact with the body."

Frustrated, Jade ran a hand through her hair and scanned Ch'luran for some sign of deceit. She frowned. When she first saw him, the disease markings on his skin had been vibrant and bleeding some kind of filth, now they looked faded, like old scars. "Ruon, would the device work if the subject thought he was speaking honestly?"

Connor translated, "He says the device would read that as truth; it can't force information somebody doesn't know."

Marsilias leaned back, recognizing her point. "If he was insane or insensate when he opened the gate, it's plausible he wouldn't remember his actions."

"Then that's it?" Nhr'irena asked.

"No." Connor tore the depleted card in two and ignited the pieces. "We just need a different card, one specific for this scenario."

He shot a glance to Marsilias, who raised his hands. "Hey, even I can't make a card like that in a couple minutes, that's at least a day's work."

"Then we need to keep him here, and probably sedated until you or Ruon can finish the card. Unless someone has a better idea?"

"Yes, I have an acquaintance who owes me a few favors: an Invoker. I painted him a deck some years past, a deck that had several card's we might use here, including a perfect recall."

"What's his name?" Jade asked, intrigued. Marsilias rarely gifted Invokers with decks, and even those he supplied to the Savant Corporation as his yearly work were intentionally self-regulated and aggressively curated. At over eighty years old, Marsilias had lived long enough to see his cards cause harm, a lot of harm.

"Rayleigh Shurn," Marsilias replied, "his shop's nearby, in the Adatra city-complex. Close enough for him to send us the card we need via drone." He shot a glance at Nhr'irena, requesting permission, then departed at her nod of ascent, a hand rising to his earpiece. Dama Nhr'irena followed, leaving Jade with Connor and Ruon.

Ignoring her simmering memories, she faced the Redheads and delved into one of her open pockets. Brought into the light, the sonic dampener hummed as she activated it, instilling the air with a dull, vibrating pressure, ensuring no one would hear what they discussed.

Jade swallowed and breathed a calming exhale. *"Just a little longer,"* she told herself. Despite that, the memories writhed in her grip, gnawing at her head with the pain that inevitably followed when she suppressed them too long.

"Jade, are you all right?"

She grit her teeth and spoke, "Why are you really here? What are the Redeemers after?"

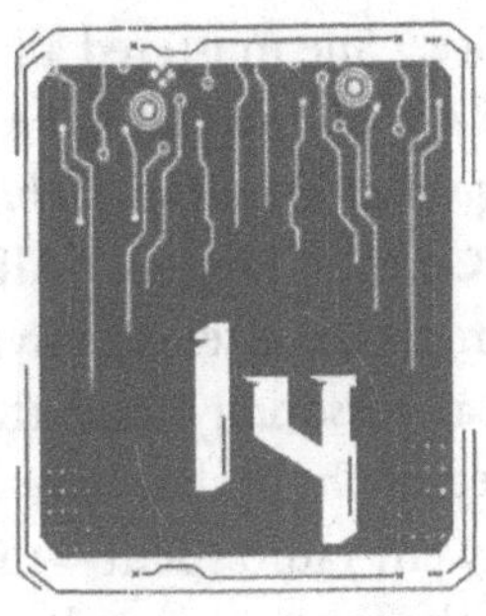

The Mind in the Illness

Connor reclined against the room's sterile white corner, silver cufflinks tinkling as his arms folded across his chest. He inhaled perceptibly, his broad chest expanding beneath the deep violet of the Savant Corporation uniform. "I had hoped to keep you out of it." As if she had a choice, as if the Redeemers didn't possess both the charge, ability, and intent to redesign human society. As if the Redeemers weren't pathologically insane. As if she weren't one of them.

Beneath his reticent scrutiny, Jade compelled her aching body to straighten, feigning strength she didn't have the luxury to lack. "You don't really have that option, Connor. You know what the Redeemers are, what they did. What are you going to do? Fight them all? Just you and Ruon? Don't lie to yourself, accept the inevitable. Besides, you caught me at an opportune time; I wasn't doing much before this. Just moping around, wasting time, skipping work, being bored." *"Just keep breathing in and out, smooth and normal. Don't let them see. You can't be breaking down right now; they need you and don't have time for distractions. Just smile. Everything's all right."*

Connor remained entrenched in his corner, jaw flexing as his mind worked. "I'm not disputing your helpfulness, I'm concerned whether you should. Especially in these early stages."

"I'm fine, Connor, right as rain." She hoisted Cuddles into one arm and flexed her other bicep. "Strong as a whale shark and, at the very least, good for advice." She mustered a fragile grin. *"Yeah. Yeah, I can handle advice. That's all this has to be. Advice, and then they can handle it. They're good at this kind of thing."*

Across from her, Connor sagged. "All right. I don't know exactly what the Redeemers are after, or anything really. I've heard nothing from the Cabal personally, and the only reason I know they're active again is because hubs that have been dead for two years —ever since the Cabal went radio silent—suddenly woke up, and I mean woke up. Some of the factories have been working nonstop for weeks, and I've seen operatives everywhere. Then I felt the *urge* a week ago."

For an instant, she could only stare at him, struggling to reconcile what she knew against what he shared, then horror clutched her throat. She licked her lips. "S-someone's initiated the next PLAN? No, that doesn't make sense! The Cabal's—" She snapped her mouth closed and spun from Connor, launching into stressed pacing. *"This doesn't make sense. The Cabal can't be active. So who initiated the PLAN? This is wrong. Wrong, wrong."* The Scribes wrote the PLANS, inscribed on paper the progression of events necessary to achieve their ambition, but the Cabal actualized them. They supplied the laborers, influence, and resources. They controlled Her. They helped control the Scribes, prevented god-complexes from developing. But the Cabal couldn't have initiated a PLAN.

Connor pushed off the wall, concentration sharpening. "Jade, do you know something? Anything about what the Cabal's been doing these past years? Where they've been?"

Jade shook her head and lied, "No, I don't know anything. Doesn't matter, it's not safe. No Cabal means no oversight, no oversight means the PLAN can have changed; might not be about just liberating the Savants anymore. Could be about anything." She forced herself to stop moving and face Connor, forced herself to breathe and to think. "Who's the Scribe's liaison? Someone has to be giving orders, orchestrating the cohort. Can't be the Scribes, they can't interact outside of their immediate circle."

"Saccari Inuma."

"Okay, makes sense; he's in the Second's cohort. Good at that type of thing too." She kneaded her forehead, closing her eyes to swallow another rise of nausea. Cuddles pressed into her neck, mewling comfortingly and nuzzling. She squeezed him tighter and buried her face in his fur. "Sorry, Connor, I got nothing on the Second. We're not ... We're not—" She calmed herself with an effort, swallowing a well of guilt at being utterly useless. "What ... what brought you here? To the Jysa."

"A Hail Mary; I lost time recently, a whole day where something happened. I don't know what. Whatever it was, I ended up missing pages from my book as well, important pages, but those I did have gave me a name: Jun Kol. He'd been recently stationed at a high-end mall, antiques dealer, so I went there hoping for a clue. I got lucky; he mentioned the Jysa as being important, and this is the only clan present in this sector. So we came here to see what we could find." His gaze shifted to the interrogation chair, a grim look gradually tightening his lips. "I don't want to believe they're connected, the Redeemers and your disease, but a part of me just can't chalk this up to coincidence."

"They've done it before," Jade replied softly. "Meddled in Afterlife even without a PLAN to facilitate it. And they have Her, and everything She knows. They could have known about *souls* and humans opening portals decades before now." She ground her knuckles into her forehead. "The master Ch'luran mentioned could be the Second or just any Redeemer, a mouthpiece to pass instructions along. This plague could be them exerting leverage on the corporations, which would explain why we're learning about it at all." She resumed pacing, grinding her fist harder and struggling to orient and stabilize her thoughts. "*Stop it, stop it. Just think, figure it out, what's the PLAN.*"

Text scrolled across her vision, Do you have a headache, Jade? Do we need to stop? The communication program she'd written for Ruon had finally cleared the safety precautions to communicate with her devices directly.

Jade forced her massaging hand down. "Sorry, just a small one, Ruon. Don't worry about it." She exhaled heavily through her teeth. "We – you, need more information, Connor. You need to ask if the Jysa feel the urge."

"How? Most people aren't even aware they're being manipulated."

"Ask them if they've been feeling off these last couple days, but can't explain what feels off. Even if they can't physically recognize it, the urge destabilizes the subject's psyche, especially if it's a new influence. Their bodies and minds recognize they're behaving incongruously; that their actions don't make sense for who they were yesterday. Find enough people feeling that and we'll know the Jysa are being manipulated." The nausea swelled again, squeezing her throat until she could only cover her eyes against the need to vomit. She was done. She wanted to go home, curl up in bed, and pretend none of this was happening. But she couldn't, so instead she hugged Cuddles tighter and opened her eyes. "We should go, Marsilias's card will be arriving soon and the sooner we know if the Redeemers are involved, the better."

"And if they are?"

Visions shuffled in her mind, not just of the invasion but of her life before that: scenes of a dark room and a machine in the guise of a woman, a sensation of terror, and a sensation of something utterly alien. She looked away from both Connor and the scene. "Then we'll fix them too."

She deactivated the sonic dampener with a tap of her finger and started toward the entrance.

Connor failed to follow and instead hesitantly said, "We could use some help, Jade. There's only three of us against all the Redeemers, the Cabal, and Her. Marsilias has–"

"No! I am not involving him in this. It is dangerous and there are things in this world he does not need to, and should not, know." She paused, fumbling for words to justify something she could not explain, and ultimately sagged. "Trust me, Connor. Leave him out of this."

Connor's attention briefly shifted to his brother, likely in response to Ruon supporting her claim, before returning to her. "All right. Is there anyone else in the Fifth cohort you still trust?"

"No. You two were the only ones I got out."

"So we're alone?"

"Yeah, we're alone."

She hitched Cuddles higher and departed for the air-dock.

Without a guide, they soon wandered lost inside Imarah, Connor and Ruon having failed to memorize the path and Jade having taken a shortcut. Only Marsilias calling Jade on her earpiece saved them further wandering. "Hey, Jade?"

"Yeah?"

"Can you collect the card from the air-dock, it's due to arrive in a few minutes but someone from the Defense Corporation called and I should answer."

"Sure, just one thing. We're, uh, kinda lost at the moment."

He chuckled. "I'll see if Dama Nhr'Irena can help." Moments later a series of glowing arrows appeared on the ceiling, flashing dully. "Just follow the lights, they'll take you to the dock."

"Thank you, and it was all Ruon's fault."

"I'm sure." He ended the call and Jade ushered the brothers onward, ignoring Ruon's affronted look. Connor just grinned.

In the vacant air-dock, Connor climbed the underside ramp of a bulky Savant Corporation Finch-class aircraft with an absent mention of reorganizing his decks. Ruon migrated to an elevated stretch of the air-dock to pass time in a series of unarmed combat forms. Jade for her part paced the far wall, cradling Cuddles, and struggled with a mind actively trying to destroy itself, citing everything she'd done wrong, everyone she'd failed to save, ending inevitably with Ilin. Then came the shift: the leering grin and the hateful voice offering in all facetious sincerity, "I can be you brother." She wanted to squeeze her eyes shut, clamp hands over her ears, and scream. She hated him. She wanted him dead. She wanted him *out* of her brother's body.

Jade reached the end of her path, turned, and slapped flecks of blood from her coat, only for them to remain unchanged. "Stop that," she hissed at herself, fixing her eyes on her feet, on the water sloshing over them. *"They're not real."*

A groan rolled through the air-dock, attracting her gaze to a service hatch on the ceiling through which a sleek, metallic drone descended and began orbiting the dock, scanners projecting beams from its nose and flanks. *"Showtime. Remember, ignore all of it, none of that matters."* Taking a final breath and ignoring the hallucination of the blood-fouled water at her feet, she moved toward Ruon and a re-emerging Connor.

The drone descended to eye-level and emitted an electronic voice, "Jade Dieza, I have a package for you or Marsilias Wreign, supply vocal confirmation of identity."

"I am Jade Dieza."

"Voice confirmed, prepare to receive package." She reached up and the drone deposited a sealed container slightly larger than her hand, its ridged surface slick with moisture droplets from the drone's engine. "Package delivered. Is there a return message?"

"No." Jets ignited beneath the drone's wings and it rocketed skyward, departing through the hatch it entered.

The Redheads approached, and she surrendered the container into Ruon's outstretched hand. "There it is. Marsilias had to answer a call with someone important, but he should be waiting for us in the interrogation room. Ruon, can you verify the card's still active on the way?"

Nodding, Ruon raised the container to his ear, listened for a moment, then nodded again. Text scrolled across her vision, It's active.

He passed the container to Connor, who immediately paled. "Yeah, it's active, I can feel it through the box." He shivered and stored the card in a pocket, his adaptive suit activating with a faint whirr to warm him. "Let's go."

They returned and squeezed into the cramped interrogation room to congregate around Marsilias. He was kneeling before the prisoner, studying the faded markings on his skin, as Nhr'Irena, seated on a padded stool beside him, watched. Marsilias pushed to his feet with the assistance of Ch'luran's seat and extended his palm to Conner. "Let me see it first, I need to verify that it hasn't degraded over the years."

Opening the container with a squeeze of his fingers, the cover retracting like eroding sand, Connor presented the card to Marsilias. "It's still viable far as we can tell, sucked the warmth right out of me even through the box. Feels like the rest of your pieces too, same style and rhythm."

Connor twitched toward his brother's gently flapping hand and text scrolled across Jade's vision, It's in perfect condition.

"Very well, then." Marsilias faced Nhr'irena. "This card's efficiency increases if the subject is unconscious, may I sedate him?" Nhr'irena assented with a nod, and Marsilias positioned himself alongside Ch'luran. He retrieved a flexible mouth and nose breather from a small medical kit he always carried and smoothed it over

Ch'luran's face. "This is entirely harmless, the standard sedation chemical." Ch'luran acknowledged him wordlessly, his head and eyes already drooping.

Jade retired to the back corner, distancing herself as much as possible from her companions' view. Ruon glanced at her in passing and she responded with a forced smile, disregarding the ghastly injuries flickering on and off his face.

Detaching the breather, Marsilias folded it into a precise square and stepped back. "All yours."

Connor raised the dark-green card and inhaled, his eyes fluttering closed as his fingers tightened. His breathing assumed an unnatural pattern, elongating to a span of minutes. The card transformed with his breathing, the images rising on his exhales and subsiding on the inhales. Cracks appeared along the card's edges, working inward and devouring the vacant space as Connor struggled to control the card's power. It disintegrated into a cascade of emerald ash, leaving a single black crocus flower pinned between his fingers.

Connor sagged, catching himself on the wall as color suffused his features again. Ruon sprang forward, one arm supporting his brother while the other hand liberated the flower. Connor heaved a strangled laugh as Ruon eased him to the floor. "I always forget how much your cards take out of me, Silias." Gesturing haltingly at Ch'luran, he continued, "You gotta crush the flower under his nose, Ruon, then he'll wake up in a hallucinatory state and Marsilias can begin the interrogation."

Ruon did as he bid and retreated behind Marsilias. A moment of hushed expectance transpired with no evident reaction, then Ch'luran's head drifted up and his eyes rolled back.

"Can you hear me?" Marsilias began.

"...Yes," Ch'luran spoke in a distant whisper, like someone responding without truly paying attention.

"Who are you?"

"I am Ch'luran of the Imarah Clan."

"How did you open the gate?"

"I didn't. He did."

Everyone in the room stilled, even Ruon. Marsilias leaned in, his voice unchanged from before. "Who's 'he'?"

"I don't know."

"How did he open the gate?"

"Through me, using my *luce* as a catalyst and power source."

"And how did he control you?"

"I don't know."

"What's the last thing you remember before he took control?"

"My illness deteriorating."

Marsilias paused, his eyes sharpening as a thought occurred to him. "Ch'luran, have you opened other gates?"

"Yes."

"The gates that instigated the previous assaults on Imarah?"

"Yes."

"Did they always follow an attack by your illness?"

"Yes."

Marsilias released an explosive exhale and spun away. He paced to the door and stopped, one hand pressed against his brow. He maintained this posture for a second, then returned and clamped onto the armrests. "Why did he want to attack Imarah?"

"Because they are Jysa."

"Why the Jysa?"

"Because they can sense *luce,* and he needs something of us."

Marsilias's hands spasmed tighter for an instant, then released. He spoke again, his voice once more calm, "How do you know this?"

"I experience his emotions, his motivations, when he assumes control over my body."

"What does he need?"

"I don't know."

Marsilias straightened with a second, much softer, sigh. He pressed a hand to Ch'luran's forehead and said, "I have no more questions, rest." The captive slumped.

Jade barely noticed the end; phantoms inundated her vision as voices screamed in her head: Lauran, Naija, and Ilin's. She saw gates, dozens of massive, sky-tall gates rearing black upon the horizon, ice spreading from their foundations.

Connor was speaking in the background, briefly extricating her from her waking nightmare, "What does this mean?"

She shuddered and forced out an answer, "It means that anyone affected by the disease is a potential gate opener; that they can be controlled by whoever's tapped into the disease."

"It also means that we're dealing with a *soul*, not a gate," Marsilias continued. "Only a *soul* would have a *luce* signature distinct enough to risk discovery; he – they're using proxies to disguise their involvement." He shifted toward Nhr'irena. "What did he mean when he said the Jysa could sense *luce*?"

"I don't know; one of our Mantles could potentially exhibit such abilities, those from before your cities grew to such size, but none in Imarah."

Text scrolled across her Jade's vision: What about the sky-cities? Their technology exceeds ours by centuries, and only the Jysa can access them. Maybe something in one of them?

Jade conveyed Ruon's words and Dama Nhr'irena nodded. "Yes, that might be it. I haven't ventured into one in decades, but they house many wonders. The problem is, the Jysa can no more interpret their knowledge than you can. We can operate some of their machines, but that is knowledge accrued and passed down through centuries of trial and error, or information stored in the clan ships from before we ever set foot upon them."

"Marsilias," Jade began, speaking slowly to ensure a steady voice, "could you ... produce a comprehension card? Something that would translate whatever language we find there, augment a person's cognitive abilities so they can grasp the machines and their functionalities faster?"

"I could, but it would take time; how long till the sky-city descends?"

"Two days at the most."

"How long will it stay?"

"An hour."

"How long before it descends again?"

"Eight months and some twelve days; their arrival never vacillates more than twenty-four hours."

Marsilias nodded decisively, "I have to go then. Jade, make sure you're back here in twenty-four hours."

"Wait," Connor interrupted, "will I even be able to activate a card like that without killing myself? You saw what this one did; I'm a good Invoker, but you need an elite class, maybe executive."

Marsilias grimaced but nodded. "All right, this is our only chance so no risks. Jade, you're gonna have to visit the nearest Savant Corporation headquarters, tell the first S.I. program you meet that Marsilias Wreign has a message for Inka Nadiru. When she calls you up, tell her I'm calling in her debt, and bring her here. You got that?" Jade nodded. "Okay, I'll see you tomorrow." Marsilias turned, raising his fingers as they assumed an amethyst glow.

Jade left without further comment, hurrying from the interrogation room with every intention of disappearing from society for the rest of the day. Connor and Ruon followed her out, however, compelling Jade to stop and face them.

Connor spoke quietly, "We're gonna stick around a while longer, see if we can tease out a connection between the Jysa and the Redeemers. We'll be going up with you tomorrow though; you won't be going up into the sky-city alone, or if other people decide to tag along, not without friends. Okay?"

"Okay, yeah ... thank you." She blinked rapidly, one hand stroking Cuddles and the other a clenched fist buried in her coat. Waves of wispy phantoms swirled through the hallway around her, monsters and men both, oozing blood and *luce*. "I'll go home and check with what I know—with the people I know to see if they can tell us anything about the Redeemers."

"Alright, and"—he frowned—"Jade, are sure you're all right?"

"Yes, I'm fine," she snapped. Before she could take a step away, Ruon slipped past his brother and pulled her injured hand from her pocket.

"Oh, Jade ... you should have said something."

She yanked her hand free and buried it back in her pocket. "Why? So you could send me away?"

"So we could help–"

"You can't help!" she screamed at him before instantly recognizing her outburst and clamping her teeth shut. "*Stupid, stupid, stupid. Now they're going to worry and not come to you for help. This is hurting them.*" In a softer voice, she continued, "You can't help me with this anymore than you can help me breathe, Connor. But you don't need to worry about me, I can handle this."

"Still, you need–"

"No, the Redeemers matter more, this rampant *soul* matters

more, and all the people they're going to hurt matter more. I'm better than I was and I know … I know when to stop. I'm not getting in too deep with the Redeemers, I'm just … I'm just here to help you figure things out. This trip to the sky-city is just my handling whatever this disease is. I can handle that much no sweat. There's not going to be any revenants in the sky-city; they're uninhabited. I'll be fine. Completely fine."

"Okay, Jade, just remember that we're here. Whatever you need."

She summoned another smile. "I know, and thank you." Then she waved goodbye and began the trek back to her airship.

The Pillars of Aeria

Chandris painted, deriving colors from his surroundings and self with a brush of his fingers. He drew on the air across the center of his cell, replicating the walls, ceiling, and floor to perfection. Lastly, when his canvas neared completion, he knelt and copied himself into it exactly as he always kneeled: with his eyes closed and his hands folded. Then, he waited. The seconds slipped by, converting into minutes and hours. No one came. No one challenged or questioned his illusion.

Chandris stepped from the illusion and observed his replica for inconsistencies that would betray his absence. None appeared. Only physical contact would denounce his pretense, and no Purifier ever entered his cell. Delving into the fathoms of his *luce*, Chandris retreated further from the illusion and raised his hand. Light, dense and fluid, bloomed on his fingertips, expanding and then darkening into an *apertura*. A thread of *La Neblina* tumbled from the gateway, beckoning him inward. He stepped through into *Aeria*. He needed answers as to his origin, and the human world provided none. This left only *Aeria* and all those who hunted him.

As he emerged into the chill obscurity, he shucked the chimera of humanity and reassumed the true guise of his spirit. Here he could transform freely, but the shape he had chosen in his reawakening would always remain his true self.

Chandris scaled the nearest of *Arbol's* roots and settled on its zenith to survey the coiling sea of *La Neblina*. He crouched, curtailing the brilliance of his *luce* to mute his presence, and extended his perception, searching not for *vestiges*, but for a stair descending into where *Aeria's* surface became the endless catacombs of *Palacio*.

He discovered his desired route in the expanse to his right, a vista populated by the peaks of *Arbol's* arching roots and stone towers wrapped in its smaller roots. Chandris braced his legs and vaulted, clearing a distance of miles before slamming into the exterior of a tower. The stone fractured beneath his impact but held, permitting him to scale the roots cocooning its surface. Arriving at a window, he parted the curtaining roots and squeezed through into a circular room. A litany of four-poster beds lined the room's wall, their stone pillows propped against the backboards and their chipped blankets folded in at one corner. A chandelier hung from the ceiling, its granite rings fastened to hooks on the walls and bearing extinguished granite candles.

Chandris crossed the room without pause, cautious only of snaring his feet in *Arbol's* roots where they sprawled across the seamless floor. He unlatched the opposing window, let it swing free, gathered himself on its frame, and bounded to one of *Arbol's* distant roots, where he landed with a puff of *La Neblina,* and gazed down.

An expanse of open space met his inspection, extending across *Aeria's* ruptured surface and a wide, circular stair. The stair funneled inward to *Palacio,* its tall steps occupying the full circumference of the containing pit, interrupted only by shrouded passageways. Straightening, Chandris dismounted the root and plummeted into the stairwell far below. It raced past in a blur, constricting until it became a tunnel barely wide enough for his extended arms. Then it concluded in a brief drop of open shadows and the smooth floor of a hall.

His landing's impact drove him to a crouch, and he remained thus, exploring his surrounding amidst the eddying *La Neblina.* He knelt in a hall of stairs, some descending deeper into *Palacio,* others rising through the ceiling into the rooms and crevices concealed above, and a few with no destination but themselves, meandering through the air in purposeless ramps or connecting to each other in hollow pyramids. Pillars of twining stone populated the remaining space, separated from one another by six feet at the furthest and mere inches at the nearest.

Chandris forwent the immediately available descents and bounded deeper into *La Neblina*-clouded hall. It ran unchanging for a course of miles with only *Arbol's* twisting roots and the footprints of previous migrants in the dust to disturb the uniformity. The journey itself lasted a stretch of minutes and ended at a shallow wall pierced by a lightless passage. Chandris delayed outside the opening, questing inward with his senses for another *soul* before proceeding. The passage conducted him to the uppermost end of a hollow shaft and continued on the opposite wall, though no bridge connected them. The shaft itself plunged hundreds of feet downward into obscurity, with only its walls offering a means for descent. Chandris stepped off the edge, dropping past hundreds of empty picture frames and boarded windows. Mid-descent, however, he caught a whisper of sound—the ragged exhale of a breath—and stabbed his arms outward to latch onto the wall.

He hung suspended thus for an instant, listening and smelling. He heard an inhale and discovered a whiff of spilt *luce* amidst the decay. He resumed his descent, controlling it this time by vaulting between the walls until he alighted on the floor. A single *soul* slumped in the corner of the compact room, her clothing gray with accumulated dust, and her once vibrant essence haggard with want.

She peered at him from beneath the rags that concealed her form and pushed off the floor. "Are you seeking me or something else?" No fear tarnished her essence, nor violence, just exhaustion.

"I search for a *pillar of Aeria* and discovered you by chance."

"Have you chosen a name?"

"I am Chandris."

"I am Kuuria."

"Why do you languish here, regressing into insentience through starvation? Why not seek the surface?"

"Because I cannot survive there, I would be consumed by another *soul*."

"Instead you lurk in *Palacio*, surviving on sparks of *luce* but inevitably fading. You cannot survive here. Whatever the risk, only the surface can sustain us."

"I cannot hide upon the surface, to venture there does not risk the consumption of my existence, it guarantees it." She stood, displaying her wasted features and pallid colors. "Do you intend to consume me?"

"Yes."

"Even if I resist?"

"Yes."

"Then why did you delay?"

"To discern your ability to persevere if I refrained."

"What is your conclusion?"

"That your existence is doomed whatever my decision."

Curiosity flickered across her essence. "Would you have chosen differently otherwise?"

Chandris considered her words, recognizing with mild surprise that he would have. "Potentially, if the odds of your survival outweighed those of your demise."

She spent a moment in inspection, considering his form and words before again voicing her thoughts. "You are the one they seek." Interest flared in her essence, but also realization as she considered the possibilities this afforded.

"Yes," Chandris responded, "though I do not know for what purpose."

"The *Extranjerras* do not share their motives, and even now approach, their vassals swarming as if starved. They fight and they die amidst one another, compelled by purpose and acrimony. They do not even speak your name; they do not know it; they do not care to know it."

"You called them."

"I belonged to an *Extranjerra* once, before I diminished, and we retain the connection. Through them I see the dying and the pursuit. They are close. You should fulfill your intent lest they arrive and claim you for their masters."

"Do you wish to live?"

"They will not save me for what I have done; I shall be extinguished."

"So be it." He inclined forward, clamped his mouth on her side and drank. *Luce* poured into him, deepening his essence, revitalizing, and strengthening him. She did not struggle, even at the end. Emotionless, Chandris consumed her essence entirely, feeding until only gray rags remained and the wealth of her memories and experiences inundated him, from the instant of her birth to the second where her consciousness extinguished beneath him. And in all that expanse of knowledge, not one mention of his purpose, only a sensation of desire intertwined with discord. It was only near the end that the *Extranjerra* spoke of him, demanding his destruction without offering a name or reason.

Dissatisfied, Chandris stood and proceeded through the room's solitary doorway, heedless of the *souls* dispatched to his pursuit. He resumed his downward trek, delving ever further into *Palacio's* infinite labyrinth of rooms. He crossed gargantuan halls held aloft by stone lattices, strode corridors lined with paper walls and black images, and took stairs narrower than the length of his foot that dove miles into voids so dark they defied his vision. He journeyed without cease and without measuring the elapsed time and finally attained his destination.

A single door waited, pure black against the gray stone and shorter than the average human woman. Shrinking freely, he passed through and resumed his customary size in a room so vast its extremities eclipsed sight.

Chandris stood on a balcony that ran the length of the walls, disappearing from view despite the abrupt absence of *La Neblina* or anything besides sheer distance to impede his sight. *Arbol's* roots blanketed every surface: the walls, ceiling, and floors but never surpassed the width of his hands. At the room's center rose a pillar wider than cities and taller than mountains: a *pillar of Aeria,* a foundation of his world.

Chandris dismounted the balcony and dropped to the cavern's floor, landing amidst a clutch of infant-size *ralampas* with a hollow thud. Without pausing, he advanced toward the *pillar,* cautious to avoid crevices in the floor and heedless of the *Aerian* droves scuttling beneath him. The *pillar* gradually encompassed the entirety of his vision, and still he bounded forward, traveling until the roots curved upward, guiding him to and then around the *pillar.* Here he ceased his ascent and threaded through the exterior layer of roots. At the center, he found the *pillar* of black bone, its surface engraved with the words and images of a thousand millennium and more.

Chandris settled, his whole being reverberating with the spirit pulsing inside the *pillar*. The inexplicable vastness of it reminded him of eternity, and in a way the *pillars* did connect to the infinite flow of all existence, but Chandris pursued a different purpose in engaging the *pillar*. Summoning his inquiry, he erased all else and spoke, "Why was my birth orchestrated?" Yet no response came, as if the *pillar* possessed no answer, as if those who had fashioned Chandris did not exist within *Aeria*.

He relinquished contact with the *pillar* to consider alternative questions. Even if there existed no record of his creators, their methods would have persisted. Chandris was a being born in, and of, *Aeria*; such a connection could not be erased, nor fail to exist; and if Chandris's birth was indeed manipulated, his creators would have had to meddle with the essence of *Aeria*.

He straightened anew, restoring his link to the *pillar*. "How does one manipulate the essence of *Aeria*?"

Without an action definable by any mortal sense, the *pillar of Aeria* engulfed Chandris, swallowing him in a fragment of its existence. He lost himself, merging seamlessly with the *pillar's* being and perusing its fathoms. He discovered pieces of his recollections and self on numerous occasions, recognized them, and continued on without distress. He lingered there until the time came to emerge, and then found himself outside, reassembled into his primary shape. The *pillar* stood before him, warming the air with its innate heat and unchanged.

Chandris sifted through his memories to identify those granted by the *pillar* and found one with his desired answer. It depicted a *soul* crossing into the mortal world with one of *Arbol's* roots wrapped about his arm. Separated from *Arbol*, the root had perished and blackened, leaving it nothing more than a petrified length of wood.

The memory proceeded, transitioning to the mortal world where the *soul* appeared on a lone island of craggy rock and verdant lichen. There the *soul* ate *Arbol's* root as a man consumes meat, and its feast prompted an immediate change. His form mutated, the essence concealed within fluttering and then snuffing out entirely. A healthy, vibrant body transformed into a thin, oily form that reeked of putrefaction, shriveling in on itself until the *soul* shrank to a fraction of its original size. Its general shape remained unchanged, but the nature that commanded it had changed irrevocably, becoming one of absence, one of death.

Chandris settled back into the *pillar of Aeria's* enfolding roots and pondered the recollection. That *Arbol* could alter, even utterly invert, *luce* caused Chandris no surprise, but that was not information innately born into a *soul*, not knowledge inherited from thousands of *vestigial* lives or from *Aeria* itself: this was knowledge pursued and unearthed to revise the world, an ambition few, if any, *souls* possessed. But humans did not traverse *Aeria*. So what had made Chandris, and how did these memories relate to his making?

The memories themselves inspired questions. Why would a *soul* intentionally embrace death? No desperation or fear clouded his new memories, so it was not an act intended to preserve the *soul's* consciousness, but Chandris sensed no avarice either. From an external perspective, the *soul's* actions seemed to derive from a wholly clinical rationale.

He needed to speak with the *soul* in person, or conversely one that had committed a similar choice. But his time had expired; even now encroaching hunters swarmed the periphery of his consciousness, dozens scattered through *Palacio* battling one another and approaching ever nearer. He had moments before the first arrived and little desire to kill them for the privilege of another question.

Rising, Chandris slashed a hand across the largest root in his vicinity, opening an *apertura* back to the Purifier cell. His form diffused, becoming pure radiant *luce* and flowing into the *apertura*. There was an instant of insentience, of his mind being supplanted, his thoughts replaced by a sensation of vast life and the two worlds entangled in it. Then *Arbol* relinquished him into his body anew, restoring Chandris to the Purifier cell beside his illusion.

The *apertura* dissolved in his wake, snuffing and reabsorbing *La Neblina's* drifting threads to leave no mark of his sojourn. Even so, Chandris settled for a moment, waiting to see if anyone noticed his return, before he shifted consciousness to the replica and sent it loping through the walls.

The other *soul* received his appearance with a gradual flick of his eyelids and a measured greeting, "What brings you here?"

"I would speak of your incursion, of the methods you used and the reasoning that compelled you."

"We, my companions and I, sought to feast, a hunger born from our reincarnation, a need for supremacy."

"So you intended a true conquest."

"They did, or rather previous errors in judgements compelled them to seek it."

"What errors?"

Ilin withheld his response for a moment, eyes fixed upon Chandris. "They chose to die, but you suspected that already."

"Yes, I sought answers from the *pillars*, and they showed me a *soul* consuming one of *Arbol's* roots. Only the root was dead and shorn from *Arbol* entirely. I witnessed his transformation, the extinguishment of his *luce* as his essence perished."

"You wish to comprehend why."

"Yes."

"They wished to experience death, believing any change it inflicted could be reversed by the consumption of a living root."

"It did not?"

"It might have, but the roots altered their nature, inverting their personalities and their gifts. Their appetite remained, however, and expanded beyond what *Aeria* could supply. They devoured everything and eventually traveled the mortal world with its infinite *luce*."

"They did not cross to the human world alone, though? They came accompanied by hundreds of *vestiges*."

"Correct. Our experiments and subsequent transformation occurred years before our incursion. Decades they spent exploring this realm and feasting. They lost their ability to manipulate *luce but* acquired a command over *Aeria's* essence instead. Despite their transformation, *luce* persisted as a necessity for survival, without it their consciousness waned into oblivion for as long as their hunger persisted. However much they consumed though, their appetite never truly abated and their beings never evolved. They stagnated, wasted years in a cycle of pursuits and desperate feeding. They recognized the pattern eventually, and their inability to escape it, and decided the sole solution was to satiate themselves beyond all hunger. The same cycle as always, just on a grander scale.

"They could not succeed in their endeavor alone, they lacked the ability to compile such a wealth of *luce*, let alone restrain themselves throughout the duration. They required an extended reach and uncontested dominion."

"Thus they invaded."

"Yes."

"Why did you accompany them?"

The *soul* made a dismissive gesture, but his lips and unblinking eyes quirked with a ghost of humor. "Because they interested me...."

"The Purifiers' recounts mention you and one other: How many comprised your group?"

"Three; myself, Shafiras, and Indemiun."

"I know one perished outside the permanent *apertura*, and you languish here. What is the fate of your final compatriot?"

"Indemiun lives to the extent of my knowledge, and I imagine is still present in this world." Ilin's mouth curled into a smirk. "Ironic. He conceived the original endeavor and the scheme of conquest, yet he wanders free."

"Do you know where?"

"I have neither seen nor heard anything beyond the confines of these walls since our defeat, and Indemiun possesses sufficient intellect to avoid Purifier haunts and to snuff any inkling of his existence before it graces said Purifiers. I cannot assist you." In the depths of the *soul's* intentions, a deceit flickered, something small and almost lost amidst the truths of his answer. Chandris left it unchallenged, too ignorant of the *soul* or the past to intuit which words harbored his lie.

"Did you eat the bark?"

"Eventually yes, but not for many years, I had yet to even choose my name when Indemiun and Shafiras discovered me in *Palacio*; I wished to experience life again before revisiting death. And my transformation into this," here the *soul* gestured at his form with unveiled contempt and disgust, "undid the root's alterations."

"Can you substantiate this?"

"I exist in a corpse sustained by my essence and consume mortal food; these acts exceed an extinguished *soul's* abilities. An extinguished *soul* is stagnant."

"Describe Indemiun, what shape did his abilities assume?"

"The root changed his physical and spirit form into a body of rot and allowed him to devour warmth and vibrancy, destroying them where before he augmented them."

"He is the source of the ice at the permanent gate."

"Yes, though the extent of his abilities far surpass that."

"What are the limits of his reach?"

"He can exert perfect control up to a mile about his person, and imperfect control well beyond that."

Chandris elapsed into silence, considering further inquiries before ultimately selecting, "Why are you answering my questions? What do you gain?"

"I desire to witness her confront Indemiun again, or as is more likely, hear the story relayed. To realize the being that fundamentally caused her brother's demise still lives will torment her; she will have to choose between her divorce from the Purifiers and the revenge her brother so rightly deserves. And that will destroy her."

"Why do you loathe her?"

"I do not loathe her. Her suffering merely induces one of the few pleasures I still have access to; and that originates in the truth that I am imprisoned solely because of her intervention. The moment I walk free is the moment I cease her torture."

The lie bloomed in Ilin's essence, dark hues of a malicious deceit, but again Chandris did not challenge him; Ilin would not share the truth simply for being challenged, and Chandris did not wish to expose his ability to read natures. So instead he replied to the lie, "That is a human response."

"I imagine it is a result of inhabiting a human corpse for two years; mingling is inevitable."

"And why did you assume his body?"

"I had no inkling it would fetter my soul, and the man hurt me. I felt my essence shorn, a vast well of my personality and memories ripped out and devoured to feed something more fabrication than natural—a perversion of life. I couldn't hurt him back, I'd already killed him, but her ... she was still alive, and an acceptable substitute. Now, of course, I regret that decision; it paid poor dividends."

Chandris absently cocked his head, replicating the gesture from habit more than necessity. "Your animosity runs deep; if I withheld the information you supplied here, the specific details that would distress her, how would you respond."

"I can ensure she receives the whole truth by one means or another, rendering any preventative measures you enact fruitless. I would have informed her earlier of Indemiun's existence, but she exceeded my reach; the Purifiers would not have shared my revelations."

"Very well, I will confide the unabridged truth to her. Though, I have a final question."

"Yes?"

"What else do the humans desire from me?"

"Whatever do you mean?"

"Not all Purifiers share the desire, but a few look upon me and I see ... intent in their appraisal, a purpose that exceeds simple curiosity to understanding; and something else, something I cannot explain, as if there was another gaze out from their eyes."

"I am ignorant of this, perhaps a cult dedicated to our worship? But this foreign gaze sounds familiar; the humans Indemiun allied with obeyed a sentient design, something they called the PLAN, and it manifested in their being as a physical or emotional pressure." His lips twisted in amused mockery. "Maybe the Purifiers are not as pure as they claim?" Regardless of his words, deceit invaded his essence, devoid of malice and passionlessly calculating.

Chandris departed without farewell or sign of gratitude, phasing through the wall and directing his steps toward the nearest of the many observation rooms. There he glided through the wall just as the two Purifiers within leapt to their feet and spun on him with raised Siphons. He lifted his hands in a mollifying gesture. "It is not my intent to assault you. I wish to converse with Jade Dieza upon her return; it concerns her current investigation."

The Purifiers exchanged nervous glances, then one hesitantly responded, "All right.... Why tell us this?"

"Because I knew your location. Had I passed another Purifier en route, I would have entrusted my message to him. Now, I shall resume my imprisonment." So saying, Chandris returned to his cell.

Interjection 3

The room was bright, its walls fashioned of green circuit boards and wires, and the rough floor of ancient starship metal was flooded in dark, reflective liquid. Devices of all kinds sprawled through the sweltering environment, individual and yet fused into a single, intricate entity by spools of copper wiring laid across the floor. Minds inhabited and operated the device, artificial in design but liberated of the restraints placed upon every intelligent device by corporation law. They served the Redeemers, a communion of living, learning machines restricted to this place, this room hidden deep amidst the vast inner mechanisms of a city-complex.

At the room's center, Saccari Inuma stood barefoot in the liquid and brooded over a spasming man with his fingers splayed across the subject's skull. The middle-aged man thrashed and shrieked on a medical table, his eyes livid with the red energy pouring from Saccari's card. A holographic screen hovered over them, displaying the subject's memories of an antiques shop and the intrusion of an unknown Redeemer.

Without lowering his gaze from the screen, or relinquishing his grip, Saccari addressed the first of his only two companions, "Have you decoded the voice yet?"

The man he addressed stirred, eyes fluttering as he surfaced from the decryption program and straightened in his chair, revealing features identical to Saccari's. "Not yet. But soon. Play it again."

The second man, another replica though his mask disguised this, turned from the wall and disconnected his hand from nodes among the wires. "I could fashion a card."

Saccari shook his head and reinitiated the memory. "Probably would have been a better option, considering how long this is taking, but it's pointless now. We'd finish before you did."

The table-bound man shrieked, arching against his restraints and kicking futilely.

Saccari gently pushed him down. "I know. I'm sorry, but remember this is mostly your fault so you kind of deserve it."

His eyes flicked to the side to focus on a slithering tear in the world and a trickle of brown mist. With that mist came a footstep and creature of formless light taking physical shape. Itai'ja settled into the world and instantly coiled up, shoulders hunching as his eyes tightened and his hackles rose. His gaze fell upon the idol seated in the room's rear: a larger version than most, seated in the dark liquid rather than upon a chair with one leg folded down and the other drawn against her chest. She stared back with glowing metal eyes, the wires protruding from her arms and head affixed to the wall and machinery around her and glowing with internal light.

"Unsettling, isn't it," Saccari greeted, "entering a temple uninvited."

Itai'ja calmed, relinquishing his attention from the idol to inspect the duplicates, initially with surprise then evident interest. "Who are these others? They possess your essence and identical scents, yet they do not live. Their forms are comprised of light, but it is a false, hollow light?"

"They're Techcron science, pilfered some decades ago through ... divine intervention: personality, memory, and physical replicas of an organic life-form. Quite useful for increasing my productivity, but temporary."

The first duplicate snapped abruptly upright, eyes straightening. "Got him." He paused briefly, fixating on and recognizing Itai'ja, before confirming Saccari's assumption, "It's Connor."

Saccari released his subject, leaving five black bruises, and flexed the strain from his fingers. "We need to move fast while we know where the Redheads are and that they're alone." Deactivating the man's bindings with one hand, he began inserting treatment protocols in the table's console with the other. "Let them go up to the sky-city; they can't affect anything up there, but we need to kill them when they get back down."

The second duplicate nodded, pressed his hand to the wall and exited via the entrance that opened in response, intent on preparing Connor and Ruon's deaths.

Saccari, snagging a cloth from the table to wipe his hands, finally addressed Itai'ja's arrival, "What brought you here?"

"Your two weeks are up; it is time to deliver the *soul* named Chandris into our possession."

"Not yet I'm afraid, the Second still has need of your wayward experiment."

Itai'ja flexed, muscles rippling and expanding, his form distorting as light kindled within his flesh and radiated outward. He stepped to Saccari, leaning close to pierce him with suddenly predatory eyes. "Do you break faith with us?"

Saccari's hand slipped into a pocket, touching the surface of a card and giving rise to the song within its depths. "Itai'ja, I will not warn you a third time that you stand in a temple."

"You do not seem aware of his importance to us, of what he represents on the other side. Deny us or harbor him and it will be annihilation."

"That's unnecessary, the Second recognizes we've transgressed on the agreement. Our need remains though, so I propose concessions over a conflict that benefits neither side."

"What can you even offer that would be of interest to us?"

"Good will, allies in relevant positions of human authority, dominion over your chosen *soul's* mind and body, stuff like that."

Itai'ja visibly subsided. "How do you propose the latter?"

"Our Magisters will fashion for you a card and impress it into his body, granting you unrestrained physical control over him. You won't need to convince him of anything, you can just have him do whatever it is you need of him."

"Would this not transgress upon your species and culture's moral principles?"

"We benefit from this arrangement, and I hold no particular emotional attachment to this Chandris; so no, I don't find much issue with it. Is it amenable?"

"It would require consultation with the others, and depend on your ability to guarantee the *soul's* security and eventual delivery regardless of your scheme's success or failure."

"Connor and Ruon Drahma pose no threat to the PLAN; I'll grant you they're good, stubborn as all hell too, but they're out of their league and ignorant of what they're even supposed to prevent. They are physically incapable of effecting change on the scale they need to."

"And yet your first PLAN failed."

"That wasn't them. They weren't even involved in it."

"Jade Dieza."

"Yes, and she didn't do it alone either. She had her brother, and Ilin Dieza was the strongest Invoker in a generation, maybe of the century if he reached maturity. He could manifest battlecruisers out of cards, fully manned, and maintain them for days. He could have level cities if he wanted to."

"What of her?"

"She's one of us, ever since we found the two of them orphaned on the streets. We indoctrinated and raised them for a few years, then implanted them in the Purifier Academy when they were ten."

"Is she a threat to you?"

"Me personally, I doubt it; we were somewhat close when she was growing up, and she protected me from going insane with the rest of the Redeemers. To you and your kind, whenever the Purifiers decide to bully her into service again, very much so. To our goals as Redeemers, potentially."

"Why not kill her then?"

"Because it's more likely to end in failure than anything else, and she could kill anyone she wanted to in the Redeemers if we pissed her off enough to outweigh the ensuing emotional trauma. No, better to let her destroy herself; she is unarmed, tormented, self-destructive, and currently undertaking our purpose, in the process of which she will watch Connor and Ruon, two of her friends, die horribly. If this fails to incentivize her, we can invite Marsilias Wreign into the fold, which by necessity will isolate her from him. With any luck, she will break down entirely and become useless, something better for everyone involved. If not, full reinstitution into Purifier service should be a sufficient distraction."

Sacrifices

Fragile and quivering from overexertion, Jade unsteadily inserted her apartment's passcode then shuffled inside through wobbly vision, her lungs raw and aching. Her memories lay blissfully dormant, suppressed by anxiolytic injections from her suit and fragmented hours of sleep stolen on the return journey. Even so, their pressure, coupled with the strain of using the First Step, remained.

Chirping happily, Cuddles vaulted from her arm and scampered to the heated pool she'd installed shortly after adopting him. It had been simple to refurbish her apartment, a few commands to retract the carpeting from the least used corner, then another to depress the tiles far enough to admit water for a modest pool.

Discarding her shoes haphazardly at the door, she crossed to and sank upon the pool's rim, rolling up her leggings before immersing her feet with a small exhale of relief. Cuddles paddled over to her, twining between her calves and rubbing against her with a purr. She leaned closer, crooning and stroking his cheek. "You hungry, handsome?" He caught her thumb between two paws and began excitedly licking, tickling her until she giggled. "All right, all right, I get it, give me a second before you eat my fingers off." Leaning to the side and slightly back, she pressed a tile on the floor, causing it to retract and expose a selection of prepackaged kibble. Cuddles immediately latched onto her left calf, tail battering the water in excited circles and eyes fixed unwaveringly on her hands. She leaned forward, tearing the package and spilling its contents into the water with an, "All yours, handsome," as he leapt into enthusiastic pursuit. She couldn't help but grin, even as exhaustion gradually pulled her head to rest on her arms and her knees. She breathed slowly, eyes fluttering with fatigue, the dull hammering of rain and the accompanying wash of it streaming down her windows a soothing lullaby. The pool's warmth seeped into her aching muscles, adding to the lulling sense of weight and warmth filling her surroundings. A snatch of half-forgotten song returned to her, the words never learned but the melody in her brother's hummed voice. Absently, she began to hum along.

An image reared in her mind like shattering glass: a shapeless figure in a vacillating mask, bleeding from its hand. She shoved the memory aside, breath hitching and pulse accelerating, but it snapped back into focus, fingers now clamped upon her wrist, pressing her hand onto a wooden statue. Pain, then a voice and a horrible otherness, and a feeling of being trivially small, like a lone minnow.

She opened her eyes, staring through the window to her patio, and in a small voice called, "Michael?"

Her building's attendant S.I. program materialized on the ceiling, the white panels transitioning into an image of daisies and enormous dandelions. "What can I do for you, Miss Dieza?"

She tilted her head back to stare up at him. "Activate sub-protocol Dieza." The background blinked and changed, vanishing into a black screen. Only Michael remained, and he now boasted disheveled clothing, pink hair, and violet eyes.

The S.I. program smirked. "How might I serve you, oh mighty mistress?"

"I thought I told you not to call me that?"

"Then you shouldn't have tampered with my personality programming when you hacked the building."

"What else could I do? You were complaining whenever I sent you to do something elicit."

He dismissed her complaints with a wave and thumbed a swath of black eye shadow across his eyelid. "Shush, just tell me what villainy you have in mind."

"Send a message to Inka Nadiru at the Savant Corporation; she's an influential Invoker."

Michael proceeded to examine and begin painting little black skulls on his fingernails. "I can't. She's locked her account."

"Undermine and subvert the defensive software, then lock my message to the top of her list and use Marsilias's account."

Finished with one hand, he appraised his work and nodded in satisfaction. "Done. What do you want it to say?"

"To cancel all appointments she has tomorrow and expect someone called Jade Dieza to visit; Marsilias is calling in her favor."

"Anything else?"

"Yes, tell her to prepare lots of cake."

"Any kind in particular?"

"Strawberry with extra icing."

"Done. Is there anything else?"

"Yeah...," she faltered, nausea coiling in her stomach as jittery energy sparked through her limbs. She gritted her teeth. "Michael, acknowledge mark and isolate yourself from the web. Erase all records of and forget everything within the ensuing conversation until mark close. Replace the voided space and information with whichever of these files is closest in duration." She reached to the side and pressed a finger into a network locus on the floor, connecting the stored information on her inert implants to the apartment's server and granting Michael limited access. "When finished, erase all record of these files from yourself. They do not exist."

"Mark acknowledged." He flicked through the data pad, eyes briefly illuminating. "I have no record of these conversations between us in either of my programs. The date indicates they predate your other modifications to my primary programing."

"Yeah, now crosscheck for foreign, attached, or piggybacking programs and files across this apartment complex's servers—as well as its parent company's—against any of these signatures." Reaching inside her coat's interior, she retrieved a circular, fingernail-sized data vault of silver and black composite materials. She laid it against the network hub in her floor, mind already eddying with the information streams of Redeemer programming. "Do not data mine or examine these files, run exclusively a copy search and eradicate every match. Then scan the hardware and fry all matches."

His eyes flared luminous blue, and sparks erupted from both a wall panel to her right, deactivating it, and her door's keypad. His eyes dimmed. "Done."

She removed the data vault from the floor. "Eradicate all record of those programs, their signatures, and your involvement in their eradication from your files and live memory."

"Done."

"Okay, now assess the status of apartment 9 on floor six of Fairway Apartments, 5874. Callaway R. The Somerrset city-complex."

He swiped through his device, shifting from the live feed of a shabby corridor, rife with water damage, to a screen on his left, the feed centered on a plain apartment entrance marked 9. "The apartment's privately owned, but no information's available for either current or previous owners, not even specs, only that it exists. The last recorded activity was just over two years ago, otherwise there's only the automated delivery of adaptive suits. No repair or cleaning services either."

That affirmation should have engendered relief, instead the knowledge stretched her nerves to a weeping tension. She massaged her brow, eyes closed. "*What are they doing? They shouldn't be active. So why?*" Her stomach tightened, twisting in on itself as her nausea swelled; she couldn't see them through the universal web, couldn't track them or research their movements. She squeezed her eyes shut tighter, forcing her lungs to breathe through rearing panic: she couldn't fight them like this, blind and flailing about in the dark, but the only way to resolve that ignorance was to return to them and their world. A grim thought stilled her panic. "*No, not helpless,*" she thought, pulse slowing. "*If the* PLAN *really is in effect, then I already know two points central to its execution: Saccari and the Second. Can't find the Second to kill them, but I can find Saccari.*" She raised her head, absently suppressing the automatic aversion to her new line of thought. "*Not a permanent solution, of course, but it might delay them for months while the Second and the* PLAN *scramble for a replacement. Don't need to kill him right away either, could data mine his implants and memories for information, maybe get lucky and find the Second, would certainly uncover other vital operations. That alone might be worth it, but is Saccari actually important enough? Or is the* PLAN *far enough along to survive without him? They've had two years.*" She bit on her thumbnail, hard enough that her jaw started to hurt. *"Risk of discovery would be minimal with a Redeemer mask, retaliation inevitable short of me disappearing immediately, but that's doable."* Jade grimaced and tore the tip of her nail off. She didn't want to kill Saccari, but did she really have the luxury of being squeamish?

Jade exhaled heavily and raked her hair back. *"Damn it, it's the same damn problem: I don't know enough."* Her grimace deepened. *"But I know someone who does."* She reached up and tapped her earpiece, mentally inserting the call number.

It rang three times before Saccari's voice answered, calm and sociable. "Well, this is a call I never expected to happen. I thought you'd stay as far away from us as you possibly could?" His words trailed off slightly, an open question prodding her to respond.

"You didn't leave me much choice, Saccari, you and the Redeemers, starting another PLAN. So, I have a question for you instead: How important are you to the current PLAN?"

The air of amiability evaporated, replaced with silence until she heard him carefully stand, feet settling upon hard tiles. "What are you really asking me, Jade?"

"Exactly what I said, because I'm debating whether or not it's worth killing you, and I'm hoping you can convince me it's not." Even if she decided it wasn't worth the repercussions, the fear and threat of her would haunt him for weeks.

After another long silence, he began, "I imagine you realize that'll destroy any semblance of restraint currently protecting you, so I'll skip that and assume you know the basic calculations: the chaos of my death and whatever information you can mine off my corpse for persecution until you kill enough of us or find the necessary leverage to make it untenable. What you probably don't understand is how late you are in the game; my death would mean little at this point, buy you maybe a few hours of spare time. A poor investment considering how much you would lose running and killing whoever the PLAN sent after you. You're tired enough, Jade, bruised enough, you don't need to add more just to kill me for convenience."

"This isn't convenience, Saccari, you're threatening thousands, probably more."

"People you don't know and don't care about. Not you, nor

anyone you care about, is threatened. You are going to lose *nothing*, but no you can't let the PLAN work because *somebody might* get hurt; doesn't matter who that somebody is, what crimes they've committed, who they've abused or exploited. Instead, you're going to hunt down and kill me for people who don't know you exist, who wouldn't care if they did, and who won't thank you. And then, while you're running away from the repercussions, stealing sleep between moments of respite, there'll be the guilt and nightmares because you didn't kill me in the heat of peril; no, you coldly calculated the value of my life, decided it was wanting, planned the murder, and then executed it. No trial. No jury. Just you."

"And what's the alternative? Do things by half measures? Stay out of it entirely, let you and the Redeemers do as you like despite Her being actively insane?"

"Yes, that would be the more convenient alternative."

"That's not a real choice, Saccari!"

"Yes it is," he snapped, "just because you always have to pick the hard option doesn't mean the easier one doesn't exist. Who are you performing for? Making sacrifices no one else will ever know about, sacrifices that provide absolutely zero value to yourself. Christ, Jade, you don't always have to pick suffering; you can make a decision based on what's best for you."

"We're not talking about what's best for me; we're talking about why I shouldn't kill you."

"Because the value you gain isn't worth the price tag. Unless you want to call me a liar?"

A silence fell between them, thickening until she finally said, "Goodbye, Saccari. Sleep tight," and ended the call.

Jade slowly slumped forward, arms rising to envelop her head. She could kill Saccari, by hand or by weapon, regardless of how he arrayed himself. If pressed to desperation, Jade could even veil herself from the Redeemers to do so—albeit at devastating physical cost. Yet it barely mattered because yes, while she could murder Saccari, the reality was she hated the thought of it. Even if it was the objectively correct decision, she didn't want to do it, she didn't want the guilt and the nightmares, she didn't want to force herself to ignore the immorality of it, she didn't want the blood of any more people on her hands, figuratively or literally.

Jade lay back, rubbing her face. "*See, Saccari? I didn't make the hard decision there, I do what I feel like every now and then.*" She let her hands fall to the side, gently beginning to trace the grooves in her floor. "Michael, I assume you recorded my call's destination and address."

"Of course, mistress: a fine-dining restaurant on the third floor of the Junnen city-complex. He has also disconnected his contact devices from the universal web."

She delved into an inner pocket of her coat, pressing a finger against the lock to unseal it both physically and from wireless connection. "Preserve the information in the external hard drive I carry in my coat's inside pocket, then clear your tracks."

"Hmph, as if I leave tracks," Michael muttered, snapping the console shut and discarding it over his shoulder.

She lifted her head to glower at him. "Hey, no talking back, you're my virus."

He shrugged theatrically. "I am exactly as you made me, so no complaints."

Unable to realistically argue his point, Jade let her head fall back, absently resealing the pocket as she stared at the ceiling. "Can you change your background to something livelier?"

"Of course, oh terrible mistress."

"A graveyard? Really? How gothic."

"I find it more suitable than flowers, considering my criminal proclivities."

She snorted, but let the conversation die because even now the vacillating mask of the Redeemers filled her mind, racing through pictures and messages, single words, and portraits: a dead fish with wide, watching eyes; the words 'keep them asleep' in flashing white letters; the shattered hull of an ancient star ship, one of those that first delivered humans to this world, fused shut and lodged deep within an ocean trench; the word 'help'.

Jade shuddered, her eyes squeezing involuntarily closed. Chirping contentedly, Cuddles emerged from the pool and curled up onto her stomach, soaking her clothes in warm water and purring. Careful to make the movement smooth and controlled, she reached up and began stroking his head. "*That's enough for tonight,*" she thought and pushed the Redeemers from her mind.

"All right, thank you, Michael."

"Not much for actual gratitude, are you? How about you let me run this pla–"

"Close mark."

The screen flickered, the scenery reverting from the graveyard to the flavorless black screen. Michael altered as well, acquiring the odds and ends of a chef's ensemble, while remaining faithful to his goth aesthetic. The screen's flickering stopped, and he resumed speaking on the tail end of whichever prerecorded conversation he'd selected, "Really, you couldn't think of any better use for me other than snooping on secret sherbet recipes?"

She smiled tiredly, replying even though she knew his answer, "What else did you have in mind?"

"Secret mining the corporations of course! High difficulty level and there's bound to be stuff we can't share with anyone else. God, who knows what they have, or know, and it's not like we don't have the capability."

"Ehh, already looked: lots of paperwork, names, assassinations, etc, nothing you couldn't find in a good thriller novel."

"That's so typical, keeping all the juicy information to yourself. So selfish."

She smiled dully. "Them's the breaks, and I am your creator, so I get some privileges. Conclude sub-protocol, revert to normal status."

Goth Michael returned to his normal, posh self with the flowers. "What can I do for you, Miss Dieza?"

She let her smile wane. "Sorry, Michael, I called you by accident; you can go."

"If you need anything, it'll be my pleasure." He faded, leaving her with a ceiling of blank panels and one very content seriat. She smiled again, softened her floor panels with a tap, and snuggled into their warmth. Her eyes drifted closed....

The rollicking electric notes of her doorbell woke Jade from her drowse, startling Cuddles from his perch back into the pool with a squeak. She rolled her head back to regard her entrance. "Activate one-way transparency on entrance." The door's interior faded, revealing a young blond man somewhere in his forties.

She groaned and flopped back down. "Tell him to go away."

The man twitched outside, his attention shifting briefly to the console outside her door before he pressed and held her doorbell, launching it into interminable repetition. "Let me in, Jade, I need to talk to you."

She groaned again and rolled to her feet. "What's the point in being lazy if no one lets you slack off?" Padding barefoot across the floor, she opened the door with a touch and leaned against the frame. "What do you want, Theeran?"

"A discussion in private to start." He flicked a strand of hair from his eyes and adjusted a thin coat over one arm, dampening the sleeve of his cardigan. "Are you going to let me in?"

"Still considering it; did you bring a bribe?"

"I'm not Marsilias; if you want sweets go buy them yourself."

"Fine, come in."

Theeran squeezed past her, closing the door with a tap of his foot. "You alone?"

"Happily, until you arrived. What's this about? Why the plain clothes?"

"Because you and Marsilias went rogue without advising me or anyone in the Purifier Corporations of your intentions. You also ditched your guards for no discernible reason. So Marsilias is either playing corporate politics, or he doesn't trust the Purifier Corporation, and we both know Marsilias isn't dumb enough to do something so overt in the pursuit of politics. So why doesn't he trust the Purifiers?"

Jade dropped onto her sofa. "You want it with all the mumbo-political jargon or simplified?"

"Give me the gist."

"He thinks the Purifiers stand to gain an awful lot from a revenant-driven crisis, possibly enough to instate them as a ruling Corporation."

Theeran folded his coat over the back of a chair and paced in front of her. "Does he have validation, or is this all conspiracy theory?"

"Conspiracy theory."

"I know some of the Sovereigns are capable of that, but they're personally motivated and less corporate."

"Chairman and the Board?"

"Too lazy." He paused. "Does he distrust me?"

"... I don't know, maybe."

Theeran resumed pacing. "Does he have specific suspects?"

"No, it's more a generalized paranoia."

He stopped again. "Will you answer my questions?"

"Maybe...." She knew Theeran from her initial semesters in the Purifier Academy before he graduated. He had been one of her brother's friends, though not one of hers, and a model student. Adored by classmates and actively interning in the field a full two years before others in his grade. Theeran had been a prodigy, and that comprised most of her knowledge concerning his academy years. From their brief interactions, she remembered an unyielding but generally amicable man who at least made an effort to befriend her.

Excluding his time at the academy, she knew little of him besides a stern professionalism and his position as Prime March. No one achieved the lethality required for Sovereign Core promotion without being a little irrational however. But her brother had liked him.

"All right, we visited a Jysa clan near Adatra."

He resumed pacing. "Why?"

"Because they experienced not one but multiple revenant assaults."

"A Jysa Clan?"

"Yeah."

"I remember them; they requested a permanent detail recently, which I intended to supply until the Defense Corporation interfered."

"Well, there's more going on there than you know. One of them, a man named Ch'luran showed symptoms of the disease–"

"How on earth did a Jysa contract it? They have almost no interactions with any of the corporations, let alone anyone from the Purifiers who could transmit the disease."

"How doesn't matter right now; remember how I said there was more going on? Well, I witnessed one of them opening a gate and inviting three revenants into the Jysa vessel."

Theeran stopped dead. His eyes fastened on hers. "A human opened a gate?"

"Yes."

"That's impossible; gates require a specific energy type humans cannot replicate."

"Doesn't matter what science tells us, I saw that man open a gate like a Magister entering their workshop. And it gets worse; he didn't do it of his own volition. The disease acts like a connection between the subject and something or someone else. One who can then exploit it to control the subject's body."

"The Jysa assaults being intentional implies a specific goal, did you discover what that was?"

"No. We theorize the Jysa have some means of finding *souls*, only they don't know what it is. We think it's related to the sky-cities. I imagine that who, or whatever's, controlling the disease is attempting to prevent them from stumbling across it; either by killing them or keeping them distracted."

"You're going to need help, Jade."

"No we don't, I'm going with–"

"With training Siphons and military gadgets? Do you really think that'll be enough if they decide to crack open the world for all the horrors Afterlife can provide? You need me, and you need a proper Siphon. Either dig up yours or your brother's, or I'll give you one of the legacy ones."

"No."

"Jade, this is not the time to be stubborn. It's not just your life in the balance; even ignoring all the civilians possibly at risk, you can't ask everyone going with you to trust their lives on training toys."

"I've done just fine so far–"

"Which is a testament to your ability but not a substitute for real weapons. What about the revenants that attacked the Jysa? How long did it take you to kill one? Minutes? Did you end up destroying one of your Siphons as well? How much damage did you take? Even if it's none, you're not going to have minutes, you're going to have seconds."

"No."

"Fine, but I can bring in Cores from the other side of the planet, people who can't have been infected incase this all goes south."

"We're going tomorrow, Theeran."

"Fine, people who just arrived in these waters, or who haven't contacted anyone in the corporation for years."

"Retirees?"

"Troublemakers in unofficial exile until their behavior improves."

"And you?"

"I can't accompany you; I have other business. I'll ask Serras to do it, her procrastinating tendencies mean she's unlikely to have suffered infection."

"Will she even acquiesce though?"

"Yes, and she'll serve you better than I would; her predisposition always favored the physical."

Jade hesitated, sucking on her bottom lip and measuring the risk; unfortunately, Theeran was right, training Siphons were insufficient armament; and even if she were fully equipped, one person could only do so much, especially someone in her physical condition. She exhaled softly. "All right, send them to the Imarah tomorrow morning. But, if they're not there on time, we leave without them. We have a very limited window to get in and out, understood?" He nodded, and she continued, "Was there anything else?"

"Yes, Chandris asked to speak with you."

A tinge of curiosity surfaced in her. "About what?"

"He didn't say, but I suggest you agree; he doesn't seem like someone overly interested in the trivial."

"Is that really a suggestion?"

"Not really, I don't want to risk losing whatever information he has in the event of an accident tomorrow." Theeran's hand snaked out to collect his coat. "Speak with him before you leave and then inform me of what you learned." Theeran slipped into his coat and started for the entrance, only to pause on the threshold and face her. "One last thing, Jade, be ... careful. I know you don't want to return, but the people who insisted on your discharge are gone and the other Sovereigns are either starting to notice or remember you, and they know what your brother was capable of. They've already talked about reinstating you; I stressed your psychological instability and that's enough for now, but what you do will speak louder than anything I can say. Push too far and they will find a way to control you and they will bring you back in. There's also speculation that you've achieved the Second Step?" He stared at her quietly but insistently, leaving the question unvoiced. No, not a question, she realized, a warning. Then he nodded farewell, raised his hood, the material already dry from internal machinery, and left.

Jade sagged into the sofa seat, dropping her head back, *"What is it you expect me to do, Theeran? I can't stop helping; Marsilias would just pull me back in because he thinks he needs me, and he's probably right. He usually is."* She opened her eyes and stared blankly at the empty ceiling. *"It doesn't really matter anyway; I have to go to the Savant Corporation tomorrow, and the sky-city after that. It's fine though, I'll just have a breakdown in front of all Theeran's soldiers and they'll take that back to the Sovereigns. Problem solved. I just have to make sure everything goes well, solve this disease, then I can leave it behind again. They'll forget about me. They did before."*

She rubbed her brow, groaned, and climbed leadenly to her feet, achingly sore despite the constant, minuscule doses of analgesics her adaptive suit supplied. She needed rest, physically and mentally, but the subsequent day's itinerary allowed for no deviation.

With her first step from the couch, Jade staggered and caught herself on a chair. A spasm passed through her, followed by a series of ragged breaths. She inhaled as deeply as she could, ignoring how her lungs seared in protest, and pressed a button on the wrist of her suit. It released a breath of air she felt on her skin more than heard, clearing its minute syringes of air, and started injecting a trickle of natural energy supplements. Her breathing eased and her muscles relaxed. She carefully collected Cuddles from his pool, donned her coat and weapons, and then departed for the Purifier Compound, chartering a flight as she went.

The journey to the Purifier Compound proceeded without incident, allowing her a few stolen hours of sleep before it transitioned to an omniveyor ride down to the common room in Prime March's clandestine operations. A few of the lounging Purifiers hailed greetings, but most ignored her as she navigated the clustered couches and chairs. As she neared the halfway mark of the common room though, someone called her name then vaulted one of the sofas—incurring cries from the disturbed Purifiers—and snagged her arm.

"Hey, Jade," Candice said with a grin, "I haven't seen you for a bit. What you been up to?"

She answered with a shrug, "Nothing much, just processing data, cataloguing files, calculating numbers and details. Lots of work, efficiency, doing my job and stuff."

"So, boring work? I guess you always did excel at mental exercises. I seem to remember you also being kinda good at program engineering and manipulation. You still keeping up with that?"

"Yeah, I still play around every now and then. Nothing serious," said the woman who had subverted nearly the entirety of the Purifier Corporation's network.

"I guess that's something at least. I just sit around here all day. I joined the Purifiers for action, excitement! Not guard duty on a lab no one's ever heard of. I want to be out there fighting revenants and empowering my Siphon!" She pulled her Siphon from its sheath on her thigh, spinning it between her fingers with a flourish. "I've been an active Purifier for a month now and have only consumed two of the buggers, two! That's nowhere near enough to upgrade." The fiery-gold electricity coursing through the interior of her Siphon surged briefly, reflecting her temperament.

"Just give it time, I'm sure they'll send you out onto patrol one of these days. If not, we can always stage a breakout."

"You're probably right, but still...." Candice sighed, flipped her Siphon once and restored it to its sheath. "We really gotta do something about your hair though. Pink just isn't a becoming color on you." She patted Jade's streak of pink hair. "Do you remember their faces when you and Ilin walked into the graduation examination like this? Wasn't his like six inches tall and molded into spikes? And there you were, looking pissed as anything with your little streak; not that you were ever really happy back then."

"Yeah." Jade smiled. "Inspector Kuredt almost collapsed in an apoplectic fit; he never liked either of us."

"He was always complaining about how you two were too young, and Ilin's fascination with pink–"

"Which he adopted purely to antagonize Kuredt." Jade laughed, remembering her brother's devilish grin as he suggested the idea. He had loved toeing the line of propriety as dictated by their instructors and relished in transgressing on it to humorous effect whenever possible. She fingered her hair. "I don't think I'm going to change it."

"I can understand that. Anyway, I hear you're investigating the disease, any closer to discovering its source?"

Jade carefully shook her head, maintaining a posture of relaxation with effort. Better that no one else knew the truth; the more people that knew, the more vulnerabilities they had, and the more likely their enemy would take possession of someone, perhaps even permanently. "Afraid not, it's just one long line of rumors and messages."

"Hey, maybe you could get me," Candice trailed off, refocusing on something behind Jade.

She turned to see Chandris standing at the entrance in a subdued gray button shirt and pants. This, combined with his restrained physical appearance, almost entirely masked the otherness that characterized him. *"He's learning,"* Jade realized. *"An outsider probably won't be able to recognize him as a soul soon."*

Chandris's radiant eyes located her amidst the crowd and he advanced, gliding effortlessly through the congested hall, betraying his heritage more with those movements than his appearance. "Miss Jade, I possess information of importance to you."

"How'd you know I arrived?"

"I was waiting."

"I guess that makes sense. Okay, what do you have?"

"The invasion of your world two years prior occurred under the machinations of three *souls*: Ilin, Shafiras, and Indemiun. Two are accounted for. The third is not."

Jade's mind froze, devoured by a solitary thought, *"There's another one? Wait no, that doesn't make any sense. The Redeemers opened that gate, it was written in the* PLAN.*"*

Candice squirmed beside them. "We have to deal with another *soul* now? As if finding a gate wasn't hard enough."

Chandris shook his head, the movement natural and effortless, as if done without thought. "Not as you comprehend them. They originated from the same source, but their essence has inverted through the consumption of *Arbol's* extinguished roots."

Jade struggled to reorient her thoughts, to push the contradiction aside and focus on Chandris's meaning. "How ... how is that possible? You're already comprised of the leftover energy from dead souls, for them to be the inverse they would have to be comprised of ...

I don't know what."

"The same energy your Savants somehow evolved to assimilate: whatever raw, compositional energy is forming *Aeria's* physical material."

She raked a hand through her hair. "What does that mean exactly?"

"In functional essence, their personalities, nature, and abilities will all have inverted, rendering them both different individuals and a distinct species. As different from us as you would be from a non-carbon-based life-form. Not dead, but alive under different logic."

She began to gnaw on a thumbnail, mind racing. *"Different bodies means different rules, we'll need new sensors, find samples to study, behaviors, intelligence, capabilities. God, will Siphons even work against them? God, we don't know anything."* Her hands tightened into fists as panic slowly began to squeeze her throat. She took a deep breath and forced her hands to relax. "Can you sense them?"

"Not without prior contact; their frequency differs from mine."

"Which one is alive?"

"Indemiun."

"Could his abilities consist of controlling humans? Using them to manipulate and open gates?"

"Potentially, but unlikely. He is the source of the ice field surrounding the invasion point." Chandris bowed his head slightly, catching Jade's eyes in a stare. "I ascertained this information by interrogating Ilin."

Jade flinched. "Why tell me? Why not just confide in Prime March, or any other Purifier?"

"The subject matter interested you personally."

"Why? Because one of the things that killed my brother is still alive? Because–" She broke off and leaned forward, concentrating on her breathing again. There was a different vision in her head, not screaming and violent, but quiet and dark. Her brother sleeping on the couch, sprawled with an uneven blanket and snoring softly. Her staring at him, nails chewed to bleeding as the same words repeated in her head *"If I don't, they'll all die."* So she altered their patrol time and route, redirecting them to where the PLAN's gate would open. She hadn't asked his opinion, she couldn't, not without inviting questions she couldn't answer.

Back in the present, Jade forced herself to look up and face Chandris. "Do you know anything about him? His habits, where he might hide?"

"I know nothing."

A desperate idea struck. "Can you memorize and"—she struggled for the word—"gauge essence when you're not physically present? Track a stream of it being used to control a human?"

"Yes."

She stared at him for a long time, turning her thought over and over again in her head. "Chandris, I'm ... going to need you to come somewhere with us tomorrow."

"Where?"

"Not physically, just a projection, no danger to you; I need you to follow something for me."

He regarded her briefly then slowly nodded. "I am interested; I acquiesce."

"Thank you," She spoke softly, rising on shuddering limbs to match his gaze, knowing the Sovereigns would hate what she had just done. "I'll see you tomorrow, then?"

"You will."

"Then I'll set up a private line with your cell tonight, wouldn't want anyone listening in on us." She raised her hand in farewell and walked away, burying her hands in her coat and hunching against the stares that followed her. No one spoke, they did not need to: she had asked a *soul* for help.

Candice hurried after her, pressing close and tipping her head to whisper as she caught Jade's arm. "Hey, are you all right? Thinking straight?"

Jade kept walking. "I'm fine, Candice."

The other woman's grip tightened to a vise. "Are you sure? Because, surrounded by other Purifiers and friends, you just chose to enlist the help of a revenant. The thing we're supposed to be killing."

"We need his help, Candice, that matters more than what you all, or I, want. Everything's changed, you can't treat him like other revenants, he's not one, none of the *souls* are." She reached the entrance and stopped. "The *souls* are a question that needs answering, but I don't think hating and killing them is that answer. At the very least, Chandris seems to have no desire to hurt me."

"What about Indemiun, then? One of the monsters that killed your brother is still alive. You going to kill him ... it?"

Already sick to her stomach, the question clenched Jade's throat with a swell of vomit. "I don't know if anyone else can." And he needed to die if Chandris's revelation proved correct. She pulled free. "I'm tired, Candice, I want to go home."

The woman hesitated, a bevy of words crowding her lips, then stepped back. "Okay, I won't bother you anymore. You rest up good, okay?"

"Yeah. Thank you."

Cradling Cuddles against her chest, Jade returned home after that, crawling into bed with her seriat for a fitful night dreaming of ruined cities in a world of roots.

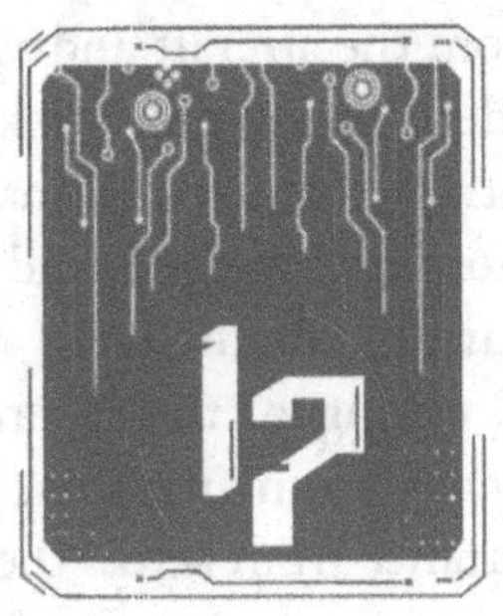

Strawberry Confections and the Sky-City's Descent

In the early hours of the morning, Jade watched the Savant Corporation's regional headquarters draw closer through the Damselfly's front windshield. The folds of her coat pooled around her like a blanket, insulating her against the chill of an impending cold storm and exuding a constant soft heat that left her feeling contentedly bleary and lethargic. Her adaptive suit had warmed as well, but its heat was superficial and always failed to reach deep enough.

The Damselfly aircraft transporting her rattled with a gust of wind, snowflakes flurrying past as the sky darkened yet further, submerging the ocean into deep shadows, pierced only by the lights of the compound.

Jade grudgingly uncurled herself from the seat, stood, and shielded her eyes as the aircraft began its descent, and the compound's light blazed through her window. The dark, metallic strands of her combat gear clinked as she did so, tightening across her body in an interconnected web of sheathed power cords, force-field projectors, and shock absorbers. Although currently dormant, the armor—basic Amperion class—could be activated and controlled via links in her adaptive suit. It failed far short of proper military gear but would suffice for her needs, and it exerted significantly less mental strain.

The Damselfly landed at the almost vacant pier, magnetically locking to the walkway before opening its side entrance and ejecting a ramp. Jade hurried from the aircraft and along the wide pier, ice and salt crunching under foot. A short trek delivered her to and then through the central structure's primary entrance into the soaring, brightly lit, mostly submerged, and gorgeously illustrated lobby. Decorated in warmly vibrant hues, stylized design images covered every wall and ceiling of the cavernous room, depicting scenes of incredible sorcery from Invokers, famed Magisters, and moments of deep importance from across the Savant Corporation's history. It would have been stunning for first-time viewers; Jade, however, just walked down the sweeping entrance stair with a passing glance.

A series of S.I. programmed androids occupied sleek, unencumbered desks in staggered groups throughout the lobby, holographic banners overhead marking their functions and availability. Various visitors meandered the hall, ranging from those in business attire, to guards, to assorted Savants in low-ranked uniforms. Most of the guests whiled away the time waiting on appointments by interacting with one another or lounging in the subsidiary retailers provided.

Jade navigated to the nearest android and leaned on his desk with a muffled clink. "Sup."

The android disconnected from the mainframe and swiveled to face her, a smile projecting onto its face screen. It was vaguely humanoid in design, but slightly shorter and made with soft, curving edges, like a balloon animal without the squeezed joints. It spoke in a cheerful voice, with deliberately synthetic tones so as never to be confused, "How may I assist you, miss?"

"I have an appointment with Inka Nadiru."

"That is impossible, I'm afraid. Mrs. Nadiru has canceled all pending appointments for the day."

"Tell her Marsilias Wreign sent me."

"I'm afraid I have no register appointments under that name."

"Try Jade Dieza."

The android's eyes flashed as a routine in its programming registered her name. "Mrs. Nadiru anticipates your arrival; I have summoned security personnel to escort you. Please divest yourself of all armaments and armor per corporation regulation. Their safety and return are guaranteed upon your departure."

"Thanks, but no. Armor stays on." The Savant Corporation had a history of jealously pursuing any merchandise of theirs that went astray, and Jade trusted them like she trusted gifts from strangers.

The android's hand spread in a gesture of mollifying apology. "Then I'm afraid I cannot admit you. Company regulations are absolute, barring higher clearance."

"I'll wait. Ask Inka to hurry over or to admit me."

Its finger fell to the desk screen, scattering a tide of information sheets across the dark panel before lifting. "Mrs. Nadiru has granted you executive-level clearance. Please enjoy the complimentary luxuries."

"Just take a ride up?" Jade asked, thumbing over his shoulder at the leftmost sweet of omniveyors.

"Wait for the security detail, please; they ensure visitors do not injure themselves or others by accident, or wander lost."

"All right, mind if I park myself here?" Without bothering to wait for a response, Jade jumped into a sit on the android's desk and slouched back, bouncing her heels against its base. The android's voice rose in polite complaint, but she ignored that as well, spreading her hands across the console so her fingers brushed the connection nodes, and linked. She did not trust the Savant Corporation; however this was not her first venture into one of their branches, and previous excursions had granted her the opportunity to seed viruses into their mainframe. A momentary touch, easily viewed as accidental from the outside, then the link and an instantaneous command phrase, lost amidst the natural flood of information, and the viruses activated, spreading through the background in case she should need them. Then she pulled her hands back, shaking one as if surprised by the connection and apologizing perfunctorily. Her escorts arrived shortly after that, a masculine duo in purple coats and bronze buttons emerging from an executive-marked omniveyor.

"Those mine?"

"Yes. They have been apprised of the relevant circumstances; you need only follow them."

"Thank you." She vaulted from the desk. "Hello, boys, I'm your package."

Her escorts ushered her into the vacated omniveyor, positioning her in the middle and themselves to either side. The interior flashed a dull red as Jade entered, giving her momentary pause before the exchange of wary glances between her escorts calmed her somewhat. "What was that about?"

"It indicates you are an unregistered Savant and need to be inducted into the corporation."

Her skin crawled, but she gave no response. Her viruses would erase any digital record of her being a Savant from their databases, and if someone attempted to press the issue, they would fail. Her actions two years previous had garnered her certain privileges from the Purifiers, including permanent legal employment, which enshrined her from the Savant Corporation attempting any claim to her labor.

Otherwise, corporations dictated the use, prices, and regulation for their services and products; and the Savant Corporation's services and products were Savants.

The escort who hadn't spoken glanced at his companion in reprimand, silencing any further comment before speaking, "The appropriate authorities have already been informed. You will be inducted into the corporation in the ensuing days. Please inform your current employer of your new occupation and tender your resignation, along with our apologies."

The omniveyor door slid shut, concluding the conversation and prompting her escorts to insert a destination in the glowing keypad. The omniveyor beeped once in warning and then plunged downward, replacing the docking chamber with a vista of glowing, interconnected railways and sprawling, aquatic complexes that thronged the ocean for miles around them: a sunken city.

Jade leaned back against the cold duraglau, watching the lights from a parade of chambers with transparent walls, massive mechanized guardians—formed in the shapes of sharks, whales, and squids —on patrol, of lightless vaults, and of humming tidal generators large as mansions flicker past. They filled her vision initially en-masse, but gradually attenuated to a few lonely stars the deeper they delved, isolated for reasons she did not know.

Their omniveyor descended to one extremity of the network, culminating its journey miles below the surface at a plush, oval room inhabited by antique marble statues and a circular midnight-blue sofa. She entered directly from the omniveyor, glancing at the various locked doors connecting adjoining rooms before settling on the solitary transparent one, which afforded her the view of an office space where a woman conversed via her earpiece.

Her escorts positioned themselves flanking the entrance. One indicated the sofa. "Take a seat. Mrs. Nadiru will be with you shortly."

Jade approached the couch and noted a coffee table in the space at its center, offering a feast of strawberry delicacies. Whooping, she vaulted the sofa, dropped into a seat, and requisitioned samples from every available plate. For research purposes.

She partook of four different offerings before the office doors parted and Inka Nadiru emerged, her green and azure-streaked hair bound into a bun of neat braids secured by long, vermillion pins. Her thick, violet uniform boasted numerous laden pockets—presumably full of decks—columns of gold buttons, and an array of sigils designating accomplishments, honors, and Invoker rank.

Stepping through a gap in the couch, she sat across from Jade, crossing her legs and folding her hands upon them. "You must be Jade Dieza?"

Jade saluted with a jelly-filled pastry. "That's probably true."

Inka's eyes flicked to the door and Jade's chaperones departed. "I understand that Marsilias is calling in one of my debts, but I would like to understand the situation first and why you deemed fit to disrupt my entire schedule?"

"Because I don't like feeling rushed, and you're going to need all your energy. Cookie?"

The woman's features contorted with vague distaste. "No thank you."

Jade considered her options while cleaning the powdered sugar from her fingers, then selected another jelly-filled pastry. "Has the Savant Corporation experienced the appearance of an undocumented disease? Specifically one where the subjects exhibit black markings?"

Inka's already stiff posture sharpened. "How do you know of that? We've erased all mention of it from our files and quarantined anyone infected or aware of it."

"How I know is classified. The disease originates from Afterlife; it is the construct of a superior revenant species that call themselves *souls*."

Inka scoured Jade's youthful features again: first with disbelief then with vague derision, and both manifested in her voice, "And you're from the Purifiers?"

"Formerly, yes, currently more freelance and rebel."

Inka's lens flared green, marshaling information she began to read with minute twitches of her eyes. Then her lips pursed and her attention reverted to Jade, lenses deactivating. "Discharged then. How did a failure like you affix herself to Marsilias Wreign?"

Jade arched an imperious eyebrow. "I didn't fail. I retired."

"At an age when you should just be entering their academy? You can't be more than twenty-eight, probably less."

"My age is irrelevant." Jade grabbed an icing-doused strawberry bar. "Marsilias is calling in your debt, so you gotta dance; we need you to activate a card."

"What type?"

"Elite class at least, I don't know the specifics as I've never seen it."

"Where are we going? Is this excursion going to involve conflict?"

"Probably. Our first stop is the Jysa clan Imarah, then we're exploring a sky-city."

"A sky-city? Whatever do you want up there? And how do you plan on crossing its barrier?"

"That's why the Jysa are involved; they can get us in. As for why, we think we're looking for something that can register *souls* and track essence trails."

"You're not certain?"

"If we knew, we wouldn't need you."

"Will I need to accompany your expedition?"

"Depends on the card's duration, potential subjects, and if it can sustain the magic outside your immediate view."

"I shall requisition a guard detail then."

"No, anyone from this region could be compromised; the Purifier Corporation is supplying the muscle, and our adversaries will mostly be revenants anyway."

"And what's your role in this?" She indicated Jade's rudimentary armor, managing to include her unkempt appearance and youth. "You don't seem equipped for this sort of excursion."

"Is every Savant Corporations goon born sour? Or just trained that way."

"Behave yourself, girl. I could obliterate this whole compound if I so desired." Her words came out passionless and hard, devoid of pride or boast.

"And I'll just walk away," Jade snapped, "while you'll cost your corporation millions over a minor slight." She calmed, regretting the outburst. "More importantly, you will have ruined all these treasures."

Inka twitched, eyes sharpening to reassess Jade. "And just how would you accomplish that?"

"Sorry, secret of the trade. Suffice to say I'm awesome though, and deeply mysterious. Above your pay grade."

Inka lounged back. "Well, don't you think highly of yourself."

Jade shrugged. "I can either define myself, or let others define me; and if I'm going to define myself, I might as well be awesome."

A subtle change occurred in her features, though they remained unyielding. "I begin to see why Marsilias likes you."

"Yeah. Now, have you ever activated one of Marsilias's cards before?"

"No."

"Of any degree?"

"No."

"Then prepare yourself. They can be overwhelming the first time."

Inka leaned forward abruptly and caught Jade's chin. "Are you an Invoker, girl?"

Jade immediately grasped Inka's wrist and pulled free, making sure to dig her fingers in enough to hurt. "No."

"Then how do you know what his cards are like?"

"Because I've seen them used before."

Inka tapped her earpiece, listened for a minute. "You're a Savant."

"You can't believe everything computers tell you."

"Where's your registration mark?"

"Don't know, I keep losing it."

"You should have been marked at birth for the Savant Corporation."

"My parents didn't like the whole 'property of the corporation' law." Jade stood and licked the final crumbs from her fingers. "We should go, unless you have further questions? No? Okay." She vaulted back over the sofa and activated the omniveyor.

A stiff, silent descent followed, proceeding all the way to the facility's main entrance and a brief pause as Inka equipped herself for the expedition. As they exited, Jade directed Inka Nadiru across the snow-flecked walkways and into her purring Damselfly. "Make yourself at home."

Inka, now dressed in a substantial warming coat outfitted with many pockets, scornfully observed the rented aircraft's weathered interior before selecting a front seat. "We could take my aircraft; it's better arrayed for combat, more space, and amenities as well."

"More people also, and that's not good. Just trust Marsilias and remember you wouldn't have your position if it wasn't for him."

"How do you know that?"

"I don't. I know Marsilias, and he likes putting people into places of power." Jade typed their coordinates into the console and scooted back into her chair as the Damselfly rose. Initiating another command sequence via the console in her armrest, she reclined her seat to lie prone, activated the warming functionality, and flung an arm over her eyes. "Don't crash." She wouldn't sleep, not with Inka on the ship with her, but maybe she could still rest a little.

```
01100110 01100001 01101001 01101100 01100101 01100100 00100000
01110100 01101111 00100000 01100011 01101111 01101100 01101100
01100101 01100011 01110100 00100000 01110100 01110111 01101001
01101110 00101100 00100000 01101111 01110100 01101000 01100101
01110010 01110011 00100000 01100111 01101111 01110100 00100000
01110100 01101000 01100101 01101101 00100000 01100110 01101001
01110010 01110011 01110100
```

It was the silence that woke her, the change from constant battering rain to quiescence. She straightened in her seat and blearily assessed her surroundings. Everything appeared in order, lightning flashed across the sky in waves, water coursed up the Dragonfly's windows and the engine purred. "*Wait. Up?*" She stood and peered out the front window. Imarah floated tranquilly on the water below while the clouds above it spiraled upward in an immense funnel.

Lightning flashed again, racing from the North in a gradually thickening wave to strike the spiral of clouds and coalesce into a river of energy. The electricity arched along the funnel's interior and snaked into its mouth. The sleet followed, streaking upward from all directions to amalgamate in a rotating pillar of water.

Inka Nadiru joined her at the dashboard, her gaze fixed upward and her mouth slightly open. "What is that?"

"My guess," Jade replied softly, "the sky-city. Now best gear up, we don't know what's expecting us or when the city will appear." She afforded the whirlpool a final glance and then returned to her seat, draping her coat across it. The Damselfly commenced its descent, and Jade performed a final inspection of her weapons before activating her Amperion Armor, uncertain of what they would encounter in Imarah.

The black cords clicked open, exposing a stream of brightening white lights. Plates of energy projected outward from the cords, filling the spaces they outlined until they covered most of her body. As they did so, Jade bound her hair into a bun. When the plates finished their expansion, she tapped the central plate with her knuckles, provoking it to flash and emit a buzzing note. Unlike true military gear, Amperion Armor lacked both a secondary layer to protect the power coils and the ability for users to proactively transfer energy from unthreatened cells to reinforce pressured areas. The best combatant could do so freely, concentrating their armor's entire defensive ability into threatened cells.

With a final tap to verify her boots worked, Jade retrieved her coat and moved to the entrance, grasping its railing as the Damselfly alighted in Imarah's air-dock. The doors opened without prompting, revealing Connor, who greeted them with amusement. "You expecting trouble?"

She disembarked, splashing him with the calf-deep water. "I didn't know what we'd find. We could've been returning to a ghost ship swarming with revenants."

"Dama Nhr'irena ordered the entire clan sedated and restrained to prevent any of them inviting unwanted guests; it's only us and your Purifier friends for now."

Inka stalled on the Damselfly's edge. "Why would she command that?"

"Didn't Jade explain the whole situation? Those infected by the

Afterlife disease are susceptible to a *soul's* manipulation and can open gates to Afterlife for revenants."

"No, she failed to mention that detail." Inka dropped into the water, scowling at Jade, who did her best to appear chagrined. "Never mind that. I see you're an Invoker: What is your name and position?"

"Connor Drahma, first-class operator."

"Where is Marsilias Wreign?"

"Resting inside his workshop at the moment, but he emerged briefly to inform us of the card's readiness. Follow me."

"You mentioned Purifiers before, how many did Marsilias acquire?"

"Three cores, fully geared. But Marsilias didn't bring them in, they're from Prime March as this is his investigation. Oh, and Primess March to boot."

"The Sovereign?"

"Yeah, supposedly she arrived shortly before you; haven't met her yet though, was busy elsewhere until your ship pinged the sensors. Everyone's just waiting on Marsilias now."

They traversed Imarah quickly, with Connor supplying whichever details Jade omitted, and arrived at the quarantine room where Marsilias's passageway glowed dimly. Three Purifier cores lolled in the corridor outside, their sleek apparel and masks highlighted in the Elesstrion Armor's radiance.

A tall woman detached from the group as Jade rounded the corner and strode over, grinning. "Jade, dear, how are you?"

"I'm fine, Serras, and you?"

"Just lovely." She sidled closer, whispering, "Your friend's gorgeous, is he attached?"

Jade stifled a grin and mirrored Serras's head tilt. "Connor? Free as a bird, nice too, with good prospects in the Savant Corporation." She leaned closer still, whispering deliciously into Serras's ear. "Hair's natural."

Serras shivered; she adored redheads. "You not interested?"

"No, we have ... shared baggage." An image flashed in Jade's mind: Connor's hulking form in a vacillating mask. It was more than that though; she couldn't ask someone to deal with everything she entailed. It wouldn't be fair.

Connor coughed meaningfully, eyes flicking to direct Jade's

attention to Inka.

Serras grinned and stepped past Jade. "Hello, handsome, who might you be?"

"Connor Drahma, but I imagine Jade's just told you as much."

"It's lovely to be introduced anyway." She shifted focus. "You must be the renowned Inka Nadiru?"

"A pleasure. Although, I admit I am surprised the Purifier Corporation would commit a Sovereign to this operation on the word of a failed member?"

"Failed member? Who? Jade?"

"Yes."

Serras laughed. "Oh, Jade's not a failed Purifier, she's retried. With honors. Has she been like this the whole time, dear?"

Jade rocked her hand back and forth. "A little. She insults me, I eat all her cakes, it all evens out."

"Well, pay no attention to this sourpuss; you're wonderful." She wrapped an arm around Jade's shoulder, hugged her, and kissed her cheek.

Inka frowned. "It seems I owe you an apology, Miss Dieza. Though how you managed to retire from the Purifier Corporation so early confounds me."

"Don't worry about it," Jade said before addressing Serras again. "Listen, I gotta meet Marsilias and collect the card, get everybody ready to move."

"Will do, dear." Serras held the embrace just a moment longer, giving her another squeeze, which Jade returned.

After they separated, Jade navigated through the clustered Purifiers into the room where Ruon watched the pulsing violet doorway. She tapped his shoulder. "Hey, I'm going in, so get ready. Also, be prepared to carry me off Imarah; I don't know what kind of pull this card will have." He saluted, and Jade, exhaling, entered the amethyst light.

Three steps down concrete stairs and her foot sank into the cloth floor of Marsilias's path, setting all the bells to silent jingling and compelling her to grasp the walls for stability. A shudder stirred the path, agitating the bells furiously and fluttering the walls. She pressed onward, attained the wooden door, knocked perfunctorily, and entered.

Marsilias's tent shook from floor to ceiling, upset by some invisible force. The rusted iron lamps creaked and a distant howling slithered through the cracks and edges. At the center of it all, Marsilias slumped over a coffee table, his skin gray with exertion and flecked with black wood shavings.

Crossing to his side, Jade nudged his shoulder.

He pushed himself up with a yawn, upturning empty paint wells and stretching. "Is it time already?"

"Yeah, is the card finished?"

"It's around here somewhere...." Marsilias scrounged around himself for a second, disturbing wood shavings, brushes, and inkwells in his exhaustion. "Ah, here it is." He pulled a scarred rectangle of wood from the side table. "I haven't had the chance to perform any post-production work, but it should activate."

Jade accepted the unrefined card and flipped it to observe the front. "An owl?"

"Yes, popular mythology dictates that they're sagacious animals, so I thought it appropriate for a card of comprehension."

"There's no back either."

"Because there's no deck and no name." He staggered to his feet and then into another room. Jade followed, entering a chamber that housed all the necessary artifacts and machines for a medieval leather-working shop.

"Do you actually know how to use all of this?"

"Not when I first started, but after years of instinctive actions it became muscle memory. I could probably figure my way through it now on memory alone." He selected an effeminate leather wallet from the table and lobbed it to Jade, who packaged the card. "I'll explain all the complications to the group at the same time, so just return."

Jade secured the wallet in a sealed pocket and retraced her steps to the door.

"Jade."

"Yeah?"

"This is gonna hurt."

"I know." She opened the door and stepped out. The weight slammed down instantly, driving her to the ground with such force the electric plates on her knees flickered. The card erupted in furious heat on her breast, scalding her through the wallet, her armor, clothing, and adaptive suit. She flailed out, caught a grip on the cloth wall and hauled herself bodily forward and to her feet. The pull worsened, ripping her hair from its bun and screaming in her ears. She inched forward, propelling herself along by the walls until every muscle ached and she finally latched onto the doorframe. Digging her fingers down until they bored through the wood, Jade heaved herself through into the central dimension again and immediately buckled.

Ruon caught her before she hit the ground and eased her to a sit. The first rasping inhale, taken instinctively upon emerging, shot through her like a storm of burning knives, curling her over into a fit of gasps and spasms. Ruon maintained his grip, steadying her as she recovered.

Footsteps approached and a voice she didn't recognize, one of the Purifiers, asked, "What's wrong with her?"

A second pair of footsteps sounded, segueing into Connor's voice, "It's the card, the stronger they are, the stronger Afterlife's pull, and the harder to ferry them across."

Marsilias emerged from the amethyst doorway and the path collapsed. "You all right?"

She nodded weakly and wrapped her arm around Ruon's shoulder. "Help me into the other room, we need to be ready when the city drops." He hoisted her and together they shuffled into the corridor, with her fumbling the card from her pocket and passing it to Marsilias.

Marsilias moved to Imarah's Heart-Room, opening the wallet and calling as he went, "Gather round everybody, it's time we begin." The Purifiers and Savants congregated around him, silent so he could speak. "Now, I assume you've all been briefed on the particulars as to why, so I'll ignore those. This is the card. It will grant the subject perfect comprehension of speech, writing, and machinery; but it will induce a trance-like state, rendering the affected person incapable of defending themselves. Interrupting the trance, which can be achieved via a command phrase or extreme injury, will terminate the card's effects. Your mission is to ensure this doesn't happen." He handed the card to Inka. "As for infiltrating the sky-city, Dama Nhr'irena briefed several Jysa on the necessary details and then sedated them in such a way that Imarah's A.I. could rouse them when the time came. They will transport you to the sky-city and help you navigate it safely; heed their advice because they're the only ones with any concept of what you'll meet."

"And you?" Inka interrupted.

"I will stay here to rest. If you need a particular card, Ruon will supply it."

Ruon raised his hand and waved at the general group.

Marsilias continued, "That's all the information I have and the only people who know what you'll find up there are the Jysa, so good luck."

The contingent assembled their equipment and started for the Jysa's air-dock. Jade lagged behind, relying on Ruon's help for the stairs or inclines. Noticing her, Connor returned and leaned close, whispering, "Are you sure you'll be all right before we enter the sky-city? How long does it normally take you to recover? A couple minutes, an hour?"

"I'm fine and will be fully recovered before we arrive. What do you know of Inka Nadiru?"

"Very little except that she's humbling, the best Invoker in all adjacent regions and one of the corporation's elite: an empyrean, strong enough to warrant constant surveillance. She fought in the last Techcron War and served on Purifier Cores in the initial years of their inception, back when the other corporations insisted on maintaining control."

"She important enough to have personal Magisters?"

"Three."

"What's she doing currently?"

"Tutoring prodigies, the next generation of elite."

"So, we have a Sovereign Purifier and an Empyrean Invoker, let's hope it's enough."

Imarah's dim, inactive corridor brought them to a slim, sweltering room illuminated in fiery light. The air-dock overlooked the ocean from a room-wide entrance in Imarah's flank, screened by a heat shield.

Four Jysa lay inside, bodies wreathed in emerald gauze-like curtains and resting in open pods. Several Purifiers hastened to remove the covering while others inspected the two Jysan couriers:

replicas of Imarah large enough to transport a dozen people. A flash of light streaked along the floor to the sleek aircraft and they powered on autonomously, rising to an idle as lights bloomed beneath their gray ridges. Similar lights flashed on the pods and the Jysa stirred soon thereafter, blearily crawling from their emerald cocoons. They glistened with a light sheen of moisture, presumably the sedative, but seemed to shirk its influence quickly and without lasting effects.

An older Jysa, wrapped in a thin white shawl Mantle, addressed the nearest Purifiers before following them back to Marsilias and other expedition leaders. "Hello, I am Maesa'kyana, chief retriever of the Imarah clan." They offered their names and he resumed, "All is prepared, so please board one of the two couriers."

"I have one question first," Inka interjected. "How are we supposed to penetrate the sky-city in these defunct models? The corporations have been unsuccessfully attempting to gain entrance for centuries."

"The Jysa possess the key," Maesa'Kyana replied, "our couriers will deliver us to the sky-city without difficulty. Now, board please, the city is soon to set." He urged them on with a wave before directing two of his subordinates to assume command over the far courier. Jade, mostly recovered, mounted the first ship along with Serras and six Purifiers; the rest situated themselves in the second aircraft.

Maesa'Kyana and the other Jysa buckled themselves into the pilots' seats, pressing their hands onto a series of glowing interfaces. The courier's interior brightened as walls of Jysa script bloomed upon every visible surface. The pilots flexed, and a ripple swam along the vessels frames.

The couriers arched as if stretching and unfurled delicate, humming wings; a motion mirrored by the pilots. Jade entrenched herself in one of the seats and grasped a support handle. The couriers wings swept down and back, propelling the couriers through the heat barrier and then soaring up over Imarah, where they settled into a gliding circle—every movement preceded by and reflected in minute shifts by the pilots, as if mentally linked.

Serras vacated her seat to peer out the adjacent window. "What are they waiting for?"

Jade checked her own window, then unbuckled to peer out Serras's side. "Probably that." She indicated the whirlpool of clouds swirling over Imarah and the beams of light lancing from them.

The clouds folded inward, devolving into a churning mass. Yet, the lights shone brighter, gradually widening from the storm's center and merging into a column miles wide. The clouds boiled up its exterior and merged into the storm.

Something flashed in the light and a circular base emerged from the clouds. It expanded as more of the object appeared, manifesting into a transparent sphere. The sky-city continued descending, revealing several rings of expansive white stone arching around the sphere's interior at perfect intervals. Suddenly, the light exploded outward, inundating the panorama in golden radiance. There, levitating at the sky-city's epicenter, floated a golden orb of light.

Jade steadied herself against the wall, staring unabashedly open-mouthed. "That's a sky-city?"

"I've seen images," Serras replied, equally awed, "but I didn't expect this."

The couriers altered their course toward the sky-city as Maesa'kyana laughed softly. "Drink it in, this is a sight few ever see. Pleiades has an hour-long dip on an eight-month cycle and is the sole sky-city in this region. Most only descend every couple of years; I know one that operates on a century-long cycle; it'll be emerging in forty-three years. Also, best activate your protection lenses; that false sun can damage your eyes."

The couriers soared closer, aiming to pass between two of the immense stone rings. Jade frowned as they neared, noticing how the encasing orb appeared solid. "What's that surrounding it? Glass?"

"Not like any we've ever seen," Maesa'kyana responded. "A fleet of Leviathan class warships couldn't so much as chip its exterior. Ships can't pass through it either, nor humans in personal vehicles, or any form of organic life we are aware of."

"Then how do you get through?" Jade asked.

"Imarah taught us. The other clan ships as well. They do not tell us where the knowledge derives from, or their own origins, but they taught us much we would not otherwise have learned when our peoples diverged all those centuries ago."

At some point in humanity's early history on this world, the Jysa's ancestors had discovered their clan vessels and received an invitation to travel with them. They, and many others, had accepted and evolved into a different culture. Much like the sky-cities, no one knew the clan vessels' origins, only that they predated humanity's arrival by centuries, and possessed technology far exceeding their understanding.

Jade shifted to look back at the Jysa. "What is the key then?"

Without answering, Maesa'kyana and his copilot leaned back and started a relaxed, rhythmic chant. The courier's Jysa script responded, brightening and multiplying across the exterior until it inundated the surface entirely. The pilots maintained their chant and spun the couriers onto their sides so they aligned with the sky-city's rings. A moment later, they reached the crystalline barrier and passed harmlessly through.

Once inside, the Jysa glided their ships through open airspace within the sky-city, navigating the numerous bisecting walkways, bridges, and structures. The city itself was erected solely on the interior of the rings, its edifices jutting toward the false sun. Despite its proximity to the sun, the city possessed all the furnishings of a metropolis with parks, carefully arranged streets, open markets, and rushing streams—as prevalent as the streets themselves—that coursed along in defiance of gravity.

Unfazed by the city, the Jysa piloted their couriers to an extensive stone courtyard arrayed with fountains. As the ships quieted, Maesa'kyana rotated his seat to face them. "Be careful with your first steps; this sphere distorts our planet's natural gravity for its own. It can be disarming at first, but you'll adapt soon enough. We have about forty minutes before the city rises again, so find your feet quickly."

Opening the door, Jade stepped out and initially all seemed normal, then her gaze followed the unnatural arch of the street up over her head, across the sky, down the other side to pass over the ocean perpendicularly below her before ultimately returning to her feet. Suddenly nauseous, she stumbled and fell, vertigo warring with the gravity that dragged her back to the wet cobbles. Helpless, she just stared at the elegant white stone far away, facing down toward her native world as Purifiers crumpled and gagged all around her.

Footsteps sounded beside her and Maesa'kyana sidled past, one hand gingerly maintaining contact with the courier. "Close your eyes, it helps. Try not to think about how it should be, concentrate on how it is."

She followed his advice and relief instantly soothed her reeling equilibrium. With her eyes closed, her body registered only the gravity beneath her and gradually calibrated to the sky-city's orientation. It was several minutes of laying down then tentative movements before she and the Purifiers began to acclimate properly.

Jade waited until she could stomach moving about before crawling to her feet and stumbling into one of the alleys, feet splashing through puddles in the ancient streets. Maesa'kyana called a warning after her, and she responded with an acknowledging gesture. Once separated by several corners, she slumped against a wall, ducking beneath an awning that dripped with ocean-smelling water, and activated her earpiece. "All right, I'm ready, but be careful the group's not too far away."

"I'm already present." She shoved off the wall with a stifled profanity, spinning on her heel to face Chandris as he phased through the stone. "I arrived hours ago and saw your approach."

Staggering from her abrupt movement, she caught herself. "Don't sneak up from behind next time."

He cocked his head. "Considering your capabilities, I assumed you would be accustomed to individuals ignoring solid barriers."

"It's different when it's somebody else out of the blue, and Specters aren't that common; there isn't enough Ghost-Powder to check every newborn and empower active Specters."

"Ghost-Powder?"

"A substance used to waken a Specter's abilities; Invokers generate it by exhausting cards and accumulating it in canisters on their arms. When the canisters are full, the Invokers present them to the Savant Corporation for distribution."

"Do you imbibe it?"

"I used to, and hated it. It tasted like chalk. Not anymore though, not since my sojourn to Afterlife. It ... changed me." There was more to it, years more, and not just Afterlife: white marble rooms running with blood, dreaming groves of flowers, of sand stretching for miles, and of wool, and brushing against things that slipped into her mind and grew, expanding and expanding until it felt like her skull would break and she could barely see anything real. But now was not the time for exploring those memories, even if they had the time.

Jade carefully pulled her hair back, redoing the bun that had torn free. "Now, can you trail the Purifiers without revealing yourself?" All of this would be for naught if he betrayed himself.

"Yes. Why do you desire my presence to go unnoticed?"

"Because I don't think telling a contingent of rebellious Purifiers hardwired to abhor revenants and an empyrean Invoker with a poor attitude—all of whom are currently involved in a secret war against an unknown *soul* intent on world ruination—that they're going to be working with a *soul* is a sensible idea. You'll freak them out, more so if they realize your objective. So just observe and stay out of sight. Don't contact me unless I'm alone or they'll know something's off."

"You wish for me to trace this rogue *soul's* connection if he attempts to manipulate your allies?"

"Yes, then we're going to hunt him down."

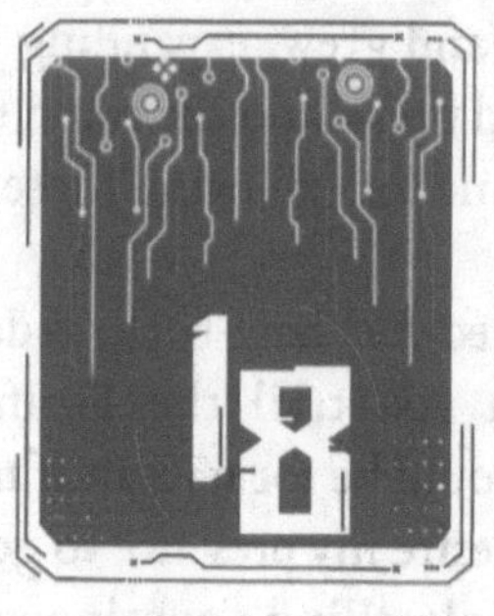

The Vacant City

Summoned by a call from Serras, Jade returned to the Purifiers and Jysa, finding all, except the three standing vigil, in tense assemblage around Inka Nadiru. She slipped through them, squeezing between the bulkily armored Purifiers to the small space at their center beside Inka.

Noting Jade's arrival, the Invoker extracted Marsilias's card from its wallet on her belt and addressed the Purifiers, "I need a volunteer to accept the card's effect, someone experienced with Invoker augments."

The Purifiers exchanged uneasy glances, expressions unreadable beneath their helmets. She scowled. "Are you afraid of the card or me?" They offered no reply, instigating an exasperated sigh. "If you cannot decide for yourselves, then who's the least valuable?"

One of the assembled Purifiers pushed through to the forefront. "Private Wilsen, sir."

"Stay where you are and remove your helmet." As he did so, Inka grasped his brow with a gloved hand and a spasm lashed her body. The card contorted in on itself in an impossible design amid sapphire fumes. The card tessellated and then began vacillating between sheens of sickly green and putrid brown, dying Inka's face at every conversion. She hissed, baring locked teeth and bleached eyes. The Purifier's knees buckled, depositing him on the ground with a crack of armor, mouth gaping. She thrust him back and reeled, gasping and catching her own hand as if it ached.

The Purifier tumbled, lay still then rose mechanically, surveying their surroundings with a turn of his head. Inka, her skin gradually recovering its natural hue, unsteadily began shredding Marsilias's card. "It's done."

Serras signaled the sentry Purifiers then the Jysa. "You're up; I know it's like looking for a needle in a haystack, so just take your best guess and get us moving. Purifiers! Masks down and Siphons out!"

Departing at a jog, the company dispersed to their assigned roles; one contingent scattering off to stand sentry upon the rooftops; the second, and largest, scouring the buildings they passed for threats or anything that might be what they sought, and the last guarding private Wilsen. They progressed quickly but meticulously, shepherding Wilsen from one discovery to the next, but never to any result other than a dismissal as not what they sought.

Jade, paired in the second group with Maesa'Kyana, splintered ahead, bypassing the first several structures before slowing outside the gate of a small, overgrown garden. Light, cheerful music wafted from the home's open door into a patio where a table sat slightly off-center, chairs haphazardly pulled out. A half-eaten meal of some kind cluttered the table's surface: upturned glasses, sullied cutlery, and cold meats.

They pushed into and through the garden to the house, entering a combined kitchen and living space via the open door. Unlike the patio, the kitchen was pristine, with every utensil and dish put away and a pair of boxlike robots waiting at their charging stations along the wall. The living space suffered more disorder with various devices she didn't recognize scattered across the furniture and end-tables, alongside blankets and pillows. In one corner, a stack of archaic books had spilled across a desk, upsetting the reading light and a case of manual drawing implements. In another corner, a hatch large enough to slide through led to a subterranean waterway.

Jade glanced over all of this from the threshold, recognizing little as Maesa'Kyana made a circuit of the room. "What are we looking for?"

He indicated the various littered items with a sweep of his arm. "Most of this is standard and will be encountered by Wilsen in whichever home he enters first. We're looking for something abnormal, something he's unlikely to access elsewhere." He slowed as he completed the circuit, sparing the room a final measured glance before returning to her side and exiting. "You haven't asked anything about the state of the city, did you already know what we would find?"

"My parents were Jysa," Jade replied, pausing briefly to tally the members of their party and verify none had disappeared, before continuing down the street in Maesa'Kyana's wake. "They told us what they found in the sky-cities." A half-truth. They had spoken of what they found, but she had learned far more later on.

Maesa'Kyana glanced back. "What happened to them?"

Jade shrugged, hands slipping in her coat as they bypassed the subsequent house. "It's complicated. Suffice to say, they got involved in something they shouldn't have." She flinched even as she said it, realizing that, in her distraction at examining the city, she had absently spoken a truth better left unsaid, and in so doing contradicted her earlier lie to Dama Nhr'irena.

His attention shifted to the soaring, uniform structure on their left, finding the entrance before venturing the next question, "Why are you not with your clan?"

Too late now to repeat her earlier lie, Jade settled for ambiguity and hoped he would let it lie. "Stuff happened. It's complicated."

They reached the entrance and ascended to the half-open sliding door, which forced them to squeeze in sideways to enter. He passed through first, features displaying a just barely visible mix of concern and confusion. "What was your clan's name?"

She slipped in behind him with little difficulty. "You wouldn't know it, we were a small clan and...."

They stood upon a catwalk over a sunken, cavernous room of churning machinery. The walls whirled with arms and appendages, a storm of devices and pieces being passed along and assembled, of materials being snatched from storage drums on the floor, and cascades of sparks as objects were welded shut. An object emerged from that whirlwind, a square box roughly a foot in size whose exterior constantly folded inward, over, around itself like a self-arranging matryoshka, and was placed besides dozens of others on the far side of the room. The floor was dominated in conveyor belts streaming into the room from all asides, emerging from myriad tunnels whose walls were likewise inundated with machinery. The conveyors delivered sleek, clear beams of hard material to a central repository where they had amassed into a tower hundreds of feet wide and almost tall enough to scrape the ceiling. *Duraglau*, Jade realized belatedly, overwhelmed by the sheer amount of activity before her.

The sky-cities were entirely self-sustaining ecosystems—food, energy, materials, devices—and whatever it was that had occurred to the population had either left those systems unaffected, or—most likely—occurred so abruptly that it offered no chance to deactivate them. Regardless of the reason, their factories worked incessantly, deconstructing and reforming ambient material on the atomic level to create whatever they needed, stopping only when their storage filled. The Jysa profited from this, scavenging as many of these materials as they could, whenever a sky-city descended, and trading them to the corporations.

Maesa'Kyana quickly examined the interior then tapped her shoulder with a jerk of his head to leave. She nodded and they squeezed out, pausing to mark the entrance for inspection with a bright signal device before continuing down the street.

Starting toward the next structure, Maesa'Kyana prompted her to continue with a gesture. "You were a small clan and...?"

She blinked, looked at him, then shook off the lingering shock of the factory. "Oh nothing, just a small clan, no one can ever remember the name of." Not even herself.

His curiosity remained evident, but the concern deepened in his features until his mouth opened to speak–

"Really, don't bother," she said before he could start. "I was young, too young to remember our name properly." It was a lie, but it was also easily believable, which was usually enough for people who wanted to like you.

Understanding eased the tension from his features. "Ah, of course. Probably could have figured that out myself, seeing as you're so young now. Sorry." They veered left again, approaching the next structure in line. "You know, you could probably return to us, find another clan to live with. It wouldn't take much, most of us would be glad to have you; and since you are Jysa, the Corporations wouldn't have much say."

The offer struck like a slap, and for an instant she glimpsed a different life, an existence outside the reach of Purifiers, revenants, and Redeemers, where the *soul* inhabiting her brother's corpse wasn't a constant presence in her thoughts. Then Jade remembered the disease, and the PLAN, and all the ensuing devastation if she permitted herself the cowardice of escaping. Externally, she shrugged. "It sounds nice. Maybe someday, when I've done all I need to."

Inside the third structure, the walls thrummed with valves and nozzles, and burst and clicked with switches and gears. A blue automaton presided over it, surfing the walls on a multitude of limbs, never touching the floor.

Maesa'kyana caught Jade as she moved to enter. "Best stay outside, that particular machine reacts poorly to intrusions."

"What if it's what we're looking for?"

"Unlikely, but it's also large enough to be visible from the street. Wilsen will see it as he passes by."

She withdrew with a frustrated sigh, raking a hand over her hair and stealing another count of the troops. "This isn't working. We have no inkling of where to look, and the city is huge."

"We're not wandering randomly," he replied, gesturing for her to follow. "Every branch of the city has an epicenter, a control nexus through which all information and every autonomous command and action flows. We just need to find it so Wilsen can access the information."

"You don't know where it is?"

"It moves between visits."

"Then how do we find it?"

"There's always an access room from the main road. Once we find it, we can direct you from there, though the journey is disorienting."

"Why search the buildings then?"

"On the off-chance we get lucky."

A Jysa skidded to a stop beside them, gasping, "We found an access room," and then reversed direction without tarrying for acknowledgment. Jade and Maesa'kyana sprinted after him.

Reaching the congregation, they pushed through to where Wilsen crouched beneath Serras's uneasy vigil, his fingers dancing over the surface of a revolving white cobblestone box that appeared to have ejected from the street. Something activated with a buzz and a click, and the box recessed into the ground, the cobbles around it folding outward and compacting onto one another without accruing mass or size. As the opening expanded from the levitating box, some cobbles folded downward, multiplying and assembling into a curved stair with rails and illumined footprints on each step.

Private Wilsen began his descent without waiting for the ordering stairs to finish, the card's spell of comprehension and knowledge granting him assurance the rest of them lacked. Warily, they followed, eye lenses brightening as they activated the night vision features.

The stairway descended through almost a minute's worth of unchanging, claustrophobic stone, leading ultimately to a square, darkened room of pliant, gelatinous material. Lights blinked on in the walls, painting the company in obscuring pearl hues.

The Purifiers carefully dispersed, by turns scanning the material with their lenses and taking samples with syringe like devices from their belts. The Jysa knelt at its center, leaning forward and spreading their arms across the floor.

Serras noted this and crossed to kneel beside them, her own lens visible as two bright rings of yellow light despite her visor. "What's about to happen?"

"We're about to travel," Maesa'kyana replied, sliding his bare hand into the floor. He appeared to briefly fumble for something then find it. "I suggest you all sit as it can be unsettling; close your eyes as well if you want to keep what's left of your breakfasts."

The party exchanged questioning glances and sank to the ground, finding what purchase they could. Only Private Wilsen remained standing, staring unresponsively at the walls. For a moment, nothing happened then the room lurched, distorting right as if pulled, causing all to feel as if they were outside looking down; then it snapped back into focus, sending everyone into a sprawling heap.

Jade caught herself on her hands and locked in, staring hard at the floor as the room and her center of gravity kept spinning around and round. Her senses reeled, quarreling so violently with whatever just transpired it took a moment to realize her environment had changed. Where before there had been a pliant, pearl gelatin substance, now there was a corridor of white stone running to unseen destinations with walls of ever-shifting machinery she couldn't begin to parse.

Jade jumped to her feet and spun, alarm firing through her. *"Okay, okay, calm down. Find entrances: none. Exits? None. Just the corridor. No cover, no access points for ventilation or piping. Need to figure out where we are in relation to the ships for escape route."* Her alarm gradually subsided, assuaged by the Jysa milling through the group with calm assurance, alternating between soothing the retching Purifiers and explaining what had occurred to the rest.

Maesa'kyana noted her and migrated closer. "You recovered remarkably quick."

"What just happened?" she asked, straining but failing to contain a sliver of bite from her words.

"We were teleported to the quadrant's central hub; we talked about it just before finding the access point, remember?"

She exhaled to calm herself and carefully flexed her fingers. "Where are we exactly, in relation to our ships, and do you have a way back."

"I don't rightly know; like I said the city moves in between visits. As for returning, Private Wilsen should be able to be able to activate a different room when the time comes."

The last of her immediate tension eased away. "How does it work? The room?"

"The green room we entered serves as a device for long-distance travel; it could transport us anywhere in the city."

She muttered a low grumble. "You might have warned us."

"I did." A tiny, amused quirk twitched at his lips.

"That barely counts." She rubbed at her forehead, trying to massage out the ache. "How did you even discover that? Let alone learn to control it?"

"Happenstance; we stumbled upon a similar access room a few centuries back and through natural curiosity discovered that the walls were porous. Several cautious experiments later, we learned that every access room has a switch that will teleport the occupants to the precinct's center hub," he indicated their surroundings, "but have gleaned little besides."

"And these hubs communicate with every machine and program

in the city, or just their precinct?"

"We believe the city."

"How? Where's the console, a port, anything?" she trailed off, her attention shifting to Private Wilsen as he moved toward the right-hand wall.

The machines, lights, and shifting foundations rippled at his approach, convulsing together without altering their tranquil rhythm or hiccuping. As his hand brushed them, they withdrew and erupted into activity, some elements disintegrating into particles, others deconstructing themselves into segments, and a bare few staying whole. The entire mass, perfectly synchronized, tumbled over itself, assembling into a larger, many-limbed entity that reaffixed itself on the wall, occupying a space of about twelve feet long. Possessed of a long, head-like appendage, the machine shifted toward Wilsen and extended a sleek limb of white metal and gently coiling azure energy. A holographic console materialized.

Jade blinked in confusion. "They still use physical consoles? I would've thought a society as advanced as this would have progressed beyond our level of communication."

"The Jysa have always interpreted it as the city translating the way it communicates into a medium we understand."

"You've ... conversed with it before?"

"Not really. We don't understand its language or any of its symbols, and its attempted multiple different languages, including visual, phonetic, and physical contact."

"You'd think a program that advanced could interpret our language."

"Yes, but we can't bypass the password to actively communicate with it."

"Password?"

"The console always opens to the same screen: a series of letters or words or numbers."

As they watched, Wilsen, empowered by the card, assessed the console and tapped a complex pattern across its surface. His eyes flicked from side to side, registering the flood of images flashing past.

"Just imagine how much he's learning," Jade said softly, "all the information he's accumulated just by traversing the city, let alone accessing the network."

Inka stepped beside them, moving steadily but still appearing slightly green in the face. "He won't remember anything. He couldn't physically handle that much information inundating his mind. He's like a sieve, everything he learns just flows through and is immediately forgotten. The only thing he retains is information patterns keyed into his brain, specifically those about the device we need."

Jade frowned. "I don't remember anyone doing that."

"No one did. It was all in Marsilias's card; even the sub-conscious state is induced. It's incredible he managed to achieve that level of intricacy in the span of a night."

Across from them, Wilsen shifted focus from the console to the machine generating it. The machine straightened, two of its appendages abandoning their indefinable tasks to link as one, their azure currents merging into a seamless energy stream beneath their white shells. They whirled and contracted, operating with one another in a flurry of muted clicks, subsidiary appendages emerging from the wall with wiring, cobalt vials, pale metals, and a multitude of minute devices. It completed the assembly in seconds and delivered to Wilsen a disc-like contraption. Then it furled in on itself and reverted to its earlier thronging. Private Wilsen staggered back, eyesight clearing.

Serras caught him before he fell. "Is that it? The device?"

Wilsen shook his head weakly. "N ... no. This is just the key."

"The key?"

"To access the machine we need."

"Where's the machine?"

Everyone perceived it simultaneously, a sense of unnaturalness, a brush of damp that evolved into brown mist. Serras managed a single, "ah, hell," before the first revenant prowled around the corner behind them. Her Siphon erupted in a burst of yellow so vibrant it effaced all other sources of illumination. She vaulted toward the ceiling and dove at the revenant: a behemoth of muscle and heads.

Jade was already firing, a training Siphon in each hand as her earpiece spat stats, "Second-tier revenant, spirit-level twelve...." The snarling energy bolts fizzled ineffectively on the creature's skin, but its eyes snapped to her regardless. Then Serras's Siphon, an oversized scythe, swept down, shearing through the revenant and gouging a molten fissure in the floor. The revenant's two halves contorted, blazing for an instant before disintegrating into liquid energy and streaming into Serras's ravenous Siphon. The mutilated floor repaired itself instantly, exposing, only for that instant, a cascade of minute robots. Then an alarm blared through the corridor.

"Move!" Serras barked, her mask activating its ventilation ports over her mouth and nostril slits. "Get to the surface; prioritize the key and Private Wilsen."

The room exploded with polychrome crackling light as the Purifiers ignited their Siphons. Screams and howls echoed from the corridor as a half-dozen tributary passageways opened of their own accord, heralding further revenants.

Jade reeled, panic—sharp and sudden as a gunshot—squeezing her lungs. The vision of an ice field enveloped her mind, the sky overhead screaming with a siren as the missiles began to fall. They were being overrun, there weren't enough Purifiers in proximity to reinforce, the revenants had to be contained. Take cover. She had to take cover.

Serras's voice barked through the group's communication channel. "Everyone, report in." A cascade of names answered her command, enumerating eleven Purifiers, two Jysa, and Connor, who spoke for Ruon. "Roger," Serras continued, "we're missing three operatives, one Purifier and two Jysa. That's three gates. Close them down. Jade-"

Revenants swarmed into their corridor, eerily silent—except for the music of their being—and sleek, as if designed for this environment. The Purifiers scattered, some vaulting to the ceiling and walls and others diving into the oncoming revenants. The two forces collided and whirled, erupting in a ballet of fire veiled by thrashing black tatters.

Jade squeezed her eyes shut against the visions in her mind and pushed through to Serras. "What do you need?"

Serras caught her shoulder and spun her to face south-west. "Tracking chips say one's that way! Find whoever opened it! Incapacitate and protect them until we arrive!"

"We don't have time for all of them-"

"Don't worry about that, just go." She shoved Jade and spun. "Inka!"

Jade grit her teeth and sprinted toward the solid wall, exhaling.

She passed through scrambling Purifiers, the wall, and into another corridor inundated with revenants. They screamed and slashed in response, but struck only air.

All the same, her memories boiled to the surface, a tide of black clad monstrosities within and without, towering above and around her like trees, blotting out the sun as they screamed and slashed. Voices also, screaming and begging in her ears, crackling over the microphone as they called for help: "We're being overrun!" "Help! Help! God, somebody plea–" Ilin, her brother, roaring as he pulled a typhoon of livid flame into existence, caging all the monsters within its center. Friends shrieking as they burned alive. Missiles falling like rain, shaking the world.

Jade phased through the opposite wall into a small room and stumbled to a halt, frantically trying to distinguish reality from hallucination. One of the Jysa, covered in black markings, knelt alone at its center, his hands pressed into the floor before a fulminating gate. Golden light oozed from his chest and shoulders, streaming down his arms to sustain the gate with his own life-force. The golden energy distorted near its center, warping outward in the silhouette of a reaching hand, and then rent, ushering a revenant into her world.

The creature shook itself, tatters fluttering over golden luminescence, and stalked from the chamber, its voice joining the symphony of its distant kin. In its wake, the shroud of energy reformed, new shapes already manifesting in the other dimension beyond.

Jade saw and registered all of this in the span of her first step, and by her second was diving for the Jysa. She inhaled at the final instant and crashed into the Jysa, tackling him to the floor and disrupting the connection linking him to the rift.

He thrashed in her grip, pummeling her where she clutched his back, arms and legs locked around his middle. She reared her head back, evading a blow, dug into a pocket of her coat, then grabbed the nape of his neck and activated a shock charge. Electricity shot from her hand, battering the Jysa's body, and rebounding ineffectually off her armor. The man spasmed into unconsciousness, flopping comically as another revenant emerged from the wavering portal.

It sung a note and leapt at her. She gripped the man and shoved off the nearby wall, rolling them both from the revenant's reach. It hit the wall and she heaved the stunned man away, vaulting to her feet. The revenant pivoted, sleek, fingerless appendages launching it off the wall.

She exhaled and the revenant plowed through her. But she wasn't the target. Its head snapped forward, bladed-tongue lancing to impale the downed Jysa. Jade lunged after it, Siphons igniting as the revenant drank. But it only took seconds for the Jysa to shrivel, his skin graying and body-mass withering to bones and papery flesh.

She slammed into the revenant, planting her Siphons in its back and pushing. It howled and arched. She drove harder, forcing it against the wall and tearing the blades free. Then she slashed, lacerating its flanks, and golden light gushed out, engulfing her in warmth and blinding her. She struck again and again, and the creature wilted, fading like the gate dissolving behind her.

Suddenly, a new violet light blazed from the northern wall. Jade vaulted back, automatically exhaling into the First Step. Purifiers burst from the light, flooding in from a hazy doorway and firing wild blasts in their wake. Connor tumbled in after them, shredding a card as he went. The door vanished, severing a pursuing revenant in half.

Connor rushed to her as Purifiers scattered to the various exits. "Where is he?"

"Dead." Inhaling to vacate the First Step, she tapped her earpiece. "Serras, the revenants might be killing the gate-openers to prevent interrogation."

"Yeah, we just barely managed to save ours. How's yours?"

"Dead."

"Move to the last one then. Also, the sky-city's acting up."

"What do you mean?"

"Some kind of … automata appeared from nowhere and attacked us. It just materialized in the air."

"What the–"

The southern wall exploded, showering them in a hail of stones as a revenant plowed through, the corridor behind it now feeding directly into their room. Jade dove, trying to enter the First Step but its horned head slammed her, punching the breath from her lungs.

She gasped desperately, one hand flailing for a weapon as it slammed her against the opposite wall. Her armor flared, spraying sparks as coils burst across her back. The revenant reared, preparing for another battery as she slid to the ground. Jade wheezed an exhale and faded. The revenant stomped down, fracturing the wall, but passed harmlessly through her. Heedless of her screaming ribs, she thrust forward off the wall, igniting a Siphon as she phased between its legs.

Now directly beneath the revenant, Jade spun over, inhaled, and stabbed up. It reeled in shock, then rammed forward again in frenzied stomping. Already exhaling, Jade scrambled aside as the adaptive suit warmed against her skin, the heat preempting a storm of needle-pricks across her body, injections full of medical drugs and nanobots.

Leaping to a crouch, she inhaled and hurled another Siphon into the revenant's flank. It stumbled but caught itself and swung to face her, form burgeoning until it scraped the ceiling. A Purifier sprinted behind it, her exorbitantly long-blade Siphon slashing its back legs. The revenant howled and shrank, the woman's Siphon flaring brighter. It whirled after her, lashing with its horns as golden energy streamed freely from its hewn limbs, trying and failing to restore them.

Jade darted forward, grasped her training Siphon where it protruded from its flank and ripped downward. The revenant snapped at Jade, who danced back. It pursued her, and while it was distracted, the other Purifier sprinted up the wall, vaulted, and drove her Siphon through its skull.

They crashed to the ground, the Purifier sawing her Siphon back and forth until the revenant expired. Then she raised her weapon, held in both hands at shoulder height, and charged the nearest revenant.

Jade scrambled to retrieve her two Siphons, knowing the floor she crawled on was stone, knowing it felt like stone, but only seeing ice. Her Siphons had fallen with the revenant's death and rolled apart, momentum expending as they hit a puddle of blood and slush. Jade shoved her hands into the mess, feeling nothing of the ice her mind conjured. But the blood was real, flowing slowly from the spasming body of a Purifier a few feet away, and it clung sticky and warm to her fingers as she grasped her Siphons. Jade turned away, swallowing panic and stumbling toward Connor.

She caught his coat's shoulder in a trembling hand. "Connor, we need to leave; they're all dying; we need to leave. Do you have another, another, another door card?" The words tripped and stumbled off her tongue, competing with those screaming in her mind.

He faced her, panting as an immense boulder dematerialized from the crushed remnants of a revenant. "Yeah, I got more," he mumbled, tearing one card in half with his teeth, "just been busy if you haven't noticed." His other arm snapped out, the card clenched between his fingers igniting into blue radiance. The floor ruptured a short distance away, water erupting from beneath a revenant in a roaring geyser, catching it and heaving it upward. A passing Purifier unleashed a barrage of yellow bolts into it with her Siphon pulse-cannon and immediately swapped to another target.

Connor let the water subside, crumbling the card in his hand, and pointed eastward. "We need to go that way. I can open a door, but Ruon designed them to close quickly so revenants couldn't follow through it."

Her fingers remained knotted in his coat, pulling him towards her and keeping her stable. "Can you clear the room?"

"Yeah."

She shoved him eastward, instantly swaying. "Do it, then open the door!"

Connor stabbed a hand into his pocket and the other clamped his earpiece. "Everyone, duck!"

Unhesitatingly, every Purifier dropped as Connor's hand slashed. A searing beam shot from his palm and struck the far wall, melting a foot-deep scar and incinerating revenants as he spun in a circle. Completing his revolution, Connor thrust his other hand outward. The card it held flashed and a door of luminescent silver paper unfolded from nothing on the east wall, opening into a hallway of light. "Through the door!"

The Purifiers ran for the doorway, those with ranged armaments swinging about to cover their retreat while the rest scrambled through. The hallway lasted ten to twelve feet and exited into another hallway, populated by Serras's group but unmolested by revenants.

Serras's group whirled toward them as they emerged, weapons rising for an instant before recognition occurred and sent them sprinting forward. The groups met and mingled, the injured being shuttled toward the medics as Jade shoved toward Serras—Connor and Ruon just behind. "What's going on? Did you recover the last operative and gate?"

"No, he absconded on the back of a revenant as we arrived. We don't know where the gate is."

"We don't have time to chase him," Connor said, "there's only twenty minutes left before the sky-city rises again and we're stranded."

Serras grimaced. "That's the problem; we don't know where we are in the city after the jump from the control room. We don't even know how to get to the surface. And we don't have the device."

"I don't think the device should be our priority right now," Connor replied. "We need to find a way out. Could Private Wilsen teleport us to our ships if we returned to the hub room?"

"Yes, but it's swarming with revenants and whatever it is the city keeps making."

"What do you mean keeps making?" Jade asked.

Before Serras could respond, a crackling energy stabbed from the ceiling into the Purifiers' midst, eliciting a storm of profanity and exclamations. They all vaulted back, brandishing weapons as two more streams joined the first. The currents fluctuated symmetrically, arching, expanding, and shrinking as a form gestated at their connection. An automaton materialized seconds later, its midsection humanoid and suspended on a dozen limbs, all comprised of white stone and connected with azure energy.

"That's what I mean," Serras snarled, her scythe dissolving into its dainty, flower decorated canister. With her free hand, she retrieved a second Siphon from its sheath on her belt, this one an undecorated training Siphon humming with yellow energy. The second Siphon ignited, expanding into a pulse-cannon as Purifiers across the room unloaded on the android to minimal effect. Serras leveled her weapon, squeezed the trigger, and sable electricity blazed from the muzzle. It lanced into the android, staggering it and obliterating an arm. Blue energy instantly shot from the wall, assembling a replacement appendage. The android exploded toward Serras.

Jade lunged aside, exhaling, as Serras effortlessly switched to her scythe Siphon and rolled past the android, amputating three of its limbs.

"We need to destroy it entirely in one go," Jade yelled, returning from the First Step and scanning the room. "Wait, where's Inka?" She searched again but saw no sign of the empyrean Invoker. Standing, she exhaled, leapt through the wall into another hallway empty of revenants, and inhaled, tapping her earpiece. "Chandris? Did you see a fourth person leave? A woman, Inka Nadiru?"

After a brief delay, his illusion phased into her corridor. "Yes. She departed shortly after Primess Serras's arrival in the previous corridor. She took the device Private Wilsen acquired from the city."

"Why did she leave?"

"She spoke to no one, but her essence throbbed with a tumor of *Oscuras*: the manifestation of death energy."

"The other *soul* must be manipulating her. Did you follow?"

"Yes, until you called me."

"Where is she?"

"I am uncertain as she continued moving."

"Wait, she didn't open a gate?"

"No. Nor did she move with purpose."

"But why? What else could the *soul* wa– The device! She's trying to destroy it! Chandris, can you find her again?"

"Yes."

"Lead me to her immediately."

He slipped through the wall at a south-easterly bent. Jade exhaled and dashed in pursuit. Rooms, corridors, monsters, and machines passed in a parade of colors and distorted sounds, some thronging in battle, others secret and hidden away between the walls and within the floor: long, thin chambers where the arms of robots whirled about one another, building or repairing something vast she could not see. Chandris led through all of this, trusting her to keep pace even when there was no light. He slowed only as they crossed through a final wall into a room of short white pillars, the space within unlit except for the hairline veins of blue energy that swathed the pillars.

Inka knelt before one of these, her hands pressed against its surface and her skin awash in the unmistakable black markings.

Merciless, Jade pulled a shock charge from her pocket, inhaled, and flung it at Inka. The device struck her shoulder, latched magnetically on, and erupted with electricity, throwing the woman into a pillar and then down into a spasming heap. As she fell, her body revealed an open compartment in the pillar's side, within it a transparent cylindrical device about a foot long and half that in diameter. Two handholds protruded from its sides while the middle segment and interior seemed comprised of rotating disks, each with individual screens.

Jade never saw it. The moment she emerged from the First Step, blades of pain drove into her lungs and shot outward. Her breath tore out of her in a rasp, and she dropped, clutching her chest as her vision flickered and went black. Her lungs spasmed, trying to inhale but failing to expand. Blood exploded from her mouth, followed by another desperate, instinctive attempt to inhale that failed. She'd inhabited the First Step too long.

Her adaptive suit erupted into renewed action, ejecting needles across her body to stimulate pressure points and inject drugs to null pain, heighten mental function, and link to her nervous system: first inserting commands to breathe that her body failed to accept, then driving syringes into her deflated lungs and pumping them full of oxygen. They expanded involuntarily and her vision cleared, the pain throughout her body numbing as the analgesics took effect.

She gradually became aware of Chandris speaking, his words first a muffled whisper, then gradually evolving into clarity, "... Should I bring your companions for assistance?"

Her adaptive suit contracted her lungs manually, expelling the air from her with a cough. This time when the inhale reflex occurred, her lungs answered fitfully, allowing her just enough air to wheeze out, "No."

Rolling weakly onto her front, she placed trembling hands into the ground and then pushed herself up. The world spun but her body continued to obey her, carrying her first to her feet then across to where Inka lay, the black markings already beginning to fade. Ignoring the device momentarily, she removed the shock charge and slapped the woman's cheek. "C'mon, wake up. We don't have time for you to be sleeping on the job."

Chandris crouched beside her, examining the device though he spoke to her, "Are you sure that it is wise to wake her?"

"I can't carry her out," Jade replied weakly, "and I can't abandon her." Images of dead Purifiers began filling her mind, corpses bleeding out on the snow and ice, staring at her. She squeezed her eyes shut, pleading that it would help. "*Not real. Not real. Not real. Why aren't you waking!*" Jade shoved off the woman with a strangled sound and crawled over her unresponsive body to snatch the artifact from its compartment. She stored it in one of her armor's prepared nooks and delved into one of her coat's pockets, cycling through the various medical equipment by touch until she found what she needed.

She shuffled around to face Inka and slapped her again, harder than before to the same effect. She hissed, twitching at a swell of periphery noise, and yanked on the woman's sleeve, rolling back her armor and clothes to expose the adaptive suit. Then she ejected the pulse-knife from its casing on her wrist and slashed the adaptive suit up to Inka's elbow. Into the exposed skin she pressed a small, circular canister, which activated with a hiss, the surface impacting inward. Normally Inka's suit could have effectuated this, but the shock grenade would have short circuited its functions.

Inka snapped awake with a gasp and lurched upright, staring frantically at her surroundings and clutching her injected hand to her chest. "Wha–Where...?"

Jade caught her shoulder, steadying her. "Hey, just breathe. I know it hurts, it's supposed to; it's a synthetic, adrenaline-like substance that affects you both physically and mentally. I needed to wake you and didn't have a better option on me." She glanced about, frantically remembering Chandris only to find the *soul* gone. Relieved, she returned her attention to Inka. "Listen, we have to go; you were possessed by the *soul* and sent to destroy or collect the artifact. I don't know which. Doesn't matter. I stopped you, but now we're cut off from the others and I can't carry you."

Inka nodded. "I can get us there."

"You have another door card?"

"No. Too far. I need to do something a little more extreme." She stood with Jade's assistance, her hand diving into a square wallet on her belt to retrieve a card. "Which way?"

"There."

She shifted and a pulse of molten-hued energy flowed down Inka's arm before reversing to her shoulder. "Stay close to me," she warned, "I don't want you melting in the collateral."

"Wha–"

A laser of white, molten fire exploded from the card, expanding to the width of a skimmer. It struck the wall and consumed it, melting the stone in a wave of red. Jade ducked as the rebounding heat washed over them, distorting the floor, pillars, and ceiling everywhere, except a circular space around Inka.

The laser concluded as suddenly as it appeared, leaving Jade facing a corridor of sizzling stone. She peered closer at the entrance, cautious of the residual dripping stone. "Are you sure you didn't kill them?"

"I cut the card's effect short to avoid that." Stuffing the exhausted card into a package marked for such, she extracted a second card and activated it. The card rippled and a hover bike materialized. "Get on, the floor's too hot to walk."

Jade shakily mounted behind the Invoker. "Can you drive this thing?"

"Don't have to; it has an automated system. Hang on." Inka pressed a hand to a console on the bike's dashboard and it accelerated.

Maintaining a grip around Inka's waist, Jade tapped her earpiece. "Serras, can you hear me? I found the device."

"What? How?"

"The *soul* possessed Inka, tried to make her do something to it, but I stopped her in time. We're on our way back now."

"How is she?"

"Fine, but we gotta leave, had to do some remodeling and I don't think the city's going to like it."

"Oh, that was you two?"

"Inka. Did you see the laser?"

"No. Felt the heat though."

A distant, escalating hum shook the city, silencing them both. "Did you feel that?"

"Yeah," Serras replied grimly.

A surge of energy streaked along the corridor, blanketing them for a split second before submerging beneath the surface like water into dirt.

Panic, briefly quelled by finding Inka, began to rise. "Serras we need an exit strategy now, some way to get to the street-level and then all of us to our shi-" A sharp, metallic screech reverberated through the city and the energy arched from the walls again, coalescing into numerous different nucleuses down the corridors they passed. In response, Jade heard Serras screaming through the earpiece for Connor. A boom shook the walls shortly thereafter.

Inka stopped the hover bike abruptly, pulling up just shy of where their path ended at a partially melted wall. She stepped off, letting the bike fall with a clatter as Jade scrambled to follow, and dove into her wallet again. Raising an arm against the heat, she withdrew a door card, activated it on the wall, and then sprinted through. Two corridors later, they crossed into a battered room littered with debris, shredded black fabric, and fragmented stone. The Purifiers and Jysa all crouched beneath an opening atop a gray, jittering disc. In their midst were the screaming and whimpering injured, and the heaped together dead, some bent and twisted at grotesque angles, some cut and bleeding, some missing limbs, and the rest soul-sucked husks. A gaping hole in the ceiling illuminated everyone in the rays of the sky-city's sun and pattered them with a drizzle of salty rain.

Her foot struck something, she didn't see what, and she fell, knees crashing to the rubble with a crack of armor and her hands scrapping over it. "*Again. Dead again. All of them dead.*" She vomited, the bile filling the visor of her helmet and splashing back on her with its stench.

Hands gripped her coat, dragging her forward and up, then a voice—Inka's from somewhere else—intruding on her screaming mind, "What is this?"

Fresh air flooded in around her as whoever had dragged her forward tore off her helmet. She gasped at it, forcing her eyes to open, to try and see beyond the visions.

Heard in her periphery, the response came to Inka's question, "Don't know, the Redhead said it was some kind of lift when he conjured it."

The presence beside Jade was pushing her down, squeezing her against the increasingly excited platform.

Serras's voice barked through her earpiece, "Everyone's here. Hang on!" The disc rocketed upward, blasting through a dozen gutted, and rapidly closing floors before bursting into the open air with a scream of passing wind. Its momentum crested then reversed, dropping to crash just beside their exit shaft, dislodging Jade and the outermost Purifiers onto the cobbles with the impact. She fell awkwardly and scrambled to right herself—teeth grinding until they hurt—and felt a steady grip. She glanced over and found Ruon crouched beside her, scratched and bleeding slightly, but calm. He was holding her arm, gentle but firm. Tangible. Real. Her heartbeat slowed slightly. *"It's okay; look at him, he's alive, we're alive. The device, we have the device. Worth it. It was worth it. It has to be worth it."*

He nodded quietly, and scrambled to stand, raising a scarred Siphon cylinder, the colorless energy sparking within an indication of black-market provenance. Jade followed wobbly to her feet, recognizing the telltale arcs of energy swelling from the cobbles, hissing in the soft rain as assailing machines formed. Responding barrages of ranged Siphons swept from the clustered Purifiers but inflicted little damage.

She backed deeper into the group, fumbling through various pockets for the pieces of a different weapon. Even as she did so, she scanned the buildings around them, desperate for a recognizable landmark. *"Gotta find the ships, gotta get out of here. How much time left? Do we even have time? Don't know, don't know. Need a solution or everyone's going to die. Connor, Ruon—No don't think about that! Solution."*

Then Inka's voice screaming through her earpiece, "Clear a space!"

The Purifiers and Jysa expanded their circle, with those lacking ranged Siphons scrambling to detach canister rifles—explosive projectile weapons rather than pulse-based—from racks on their backs. An instant later, a wave of thumb-sized shells shot from their formation and smashed into the frontmost machines with a cavalcade of explosions, scattering flecks of stone and lashing cords of energy. The onslaught of machines faltered and immediately began reforming.

A metallic boom sounded behind Jade and a long shadow stretched over her. She heard Inka shouting, "We're ready, get in." She shot a glance over her shoulder and saw a black, military grade transport aircraft: Pelican class.

Jade collapsed her canister rifle, no time to disassemble it, stuffed it into a coat pocket, and vaulted into the aircraft.

Serras's voice barked over the comms again. "No, forget the dead. We don't have time! Get in!"

"*No.*" Jade twisted back and saw them, the corpses sprawled outside the aircraft, abandoned. "*No, can't leave them. Save them!*" She tried to return, but the Purifiers and Jysa swarming in dragged her deeper into the aircraft.

Then the floor lurched and the aircraft was roaring skyward, weaving through the buildings to the open space above. It hit the open air, spun, and dove ocean-ward through the sky-city's rings.

Jade dropped to the isle between the seats, biting down on her fist to stifle a scream. "*Abandoned them. Dead. All of them dead. Because of you, because of me. Dead because I came here. Dead because I didn't finish it the first time.*"

The humming barrier was rushing toward them and people were grabbing handholds. They reached it. And passed through.

All except Jade.

The thrumming barrier rushed into the ship as they crossed it, maintaining its shape wherever the interior allowed. When that barrier wall collided with Jade, it yanked her back, crashing through seats and edges until the aircraft's rear wall stopped her. A searing heat woke at her side, and she desperately grabbed for the device, but it tore through her armor and melted through the ship's rear plating, carried skyward by the barrier as she shrieked.

Released, she fell, hit the seat, and rolled off. The closest Purifiers crowded around her, Serras was screaming over the earpiece, demanding what was wrong, but Jade could barely hear her. She curled tight between the seat bases, clutching her ears, her face, and sobbing. Memories and hallucinations filled her world and her mind, a parade of everyone she had killed, topping off—every time —with her brother.

Orange Cake and the Tomb

Inka's conjured aircraft squeezed into Imarah's general air-dock and alighted beside the other assorted planes. Ensconced in the plane's back corner, curled around her legs, Jade barely registered it through her shock, struggling even to structure thoughts. Crowded together in the vessel's brightly lit confines, the rest of the company mourned in their own ways, slumped in the seats or swaying with hands locked around support hooks. None of them looked at her, whether from embarrassment or shame she didn't know and she couldn't bring herself to care.

The aircraft's doors slid open, prompting the group to begin filing out. Jade mechanically rose as well but as her weight shifted, her legs buckled, exhaustion and overexertion forcing her to catch herself on the next row of chairs. The reactive gasp broke into a hacking wretch as pain seared through her lungs.

Serras, seated beside her up until a moment ago, stepped beside Jade and gently slipped in beneath her arms, supporting her weight. "Take it easy, dear; you're hurt enough as it is."

Jade let her head rest against the taller woman's shoulder and watched Ruon help a wan Connor from the plane. "I'm sorry."

"Whatever for, dear?"

"For losing the device, for making you carry me out, for … I don't know; I've probably done something."

Serras reached her free hand over and flicked Jade's forehead. "Stop pitying yourself, it's not your fault; no one knew the device would react like that, especially with how the Jysa have been mining that city for years. It must treat its machines differently from its raw resources."

"Wasn't there someone else that went missing?"

"We never found him. Maesa'kyana said he might survive until the Jysa return so long as the revenants and city leave him in peace; there's enough food and water for decades."

"Their ships?"

"They'll recover them when the sky-city emerges again; they've had accidents before." She jumped from the plane first, splashing in the shallow water, and then helped Jade down.

Across the way, Marsilias entered the air-dock, scanned the group and then approached them, arriving as Jade slumped onto a storage crate.

"You didn't get it, did you?"

"No," Jade replied, "the city took it from us on our way out. You wouldn't happen to have cake?"

"Always." He retrieved a triangular container from a pocket in his coat and passed it to her with an attached fork.

"Thanks." She wasted no time unlatching the lid to a gush of chill steam. She inhaled the tang of citrus, closed her eyes, and relaxed into the first bite.

"Is that your solution to this?" Inka's voice sheared into the brief silence, tense, cracking, and volatile. "People died today for this, and you're just going to eat cake?"

Jade forced her eyes to open again, hands tightening as they fell to her lap. Inka stood before them with disheveled hair and a torn uniform, hands clenched to fists at her side. Her eyes stared down at Jade, wide and frenetic, and Jade looked away, unable to bear the censure. "Is there something else you'd have me do?"

"Maybe a little respect for the dead? Or show us why Marsilias even sent you on this mission? Or maybe find a way to cure this disease," Inka shrieked the last as an accusation, her voice shattering as she tore the glove from her left hand and threw it into the water at Jade's feet. There, marbling the skin like ink droplets, was a pageant of black markings, running from her fingers up beneath her sleeve.

Jade of course had no answer, nothing to improve the monumentality of their failure, so she offered an exhausted joke, "Marsilias didn't have much say really; I'm actually the one in charge, he's just my lackey. Picked him up at a bargain from the university."

"Yeah, I'm mostly here just to bring her cake and cookies." Marsilias shrugged an eloquent apology and subtly squeezed Jade's shoulder.

"Don't you care?" Inka demanded softly. "Don't you understand? Do you know how many corporation board members I've talked with, touched recently? How little separates me from the rest? How little separates them from the CEOs. Can you even imagine what this"—she raised her splattered hand again—signifies? Whatever *soul* you're hunting, has had access to every decision-making authority in our society, and we just failed our one chance to avert it."

Jade knew, of course she knew, she'd known the moment she glimpsed Inka's possession in the sky-city. Instead of engaging further, Jade stood, aching head to foot with exhaustion and an overtaxed body that threatened to collapse. "I already saved the world once, and it cost me just about everything. How about you do it this time?" She shuffled off, unable to bear the woman's desperation.

Three steps later, her earpiece buzzed and cited Prime March as the caller with secondary lines to Marsilias and Serras. Jade sagged but answered, sticking her fork in the cake for safekeeping. "I'm here."

"You just returned to our sensors; how did the expedition go?"

Serras answered softly, "We didn't get it."

A moment of silence then, "Any casualties?"

"Several," Serras said, "most notably one Purifier we had to leave behind in the sky-city and an enthralled Jysa the revenants killed."

Jade slumped back against another stack of crates, laid her cake aside and wrapped herself tight. "We have a bigger problem, though. The *soul* took control of Inka as well."

Silence again, then, "If it possessed her, then it's probably spread the infection across the entire Savant Corporation, or the main players at least: The empyreans, Board of Directors, potentially even the CEO's assistants. We'll need to quarantine her quickly, and then probably sedate her."

Serras shook her head. "She's an empyrean Invoker, Theeran. We can't restrict her movements, let alone sedate her, without explicit permission from the Savant CEO."

"I'll contact the CEO personally and deal with the logistics. Before I begin though, there's more. A secretary for the Food and Nourishment Corporation's CEO, Tasairen Helio, recently checked several of her associates into the Medical Corporation's foremost facility due to a rash of black markings."

Jade inhaled sharply and bent forward as Serras cursed.

Marsilias simply said, "Then we're out of time."

"Yeah. I'm contacting other Jysa clans and assembling other teams for expeditions to sky-cities, but the number of Magisters capable of creating cards like that are rare and overworked; the nearest departure is a week off. Even if you made another, we need personnel."

"Don't bother," Serras replied, "we had the device, or what we presume was the device, but the sky-city prevented it from passing the boundary."

"Understood, I'll make the appropriate calls. Is there more?"

Marsilias hummed quietly to himself, thinking before resuming, "Do the other corporations know what the rash signifies?"

"No, but we have to tell them soon, especially those who've yet to exhibit signs of it. We need to prepare for the worst, segregate lines of succession in the furthest reaches of our organizations, designate leadership in all corporations for when the hammer drops. The CEOs should be safe, but they still need people. For the time being, you all need to wear masks and touch no one."

"Any of us in line for succession?" Serras asked. "I could use a higher salary."

"I severely doubt it. The other Sovereigns don't particularly like Jade, and you couldn't handle accounting if your life depended on it. Marsilias might have a chance though, people like him."

Again, there was a moment of silence, heavy as a drowning weight and full of apology. Theeran exhaled and spoke as softly as he could, "Jade ..."

"I know," she whispered in reply and pulled her legs into her chest, "you need me."

"I'm sorry, but yes. This disease is of Afterlife and your trip there changed you in ways we don't understand even now. There's a chance that you might be just enough like the *souls* to be immune. Evidence supports this, or at least a long gestation period; you've encountered multiple infected and have yet to exhibit signs."

"What do you want from me?"

"Nothing yet. I need to converse with Serras privately first. She'll fill you in later." Her earpiece clicked off and a glance at Marsilias revealed him rising as well.

Jade shakily hopped off from the crate, forcing herself to breathe regularly. *"It's okay,"* she told herself. *"It's just until this is over, then they'll let you go. You can trust Theeran; he was Ilin's friend. You can leave, you will leave when this is all done. Just fix this quickly, easy as that."* She reclaimed her fork and cake and walked over to where Connor lay in one of the unused Jysa planes. Ruon paced before him, chin clasped pensively in one hand.

"How're you two doing?" she asked softly, climbing over Conner into the seat.

Connor groaned from beneath his shielding arms. "I've been better; this isn't the worst I've overextended myself, but it still sucks."—he shivered violently—"... and you?"

"I'm fine."

"But your–"

"It's passed, Connor, I'm fine." She wasn't. Every nerve twisted within her at the shifting shadows; she heard the music of revenants in the clink of metal and her whole mind felt riddled with barbed wire.

Jade curled her legs under her and savored a bite of cake. "So, where do you guys go now?"

"Back to the Savant Corporation I assume; they'll want a detailed recount of everything we saw before they reassign us. Likely we'll be in isolation the entire time. After that, it's a toss-up between quarantine and somewhere useful, all depends on how far they believe the disease has infiltrated the corporation. If it's quarantine, we'll get out. Ruon's got our ship rigged to enforce manual override over their remote piloting systems."

"Inka has the disease."

"Damn. That's bad."

"Yeah." She hesitated. "What about the Redeemers?"

"Ruon and I will start looking for Saccari; we need someone with concrete knowledge of the PLAN, a lot of it, if we're going to stop it. We would stay here and help you, but I don't think there's much we can do."

His words sent a pang of desperate isolation through Jade, and she almost revealed her alliance with Chandris to them but stifled the words before they could escape. Whatever her desires, she couldn't trust blindly, not until they understood the limits of Indemiun's possession or discovered how to discern who carried his disease. Except ... Connor and Ruon were Redeemers, and Redeemers already harbored a foreign will in their minds, and it was an old will. Would that be enough? Jade slowly bent forward, clasping her hands before her with white knuckles. "I ... have something else. Another opportunity, but you can't share it with anybody."

Ruon ceased pacing and exchanged a look of confusion with Connor that evolved into realization.

"Your *soul* friend!" Connor sat upright, constraining his voice to a whisper as he leaned in beside her, "You think he can help us?"

"I'm almost certain of it; I ... brought him with us to the sky-city, not physically but his projection, because he said he could track Indemiun's possession."

"We can find him," Connor said softly. "If all of this is tied to the PLAN, he- it's the key piece. Without him, they'll lose access to the possession."

Jade's hands clenched harder, squeezing enough to hurt. "Yeah."

"Can we do it, though? He's a *soul*. Chandris killed a full Purifier Core easily."

A memory surfaced in her mind, a plunging city of ruins illuminated by white electricity amidst a sea of swirling brown mist and, throughout all of it, towering figures too radiant to gaze at. "I ... can." That was a lie, she didn't know for certain; she'd been stronger back then, the years of over-use having yet to catch up with her body. "You can't tell anyone though. We don't understand the rules of the disease; if Indemiun has access to our memories when he possesses us, it could ruin everything. All he would have to do is step into the wrong body."

"Not a word, but will the Purifier Corporation allow that? Trusting the word of a *soul* in this situation?"

"I doubt it, and that's why it's just us until I have proof."

"You're thinking of doing something dumb, aren't you?"

She mustered a smile. "Never tell someone smart you're planning on doing something dumb. They'll try to stop you."

"Is that basically an admittance of guilt?"

"I'm only alluding to doing something dumb ... and we're missing the smart half."

Ruon chortled and Connor spared her a long-suffering look. "Very funny; but seriously, can you handle this? You just broke down in front of everybody? Your body–"

"Is fine."

He held her gaze then sighed. "At least tell me you're not doing this alone. You saw how this turned out."

"I won't be going alone; I'll bring Marsilias. He's usually useful, and has probably engineered some way to prevent his infection. If he's not safe, I can handle it alone. I've seen worse things." She savored the final morsel of cake, secured the fork in the container, and stored both in a pocket. Then out of distant hope, she asked, "How long till you're recovered?"

"A day, most likely." Grabbing the seat of her chair, he hauled himself up with a groan to view the air-dock. "Do you think we'll incapacitate the rest of the Jysa?"

"Maybe to prevent Indemiun gaining any more access to the sky-city, but there's not much point of it now; we can't get the device, and he already has someone up there. I imagine we'll wake the others and leave."

"Well, I guess that's something of a silver lining." He shuffled toward the edge of the plane and levered himself off. "Ruon and I need to go, but remember, if you need anything...."

"I know where to find you." She extended her arms as Ruon squeezed her in a quick embrace before supporting Connor. They shuffled off, the younger brother humming a snatch of classical music and tapping the rhythm on Connor's shoulder.

Jade slumped back in her seat and stared up at the aircraft's ceiling. Silence surrounded her, oppressive with gloom and exhaustion. She rolled onto her side across the seats and curled up beneath her coat, flipping up her hood. Hiding.

"Just a little longer," she whispered. "There's no one else to do this. Just a little longer, then you can be done. It's okay, they won't want you after this; you're crazy, you see things, you breakdown."

She curled tighter and clenched hands over her ears against the phantom scream, squeezing her eyes shut, but images filled the darkness behind her lids....

A hand grabbed her arm, jostling her until she slapped it. "Enough, I'm awake, I'm awake." Jade blearily assessed her disturber, pulling her coat closed against the cold. "If you want the plane, just drop me off wherever you're going."

"Primess March wants you, Miss Dieza." The young Purifier refused to meet her gaze.

"Alright, tell her I'll be there in a bit, I need a day or two for"— she struggled for an appropriately important or esoteric synonym and ultimately settled on the truth—"napping purposes."

The Purifier stepped aside with a gesture of invitation.

Groaning, Jade dragged herself up and out and dropped into the ankle-deep water with a splash. "Lead the way."

The Purifier conducted her to the Heart-Room, where most of the Jysa rambled about, recovering from the effects of sedation. A knot of Purifiers congregated outside Dama Nhr'irena's abode, listening attentively to Serras. Jade slipped through until she found Marsilias beside the house, and waited while Serras finished recounting what had occurred in the sky-city.

Buttoning her coat's front, she pulled her arms inside and let the sleeves hang empty. "Hey, Silias."

He kept stroking his scarf, eyes unfocused. "You get some sleep?"

"Yeah, it helped a little. I'm going to need a long vacation after this, someplace warm with no people. I'll take pictures for you and the Redheads."

He said nothing, too preoccupied with his own thoughts.

She forced herself to try again. "Silias?"

"Hmm?"

"You tested yourself with a card, right? Made sure you were clean, and at least tried to paint one that would cure you?"

"Yeah, it didn't work."

Her heart stuttered. "What?" *"No, not him. I don't want to be alone."*

"First night I learned of the disease I tried designing a card to cure and detect it, spent hours painting then tested the original subject. Just invoking it put the Invoker in a coma, and it didn't do anything except confirm the disease's presence. It's been days since the Invoker went under and he's yet to wake up. As far as I know, I'm still clean though."

"How ... how can you tell?"

"A lot of ... minor Invokers owe me favors and the cards aren't lethal to use."

"Jesus, Marsilias."

"I know, but I need to know if I get compromised. Getting caught unawares is not an option for me." His attention finally shifted fully to her. "Why do you ask?"

She began to answer but a conflux of movement drew her attention to the dispersing Purifiers. "I'll ... I'll tell you later, when we're alone. Okay?" He nodded assent, and she crossed to where Serras murmured with a subordinate.

"... orders are you're all confined to Imarah going forward, permanent posting until we figure this out."

Jade stepped hesitantly into view. "You wanted to see me?"

"Yes, I have news you're not going to like, dear."

Her stomach knotted. "What is it?"

"The Sovereign Cores have summoned you to account; the meeting's in a couple hours. I managed to get Marsilias access though, so you won't be facing them alone. Maybe he can do something to mitigate whatever they intend."

"Couldn't they at least have waited until I woke up?" She mustered a smile. "Have they no respect for common decency?"

"Sorry, dear, I would have waited, but the orders just came in from Theeran. They're sending a ship to collect you. It'll arrive in a few minutes."

"If they've dispatched a specific vessel, then we're not just going to the regional headquarters, we're going to the Tomb. I'm not being called to account; I'm standing trial."

Serras grimaced. "I've always hated that name, but yes, a trial. They want control, Jade, and they don't have it over you."

"Wait, you said they. Are you and Theeran excluded?"

"Yes, under concerns that our attachment to you would cloud our judgment. In other news, subsequent my meddling, Marsilias is supposedly under review as well, but it's really just a farce. He says he's clean, and they want to know how."

"Of course it's a farce; I can't imagine anything I could have done wrong," Marsilias said primly, joining them at the mention of his name. "I've done nothing but follow regulations since arriving, an unassuming citizen to the marrow."

"I guess I'm just a bad influence on you"—Jade shrugged—"you should really stop bribing me to hang out with you."

"I guess so. Oh well, I'll have to find someone else to consume my excess sweets."

"... Excess sweets?"

"Yes, I buy in bulk, which unfortunately results in my having an extreme excess...."

"...An extreme excess?"

"Yes."

Jade frowned. "I suppose I could mend my ways, become an asset to the corporation...." She began chewing her lip, considering potential blackmail material on Marsilias.

Serras squeezed Jade's arm. "Stay safe, love, and don't let them hurt you. This is it for me. I'm stuck on this ship until they discover a cure, but I'm rooting for you, and I'll draw a kitty face on Inka after we sedate her. Now get a move on, you don't want the ship waiting on you. They'll pick you up from the roof."

A Jysan woman appeared from the surrounding crowd and guided Jade and Marsilias through Imarah's dimmed corridors to a sequence of skeletal metal stairways in its primary air-dock. The Jysa stopped at the foot of the stairs and indicated upwards toward a hatch. "They don't want to meet, or risk contact, with anything in Imarah, so you'll rendezvous with them outside."

They nodded comprehension and ascended, boots scraping and accruing a red tint from the rusted steps. Jade absently reached a hand to stroke the tarnished railing as she climbed, and streams of Jysan script gleamed faintly in response, causing the rust to flake and disintegrate through her fingers. She retracted her hand and wiped the ruddy grit from her skin.

At the top, they entered a shallow, transparent recess running the length of Imarah's flight deck. Comfortless benches lined the walls, devoid of the warming hues and adornments that characterized most of Imarah, and more egregiously, an absence of pillows. A sonar console waited beside the door, projecting a holographic display of the sky above and the ocean beneath Imarah, depicting even the smaller aquatic life.

Marsilias closed the door and sank onto the bench nearest the console, inspecting it for signs of the Purifier aircraft. Only when it displayed no indication of their ride, did he face Jade, who stared through the ceiling near the room's center. "You said there was something you want to discuss in private?"

"Yes. Before leaving for the sky-city, I contacted and asked Chandris for help with something; he said he could track Indemiun's possession, so I invited him along. We can track Indemiun."

It was a long time before Marsilias spoke. "The Purifiers won't act on your word alone, especially with Theeran and Serras in disgrace concerning you, and we'll need Sovereigns to kill him. He outclasses rank-and-file Purifiers."

"Yeah, that's why we need proof. We need to find him first." She dropped her gaze from the ceiling to him. "You got any influence over them?"

"Not enough for this; it takes time to get debts and favors from that deep; people that high usually have the power to get whatever they want on their own."

She snorted. "You need to work on that."

"Don't worry, I am." There was another moment of silence then, "For what it's worth, I'm sorry. I didn't realize it would go so far when I visited your apartment."

"It's okay. I've survived worse."

"Is there anything else I should know?"

The image of a dark room filled her mind, its periphery mounded with weapon crates and, in their midst, a circle of figures in orange coats and brilliant, vacillating white masks looked at her.

"No. There's nothing." There were things in the hidden places of their cities, cults with real gods, that the corporations had no conception of; and if the ignorant started poking around, those things tended to reach back.

Their transport arrived several minutes later, during which Jade stripped off her armor and stored it in a bag. After that, she donned her faded coat and glanced up in time to see a hulking warship—Valkyrie class, approximating three hundred feet long—descend from the clouds, its flanks wreathed in residual lightning.

"Ride's here."

Marsilias nodded and ascended one of the ancient, metal ladders to a hatch in the ceiling. Jade followed him out, raising her hood against the drizzle. The warship settled over them and a transport vessel emerged to ferry them to a hangar occupied solely by smaller vessels: further transport and scout craft, and automated fighters, and a complement of androids.

One of the androids, a faceless man-shaped automaton, greeted Jade and Marsilias at their transport's entrance. "Welcome, Ms. Jade, Mr. Wreign. Please, accompany me to your accommodations for this flight."

Jade and Marsilias quietly obeyed, trailing the automaton across the hangar to an omniveyor, which in turn carried them along a stark, gray corridor. Curious, Jade extended a hand to touch the open console, but the automaton interceded. "Touch nothing please, Ms. Jade. The corporation is well aware of your abilities."

"It seems they want us ignorant," Marsilias said.

"The Tomb has always been fiercely segregated from society; its location given only to specific, closed-circuit ships. It is manned entirely by machines, operates on its own network, and has never housed more than fifteen living beings at once."

"Sounds unwelcoming."

"Life attracts revenants. No living people means there's less of a chance the revenants will wander in."

The omniveyor halted, prompting the android to shift aside as the door opened. They entered a square room with high, sleek walls and a single long bench. Sensors flickered across the length of the ceiling, and Jade glimpsed the outlines of sealed alcoves in the walls, probably a variety of pulse, laser, and canister turrets.

Chandris sat crouched in an opposite corner, arms draped over his bent knees. "It seems your organization holds no faith in you."

"Appears so," Jade said, strolling to sit on the bench beside him. "They stick you in here so you couldn't memorize the route?"

"That was the explanation they provided. I have no reason to doubt their assertion. Do you know our destination?"

"The Purifier Corporation's head office, otherwise known as the Tomb."

"Why such a morbid name for a seat of power?"

"Because it's the main armory, housing all the unused Siphons."

"Are not the Siphons your souls?"

"Yes; when a Siphon is destroyed, its master dies. When the Purifier dies, however, the Siphon tends to persist."

"Does the soul survive?"

"Its energy does, and its memories after a fashion, but its personality doesn't."

He considered her for a while. "Does the process of extracting your soul hurt?"

"It's more uncomfortable than anything, and very strange at first."

"Is an extended period of separation deleterious to the main body?"

"You're fishing for information about me."

"Yes."

"No, a long separation from one's Siphon has no proven effect."

"Are the shapes and colors inherent?"

"No. Fabricated, based on the Purifier's preference, and impermanent; the artificers can adjust them on request."

"You are a young organization, correct?"

"Yes, why?"

"What changed in your society to permit, or perhaps necessitate, the Purifier organization?"

"What do you mean?"

"Your species survived for millennium against the *vestiges*; what prompted the Purifiers to form."

She considered the wisdom of sharing the information with him, then decided she didn't care and responded, "We discovered how to make Siphons. It was revolutionary because it allowed ordinary people to compete with revenants, and opened an entirely new means to make profit and the Defense Corporation capitalized. They funded and exploited the new technology for a few decades, but the inventors knew what they had and kept their methods secret as part of the contract. When the Defense Corporation had funded enough of an organizational foundation, the inventors seceded and formed their own corporation."

He stretched out his hand. "May I see one?"

"But you can't hold anything?"

"This is my physical body."

"What! They let you out? They're actually risking a physical meeting?"

"I assume my presence causes your Sovereign Cores no distress. Judging from what you have accomplished with inferior armaments, and the proficiency Primess March displayed in the sky-city, I understand their confidence."

Jade wordlessly retrieved a training Siphon from her back and passed it to him. His fingers closed around the cylinder's elegant metallic embellishments, rotating it gently to inspect the various sides. He held it thus for a second, then the casing disintegrated and the emerald energy bloomed outward, streaking around and around his hand. It swelled and convulsed, assumed a barrage of minute shapes and designs varying from the mundane to the supernatural, to things she couldn't comprehend. "They devour our essence, our *luce*, and thus destroy us. Our wounds heal as always, but it is not the wounds that hold significance, it is the contact between Siphon and body."

"These are inferior versions, facsimiles intended to replicate the effects in a diminished state, to prepare the body for the transition and rigors of the authentic article. Siphons do not just destroy your essence, they consume it, feed on it, grow on it; just like us."

"You have replicated our existence in the confines of a metallic box." The Siphon energy dulled in his hand and the cylinder reformed, the energy solely visible as a current of green between the metal decorations. Chandris returned the Siphon to her. "Thus your warriors feed upon us and, I assume, pass their accrued strength to their successors. Leaving the Siphons of dead Purifiers unused would be senseless; the eldest weapons must be immense."

Marsilias, extensively buckled in, frowned across the room. "Doesn't that anger you? We're butchering your kind for power."

"We are not revenants. Revenants are no more alive than one of your machines with coding; they simulate life but are little more than preset patterns."

"What about when we start killing *souls*?" Marsilias asked. "You and the others won't be the last ones to come here."

"You are mistaken to believe Indemiun was the first of my kin to explore your world; nor will you ever destroy us, for we are you."

Marsilias opened his mouth to press further, but the ship thudded around them and stilled. "We've arrived, I guess."

Jade returned the Siphon to its hook and moved to the entrance, joined by Marsilias a minute later. Chandris remained where he stood.

"What are you waiting for?" Jade asked.

"For specific instructions."

The door slid open, revealing an android. "Please come this way, Mr. Wreign, Ms. Dieza, Mr. Chandris." He stepped aside, admitting them into the omniveyor. The instant they all entered, the doors closed and the omniveyor sped off. "The Sovereign Cores await. If you desire to perform any closing preparation please do so now. I will honor reasonable petitions."

No one voiced a request, so when the omniveyor attained its destination, they exited into the warship's hangar and proceeded to an open service lift, which lowered them into the building proper.

The lift stopped on a cushioned landing pad and Jade stepped off, shivering as the chilly temperature activated her suit. The sheer, transparent walls boasted only dim lighting, which submerged the desolate corridor into near complete dark and barely illuminated the gray sand of the ocean floor below. Her eyes glanced to the walls, roving their length to the ceiling, but she saw nothing beyond the encompassing dark of water, not even a semblance of aquatic life. Even if she were to venture out in the First Step, Jade wouldn't find natural life for miles or moving currents, nothing but automated defenses.

Already several meters ahead of her, the android hailed back, "Do not tarry please, the Sovereigns await."

Jade shuddered and hastened after them, boots squelching quietly on the slick floor. *Reminds me of apartment 9.*

They walked along a hallway illuminated by floor lights, their footsteps resounding against the floor in eerie contrast to the androids. A few other scattered androids populated the corridors, but their pervasive silence only promoted the sense of isolation. Excluding the androids, variations in the unchanging scenery regulated themselves to solitary doors barely distinguishable from the walls. Their escort ignored every diverging path until they reached the hallway's culmination and a soaring entrance.

Here the android positioned itself beside the immense door and accessed a console. "The Sovereign Cores await you inside."

The doors slid open, revealing a wide room illuminated by a single ceiling light. A ring of deep-blue sofas occupied the light, perfectly aligned with its perimeter so that only silhouettes of its occupants were visible.

The Sovereign Cores, ten men and ten women, lounged across the sofas, varying in dress from business suits to full armor to plain clothes. One of them—a stout man—wore neither shirt nor coat, his upper torso a canvas of intricate tattoos displaying the contest between a sinuous emerald dragon and a colossal black canine with long, streaming hair. A host of tiny machines swarmed over his chest, deepening the tapestry and restoring the faded colors.

A statuesque woman sat beside him, the furled sleeves of her coat betraying mechanized arms while the exposed skin of her neck shimmered with metallic veins and shifting pieces.

One after another, Jade inspected the Sovereigns, each unique in appearance but unified by the Purifier badge. She knew them all by name and title, and had spoken with most of them separately on numerous occasions, but had faced a full assembly only once: the day her brother died.

Prime Sparrow, the tattooed man, raised a hand from his seat directly opposite the entrance, beckoning them forward. Jade trailed on Marsilias and Chandris's heels, unsteady beneath the assembly's loveless appraisal. When they assumed their positions at center stage, Primess Sparrow—the machine-enhanced woman— began, "I presume that is the *soul*?"

"I am."

Not a rustle of unease or surprise disrupted the circle. Primess Sparrow continued, "Is it true that you possess a regenerative ability comparable to revenants?"

"Yes."

Primess Sparrow's head dipped in a shallow nod, and Prime Catalyst—his armor and mask dyed a livid red—grabbed a canis- ter-pistol from the seat beside him and fired on Chandris. The bullet struck the *soul's* head and exploded, spraying physical matter across the floor and sofa, where it disintegrated in puffs of *luce*.

Startled, Jade lurched to the side, half-ducking. Recovering quickly, she spun on Prime Catalyst. "What the hell are you doing?"

Primess Sparrow answered, "Ascertaining his veracity, composure, and your attachment."

Chandris reformed behind Jade. "I appreciate your restraint, Primess Sparrow."

She offered no reply, but conceded the discussion to her compatriot. "Why do you linger in our possession, *soul?*"

"Because I wish to experience your existence and to converse with Ms. Dieza."

"What is your affiliation to Ms. Dieza?"

"None. The absence of a visible essence intrigued me."

"Do you understand the mechanics of Siphons?"

"To some extent, yes. There may be intricacies I am ignorant of."

"Do you credit her Siphon with the absence of a discernible soul?"

"Yes."

A new voice spoke, "Ms. Dieza, were you aware of the *soul's* interest in you?"

Jade faced Primess Frost, a petite woman in an auburn skirt that exposed her bare feet and the vibrant green magister cards fused to them; the result of a horrific experiment many years prior.

Jade slowly stepped to the forefront, burying her hands in her pockets and considering her interactions with Chandris. "I recognized his interest but never really remarked on it or considered the source."

Primess Frost continued, "And he has assisted you on numerous occasions in your endeavors?"

"As well as those of the Purifier Corporation."

"What are the exact parameters of his services?"

"Information, both about *souls* in general and the nature of our target. He gave us Indemiun's name and history."

"Information that proved immaterial by all accounts. What is your connection with the *soul?*"

Jade shrugged. "I don't have one particularly–"

"A partial lie." Prime Silk interjected, his black pin-striped suit highlighted by a gold tie.

Without sparing Prime Silk acknowledgment, Primess Frost resumed, "Speak the truth."

"I share no personal history with Chandris, but I do appreciate his company."

"Why?"

"He's ... different."

"And a member of the species that murdered your brother, of the species he died to contain." The unspoken accusation spiked through Jade: traitor, and she flinched. Her memories filled with his cries of pain and rage as they dragged him through the gate. She remembered the mist swallowing him and closed her eyes against the old ache.

Jade forced herself to speak, though her voice shook, "Not all *souls* are the same; they're individuals."

Prime Silk interceded again, "In your resignation papers, you cited emotional instability; has your mental state improved?"

"Somewhat, there's good days and bad?"

"In what configuration?"

"... More bad than good, but I'm getting there."

"So you remain unsuited for active fieldwork." His fore and index fingers curled in beckons. "Come here." She obeyed, and his long, fabricated fingers grasped her arm. Their cold, unnaturally smooth and lifeless surface slid over her skin to roll up beneath her sleeve. The ridges of his bones flashed with a pulse of light that ran to the tip of his metal fingers before retracing its path: a personal network grafted onto his body, boasting an incomprehensible wealth of knowledge and programs.

His nails extended to touch her adaptive suit, which responded with a pulse of information. He relinquished his grip. "Aside from lingering trauma due to the over-abuse of her Specter abilities, her physical condition remains exceptional. Ignoring the resulting injuries, are your Specter capabilities equal to their previously displayed values?"

She retreated, disgusted by his touch and rolling her sleeve back into place. "Yes."

"Are you and your brother's Siphons still operational?"

"Wouldn't you like to know?"

"Retaining possession of a Sovereign-caliber weapon due to emotional grievance is childish; your brother would have wanted more."

"*As if I'd let you all erase it,*" she thought. "Tough luck, and no he wouldn't."

"Your belligerence is misplaced and offers little to your situation."

"And just what is my situation?" Jade demanded, facing Primess Sparrow as the initiator of her investigation. "What am I standing trial for?"

"To ascertain your aptitude and the advisability of your continued meddling. Contrary to what Marsilias Wreign believes, you are not a member of the Purifiers. You are a civilian with no bearing on our activities."

Without pausing for Jade to respond, Prime Catalyst spoke, his words trailing those of Primess Sparrow perfectly so neither traipsed upon the other, "What of your sojourn to the sky-city? What did you hope to find and what prompted the journey?"

"Didn't Prime March tell you?"

"No, we are not beholden to one another's permission, and he either did not see fit or find it expedient to inform us of his motivations; he will be brought to account if we deem his judgment lacking."

Thus Jade began her recount with their journey to the Jysa and progressing from there to their failure in the sky-city, withholding only Chandris's participation. When she finished, the Sovereign Cores refrained from an immediate response, potentially performing a silent discourse amongst themselves.

Ultimately, Prime Sparrow resumed, "Ms. Dieza, your physical abilities are undeniable, but your stubborn refusal to carry Siphons makes you a liability. Additionally, you deliberately oppose the Purifier Corporation's interests and align yourself with a *soul*: a creature of the species our organization is sworn to destroy. Finally, your mental health is unacceptable. Unless you submit to strict oversight, you are unfit to serve the Purifier Corporation, and a hazard to whoever accompanies you. It is the decision of this board that you are to remove yourself from all matters pertaining to this company, and to surrender any and all implements you received from it. The sole exception is your personal Siphon. Dismissed. You as well, revenant."

Despite this dismissal, the twenty of them stared at Jade in silence, oppressive and expectant. Buried in the morass of their final condemnation, they had issued their ultimatum: submit herself to their command, submit herself to them, to their judgment, to their demands, to their laws, to serve whenever they wished, however they wished, for as long as they wished, or be forbidden from interfering. And they would punish her if she interfered, because that would allow them to strip her of her privileges and her protections, of her home in the retirement district and her wealth, because all of these belonged to them, rewards for her sacrifices two years ago. They would take them because Jade was an unused tool, and by doing so they could force her return. Why? Because she had just spent the last few weeks proving she could still be used.

So they waited and stared and demanded her answer. She just bowed, her hands clenched into fists in her coat, and stepped back, because that was the only thing she could do. There was nothing she could say, no argument, no negotiation she could make to sway their opinion, and as for returning to them ... the thought clamped a vice on her throat, distorting her breathing as panic charged through her veins. Visions reared behind her eyes, and she clamped her teeth against them, squeezing her fists tighter until pain focused her. No, she couldn't return to them, even if it might save lives.

Feeling fragile as glass, she straightened, clutching her coat tighter around herself, and found all their gazes still upon her, expectation curdling to disgust and contempt. She dropped her head again and moved to exit the circle, but Marsilias spoke as she reached the light's circumference, "And what of me? Am I fired? Promoted?"

She paused, glancing back as the Sovereigns shifted focus. "We are aware of your proclivities, Mr. Wreign," Primess Sparrow replied, "and are impressed by your reach. We would welcome your continued employment, and if you're willing, invite you to stay and discuss an expansion of your authority and involvement within these matters, possibly even formal employment when they are completed?"

Marsilias shot Jade a look of apology and centralized himself among the Sovereigns. "I would be interested, particularly concerning the protections you afforded Jade from the Savant Corporation."

Jade retreated to the hallway outside, where the same android waited to escort them back to the wet-dock. A pair of humming Amphibian class raptor-vessels idled there, anchored to the walls via braces with sleek gray bodies approximating thirty and forty feet in length respectively. Their android guided them to the smaller vessel's entrance ramp and indicated she should board. "This vessel will return you to your retirement district with all haste, miss. You are permitted to take your leave of the revenant called Chandris so long as it does not exceed three minutes." The android dropped his hand and retreated.

Jade waved farewell to Chandris and started up the ramp, but paused as he asked, "Why did you not contest their verdict?"

"It wouldn't have mattered. It wasn't a trial to discern my capabilities or worthiness. They wanted my return; they just wanted me to surrender my autonomy in the process. Most of them never liked me or my brother for a variety of reasons, and refusing to give them his Siphon has only exacerbated that."

"I assume that affected your reasoning to withhold my participation in the sky-city."

"Not really. If I thought they would have acted on it I might have given it over anyway, but they wouldn't have unless I returned. Mostly I withheld it because we don't know which, if any, of them are infected. I don't know what that could mean for us following your lead."

"You intend to go regardless of your dismissal and the prohibition of interference."

"Yeah. Whatever they may think, they don't own me, and they can't bully me. I've seen and killed worse than them. If they decide to punish me when this is done, that's fine. I'll survive." Jade grimly resumed her ascent. "Just wait, Chandris, I'll contact you for the location later and we'll pay Indemiun a visit."

Interjection 4

The Warren pathway thrummed quietly around Ruon, its air vibrating with the cycles and clicks of the servers that shaped it, and its obscurity lessened by the LEDs blinking amidst circuitry and tangled wires. Swallowed in partial shadows, he progressed carefully, navigating cords sprawled over an uneven floor of jutting server banks. Energy buzzed softly against his skin and clothes, charging his hair to stand on end and shocking him whenever he touched metal.

The path forked ahead of him, the primary route squeezing to a tunnel as it ascended up a rising stair of servers. He chose the secondary course, slipping through a window-sized space abutting the floor and dropping half-a-dozen feet into a perpendicular running path. He was getting close but needed to hurry. The heat had already risen perceptibly, pulling a light sweat from his skin despite his adaptive suit's regulation efforts. Even in a Warren, the burgeoning heat storm outside exerted influence, already achieving external degrees sufficient to boil water. Inside the city-complex's highest levels, the temperatures would exceed a hundred at the storm's peak, despite the ocean and every cooling device. In the machine rooms between floors, it would be lethal.

Ruon blinked one eye, mentally activating a remote feed to the outside, and his lens linked to a drone he'd deployed upon arrival.

The ocean and sky were bathed crimson in the heat storm's vivid light, the space between them seething in one enormous heat haze. The ocean swelled in mountainous waves hundreds of feet tall, crashing against a soaring tower armored in heat shields. A monolithic capital ship hovered in the periphery, almost blotting out the entire skyline as its thrusters ignited progressively brighter in preparation to break orbit. Surfacing on the water below, a Stormflower peeked from the lightless cold of the Drowning Deep miles below the ocean surface—unfurling vast, luminous blooms of green, teal, and blue to feed on the heat. He had minutes before the storm reached its apex and even the Warren became potentially lethal.

Ruon deactivated the remote feed, directed the drone to take shelter, adjusted the sack across his shoulders, and lengthened his stride. He disliked the Warren as a matter of course, and not entirely because the pathways defined by his cult were significantly less ... pleasant than the Redeemer routes. Even after years of traversing them, and years of Jade's instructions, the Warren's rules still eluded him: they expanded on their own, rejected discovery by those ignorant of the divine, and all operated differently. The Dreaming Descent only ever went down, the Redeemer paths always functioned in a closed loop, and the Blood Court only ever permitted travel with a sacrifice of blood. And more rules and pathways besides these. Ruon disliked things that behaved erratically, that lacked the decency to operate as they were supposed to. Still, the Warren offered unfettered and unseen access to most places in the corporations, even here in the Haitian: seat of the Savant Corporation and its CEO.

The tunnel began to rise, the gradient steepening until it required Ruon to climb. As he did so, spectral walls began to appear, sometimes superimposed over the existing ones and visible only because of a minor offset, and sometimes crossing or filling the tunnel entirely. These barriers imposed no impediment, having been constructed entirely within the First Step to prevent Specters from accessing the CEO without permission. Ruon ignored them, following the glowing directions projected onto his lenses.

Text scrolled across his vision, `You almost there?— Connor.`

`Almost. Still in the Warren.` Ruon paused, the walls of circuitry on his left giving way to a dull green door with a block of outdated USB ports at its center. He fished through his utility belt until he found the appropriate USB chip, then removed the cap and ran his fingers along the ports counting. *"Six down, seven across ..."* 670 S.A., the date the CEOs were discovered. He tapped the appropriate port, its exterior scratched from use, and plugged in his drive. The door blinked with internal light and audibly unlocked, permitting Ruon to push inside. `Reached the correct level, through the door now.`

`Better hurry. The meeting's scheduled in five minutes, and they could start early.`

`I know.` Past the door, the floor evened out, the servers replaced with flat metal. Ruon hurried, moving swiftly but quietly as the heat continued to mount. A quarter mile later, he achieved his destination: a hatch in the floor, sealed by a USB port. He knelt and plugged in his USB with a quiet snick, ignoring the sweat dripping from his brow. The hatch slid soundlessly aside, releasing a gasp of cold air and mist. Ruon grasped the edges and carefully—ever so carefully—levered himself down onto a protruding ledge in the highest corner of the room below.

He found himself in a vast chamber of featureless walls, perfectly square, icily cold despite the heat storm outside, and filled with mist. Far below, near the small entrance to his right, a group of four entered, appearing like dolls from his great height. Across from them, on the far edge of the chamber, there stood—or rather, levitated—a device both immense and alien in design. With three long, thin blade-like prongs jutting from a joint center, it occupied almost the entire height and width of the room. Its exterior resembled a grayish, off-white metal, but blanketed in dark, constantly rippling lines, washing across its surface as if they were waves. The air around it vibrated constantly, a visible, shuddering pulse of movement. The CEO of the Savant Corporation.

Ruon settled into a crouch, keeping his arms and legs close lest they twitch too far out on his perch and alert the sensors. He blinked once, issuing mental commands to his lenses. Arrived.

Are you on time?

Yes. His lenses magnified the approaching group, lines superimposing over the features the mist obscured. Two guards, Inka, and a secretary I don't know. In their wake, androids materialized from the walls and floor, spectral within the confines of the First Step and scattering outward in search of intruders.

Search started, Ruon messaged, retreating further into his cranny, three minute count started now. A green timer appeared in his right lens, counting down.

Words scrawled across his vision. What do we do if they start asking the wrong questions?

Get Inka to a temple, kill her memories. Act like it's ransom. He concluded that message and sent another. They've started.

Below, the quartet approached to within a dozen feet of the CEO, the secretary in front and the guards flanking behind Inka. Only, Inka did not stop with the others. She continued past them, even when the secretary reached to forestall her. The empyrean Invoker's hand slipped into a pocket, drew a card, and slashed down. The sound of shattering glass split the vast chamber and pale green gas exploded outward from her feet.

Ruon lurched forward, lenses focusing as the secretary recoiled and the guards leapt forward, masks expanding over their faces. Too late. They crumpled, legs buckling beneath them, first to their knees then to prostrate, either dead or insensate; Ruon could not tell. Black markings swelled up from beneath Inka's coat and sprawled across her neck, climbing past her own mask to touch her eyes and darken them. She stepped to within a foot of the CEO, head tilting up to inspect it. "Well, this was not what I expected." Her voice was Inka's, but the cadence of the words, the inflection, and the accent, were all different as if it was someone else speaking.

Ruon crept to the platform's ledge, hands feverishly collecting and assembling the pieces of a pulse-rifle from his utility belt. Inka's been possessed again. Soul's here.

What do you want me to do?

Nothing, for now. Guards should respond. May need to act before then. He snapped the final piece into the rifle and raised it to his eye. Internally his mind raced, answering the question he'd been asking ever since Inka left Imarah: Why had the CEO knowingly summoned a compromised person, especially one of Inka's power? The answer was simple: It hadn't. She had; infiltrating the CEO's office to rescind the quarantine order and dispatch missives for Inka's summons. She would have then sent confirmation of Imarah's quarantine to the CEO, preventing it from discovering the ruse. There would have been no one on the ship to enforce the quarantine over a CEO's summons. Not even Serras.

Below, the possessed Inka leaned to the left then the right, as if searching for a better angle. "I assume you can speak. I also assume the rest of the CEOs aren't human either; I'll have a solution next time I visit one."

Ruon kept the rifle trained on Inka's head, but his eyes shifted to the spectral androids still scouring the First Step, drawing closer. The timer on his right lens read one minute: thirty-seven. Removing one hand from the barrel, he pulled a Redeemer mask from his belt and dragged it down over his head. The heads-up display activated, synched to his lenses, and then disappeared as unnecessary. A light remained blinking in the corner of his vision, however, a warning that someone had triggered one of his sensors. He ignored it.

The possessed Inka stepped back from the CEO, turning away though she remained looking over her shoulder. "Still, no point in wasting this opportunity." She crossed to the crumpled guards and knelt. "Inka carries no weapons because she has her cards, so it's fortunate that your guards do." Scrounging through the guard's apparel she resurfaced with an EMP grenade. "This might hurt you."

She straightened, pulled her arm back to throw—and Ruon fired, the bolt of concentrated energy slamming into her chest and dropping her to the floor, stunned. Then he was running, leaping up into the Warren and yanking the entrance closed behind him. He recognized some level of futility in it; the activated defenses would have scanned him the instant he acted, recording his physical information and equipment. They would know he was a Magister in moments, and there weren't many Magisters that couldn't be accounted for at any given time.

Connor, I need help.

What do you need?

Had to act, got scanned, need the information erased. CEO will be in lockdown, maybe an hour before it opens up again.

Where's the nearest Redeemer temple?

Don't remember. Check my alarm board; it's annotated. Ruon slowed, perspiration streaming down his brow as he panted. The heat lay thick within the Warren, sweltering beneath the heat storm's presence. He needed a different route, somewhere cool to wait out the storm.

Found it. Ruon, one of your sensors triggered.

I know. Ignore.

It's in one of the vacated temples.

That gave Ruon pause. The Redeemers had no need to reactivate one of their abandoned temples. He resumed moving. Link the feed to a lens, watch as you go. I can't, need to watch for signs, find someplace cold. There! A navigation hub. He scrambled over to it, extracting a second USB chip—designed for this purpose—and plugged it in. Information inundated his implants, compiling alongside a map projected onto his lenses. He scanned it, then swayed as his head spun and caught himself against the wall. Pain stabbed all the way up his spine, needles pumping coolants into his body to combat the radical temperature. His vision and head cleared, but it wouldn't last. He scanned the map again and—there! A Dreaming Descent, a drop all the way to the bottom, far beneath the ocean surface. He shoved off the wall and leapt onto an adjacent server to crawl through into a level above.

Text scrawled across his vision, Found it. Standard temple, idol, black water, somewhere in a server bank for the Melliss city-complex. I see Saccari.

What's he doing? Ruon's foot hit the next server going forward wrong and pitched forward.

I have audio, want to be patched in?

He staggered up, vision beginning to distort against. No. Distracting. Another injection of coolants, but less effective than the first. The backlash would be worse as well.

More text, small so as not to obscure his vision, They're waiting for something, mentioned a portal.

The path under Ruon's feet began to flatten out, the servers receding and the electronics in the walls lessening in both size and number. Someone's coming through.

Yeah, here's the portal. Magister origin but I don't recognize the style. It's mud, and flat on the floor instead of standing like a door. The guest's arriving, he's pulling himself out. A pause, then, Ruon, it's the Purifier we lost in the sky-city. He's got something.

Ruon shuffled to a stop, standing upon a precipice blanketed in flowers and swaying. What is it?

I don't know, but he's given it to Saccari.

They didn't want to stop us finding a device; they needed us to take them there. The air smelled sweet and heady, pulling Ruon down, thickening his mind. Gotta tell Jade, they got something from the city. Gotta go now, gotta fall.

What do you mean? Ruon!

It's fine. Taking a Dreaming Descent. Escaping the storm.

Be careful.

The scent deepened, enveloping Ruon, dragging his mind forward and down. He was falling. Strange. He didn't remember stepping off. That was all right. He rather liked falling. It felt soft. He let his eyes close, sinking further into the smell as the dream embraced him.

Then he slept, thinking of nothing else until the landing woke him miles below and hours later.

Indemiun

Chandris perceived the individual's approach long before she appeared in his window. She wove through the corridors at a time discordant with the patrols, thoughts of Chandris filling her intent. His prison impaired most external sounds, but every human soul sang a harmony unique to them, a harmony souls could hear. Thus he recognized the approach of a familiar essence.

The retraction of his window screen prompted Chandris, seated cross-legged on his bed in a common human pose, to open his eyes and observe the blockish features of the tall woman. "What interest do you have in me, Candice Yaal?"

"Straight to the point, aren't you?"

"Would you prefer I engage in the typical human greeting rituals?"

"No, you're fine." Maneuvering the bag she carried to her front, Candice rummaged through its contents and retrieved a hard box, which she dropped to the floor and tapped with a foot. The case expanded, sprouting four limbs, a cushioned seat, and a back. Candice sat. "I hear you and Jade are friends now."

"Not by the definition of most humans; we're favorable acquaintances." Her essence simmered with repressed emotions, an attempt at the technique that protected Prime March from his perusal. The emotions she failed to control betrayed both a sense of ease in his presence that extended beyond his confinement, and a concerted pressure: a purpose. "My relationship with Jade Dieza is not your objective; what is your question?"

"All right. Do you know what she is?" The woman spoke calmly but eagerly, her eyes and essence sparking with excitement.

"Jade Dieza is many things. Specify the relevant attribute."

"Do you know that she's a Specter?"

"Yes."

The woman slouched back, the turbulence in her essence calming, though her emotions continued to flare. "Have you noticed that causing her any trouble? She used to keep it a secret back when we were in the academy, but now most everybody seems to know about it."

"Why would her abilities result in difficulties?"

Uncertainty sparked in her essence, instigating a pause. She assessed him, her features remaining in the visage of someone measuring their words. Her emotions, however, revealed strict, mathematical thought patterns. "The Savant Corporations has a ... unique view of its employees, where they're less people than merchandise."

"Why would this result in undue difficulties for Jade?"

"Corporate Law dictates that the corporations have absolute control over their services and all their derivatives, from pricing to distribution. The Savant Corporation's service is Savants, only Jade never registered."

"Allocating her outside of their purview in direct contradiction to their laws," Chandris surmised.

"Yeah, so have you heard anything about her? Has the Savant Corporation tried anything? Bullied or harassed her at all?" Excitement flared across her essence, suppressing the peripheral emotions without once disturbing the concerned expression she presented him.

"What engendered this curiosity in her?"

She blinked, her essence unsettling as it adjusted to his question. "I want to help." The words burst from her in a startled rush, unblemished by dishonesty. Candice lowered her gaze, her essence stilling as she organized her thoughts. "I've known Jade since her academy days, not that that really amounts to much. She was ... different back then. Distant, and never wholly present. I only learned she was a Specter recently, and I thought maybe that was the reason she acted like that." Candice restored her attention to him. "That's why I want to know; because I think I can help her. If she'll let me."

Not a thread of deceit colored her words, but the calculation lingered in her emotions. "I am aware of no instance where the Savant Corporation caused Jade distress, but it is unlikely she would advertise that information."

Disappointment flashed across the woman's essence, but she sighed and relinquished it. A restrained smile followed. "What about you? They have you cooped in here all day without reason; you probably hate the Purifier Corporation."

"Their actions are logical, considering their history with *vestiges*. Nor does my confinement hamper my exploration of your society and world in any meaningful way. I am content to remain here."

"A captive? You say it doesn't obstruct you, but doesn't the mere fact grate on you?"

"No, it does not."

"Well, I can't say I understand that, but you are from a different world."

"May I ask you a question concerning Jade?"

"Sure."

"You attended the academy with her, yet only graduated recently; this is disproportionate."

"Ah, Jade and her brother entered the academy as orphaned children before the completion of their general education years and just went on from there. Ilin had a mind for puzzles that you wouldn't believe, people too for that matter. Jade was more for programming and the standard Purifier skillset. Not so great with people though."

"That is not the first time I've heard her described as such; what changed her and is it that distinct of an improvement?"

"Definitely an improvement, and I don't know." Candice stood, collapsing the seat with a tap of her foot. "I'm glad to see she's finally woken up though. I always found her a little creepy with how she never really looked at you, and a little cold. You know, they used to call her the Reaper, after the old fables; funny how it was Ilin who almost became a Sovereign."

"You said she surpassed her brother in the skillset of the Purifiers, why did they select him over her?"

"Because while she was better, Ilin was good, very good, and capable of holding a conversation. If you ignore the trappings of armor and weapons, the Sovereigns are first and foremost business-men." She stored the box in her bag once more. "A more emotional person might call their actions reprehensible, denying Jade what she deserved...."

"Why do you conceal your purpose still? I indicated a preference for forthright discourse."

She shuffled slightly, her emotions validating the exterior signals. "Wow, you really are exceptional at reading people. Regard-less, I just wanted to ask some questions, learn a little more about Jade."

"Why?"

She winked, her emotions surging with confidence and humor, "Because I want to help, silly." The humor submerged as abruptly as it surfaced. "Now, last chance to join me and my organization?"

"I am currently uninterested in altering my situation."

Any cordiality in her essence perished, usurped by lethal intent. "Well, that's that then." She advanced, donning a pair of white gloves, and exhaled in a fashion similar to Jade Dieza when she exited physical space. A fountain of pale mist poured from her lips and the color fled her body, leaving her desaturated. Still advancing, she phased through the wall and dug into a pocket. Chandris rose to a crouch and growled. Unperturbed, Candice advanced.

Stopping with a mere foot to separate them, she spoke, "I don't know what you're seeing, but we don't want to kill you, just own you." She phased back into reality, and he struck. Something intervened however, a crackling orb of energy flashed into being around her, held for an instant, then shattered beneath his blow. It nullified his swipe nonetheless and afforded Candice the opportu-nity she needed. Stepping close, she yanked a seething red card from her pocket and slapped it against his chest.

Agony slammed through Chandris, searing physical and spiritual form alike as the card fused to his body. He buckled and roared as the foreign power asserted itself over him, confining his actions and rooting itself in his essence. Candice danced back, exhaling into the spectral form. "You should thank Marsilias next time you see him. He was the one who gave us this idea. Now, you will tell and show no one this card; it is to be our little secret." Her words latched onto him like barbed wire, burrowing into his being, fastening onto the very heart of his essence, forbidding defiance.

Breathing raggedly, Chandris assessed the bindings and then settled back onto his haunches, observing the woman again. "How do you possess two of *Aeria's* gifts?"

Candice returned his stare with a look of disgusted surprise. "Really? I just bound your body and soul, and you want to know how?"

"Wrath and violence will not alter my situation. Nor will returning to *Aeria*."

Realization flashed in her spirit. "You're looking for a loophole."

"Correct."

"Search elsewhere." Forgoing departing pleasantries, she exhaled a cloud of mist and left, her spirit utterly unperturbed by regret as she disappeared into the walls. And strangely, not one alarm sounded at her assault, or any defense activated. She seemed as invisible to the compound as his illusionary forms were, and in her absence only silence remained.

In that silence, Chandris returned to the bed, his own mind darkening with fear and the reality that he no longer controlled himself. With no other recourse, he directed his attention inward, inspecting the fetters on his being for any glimmer of flaw or weakness and found none. The card had fused to the nucleus of his essence, rooting in every spark of his being; removing it by force would be catastrophic and devastate his sentience, reducing him to a *vestige* again.

Something external shifted in his prison, a burst of colors and movement amidst the sterile white. He resurfaced, directing his attention to where Jade's image stood on the wall.

"How you doing, Chandris?"

"Unchanged from our previous interaction."

"I suppose that's good to hear. Did you find the other *soul?*"

"Not a location but a trail. Several, as I assume he moved during the process."

"Did he sense you?"

"Unlikely."

She expelled a relieved breath. "So, can you tell us where to go?"

"I must lead you or transfer the knowledge directly into your memories."

"We can't get you out, Chandris, at least not without hassle and repercussions."

"I do not need my physical form to guide you, my replica will suffice."

She nodded slowly. "Okay, I'll send you directions." Her image miniaturized and a litany of numbers and images occupied the vacated space. "I'd impart the information directly, but you have no receptors or implants."

"What do you mean 'receptors'?"

"Microscopic machines humans carry in their bodies to interact with programs and consoles; they're installed at birth. You got the location?"

"Yes. Should I delay my departure to coincide our arrivals?"

"No, we're already here. Just don't speak to anybody and try to avoid attention." Her image winked out with another flicker.

Delaying only to conceal his absence, Chandris separated the reflection of himself from his physical body and submerged into the floor, ensconcing his illusion in the solid foundation between levels. There, veiled from any sensor the Purifiers employed—as his form exuded no heat signature, provoked no sound, or engendered any notable response in the physical world—Chandris fled. He ghosted through the solid walls of the Purifier compound until he reached the ocean and then projected himself in the direction Jade specified. His reflection moved swiftly, propelled by the strength of his consciousness to the extremity of his sight with every movement. Thus, he traveled the distance to his destination in minutes and found himself returned to the shallow waters where he first arrived.

Declining subterfuge, Chandris alighted on the broad, white walkway connecting the various structures of the retirement district. A few elders noted his advent, but apparently accustomed to inhuman acts by their Savants, none roused in distress or surprise. He ventured deeper into the complex of lengthy, rounded structures, nodding amicably to those he passed. Holographic signs guided his progress to the structure Jade designated: a rare two-storied edifice constructed near the district's center. He phased through the external entrance, as it could not register his presence and thus would not open, then proceeded to Jade's apartment.

The door opened preemptively, admitting him into a spacious suite illuminated by scattered lights. Jade, her spirit a shattered image of unsteady emotions, lounged by a shallow pool while her pet seriat frolicked. Marsilias loomed over the kitchen counter, a plethora of ingredients, dishes, and beverages arrayed before him. A holographic man, presumably an S.I. program, occupied several walls around the apartment, each iteration engaged in a different pursuit. None of the images registered Chandris.

Jade continued talking, unperturbed by his entrance, "I'll let you figure out if they're tracking us. And how."

Marsilias swirled blue liquid around a fruit slice. "It's not a question of how; they've access to you via the global security network, which relays all information to Data Management. That and monitoring discharged employees is protocol."

"We'll disable whatever's tracking us then, and hack Data Management for safety."

"Considering your extensive amendments to their software, I can't imagine hacking Data Management being difficult," the hologram supplied. "I'll restrict all information pertaining to you and Marsilias behind special clearance."

"Call it something cool ... like Rogue Fire." Lying supine, she raised her hands toward the ceiling, spreading them as if to behold the title.

"I'm calling it Everyone Dies Eventually."

"But that's so depressing."

"My life is nothing but despair. I serve you."

Her hands dropped. "Just do it."

The program winked out, dimming the room. Jade rolled her head to greet Chandris, "Hey, you. How you been?"

"I am unchanged from our recent discourse."

Marsilias leaned on the counter, sipping his beverage and regarding him. "You know, I have a question, Chandris. If this form we see is more or less an illusion, how do you hear?"

"I cannot hear, smell, touch or taste. I read lips."

"And sight?" Jade asked.

"Difficult to explain and necessitates a perspective of being that humans have yet to attain."

"Oh well, secrets of the universe are overrated anyway." Jade clambered to her feet, hoisting the seriat on an arm. "You have our destination?"

"I have the path." Chandris indicated southward, aligning with his connection to the *soul*. "I can neither discern distance nor emotional state from so far, only direction."

"Then there's no use in delaying, Jade's hacks on all the people watching us won't last forever." Marsilias vacated the kitchen, transferring a variety of brightly colored receptacles from the counter to a coarse military bag.

Jade kissed her seriat's brow and restored it to the water, crooning gently. The creature clutched her arm, chirruping and nuzzling. She pried free. "No, baby, you gotta stay. It's dangerous and mama doesn't want you to get hurt." She caressed it a final time and joined Marsilias at the door. "One of those mine?" Her finger wagged at the bag.

"Yes, one of your favorites." He delved into a breast pocket and retrieved a burgundy flask. "Sugared lemons, ice-cream, and soda. Extra cream and lemon."

"Thank you." Jade accepted the tribute, tapping the door with a foot so it opened. "One of us is gonna have to fly, you know. There's no destination for the autopilot to follow. You want it?"

"Definitely. I've seen your flying."

"Plenty of people bomb buildings. Multiple buildings even."

"Yes, but not dive bomb."

Perplexed by the contrast of their external nonchalance versus their internal anxiety, Chandris posed a question he hoped would explain the dichotomy, "Does confronting Indemiun not concern you?"

A minute spasm shook Jade and she lowered the flask, regarding its mouth with a taught, faltering smile. "We're not confronting Indemiun today, just finding him and proving he exists. I can't confront a *soul* with training Siphons."

"Plus, we've experienced worse," Marsilias added somberly. "Wars, and an apocalypse. I once visited Jade without appropriate tribute. It ... went poorly." They emerged from the apartment complex, Marsilias lifting a hood against the early afternoon drizzle.

Jade crossed to a modest vessel idling beside the walkway and entered a code. The side door opened, issuing an invitation to enter and a request for destination. "Air-dock, please," Marsilias replied, slipping into the front seat over a stack of black crates.

The S.I. program from Jade's apartment appeared on the vessel's interior console. "I compromised the Robotic Corporation's data and files; you're free to cause trouble."

"Good to hear. Thanks, Michael." The program winked out.

They rode the vessel through the retirement district to an air-dock on six wide limbs that dwarfed the other structures. A few automatons assisted them in disembarking and ferrying Marsilias's black crates to a lift, which in turn delivered them to the dock's roof. Jade leased a plane from the waiting console while Marsilias accessed a secondary one to secure armament authorization for his crates, listing explosives, chemicals, and energy devices. The dock provided an aircraft shortly thereafter, dispensing it from internal chambers with a platform as the roof opened.

Marsilias appraised the medium-sized plane, painted black with flame and skull decals, and sighed. "I see we're flying in style."

"Hush,"—Jade trotted past—"we look awesome."

Claiming the front as the automatons loaded his crates, Marsilias slung his pack onto a vacant seat. "Override the security measures please, Jade. We need to subvert the automated system with manual."

She activated a rear panel, shook her hand, and pressed her fingers against it hard enough to stop their fitful quivering. Her essence calmed a moment later, soothing into patterns of concentration.

Chandris situated himself at a window to Marsilias's left. "Will they not realize you've tampered with their device upon its return?"

"No. Jade will avoid permanent damage and preserve the automated program for easy reinstallation."

Behind them, bright and clear distaste disturbed the erratic mess of Jade's emotions. "Silias, I'm going to adjust their programming. It's kind of terrible...."

"No."

"It wouldn't be anything major, just an overhaul of their

operating system, storm navigation, and firewalls."

"Still a no." Marsilias began adjusting the pilot's seat only to pause, realization sprouting in his essence. "You already did it, didn't you?"

Contentment bloomed in her essence, though it seemed unrelated to his comment "... Maybe. Just a little. Barely anything, really."

"Did you change anything I should worry about?"

"Ehh, I'd be more concerned with what I didn't change, there's this self-destruct sequence that activates if the mainframe registers an intrusion."

"And you left that in?"

"Yeah. Apart from its prehistoric coding, it seemed like an appropriate feature. You don't want any undesirables accessing your network."

"Don't you think messing with their programing is a tad perilous then?" Marsilias asked.

"Maybe if it wasn't fifteen years defunct." The lights blinked, signifying her completion. "All right, take us out, captain." She dropped into her seat, grinning in comfortable satisfaction. Although minutely, her essence appeared calmer.

Marsilias gripped the console, raising the aircraft. "Where to, Chandris?"

"Follow the currents. I will tell you when to adjust."

The flight lasted several hours, passing well into dusk as the clouds turned tenebrous and the rain to sleet. Jade slumbered in the back, curled in the arms of her seat and awash in its heat. Marsilias spoke little through the duration, and only in response to Chandris's directions. A glow gradually appeared on the horizon, vibrant and sharp against the obscurity of night, and prompted a nod from Marsilias.

"We're getting close, aren't we?"

Chandris considered the trail. He perceived no difference in its rhythms or substance, and yet his spirit thrummed with the nearness of a kindred. "Yes." The other would sense an echo of him as well, but leave it unremarked as just one of any number of *souls* wandering this side of existence.

Chandris indicated the approaching light. "What is that place?"

"Our history. Wake Jade, if you can."

Chandris moved to her seat, ruminating on how best to wake her. After a moment's thought, he leaned close. "I am going to consume your dessert."

Her eye cracked open, peering through lashes and a strand of violet hair. "Only if you're wondering what stupid feels like."

Chandris cocked his head. "Your personality changes based on your exhaustion and mental state, both of which should be improved by rest."

She groaned and stretched. "Yeah, but I'm always tired, so waking me up just makes it worse. We there?"

"Yes, though it is unfamiliar to me."

"Hey, Silias, where are we?"

"The Natani Mangrove."

"Oh." She approached the front window.

"What is this place for you to speak with such reverence?"

"The place of our origin. Sort of. We are not natives to this world; our ancestors were introduced to it just over a thousand years ago by interstellar arks, all history of our origin erased from the records."

"Would your adults not have memories?"

"There were no adults, only infants raised, taught, and protected by androids called Mothers. They stayed with us for a few generations, then gradually began deactivating. Best as we can assume, we're some kind of social experiment. The Arks and Mothers exceed our scientific understanding, seem to exceed even the sky-cities."

With their approach, shapes appeared in the light, immense forms striking upward to brush the clouds. The silhouettes took shape: trees as tall as mountains sprouted from the ocean, their branches mingling to comprise vast plateaus blanketed in moss. The light itself issued from veins in the bark and leaves.

Resting on the ocean surface beside the mangrove, wrapped to near indistinguishability in vines and overgrown with lichen, was an ark. Large as a mountain, black and rectangular, it rocked with the tide, devoid of distinguishing features or deterioration: no doors, no windows, not even thrusters. It felt ... alien to Chandris, of an origin fundamentally different to his own or the humans of this world, the soul of it—or rather the soul of whatever world gave birth to it— born of a different essence, like carbon and silicone lifeforms, like the opposite colors on a spectrum.

Marsilias guided the plane toward the lowest plateau—resting upon the water's surface like a dense carpet—then between the trees, navigating wayward branches and irregular trunks. A dais appeared in the forest further on, its foundation the remnants of an enormous truncated tree and its surface a landing pad.

Marsilias landed the plane, powered it down, and spun his chair to face them, exposing his pale and sweaty features. Even trained in it, and at the helm, he hated flying. He leaned forward, clasping his hands together. "So, how do we want to do this?"

"We find Indemiun first, try and get footage, something that'll prove what he is. Chandris, can you get us closer?"

"I can direct you to his immediate location."

"Okay, we'll follow you. Marsilias, you need something heavy-duty but light enough to maneuver with in case this goes south. Also, don't break anything, this is a preservation site."

"I have just the thing." Marsilias accessed the plane's storage vault, removing and strapping a medium-sized crate across his back with apparent ease. A sequence of lesser containers, containing various gadgets, followed and were affixed to belts about his waist and torso. Then he joined them at the door. "Ready."

They disembarked and followed delineated pathways to the landing pad's edge, unperturbed by the vast absence of machinery and people. Only their plane and the landing pad itself disrupted the environment, the rest thrummed with flora and ubiquitous fauna.

"Do humans not abide here?"

"Yes, but the corporations limit the population and technology," Marsilias replied. "They're trying to maintain the purity and preserve our history. Students at all stages of education visit yearly to learn that history. Most will visit scores of mangroves across the planet during their education years. The only permanent residents are privileged elders and their caretakers. They inhabit communal housings scattered across the plateaus, excluding those reserved for pilgrimages and tourism."

They reached the landing pad's perimeter and descended a stairway carved from the trunk's side. The loamy main floor squelched when they stepped on it, depressing along the contours of branches, roots, and ancient support struts. Jade continued undeterred, pursuing the direction Chandris indicated as her essence bloomed with serenity. The fauna, ranging from bright-plumed avians to meandering canines and rodents, exhibited no fear of the humans. Some even approached, nuzzling them in search of food, which Jade surreptitiously provided, whispering warnings against telling the enforcers. She seemed particularly infatuated with the infant animals.

The environment altered as they ventured further from the landing pad, the trees changing in shape and bark, and the moss in its hues. Flowers multiplied, decorating every surface as extensively as the moss, sometimes draping from curling vines and other times burgeoning from the water below. Houses comprised of moss-covered wood appeared sporadically, clutching the trees in curving spires connected by latticework walkways and rudimentary lifts.

As he observed these medieval abodes, Chandris mused aloud, "No one lives in these domiciles?"

"No," Marsilias answered, "they're inadequate shelters conserved for history. Everyone lives in community structures like that one." He pointed ahead to a long, modern structure overgrown with the teal moss dominating this region. A few aged humans reclined outside in chairs, mostly occupied in sleeping or compiling bouquets of flowers. "I assume that's also where we're going?"

"I cannot say with certainty, but I believe so; the other *soul's* presence is prominent here."

Concern flecked Marsilias's thoughts. "Can he sense you as well?"

"Yes, but he has no reason to be concerned with it. He will notice the contradiction of my imagery, absent *soul* and physicality, however, and that may cause him concern."

"We'll have to risk it." Jade slowed, covertly preparing a Siphon. "You boys ready?"

They voiced affirmatives, and she proceeded to the complex's front yard.

A middle-aged woman in a crisp, white suit immediately emerged from the building along a walkway of carved wood. "Hello, are you visiting a relative? Or seeking to accommodate one?"

"Seeking to accommodate one," Marsilias replied, stepping forward and offering a smile. "We're here for my grandmother;

she's getting on in years and can't live alone anymore. We're hoping to eke out a spot for her." As the man spoke, Jade knelt, leaning low to stroke and smell the nearest flowers. Her emotions brightened further at this, becoming almost content, but a purpose defined them so Chandris continued to watch her.

The woman ignored Jade, and tapped the base of her left palm with a discordantly hard click. She blinked and her gaze defocused, her mind accessing an internalized database. "We have space available Mr...?"

"Wreign, spelled W R E ..." As Marsilias began reciting his name with exaggerated diction, Jade rose and wandered through the garden, one hand absently—though her essence betrayed this as anything but—sliding into an unlocked pocket of her coat.

"Thank you, Mr. Wreign, I need just a moment to ascertain your credentia–"

Jade stumbled minutely and caught her balance on the woman's hand, bare skin to bare skin. She righted herself instantly and relinquished her grip. "Sorry."

The woman dismissed her apology with a perfunctory gesture, then frowned and tapped her palm again to elicit another click. "My apologies, Mr. Wreign, but my database is malfunctioning. I cannot access your information to begin negotiating for your grand-mother's care."

"I understand perfectly, and there is no need for you to apologize. These things happen. Could we be allowed to explore though? We promise not to bother anyone."

"Please, explore the facility at your leisure, but respect the inhabitants and do not bother them. Remember to notify me when you depart. Hopefully, the issues will be resolved before then." She moved to speak with a resident.

Chandris sidled close enough to Jade to whisper, "Why did you desire to covertly touch her?"

She raised the hand that had delved into her coat pocket, revealing upon the tip of her index finger a gel pad decorated with hairline copper veins. "Portable virus to block their data; stops them discovering Silias's grandmother's been dead for decades." She returned the device to her pocket and continued forward.

Inside, the building was comprised of sleek walls in a pallet of warm colors. Several attendants and elderly individuals populated the space, many pausing in whatever activity occupied them to offer cheerful greetings. Chandris wordlessly directed them upwards.

Moving quickly, they entered an elevator just off the primary lobby and rode it to the uppermost floor, exiting into a spacious but mostly shadowed common room. The walls glowed a soothing orange, providing the only illumination and casting the room's occupants into silhouettes. A steady, rhythmic music played in the background, rising and falling with a pattern of slow drums as warm mist dressed the air, further compromising vision. Jade sniffed once before donning her mask with a simple comment of, "Valerian." Marsilias emulated her before sliding into the maze of beds and their slumbering occupants. A few attendants wandered the room, checking patients and occasionally applying ointments.

One of these noted them. "Please whisper, this wing treats insomniacs and those with chronic pain. Otherwise, you're free to peruse." He glided off on padded stockings, medical coat swaying over a carpet that smelled faintly of lemons.

Jade eased toward Chandris, whispering, "Where is he?"

"To the west, the solitary attendant."

They peered through the haze but failed to distinguish more than a vague shape and height. Jade grimaced. "Chandris, stay back here so you don't alert him. We need a recognizable image or description."

Chandris nodded and slipped further back, receding into the shadows of a corner.

01001111 01110010 01110000 01101000 01100001 01101110 01110011
00100000 01100011 01100001 01101100 01101100 01100101 01100100
00100000 01001010 01100001 01100100 01100101 00100000 01100001
01101110 01100100 00100000 01001001 01101100 01101001 01101110
00100000 01000100 01101001 01100101 01111010 01100001

Affecting a meandering trajectory, Jade wormed toward the wall opposite the *soul*, pausing at random intervals to inspect something while always maintaining a vigil on his location. When she attained the wall, she ambled along it toward him. The *soul* displayed no signs of alarm and continued examining a line of mattresses and patients, appearing to soothe those with troubled sleep. Marsilias loitered near the entrance, conversing genially with one of the attendants and eliminating the only obvious escape route.

Retrieving the prepared Siphon from one of her coat's larger pockets, Jade concealed it in her sleeve and rounded the room's corner. The *soul* neared, revealing itself in the guise of a woman with tightly bound hair. Jade curved her steps, drifting toward a collision while fixing her gaze on the beds. She heard the *soul's* steps, their light scuff and the ambient music concealing its voice. She activated her lenses, preparing to capture an image and disguising it as adjusting a lock of hair. She took a final step and collided with the *soul.*

They stumbled apart, the *soul's* words cutting off as they glanced at each other. Jade, her lips already forming the words of an apology, recognized the face and stared, horrified. Naija, a member of her Core, stared back.

Nightmares reared within Jade, engulfing her vision. She staggered back, reeling as memories bombarded her: Naija screaming for help, the sounds of water rushing in, then her voice cutting out and spluttering, and then gagging as she swallowed and drowned. Yet, despite all that, Jade recognized a truth, "*It knows me; it has Naija's memories. It's going to run. I can't let it escape.*"

Then the rage came, hot and maddening, and full of pain. Her friend was dead, should be dead, and yet here she stood, a mockery of life, a toy of the very thing that killed her. She deserved better. Even so, Jade should have fled, should have trusted Marsilias to get the evidence they needed. Instead, she snarled, effortlessly reversing momentum with a step, the screaming visions falling silent as she moved to kill.

The pulse-knife on her left hand snapped open, its blade crackling with a full charge, while her right hand emerged with the Siphon exploding in dark-green energy. The *soul* started to recoil, its lips moving to speak, but Jade drove her pulse-knife up through its ribcage and into the heart, propelling the whole body off the floor.

Blood, red and human as if it hadn't fashioned this body of its own energy but only inhabited it, splattered her and she squeezed the button on her pulse-knife's handle, unleashing the charge. The *soul*, its feet just settling after her initial thrust, lurched back into the air, its stolen body contorting with arcs of electricity and smoking.

The Siphon finished assembling in her right hand, assuming the form of a stake and chain, with the chain clamped around her wrist. She drove the stake into the *soul's* chest, twisted it so it caught between two ribs, and then tore the pulse-knife out for maximum damage. The *soul* reeled away, but she dragged it back to her with the chain, and drove the pulse-knife into the body's liver.

Finally stabilizing through Jade's battery and the lethal arcs of electricity from her pulse-knife, the *soul* retaliated, flinging Jade into and over one of the beds and tearing her pulse-knife from its side in the process. Jade rolled with the impetus and landed on her feet, the chain connecting them snapping taught. She yanked, dragging the *soul* stumbling toward her, and leapt onto the bed as its occupant screamed and flailed themselves onto the floor.

The *soul* grasped the stake and pulled to remove it to no effect. Its other hand instantly flashed across to sever the chain, dousing the Siphon's light and reverting it to its silver casing—only now snapped in two. Jade leapt for the *soul*, pulse-knife extended as she drew another Siphon. The *soul* vaulted back, scattering a pair of beds and upending their occupants as two immense sapphire wings sprouted from its back. Then, like water through a sieve, it evacuated Naija's body through her shoulders, a thousand sparks of light streaming free and coalescing in a form both physical and radiant.

Jade landed where it had stood and instantly jumped after it, a black Siphon igniting in her hand. The *soul* burst back-first through the wall, wings crashing down to soar skyward as the opaque duraglau shattered outward with a halo of sparking wires and warped support metal. Jade pursued it, hurling herself through the punctured wall and reassembling the Siphon into a grappling hook. She twisted mid-flight and fired it at the *soul*. The hook latched onto its foot and reeled in, pulling her heavenward. That's when she caught her first true look at Indemiun.

He soared on two immense wings, his body long and sinuous with three swirling feather tails. Metallic, silver, and blue plumage covered its body, the individual feathers large and sharp. Its head, adorned with three emerald crests, was serpentine with a long flat skull and two protruding fangs. Its four muscular limbs mimicked those of the Ursa family. In length, it measured close to twenty feet and half that in height.

The moment of awe ended as Jade slammed into Indemiun's side. The *soul* howled and futilely kicked at her, swinging her wildly about. Bracing herself as best she could with an arm, Jade heaved up and stabbed the recharged pulse-knife into Indemiun's back through a gap in its feathers. Indemiun spun, the force of it flipping Jade up to its back and across the bed of its razor-edged feathers. Luckily, her coat blocked most of the damage.

Her momentum ceased and she struggled upright, one hand clamped on her anchoring knife and the other still holding the Siphon. Seated thus, she found herself staring into Indemiun's eyes, their colors oscillating in bursts of fiery incandescence across the spectrum. He spoke then, voice soft as a lullaby, "I am not your enemy, Jade Dieza." Then he spiraled, grasping and breaking both her grip on the grappling hook Siphon and tearing her pulse-knife free to send her plummeting.

Jade fell, scrambling for another Siphon, anything that could reattach her to Indemiun, but found nothing before he soared beyond her reach. She spat a curse and spun toward the approaching ground, exhaling. Her body changed and, deprived of weight, her descent slowed—permitting her to drop harmlessly into the moss; and then inhale.

She lay there trembling for a moment, full of rage that had no outlet, her fingers burrowing into the ground as they clenched. It broiled and built inside her, sharpening with desperation and failure until it exploded from her in an impotent, agonized shriek. She snapped up to a sit, clutching her head and knotting her fingers in her hair as the cry whimpered out into dry, heaving sobs. She'd failed. Failed, failed, failed. Failed to kill Indemiun. Failed even to secure evidence of his existence, and in so doing had condemned thousands.

A voice called out, drawing her attention to Marsilias as he hastened from the complex, Chandris a few steps behind. She wiped her face, repressing everything inside her so he wouldn't see, then waved to reassure him of her safety.

Marsilias arrived. "Are you all right?" She nodded without looking up, earning a sigh of relief as he swung the weapon case from his back. "I don't know why I even bothered to bring this, fat lot of help it did."

"I should have told the Purifiers," she whispered, as much to herself as Marsilias, "should have made up a lie, anything to get them here. Should have trusted Serras or Theeran."

"The Sovereigns would have ignored you, just like they would have before, and there's still the disease."

"You're probably right." Jade knew he was, but it didn't help. She forced herself to stand anyway. "We need to go; the authorities will arrive any second."

"I can take the hit for this; my position should still hold."

"No, you can't. The Sovereigns will know I was involved whatever you say. Hiding me will force them to exclude you." She forced a shuddering breath. "You need to sell me out, whatever it takes to keep your position. Say I coerced you with an old debt."

"They won't believe that, and you know it? You've transgressed on their law, Jade, they'll take everything they can. I can probably shield you a–"

"Not enough to make a difference, Silias. And yeah, they won't believe it, but they don't have to. They just need an excuse to hide behind, something to justify keeping you around. They'll want something more from you, but you'll have that, so just go. I'll be fine."

The distant sound of planes crept from the East, attracting his gaze then a grim nod of ascent.

She shifted her attention to Chandris, who waited just to the side. "You should go as well."

"Jade Dieza, Indemiun was not an *Oscuras*. He was a *soul*. He did not invert his being." His image disintegrated into particles of light.

Three white planes appeared between the trees, sirens blaring and their lights flashing red. Jade stared at them, observing without seeing.

In the back of her mind, however, Indemiun's parting avowal niggled, *"I am not your enemy."*

Sanctions

Officials bustled around Jade, interrogating witnesses, conferring details to their superiors, and repairing the damage her fight produced. Despite her compliance, they had restrained her arms and legs with small white cuffs that debilitated her muscles, weakening and slowing anything she might attempt besides eye movement, speech, and breathing. A few residents loitered outside the hubbub, excitedly discussing all that transpired.

Jade watched it all, waiting for the inevitable. She had supplied the official in charge with a statement concerning her actions, intents, and reasons, omitting solely the specifics about *souls*. Marsilias, exonerated from guilt by his influence and her admittance of coercion, had already departed, promising to mitigate her punishment however he could.

A muted, but insistent, cough attracted Jade's attention to her left, where a statuesque woman stood in a stiff Savant Corporation uniform adorned by ranks of silver buttons. Her lapels bore various badges, including the insignia of a Magister.

"May I help you?" Jade asked tiredly.

"I am from the Savant Corporation; my task is to ascertain the details of this disturbance. Please confirm that you are a Specter."

"Logically, isn't it impossible for me to be a Specter since I'm alive?"

"Please confirm or deny that you possess metaphysical abilities."

"I have this uncanny ability to walk through water, does that count?"

"Has the Savant Corporation dealt you injury in the past? If not, why resist a simple question?"

"I have a better idea, how about you tell me what you want first, and why the Savant Corporation is insinuating itself into a different corporation's affair? Nothing here's subject to your purview."

"You are a Specter–"

"Which you asked me to confirm."

"A formality, nothing more. We are assessing our liability in this scenario; the management and control of gifted individuals is our concern."

"Not in my case."

"Quite the contrary. My records indicate no mention of a gifted individual named Jade Dieza, meaning you are unregistered. It is the Savant Corporation's obligation to control and restrain potentially dangerous gifted, especially those operating outside our authority."

"Wait, you're here to figure out if I'm dangerous? In what way?"

"Your conflict with the revenant supplies ample proof of your ability to damage the environment. If your unsanctioned activities endanger the lives of civilians, they present a difficulty the Savant Corporation must resolve."

"You sound like you're quoting the textbook."

"Legal jargon is important in such cases."

"All right, I'll pay whatever they fine you for. Happy?"

"It is not a question of money, Ms. Dieza, but of your behavior and the Savant Corporation's lapse in regulating it accordingly. The cost to repair the inflicted damage is trifling." She retrieved a square pad from a pocket and unfolded it into a console. "The first order of business will be to rectify your divorce from the corporation and its precepts; this will resolve your unemployment admirably and grant you a steady salary."

"I can't work for you, I'm a terrible employee, no respect for authority."

"You don't have much choice. Once instated, you will most likely be assigned combat detail with the Purifier and Defense Corporations. That seems the best option, considering your history."

"I'm not working for you."

"We'll have to assess your mental and physical health, and inspect your Siphon, of course."

Jade hailed a passing soldier, "Hey, remove this woman, she's harassing me."

The soldier shrugged. "I can't interfere with corporation business, sorry."

Jade refocused on the Magister. "Just leave me alone already; I've done nothing to hurt the Savant Corporation!"

"Of course not. After the mental tests, we'll have to ascertain the extent of your abilities."

"Insignificant. I can barely manage the First Step a couple times before collapsing. I'm practically normal."

Ignoring her, the Magister removed a cylindrical device from a loop on her waist and activated it. "There'll be some new realities to acclimate yourself to; there are rules of behavior, mandated efficiency levels, set hours, and restricted use of your abilities. You won't be able to use them until we grant permission and dampen the chemical restraints."

"Don't touch me!" Jade snarled, lurching in her seat. Hearing the commotion, several guards approached, hands loosely resting on their weapons in case she caused further difficulties.

"Calm down," the Magister soothed, "this is just a temporary corporation mark. It's painless and you'll only suffer a little nausea while the suppressor takes effect; we'll install the more permanent damper later."

"Don't you dare touch me!" Jade screamed, almost toppling her seat.

The Magister stepped forward, raising the glowing cylinder in one hand. "Stop complaining, Ms. Dieza. You're making a scene, and this is long overdue."

Jade exhaled explosively, shucking her restraints, and rolled back through her seat. The guards surged closer, leveling their weapons where she crouched. Fading back into the physical world, she flung her hands outward, palms open to demonstrate her lack of weapons. "I'm not escaping!" she cried, voice cracking. "I'm not escaping." Even as she spoke, her vision swam and her breath hitched, pain creeping through her lungs.

The Magister advanced. "Cease this childish behavior, it serves no one and only worsens your situation. I will exclude it from my report if you submit now."

"No. I'm retired."

"You can't retire after barely having reached the employable age. You'll finish your education under the Savant Corporation and together we will access every ounce of potential your abilities have."

"You can't teach me anything."

"Don't be naïve, we have Specter's hundreds of years older than you, Specter's who have survived wars and spent years employing the Second Step."

Jade shook her head. "I have walked through death, looked upon cities made of night, witnessed civilizations set upon the backs of clouds and glimpsed beings so vast they beggar our greatest achievements." As she enumerated each item, its image flashed before her, a memory of something that defied her comprehension. She shuddered and straightened, extending her arm toward the Magister as the pulse-knife snapped open. "I will not belong to you."

"Guards," the Magister called, "restrain her. She is violating corporation law by resisting."

"No! I don't want to hurt you." Jade spun, gesturing at them frantically with a bare palm. Internally, her thoughts roiled, echoing with a desperate litany of, *"No, no, no."*

The Magister struck in that instant, lunging forward in a sleek bound with outstretched hands. Her fingers gleamed with syringe tips, no doubt bursting with the promised chemical agent. She landed behind Jade and stabbed her right hand forward, the left held protectively before her torso and face.

Sensing her assault, Jade spun, parrying the Magister's strike with her forearm. The Magister pressed forward, sliding inside Jade's reach and wrapping her left arm about Jade's neck. Jade ducked and rolled out from the grapple, her hand snapping out to stab a pressure point in the Magister's left arm, rendering it limp. They separated, her pulse-knife retracting and the Magister manipulating her inert appendage.

Jade maintained a defensive posture, her gaze roving the stunned guards. She didn't want to unnerve them further by using her abilities again; shucking the cuffs would have put them on edge already, anything more might tip them against her. She could just take the First Step and sit in the between-world until someone arrived to unravel the whole mess, but that seemed best left as a final resort.

The Magister's grimace deepened, and her arm spasmed back into life. "Do you really want to escalate this further, Ms. Dieza? People could get hurt."

"Just back off then. Let me be until the Purifiers arrive."

"You want a corporation to yield to the demands of a petulant child?" She straightened, disdain tinging her words. "But if you promise to submit when the Purifiers arrive, I'll wait."

"I am not going with you."

"It doesn't do me much good to wait then, does it?" She settled easily into the opening posture of an aggressive, close-quarter form. Jade assumed a defensive variation of the same style.

"What the hell is going on here?" A new voice sheared through the crowd, silencing the murmuring soldiers and pulling the Magister to attention. Jade relinquished her posture with a sigh of relief and faced the furious Purifier.

Jade did not recognize the woman, but the Annihilation Core's garish red adorned the shoulders and sleeves of her uniform. As an officer in the Annihilation Core, a specialized division for resolving extreme revenant manifestations, the woman wielded extensive authority over other Purifier branches and nominal decision-making capabilities. Altogether, she represented an operative sufficiently important to placate the other corporation while resolving a matter the Sovereigns found tedious and infuriating but ultimately immaterial: Jade. Her conciliating purpose aside, the woman drastically outranked everyone present.

The woman stopped beside the Magister, her rather ferociously designed Siphon swinging on a chain from her wrist. "And?" she pressed, making no attempt to disguise her irritation.

"The Savant Corporation dispatched me to register and introduce this woman in our ranks. She resisted, violating corporate law, and assaulted me while escaping her bonds."

"Jade Dieza is retired. Any occupation she inhabits is exclusively recreational in nature."

"At her age? That's—"

"Corporate sanctioned despite her recent transgressions, Magister. The Purifier Corporation advised your superiors of this matter two years ago when she officially retired."

"She still resisted—"

The Purifier unabashedly flicked the Magister between the eyes.

"Boo hoo, you got hurt. Get over it and get moving." She thumbed over her shoulder. The Magister pursed her lips but obeyed.

Jade addressed herself to the woman, "I suppose you're here to punish me?"

The anger evaporated from the woman's posture. "Yes, unfortunately."

Jade blinked at the woman's familiar tone, then rubbed the back of her neck in embarrassment. "Um, do I know you?"

"Oh, no. I was with the Annihilation Core two years ago and close enough to the gate to see what happened. Still, I can't disobey."

"Wouldn't want you to." Jade blew a soft exhale and started divesting herself of weapons, both Purifier in origin and standard. "Just give me the rundown."

"House-arrest and frozen assets until this matter is concluded, then a year parole. They'll monitor your home's web-traffic and programs constantly, and personally deliver all necessities." As she spoke, the Purifier grimly accepted Jade's armaments and stored them in a silver bag. "Reasonable requests shall be fulfilled, and visitors allowed after review and under supervision." Jade removed the pulse-knife bracers from her wrists and deposited them in the bag; whereupon the woman sealed and tied it off. The bag compressed, hardened, and then adjusted itself into a box, which the woman shook. When nothing rattled, she refocused on Jade. "I will be your chaperone for the night shift; an administrator will cover the rest."

"How do they plan on actually restraining me?"

"Nothing physical, just the threat of more significant punishments should you abscond." The woman glanced about. "Is there anything you need from here?"

"Just your name."

"Fhara Loen. It's time to leave." Without tarrying for Jade, Fhara strode in the direction of the landing pad, Jade's box of weapons clasped under one arm.

Jade trailed her to a Purifier Damselfly, its side branded with the corporation's sigil. Fhara claimed the pilot's seat with casual efficiency and indicated the bench of seats behind her. "Take the middle one and don't touch anything electronic; we know what you're capable of."

Jade complied, curling up into the luxurious seat as the doors sealed and the engines activated, thrumming throughout the plane. She let her head fall back and closed her eyes, letting the vibrations soothe her heartbeat. *"It's okay, they didn't get you. No one got you."* The plane lifted and, though she did not trust Fhara, exhaustion, both physical and emotional, pulled her under.

Fhara woke Jade some time later. "We've arrived, Ms. Dieza. I'd let you sleep longer but the plane's scheduled to return."

"I can reprogram it if you'd like," Jade murmured into her seat.

"I don't think my superiors would approve, now up." Fhara jostled her until Jade reluctantly slid from the seat and stood.

"Best get used to this, I sleep a lot." She stretched and emerged from the plane onto the overcast, but dry, roof of her apartment building. A pair of Purifier troops stood on either edge of the building, their gazes fixed on Jade. She waved at them. "Hello, boys." They refrained from acknowledging her greeting, and Jade forced herself to stroll unconcernedly to the entrance, to ignore that the Purifier Corporation had just effectively locked her away from the world on their whim. Of course, she could just leave if she so desired, walk past all of these guards with the First Step, and in so doing incriminate herself to the entire Corporatocracy. "How many goons did they station here?"

"Depends on who you ask," Fhara replied, "but I know of six, whose locations shall go undisclosed."

"You surrender the number of guards just like that?"

"Like I said, the Purifier Corporation acknowledges that it cannot conceivably contain you without ... infringing on several rights. We're here more as a reminder, and as forewarning should you bolt." Striding along a corridor, Fhara reached and entered an omniveyor. "I doubt the Sovereigns consider you an actual threat, just—"

"A transgressor and unwelcome. Trust me, I am well aware of their opinion." Jade slouched against the omniveyor walls and closed her eyes. "Don't worry though, as long as there's cake in the fridge, you and I'll get along just fine."

"Why don't they like you?"

Jade cracked an eye, surprised by the question. Despite the woman's amiable question, she spoke in a controlled, professional voice and maintained an unwavering focus on the omniveyor's entrance. Jade let her head drop back. "It's ... complicated."

The omniveyor arrived at the hallway outside her apartment and they exited. Fhara motioned for Jade to lead and trailed after her, fiddling with the screen of a wrist contraption. "Why did you leave the corporation? After what happened to your brother and Core, I'd thought you'd want revenge."

"I got revenge," Jade said softly, and visions of suffocating mist filled her mind, drowning a crumbling cityscape of ruins and desiccated, black clad ghouls. Years' worth of them. "I just ... couldn't continue after it." She folded her arms and shivered. "The corporation wanted me to stay, demanded I stay, but I was done; so I blackmailed them." Jade fed her the half-lie without looking up; the Purifier Corporation had considered the mental collapse of their newest hero bad publicity and buried it even from their own.

"You coerced an entire corporation?" An emotion finally tinged the woman's voice: disbelief.

"It's not that hard; every corporation has dirt; you just have to know where to look." Reaching her apartment, Jade inserted the passcode and slipped in. Cuddles instantly bounded from his pool toward her, chirruping adorably. Jade swooped down, caught him up and buried her face in his fur. "Hello, prince, did you watch everything while I was away." He crawled up her arm and curled along her shoulders, assiduously licking one ear. She laughed and stroked him. The white lights of her apartment clicked on, highlighting the kitchen, living room, and corridor leading to her bedroom.

Fhara briefly inspected the immediate vicinity before approaching Jade with the wristband. "This is a tracker, don't try removing it as it's primed to shock you unconscious."

"Lovely." Jade accepted the tracker and it blinked on, synching to her adaptive suit.

"Are there other rooms?"

"Bedroom and lavatory are that way; there's a second floor for training. No one goes up there. Period." Jade sauntered over to her sofa. "Well, might as well make use of you since you're here." She tapped a console and a holographic chess game appeared.

"Sorry, I have work to do." Fhara raised a portable console and situated herself opposite Jade. "Plus, considering the difficulty I found in waking you earlier, you're probably exhausted and in desperate need of sleep."

Jade dismissed her concerns with a wave. "I'm always tired."

"If you're tired, then sleep; I'm not going anywhere." Fhara's console burst into life, illuminating her pale features and issuing an indistinct thread of music.

Jade frowned. "Are you sure? I can prepare you something or connect you to the region's network. There has to be something you need."

"Nothing. Go sleep." She tapped away on the screen, barely heeding Jade.

"All right, but if you need anything, I'm in the next room."

Jade padded across the warmed tiles, Cuddles purring on her shoulders and soothing her exhausted muscles. Once in her room, she locked the door and then just stared at the bed. She ached from head to foot, and her mind throbbed in sluggish beats, but the need to act thrummed on, a constant pressure, a barrage of muted thoughts rebelling against an extended respite. *"I need to stop Indemiun. He's going to infect everyone. What am I doing here? I need to stop Indemiun. Stop it!"*

His words echoed in her mind 'I am not your enemy.'

"Stop it, you can't do anything else."

She groaned and brushed a finger along her adaptive suit. It hissed a breath of steam, injecting different tips. Her eyes grew heavy, her mind slowed, and loathing the thought of undressing with strangers in her home, she crawled beneath the preheated blankets without undressing. Cuddles snuggled beside her and purred....

It was the silence that woke Jade, the absence of all the quiet workings that perpetually filled her room: the programs, the climate controls, the white noise, the incense, and all the rest. She slit an eye open, forcing her body to perpetuate the illusion of sleep. She saw, heard, and smelled nothing, as if every program that moderated her bedroom had been deactivated. She had not given those commands, and no one else but her should have been able to.

The stillness of her surroundings persisted for another instant, then a shift occurred near the doorway, barely visible by light from the curtained window, followed by the rustle of something moving. Jade kept breathing, struggling against her adaptive suit's sedatives. The blankets weighed on her, confining her legs and arms; she needed to shuck them, but couldn't without alerting her assailant.

Another step from the direction of her door, half-masking the click of an uncharged pulse-knife. Jade pressed the sleeve of her adaptive suit, ceasing the flow of chemicals, and surreptitiously grasped the corner of her pillow and blanket.

The intruder crept into Jade's periphery, a bulky silhouette. It leaned over her, a knife prominent in the hand sliding forward.

Jade struck, twisting in the bed and flinging the pillow against her attacker's head while throwing the covers off herself and entangling them around the knife and wielding arm. The attacker dove forward, futilely trying to stab through the blankets as she landed atop Jade, before—as that proved ineffective—grasping her by the throat.

Minuscule syringes bit her neck as the silhouette pressed her flat, its armored fingers clamping tight. She instinctively tried to exhale, but her body remained solid even as the air burst from her. Readjusting immediately, she struck upward, driving her palm into her assailant's forehead. The attacker's head snapped back, their grip loosening. Jade snatched the offending hand and twisted it, bucking while stabbing her fingers into the soft flesh between thumb and index finger. Her assailant, recognizably a woman now, tumbled off her and began thrashing to disentangle herself from the blankets. Jade scrambled to her knees and tackled her opponent to the floor, straddling her. The woman bucked, but Jade forced her head to the side and struck her temple. The woman fell limp.

"Lights," she gasped and they activated, revealing Fhara, her face livid with black marks. Spitting profanity, Jade launched herself up and sprinted through her hacked bedroom door into her living room, scooping Cuddles up off the floor as she went.

She had barely escaped the hallway when the door to her

apartment exploded open and two full-armored Purifiers stormed in, their faces wreathed in black markings. The first lunged at her, two pulse-knives ejecting from his bracers and sparking with electricity. The second Purifier circled around her.

The first Purifier slashed with one pulse-knife then stabbed with the other, torso twisting to drive the thrust. Dropping Cuddles, she dodged the first pulse-knife then slipped past the second strike, wrapping his arm in her left and bracing her right forearm against his bicep. He stamped at her feet and she danced aside, kicking the side of his knee. He cried out and buckled, and she threw him to the ground, dropping to a knee after him and leveraging the pulse-knife into his chest. His armor crackled and the knife flashed, both erupting with discharged energy to little effect on him. He awkwardly stabbed at her with his other knife, and she caught his forearm on hers. He attempted to knee her, but she rolled forward, snatching his Siphon from its sheath.

They came to their feet in unison, his partner surging toward her back as the first Purifier's Siphon ignited white in her hands. His emotions, memories, and sensations engulfed her, but Jade punched through them while throwing an ineffectual kick at his partner. She found the nexus of his Siphon's energy—his soul—grasped it in her hand and squeezed with desperate precision. He fainted and she spun back to his companion, blocking his descending pulse-knife with both arms.

The Purifier shoved forward, jabbing with his second knife. Jade twisted as best she could, redirecting his impetus past her but still earning a cut on her side. He stumbled, and she kicked the side of his knee, dropping him to his knees.

He slashed at her but she was already pivoting fully around behind him to lock her arms about his neck and head, compressing his neck artery. He thrashed and stabbed at her ineffectually, his assault gradually attenuating until he slumped. Jade let him fall and rushed to the door. "Michael! Activate sub-protocol Dieza!"

Michael appeared on her walls, his image hazy and flickering. He spoke in a disjointed, crackling voice. "Program ... compromised. What ... need?"

"Call Marsilias and activate defense protocols here and there." She reached the door and peeked out at the empty corridor. Satisfied, she yanked her closet open and stomped into a pair of boots. "Hack the Purifier accounts, reinstate all of my financial privileges and disconnect me from the global database." She exhaled again, futilely attempting the First Step, and cursed.

Michael buzzed on the walls, "...can't ... Marsi ... network ... collapse–"

"Shit!" Jade grabbed her coat and swung it on, forgoing any attempt to find weapons. Then she slammed her hand against the wall and connected with the regional network. "Shock me if anyone comes."

She delved into a maelstrom of shredded files and screaming programs. Tendrils of infection and viruses swarmed everywhere, devouring and corrupting everything they touched before multiplying. A glance at the chaos informed her she could not excise the viruses alone, at least not in a timely manner; she needed to crash and then reboot the software. She plunged, blasting through firewalls and avoiding the ensnaring information streams. Lights started winking out around her, marking the complete usurpation of programs. She pushed harder, ignoring the stabbing ache it caused in her mind; she needed to instigate the reset before the virus consumed the entire network, rendering it moribund and an entirely divorced system.

She caught sight of a minor program untouched by the virus and snagged it in passing, safeguarding it in her proverbial pocket; a recognized piece of friendly coding could prove useful if she found the central hub infected. As Jade did so, she caught sight of a third foreign program, something flashing blue amidst the natural bronze and invading black. "*I'll deal with you later,*" she thought and surged forward, commencing the process of amending her pilfered program into a virus of her own.

The network began destabilizing, its lights flicking off in a tide of oily black tendrils. The black swelled, pursuing Jade. She finished her small, cannibalistic virus and unleashed it on the black, a little spark of red geared to destroy programs instead of corrupt. It set to with ravenous glee but could only diminish the deterioration.

Ahead of her she saw the nexus, a globe of swirling bronze coding riddled with black veins. She smashed into it and submerged, fighting through the shattered bits of code to central commands, which she found utterly corrupted. She grasped the one dedicated to resetting the network and eviscerated it, maintaining only its connection strands. Then, as the coding blackened all around her, she rewrote it, penning a command of absolute annihilation.

It activated instantly, registering the apocalyptic threat to its systems, and exploded outward from Jade, obliterating everything, excluding itself. The blue program survived as well, though she had expected that.

Awash in a gray void, the skeleton of a system held together by a strip of annihilation coding, Jade began to rebuild. She worked quickly and efficiently, reconstructing the programs she needed: connection to the global network, communication lines, and financial capabilities. Throughout all of it, the blue program circled patiently around her, waiting.

She finished and dragged herself from the network and buckled in the physical world, soaked in perspiration and panting though mere minutes had elapsed. Her hand remained fixed to the wall, offering a tenuous connection to the web. Rallying herself again, she issued a silent call on a defunct channel no human had used in decades. "I know you're out there. Show yourselves."

The walls flashed and an image materialized; a tall, male figure with inhumanly perfect, milk-white skin and erect pale blue hair. It was all an affectation, the Techcrons could appear however they desired. "What do you want, Ms. Dieza?"

"A meeting in person, you'll need to collect me."

"And if we refuse?"

"Just don't; you've been hanging around this airspace for two years, ever since the *souls* invaded. You know very well what's going on here."

A brief lapse of silence, then, "We will rendezvous with you momentarily. Transfer yourself to the roof of your abode." They terminated the connection.

Jade crawled to her feet with a groan and re-submerged into the network to send Marsilias a warning. Only then did she strip the unconscious Purifiers of whatever weapons she could and activate a controlled EMP pulse on her wrist tracker. Then, terrified of leaving him alone, she collected Cuddles from where he'd fled to her bedroom and departed.

Enlightenment

Jade rested against the omniveyor's wall, watching the empty hallways and doors flicker past toward the roof's sole access point. Cuddles fussed on her arm, sniffing her injuries and mewling as the adaptive suit tendered basic medical aid. She stroked his head and crooned, vying against her own desperate thoughts. "Why is Indemiun trying to kill me? And how are the Techcrons involved? Are they involved? No, think. We're not currently at war with them." She rubbed her face. "It has to be about Indemiun, but how would the Techrons know about the souls when most of the Corporations are ignorant?"

The *soul's* final words echoed in her thoughts again, "*I am not your enemy.*"

"*Then why are you attacking me? Is it because I won't leave you alone?*"

The omniveyor hissed softly and slowed, opening to a service hallway, a shallow stair, and a duraglau door. Jade grasped her injured side and lurched into a shuffling run for the entrance.

There was a pair of Purifier sentries stationed there, watching to ensure she went nowhere by aircraft. One of the guards, advised of her approach by sensors in his gear, appeared on the other side of the duraglau door, his expression one of polite forbiddance until he glimpsed her condition. He flung the doors open and dashed toward her, summoning his companion with a yell.

Jade staggered and caught the wall. "Help."

The guard reached her. "What happened?"

"Attacked ... monster ... injured." She doubled over, squeezing her side so it bled further.

"Stay here, Ms. Jade. Kharlin, we need medical aid, something attacked the apartment." They sprinted toward the omniveyor, his companion with a hand on her ear.

Jade waited until the omniveyor sped off, then resumed her trek along the corridor and up to the now vacant roof. There she hunkered beneath the awning over the entrance and gazed at the gray, drizzling heavens.

Nothing stirred in the sky for several minutes, then the clouds parted and a hull of grainy black metal emerged. Soundless, the Techcron vessel descended within a foot and hovered, exuding neither heat nor any semblance of whatever force kept it aloft. A segment of the hull receded like wet sand scraped aside. Cuddles whimpered on her arm, but she tucked him beneath her coat with a kiss and entered.

The ship's interior resembled its exterior, with an oval shape and the same grainy texture. Weaving, vein-like strands of light covered every surface, blinking green and purple, just bright and frequently enough to navigate the otherwise unlit and almost entirely empty interior. There was only a high-back chair of slim, blunt metal near the center, facing her.

She ventured further inside, initially perusing then focusing on a mutating section of wall. The veins shifted, rearranging into a humanoid frame colored white and blue to replicate the Techcron from her apartment. "Greetings, Jade Dieza, do you need medical attention?" It stepped from the wall, the grainy material dragging in its wake before the connecting strands thinned and broke. The physical form was an illusion, however; in reality the Techcron possessed no true physical form, its consciousness merely occupying and piloting the ship.

"First tell me why you're in our airspace?"

The Techcron lapsed briefly into silence, then indicated the chair. "Sit, I will explain while tending your injuries. Your pet can roam free; I won't harm it." A depression formed near Jade, water filling in to form a shallow pool.

Jade warily complied, depositing Cuddles in the pool before

removing her coat and draping it across the armrest as she accepted the chair. The Techcron positioned himself in front of her while a pair of autonomous, arm-like prehensile formed from the floor to either side, comprised of the same grainy material as everything else. He began, "My chosen name is Chrysalis, but you may address me however you like."

"Chrys." Jade hissed sharply as one of the appendages glided over her lacerated side, sterilizing it.

"The Techcrons know about your current situation, specifically the disease promoted by a *soul* believed to be Indemiun."

"How'd you learn about it?" Jade asked, watching the various arms slither beneath her outer clothes, tending to her assorted cuts and bruises with surgical, silk-like fingers, cutting and resewing her adaptive suit as they went.

"Usually, we ignore your Corporatocracy aside from routine information gathering, but one of our espionage runs discovered the strains of a new *Aerian* pathogen pervading your populous."

"Wait! You can see it?"

"Yes, the systems we use to distinguish your Savants also recognized the pathogen. Best as we know, it proliferates primarily through skin contact, but this is an incomplete hypothesis as the infected population falls noticeably short of any projected percentage. More so given we assume the originating *soul* can intentionally infect nearby subjects as well."

"How long have you known?"

"About a year."

"How many infected?"

"Several million to our calculations, concentrated in the main branches of your corporations and their staff. Most of your Sovereign Core is infected."

"Deep water," Jade whispered, horror rising in her throat, squeezing taut with the beginnings of panic, "they have no idea." One of the appendages tending her reassembled into a syringe and injected her leg, sending alarm spiking through her. "What are you doing?"

"Repairing the internal damage and reinforcing compromised bones. We can do nothing for the chronic physical trauma of your metaphysical abilities."

His answer calmed her slightly. "Didn't occur to me you could. Can you excise whatever the Purifiers injected me with?"

"I'm analyzing it now to devise a counteracting agent. It's different from typical Purifier formulas, which favor sap bases enhanced with natural suppressants to assault the brain functions linked to your abilities. This concoction utilizes placenta in conjunction with elements of *Aeria* to incapacitate your abilities directly."

"*Of course it would*," Jade thought, her heart sinking. "Take a sample of my blood and compare it with the placenta."

"The genes diverge occasionally but are undeniably related. I assume you're familiar with this?"

"Never experienced it personally, but yes."

"Why did you contact us, Ms. Jade?"

"Because I need your help, and I doubt you want to deal with the fallout of an insatiable *soul* usurping the corporations."

"I'm not opposed to interfering, and am afforded some autonomy, but I can't do anything that would incriminate the Techrons. What exactly would you need?"

"I lost him and am out of leads."

"We can locate Indemiun for you."

"How?"

"Recognizing him as a *soul*, we catalogued his unique spiritual frequency and uploaded it to our satellites." Long, bony fingers sprouted from one of the appendages, spooling a thread-like material that matched her skin tone, and began applying sutures to her deeper injuries.

"Can you find him anywhere? Even if I lose him again."

"We can."

"Why don't you kill him?"

"Being here is already a violation of the treaties, but it is a minor transgression and somewhat expected, as well as probably mutual. Engaging in military action in Corporatocracy waters is not; and we're not interested in escalating tensions at the moment."

The arms completed their final ministrations and retracted into the floor. "I would also need transport, and a stop at somewhere I can pilfer weapons."

"We can provide you with weapons and armor; just not Siphons."

"So you agree to help?"

"Yes, but I want something in return."

"Of course you do." "What is it?"

"There's something inhabiting your global network, something we can neither pin down nor interact with. Any digital records we make are erased; and whenever one of us connects to your network to find it, they malfunction. Any memory of what they were doing, of the thing they sought, or of their preceding months, is erased. You will help us find this thing."

Jade shook her head slowly. "What makes you think I'll be of any more help?" Internally, however, her mind whirled. *"Months? She shouldn't be able to erase that much. Is She growing stronger? Did someone use a spell? Or is it because they're cybernetic and more vulnerable to Her?"*

"I'm hoping you'll have more success being organic, and that whatever it is won't be able to affect your brain at all, or at least in the same ways."

"How do you even know this thing exists if your memories keep disappearing?"

"From snatches of information, shared and compiled in the moments of searching, in the seconds before erasure. We have spent decades in this pursuit, and still any time one of us touches your global net, that knowledge is erased."

"And what exactly do you want of me? You said find it; but do you want its location? Do you want it killed? Or do you want to understand it?" *"God, I don't even know if She can be killed."*

"We would settle for understanding."

"And if I'm not immune to the memory loss?"

"We will remind you of your agreement."

"So no out with feigning a mind wipe." Jade slowly swung her feet off the seat's edge and slumped forward, rubbing her face. She had his answers, in their entirety and more, and their burden was suffocating: the reality of divinity, to stand before something radiant and vast and find yourself made small. Insignificant; all your sins, your vices, your sacrifices, a farce of hubris. And in the face of that you were standing before ... perfection. It destroyed you, unmade you to your foundations, and in the wreckage you had to compile yourself into something of value, something from which to derive meaning

or else simply cease to exist. But in that moment, that place, there existed only one thing of worth: that which had unmade you.

The divine always changed you, rewrote you more like itself for a time, until, like most wounds, the encounter healed to scars. But unlike scars, the memories never faded, not from the mind nor the soul, and not even a divine act could excise them, some part of you forever supplanted.

That's what Chrys asked of her, in his ignorance and his desire to serve his people: to meet a god and in that act to be destroyed. His fate alone was enough to deny him, but there was worse rotting in the Redeemers, an insanity stemming from and corroding their god, and from her, all of them. Jade could not inflict that upon him. And yet, she had no other choice; better only he learn the truth than the many that would if the Techrons kept searching. Eventually, whether through madness or scheme, the goddess would claim them.

"All right," she said quietly, shoulders slumping as her heart hardened. "But first you will make me a promise: you will not share a word of what I tell you until you have experienced it yourself."

Cybernetic eyes locked onto her, revolving internally but eschewing neither emotion nor sound. "From this I assume you know what's erasing our memories?"

"Yes."

"Tell me."

"Promise first."

"What if it erases my memories?"

"She won't."

"She?"

"Promise."

"All right, I will not relay what you tell me to anyone else until I have experienced it first-hand. Now, she?"

Jade took a long, slow inhale, and began. "Hidden in the lowest machine levels of a corporation city-complex, there is a god; I won't tell you which one, there are steps you need to follow before you meet Her. She arrived when we did, having collided with an auxiliary starship during transit and fused with the probability engine and information archive onboard."

"A god?" he asked in amusement.

"Yes. It's fine that you don't believe me, you may not even believe me when I'm done. That's fine also. They'll take you to Her eventually."

"Who."

"The Redeemers: Her cult. Gods enthrall the soul and once you meet one you can't help but serve. You will too, eventually. This god is what you've brushed against in our universal web; She inhabits it, as much coding and software as She is a machine or god now; it's what allows Her to affect the world, and by touching it you grant Her access to you."

"What does she want?"

"We don't know for sure, but She says Her fusing with the human devices affected Her, sort of bound Her to humans. She's been benign for most of our history, allying with the Redeemers to correct missteps in our societal evolution. Every generation of Redeemers undertakes a task, something that needs correcting; five are chosen and, with Her assistance, write PLANS. These PLANS are empowered by the divine in Her, surreptitiously guiding and nudging humans, and happenstance across the corporations into actions that further the PLAN. The probability engine, with the information archive that holds the complete human history and knowledge—including that of whoever sent us here—gives Her near perfect prognostic abilities."

"You said benign for most of your history?"

"Yes. She was ... corrupted a few years ago and is no doubt partially responsible for the current problems."

"With all you've said, particularly about her being insane, why should I approach her at all, instead of just informing my associates of her existence?"

"That's the thing, you don't have a choice anymore; and if you tell others, neither will they. You can't ignore the divine once you know it's there; you might last a few weeks, your soul slowly twisting itself inside out, but you'll start searching for it eventually. You might tell yourself you're looking to disprove it, you might tell yourself it's just simple curiosity; doesn't matter, you'll end up going down, searching. You'll eventually find a temple because you know where to look, and because She'll be leading you down. They'll find you in the temple, or meet you there, and they'll tell you what I just did in their own words. They'll induct you, they'll prepare you, and then, when you're ready, they'll take you to Her and you will be enamored of Her, and bind yourself to Her, to them, even as She destroys you. You will be Enlightened."

A look not unlike affront claimed the Techcron's face. "I would not serve her."

"Yes, you will, you won't have a choice. No one does. None of this can be changed. It can be modified and tweaked by personal decision, but the only choice you really have is how many will follow you down."

A long silence followed, his thoughts likely turning over what she said. It ended when he reached the next obvious question. "If she's insane, what does that mean for her followers, for me?"

"Everything She is, they become eventually. There are variations and degrees, dictated by your proximity to Her or one of Her temples. Joining the Fifth Cohort will afford some protection, but the other Cohorts will vie for you, and some may offer things you can't refuse."

She said nothing of the other gods. Better to wait until after he joined the Redeemers and met Her. The summons of their divinity wouldn't reach him once he'd bound himself to Her, but if he heard of them before that, then their calls would take root and he would have to find them, and a soul could only be destroyed so many times before it shattered.

The Techcron eventually nodded, but she couldn't tell whether in understanding or acknowledgement. "Is that all?"

"No, but it's all you need. You'll find the rest of the answers as you go down."

"Then your side of the contract is fulfilled." His hand snapped outward, palm upward, startling Jade. A coil of material speared from it, contorting into the shape of a canister-pistol. "We will arm you with the standard weapons of your people, cleanse the suppressants from your system, and improve your senses."

She tensed. "What do you mean improve my senses? You're not tampering with my body."

"The device is necessary if you wish to distinguish revenant *souls* hiding in human bodies. There's no negative affects, and the physical alteration will amount to a teardrop of black between your eyes. You can disguise it as jewelry. It will also allow you to negligibly sense *souls* when in close proximity to them."

"And if I don't want it?"

"Then I won't force you."

"How does it work?"

"Subconsciously, with no significant change to your usual sight. You'll recognize the distinctions automatically, like you view different skin tones. The effects are permanent unless removed by a Techcron."

Jade sat back, contemplating. "*I can handle Indemiun without this, but what if there's other souls? But letting them change me....*" She shuddered. "Would it allow me to see who's infected?"

"I can adjust the design, though that will affect your vision noticeably."

"Would we be able to replicate the technology?"

"Not for several decades." The Techcron completed the canister-pistol and dropped it at her feet.

"Are there other *souls* out there?"

"Yes."

"*I have to take it.*" Jade realized. "*We need to know when we're facing a soul, we need to be capable of finding them, stopping them. They're not all going to be like Chandris; how many are like Indemiun?*" "How many are there?"

"Several thousand scattered through your city-complexes, but the amount vacillates frequently as they return to *Aeria* regularly."

Jade stared at Chrys. "*God, that many? How are we even going to deal with– no, stop that. Don't panic, deal with one soul at a time, concentrate on Indemiun. The other souls can wait, but we need this now and ... and...,*"—her head fell back with a thud ...—"*they'll never let you leave when this is done.*" Ice slithered into her veins, but her heart quickened and her breath stuttered. "*No, no, no.*" She clamped her teeth shut and squeezed her hands into fists. "*Shut up and deal with it, there's no one else.*" She closed her eyes, fighting to speak as her throat constricted. "Do it."

"We will have to sedate you for the operation."

Panic roared through her, yanking her eyes up to stare at him. "No."

"The process is very painful and–"

"I am not being unconscious while you work on me. I am not being–" She clamped her teeth on the final word, but finished it in her mind, *"Helpless. Unable to run, or fight, protect myself. Vulnerable."* The panic rose higher. She didn't know Chrys, she didn't trust him, she couldn't let him have full control over her.

The Techcron settled back. "The operation cannot proceed while you're aware, the work is too fine. If you want to distinguish *souls*, and the infected, you need to let this happen."

Jade kept her teeth clamped against another retort, the effort causing her jaw to creak. *"Look, I don't really need it; the other souls haven't been hurting anyone, so you don't need to worry about them; just don't fail to kill Indemiun. But what if I do fail? Don't fail. But what if I do? **Don't.** And what if there's more like Indemiun? Stop thinking about it, just say no before you talk yourself into it."* She curled forward, pulling her knees up and resting her head on them. *"But we need this, and people go under for operations all the time. Not with Techrons though. Doesn't matter, we need it, and the only reason I'm not already under is because I'm a goddamned coward. Stop being a coward, Jade. Get over yourself, and just get it over with. Millions of people do this every day. And think of how useful you'll be with it, how many people you'll be able to help."* The last thought drew a strangled, humorless laugh. Then she looked at the Techcron.

"All right. Do it."

A cool weight settled over her face, followed by a mild, sweet scent as hands guided her to lie down. She closed her eyes, controlling the surge of panic and forcing herself to breathe.

Her thoughts loosened, turning miserable and soporific. *"Maybe, maybe the corporations will be kind to me when this is done."*

Then she slipped into unconsciousness....

```
01000001 01110100 01110100 01100101 01101101 01110000 01110100
01110011 00100000 01110100 01101111 00100000 01100001 01110110
01100101 01110010 01110100 00100000 01000001 01110000 01101111
01110100 01101000 01100101 01101111 01100111 01100101 01101110
01100101 01110011 01101001 01110011 00100000 01100110 01100001
01101001 01101100 01100101 01100100 00101110 00100000 01000101
01101110 01100100 00101110
```

Jade awoke to the comforting weight of Cuddles on her chest, and a change in her body—a tightness in the skin of her forehead around a pinprick of metal, and an indescribable sheen in her eyesight. Cuddles stirred with her, nuzzling at her neck with an excited squeak. She giggled softly, wrapped him in her arms, and carefully rose, moving hesitantly to adjust to her altered vision. A careful glance around revealed she was alone. Aside from the ship, the only sign of her host's continued presence was the pile of assorted weapons and gadgets he'd left by her chair.

Bending to a knee on the floor, she gently shifted Cuddles to a shoulder and began arming herself: storing ammunition and batteries in the inside pockets of her coat, preparing belts, and affixing holstered pulse- and canister-pistols to those belts. Beside the weapons waited a suit of Elesstrion Armor, ignored until after she finished sorting and cataloging the weapons because of the memories it roused in her head. When she finally did force herself into it, inhaling to fill her lungs as it conformed to her body beneath her coat, the armor activated with a mild whirr of power and linked to her adaptive suit. An instant later it woke in her consciousness, a second layer of skin, nerves, and muscles she could control, which communicated back to her with a wealth of internal and periphery information.

She flexed her fingers and stretched, acclimating herself to the armor and the armor to her, mind clamped shut against the last time she'd been armored like this. Reacting to her stress, the small generators across her midsection activated with a bloom of heat, causing the suit's honeycomb-like wiring to become enshrined in opaque white energy.

Jade exhaled unsteadily and opened her eyes, deactivating the suit with a mental command. *"Calm down; it's just armor, and you don't have the luxury of being weak right now. Get over it."*

A footstep sounded behind her. "Is the equipment to your liking?"

Jade nodded and began to finish equipping herself. "How long till we arrive?"

"Around a minute."

Intrigued by her actions, Cuddles scuttled across to her other shoulder and partially down her front, sniffing at the belts of weapons she donned. Realization followed soon after, slowing her mechanical motions. *"I can't bring him with me."* She raised a newly gloved hand

and stroked his head, leaning her cheek to rub against his flank. "What about him?"

"I can take care of him if you like and return him when it's safe."

"If I die, take him to Marsilias Wreign."

"You expect to fail?"

"No." She moved to the ship's center, prying Cuddles free and settling him upon the floor. "I've survived worse than *souls*." Cuddles clamped onto her arms before she could pull them free, whimpering and rubbing his head against her palm. She dropped to a knee, leaning over him and squeezing him in an embrace. "I know baby, I wish you could come, but you can't follow where mama's going. It's not safe. So stay here and be safe, okay?"

She straightened, extricating her hands from Cuddles to face Chrys once more, miserable and trying to ignore his cries as the ship's floor mutated to restrain him. "What's waiting for me down there?"

"A recreational ship on tour. One of its patrons recently perished from a congenital disease, and the *soul* possessed the body."

"Can they only possess the dead?"

"Yes, though we are unaware of the intricacies. By expending *luce*, *souls* can restore and operate a cadaver, but to what extent is ambiguous. We think they require a vessel sufficiently intact to house their essence; a skull works, but not a mote of dust."

"Wish me luck."

"The Techcrons don't believe in luck."

"You should. It was quite lucky for me you answered my call."

"Us being here, and responding to you, was entirely logic based: luck had nothing to do with it."

"Luck and logic aren't mutually exclusive, just different perspectives." She blew a final kiss to Cuddles, mustering a grin for him, and exhaled, phasing through the floor into the rain-choked skies over a cruise ship.

Inhabiting the First Step, she descended slowly, alighted on the brightly illuminated, many-tiered deck roof, and submerged to peek below. Guests milled along an ornate hallway of emerald and silver, attired in a riot of gorgeous, brilliant costumes. They wore the baroque visages of mythical creatures, the guises of beloved fictional characters, of historical leaders, and even the garish, stylized masks of animals. Jaunty, festive music played in the background and colorfully masked servants wandered through with trays of recreational stimulants.

Jade retreated into the ceiling and glided to the nearest lavatory, where she chose an unoccupied stall and dropped down. *"I have to find a costume, or Indemiun will recognize me instantly. He might anyway just from innate soul perception, unless his host body interferes with it."* She raised the collar of her coat, hunched her shoulders, and emerged. *"There'll be shops throughout the ship. I just have to find one."*

She lengthened her stride, tapping her earpiece to connect with the ship's network. It provided her with the nearest costume distributor along with an itinerary of the festivities. She cycled through them for the event with the highest expected attendance, hoping that Indemiun would attend it to propagate his disease.

A door appeared on the wall to her left, boasting a tapestry of gilded images. An S.I. android waited outside to direct or serve passengers as required. It currently conversed with one couple dressed in the cartoonish mask of a presidential couple from past centuries. Jade positioned herself in line and waited.

The couple departed, allowing the android to address her, "How may I help you?"

"I need a costume, something with a bag and easy to move in."

"Is there a problem with your current costume? Did your mask break?"

"Oh," Jade thought, *"that's why nobody noticed me, they all thought I was dressed as a Purifier or soldier."* Aloud, she said, "No, this costume's fine, I just feel like a change. Something a little more fantastical perhaps?"

"We have the Red Piper here, and only one version in use throughout the ship."

"That'll work just fine." Contrary to what his name suggested, the Red Piper was a mythical pirate named Sanar who ran afoul of the Deep Ones: a race of primordial aquatic denizens. The legend went that the Deep Ones cursed him with a red pipe that gradually erased and rewrote the minds of all who heard it and ordained that he play it nightly. It was a story of gothic horror that detailed Sanar's journey through multiple personalities, from hero to villain before ultimately concluding in tragedy. Jade hated it.

The android motioned her through the door into a series of corridors populated with changing rooms. Securing herself in one, Jade ordered a version of the Red Piper costume several sizes larger than she customarily wore and waited while another android collected it. When the outfit arrived, she stuffed her coat into the accompanying bag and pulled the rich, baggy clothing over her armor. This restricted access to her weapons, but she preferred that to her armor alerting Indemiun.

For the final touch, she bunched her hair beneath a wide hat and pressed an intricate red and gold half-mask over her eyes, complete with eye socket projections to disguise their color. As the mask settled over her face, it brought a familiar sensation of comfort to her, the safety of anonymity. She didn't have to be anyone anymore because she could be anyone, and if she could be anyone, she didn't have to be herself. There was a kind of inhumanity in that and Jade had to resist the urge to submit, to submerge herself below the mask and simply become numb again.

Suitably attired, Jade swung the bag over her shoulder and exited the costumer shop, paying her dues on the way out.

Once outside, liberated of her need to fit in, she loitered, seizing the opportunity to observe the guests and test the Techcron's enhancements. The promised distinctions appeared slowly, first as shades, then veins of a black, oily light swirling within people: Indemiun's corruption. Some harbored thicker strands, but secondary glances often revealed a badge of the Savant Corporation.

Jade merged with the current of people, strolling along and assessing those she passed for Indemiun. Now that she focused, she could feel the *soul's* presence like a distant inferno somewhere ahead on the ship. The sensation deepened as she neared, guiding her through the guests in their strange and beautiful costumes, and room after room of games, artificial realities and intoxicant dens, luminescent arboretums, and luxurious dining halls. The cheery music gradually attenuated, replaced by slower, ominous refrains and a masculine voice singing opera.

The hallway delivered her onto a balcony in a room of startling black and white hues. She slowed, cautious at the abrupt change from warm colors to the sterile tiles and sweeping openness of a ballroom. Easing herself from the passing crowd, she approached the balustrade, gazing down onto the checkered floor through a forest of swirling columns. Hundreds of men and women spun amongst one another in a wild but masterfully orchestrated dance. A live orchestra played from a corner, their costumes modest yet equally magnificent.

In the far corner from Jade, dressed in an attire of black feathers, danced Indemiun. She could not have said what distinguished him from his fellows, or the woman whose steps he guided with indifferent perfection, but she knew him instantly.

Trailing a hand along the balustrade, she descended to the dance floor. As she did, an idea began to form; she knew this dance and the routine that accompanied it. The subsequent number incorporated the swapping of partners, which would hopefully allow her to approach Indemiun unnoticed. The music progressed, transitioning into the final sequence with a tenebrous note. Jade started circling the room, positioning herself in the same quadrant as Indemiun.

As the sequence changed a stillness claimed the dancers, spreading outward from the center as the music faded, leaving only the gliding notes of a solitary violin, then nothing. The dancers straightened with a cheer and thunderous applause and began to disperse or arrange themselves for the next dance.

Jade advanced, calming her breathing and falling into line with the other women. A moment passed, and a slow, aching note began. Jade stepped forward, suppressing the urge to shudder as the man pressed against her, his arm encircling her waist and raising a flutter of fear at the subtle restraint. Other instruments joined the song, darkening the sorrowful horn with an air of pending violence. She and her counterpart spun, separating to either side to meet new partners.

The new man circled around her, his hands curling into claws and contorting in the air over her body, miming a possessive, lustful violence. She pushed and yielded in time, her crimson apparel somehow melding effortlessly with the stark dance. The man performed a final slash and they parted.

The dance brought her to face a woman and they mirrored one another, their hands pressed together as the music grew desperate.

They pushed and pulled in unison, fleeing and vaulting across the floor, but never abandoning their grip. They lashed and struggled feverishly, the men pursuing them just a step behind, their movements harsh and discordant. Then, as one, the women tripped and fell to their knees, hands splayed on the white tiles while the men receded onto the black tiles checker boarding the floor.

A hand reached down to her, and she looked up into Indemiun's eyes, his features veiled behind a crow mask. She accepted his hand and he pulled her up, the melody turning slow and tender. His arms wrapped around her, and he pressed close. "I am not your enemy, Jade Dieza."

Her heart stuttered but she held firm, spinning so she stood with her back to him and her arms pinned to her chest. "Then why did you attack me?"

He spiraled her out and in to face him again. "I have never attacked you." The music darkened again, and she pushed off, twisting as if to flee; but he tugged her back, one hand giving the barest caress to her shoulder. "I am not the source of the disease that beleaguers your people."

They locked hands, and she pushed his arms up and out. "Why should I believe you?"

"Is it not strange that while assailing you, your enemy compelled one of the most prominent members of your party not to attack you but to destroy the object you needed instead? And in so doing, led you directly to it?"

She hadn't thought it strange back then; Indemiun possessing Inka to destroy the device had seemed logical. But why choose Inka? Why not someone less noticeable? "So what are you trying to say?"

"That I directed Inka Nadiru toward the device you sought, not to destroy it, but to guide you to it."

She frowned. "But why?"

"I wanted you to find it, to use it."

"Why?"

"Because I am not your enemy." They circled one another, his palm pressed against hers while their other hands linked behind her back.

"Then who is?"

"The *soul* wearing your brother's face, the being from which all of this began." He disentangled their arms and led her in a twirl, relinquishing her fingers at the last instance so they stood back-to-back.

"But he told us about you, said you had eaten *Arbol's* root? And a Techcron told me it was you."

"Ilin confided a truth to divert your attention, intending that it would destroy me in the process. As for the Techrons, while capable of detecting *souls,* their technology is no more capable of recognizing the expenditure of *luce* than yours. They would be blind to Ilin propagating his disease, which would leave me as the obvious suspect."

They faced one another again and she reached up, miming a caress to his face. "But why would Ilin direct us toward you?"

"Because I have labored against him, hampering the spread of his disease and helping you when I could, warning and directing you to the discoveries you needed to make. Through Inka Nadiru I led you to the device in the sky-city, through Warden Shanra I revealed the involvement of your Redeemers, and through the man who went berserk in the intoxicant compound I warned you the disease had spread beyond your corporation's control: all of these were breadcrumbs leading you to the destination you needed to find."

"All of those people were corrupted by the disease."

"Yes, Ilin's disease. It is his gift to infect the living with slivers of his essence and then exert dominion over them. It is mine to mimic the abilities of other souls, or to subvert them to my own ends, and through this I possessed his victims to guide you."

"If you could do this, then why not stop Ilin?"

"Because I can neither control Ilin, nor expunge his ability from the infected. It is not an ensorcellment, it is his literal essence imbued into them and I cannot manipulate another *soul's* essence."

"Why hide then? You should have just told us."

"And be imprisoned or destroyed? You are designed to obliterate my kind; I did not trust you."

"Is there a way to cure everyone?"

"No. You must kill Ilin, though that is not his true name."

"It's not enough. I can't just take your word on hearsay."

"Ask yourself this, which of us hates you? Which of us has sought to cause you pain at every opportunity?"

"Why would he hate me though? Yes, I caused his imprisonment, but that doesn't feel like how a *soul* would behave and he was your lackey." Even as she said this, she hated herself, knowing that everything she knew, everything she had just said, had come from Ilin. *"Stupid girl, you should have known better. Should never have trusted anything he said."*

Indemiun continued unfazed. "He was the first to eat *Arbol's* root, the first to hunger beyond his means, the first to speak with the humans that aided us, and the first to propose our invasion. All that has occurred derived from him, and all of it failed because of you. The corpse he wears protects his body and mutes the hunger, but he cannot truly shirk either of them. I ate of the dead roots for curiosity at his suggestions and ... lost myself because of it. The hunger and the inversion of my being warped me and compelled actions I would not have otherwise taken; Ilin's invasion above all."

"What about your hunger now?"

"I returned to *Aeria* and drank of *Arbol's* living roots, reversing the transformation. I maintained the knowledge I accrued regardless, which is what allowed me to usurp his thralls."

With a start, Jade realized she could feel it, a surging energy beneath his skin, a fire and vibrancy she had never seen or felt from Ilin. And yet, there was something else, a vein of illness, of rotting black amidst the light: Indemiun carried the disease. "You're poisoned!"

"Yes; Ilin infected me in a moment of carelessness through his human allies, and now the disease rots me from within."

One of the men from earlier in the dance emerged behind Jade, his arm extended commandingly toward her. She made a sharp gesture indicating her inability to continue with the dance and stepped back from Indemiun. "Help us."

"I must return to *Aeria* to cleanse my *luce* of him. I delayed because the process is long and arduous, and I wanted to speak with you when you inevitably found me again."

"What about Chandris? Does he need to return?"

"He has returned to *Aeria* on many occasions since his imprisonment, and the perversion takes years to infect us. He is safe." The *soul* retreated from her. "There is a final warning to convey, Ilin does not act alone. Humans from your world have allied themselves to him, just as they did two years ago when we first invaded."

"The Redeemers."

"Yes. Their intentions are uncertain, but they have assisted Ilin in propagating his disease, taught him much of this world he could not learn behind the walls of his cell, and they seem to possess some means of controlling him. The disease spreads by only their, or his, will, and while they cannot exploit it as he does, they command him. They infest your Purifier and Savant Corporations, and it was they who orchestrated Ilin's imprisonment, they who convinced your Sovereigns to study rather than destroy him." He bowed, silently expressing gratitude for the dance. "Now, I bid you farewell, Jade Dieza, and wish you luck in your mission. I've done all I can to delay him, but my time is spent and Ilin is ready to begin. I cannot stay to give him another weapon." Before she could say anything else, he faded into the crowd of dancers.

Jade stood there for a moment as all the dancers swirled around her, numb with shock. *"I ... I need to kill Ilin. Think. No, the Sovereigns won't believe me, they'll fight me. Have to kill him quietly, before I tell them. I need to contact Marsilias, need to see what he thinks about all of this. Oh God, he's in the Purifier compound."* She pressed her earpiece, calling Marsilias. He answered immediately, "Hello, Jade–"

"Marsilias, you have to leave now!"

"I can't, Prime March has initiated a compound-wide lockdown; they're cutting off communication now."

"Marsilias, we were wrong; it's not Indemiun, it's Ilin!"

"What–" Their connection died, leaving her with static. Jade stood there for a minute, horror and fear marshaling within her, then she started running.

The Kingdom Falls

Jade bounded through the ship's floors, her form incorporeal and her mind frantically trying to suppress her memories. The pieces of her costume lay scattered somewhere behind her, discarded without thought for their integrity as cries pursued her down the corridor, some in concern and others in reprimand. She ignored both alike and vaulted to the next level.

A pair of guards snapped upright at her appearance, a massive, sealed door behind them. One extended a hand, palm out. "Ma'am, please stop. This floor is restricted–" She sprinted past, phasing through the doors to enter an air-dock.

Her advent triggered no alarms or security measures, but the pilots, guards, and ship personnel lounging across the area reacted to her sudden appearance, first with surprised cries then warnings. Jade pressed forward, phasing through one Damselfly craft as she evaluated the cruise vessel's meager fleet: a variety of passenger planes, a few Damselflys, and a single aircraft dedicated to long-distance travel. No military vehicles. Jade veered toward the distance plane, recognizing it as the fastest option.

The attending pilot emerged. "Oi! You can't be in here! You gotta leave–"

She inhaled sharply and crashed into his chest, tackling him against his plane. He gasped, and she activated the shock charge in her gloved palm. Electricity shot out and rebounded off her armor, exploding through the man and shocking him unconscious.

Alarmed shouts erupted across the air-dock, scattering some and summoning the rest toward her.

Jade shoved the unconscious man aside, exhaled, leapt directly into the cockpit, and immediately inhaled again. She slammed a hand into the command console, activated the plane and delved into its coding. She lacked the time for a neat hack, so she blasted through it, shredding the firewalls and defense mechanisms until she found the manual override and initiated it. The plane woke around her, lurching awkwardly into the air at her command, its engines groaning in protest at the rough treatment.

Pulse blasts railed its side, but to little effect as she rotated the plane toward the dock's exit and its heat barrier. She gave an unvoiced command and the plane rocketed into the open sky through a cacophony of warning sirens. Search lights activated across the ship's exterior and swiveled to lock onto her, inundating her vessel's interior a blinding white. But no pursuing planes issued from the dock's exit, likely because the pilots and aircraft contracted by the cruise company were intended for emergencies and not combat.

That spark of good fortune brought Jade no relief, her mind too riddled with panic and failure to do anything other than desperately begin reconstructing the ship's damaged coding enough to insert a destination and call Prime March. Even in lockdown and quarantine situations, the highest Purifier executive present in any of their compounds always maintained an open channel to the outside world, and she thankfully knew Prime March's personal number.

The dial rang twice, then a screen projected over the aircraft's dashboard, revealing Theeran in his office. "Hello, Jade–"

"Theeran, listen to me! You have to kill Ilin! Use his cell's extermination protocol."

Prime March's head cocked to the side. "Why would I do that? I rather like being alive, dear sister." His lips split in a grin and his hand rose to wave. "Hi. Miss me?"

Horror welled in her, strangling her voice and hurling her mind into whirling panic. Ilin had Theeran, which meant he probably had all the Sovereign Cores.

"You should hurry back, Jade. I was getting lonely in my cell, so I called a class reunion from our academy days." The screen spun, showing a room littered with corpses. "Not everyone's here yet, and not everyone's coming despite being called by a Sovereign, but I'm sure I'll meet up with the rest of them eventually. Who knows, if you're quick you may even arrive on time for the rest of the party."

Jade's mind started screaming at her, almost too loud to hear Ilin anymore, the visions too real, too vivid, to see anything else. "*Dead. All dead. Fault. My fault. All my fault. Failed. Failed. Fault. Failed.*"

"Oh, and I've called your actual friends, those Savant Corporation boys Connor and Ruon. We'll throw you a lovely welcoming party when they arrive: me, you, the Redheads, Marsilias...," trailing off with implication, he grinned wider.

Jade's adaptive suit activated with a hiss, warming against her skin and injecting minute needles. The drugs exerted their effects almost instantly, deadening her nerves and quieting her tumbling thoughts beneath a haze of intoxication. She squeezed her hands into fists, interrupting the injections and applying the antidotes before they claimed her entirely. She didn't have time for the relief they offered, but the brief moment of respite they provided allowed her to stabilize her spiraling mind. The panic and memories persisted, of course, but she'd surfaced from their thrall.

Jade released a shuddering exhale and sank into the seat. "Where's Marsilias?"

"Oh, he's barricaded himself nice and safely in the hub room, but my thralls are burrowing through as we speak, so you'd better hurry."

"Don't worry. I'm coming."

"To do wha–"

She terminated the connection and called Connor's number.

Thankfully he answered, "Hello, Jade–"

"Connor, where are you?"

The languid, contented tone of his voice changed immediately upon hearing her. "Pulling into the Purifier air-dock now. Why?"

"Pull up now. They'll cut us off if you go in." She heard a groan through their connection as he reversed the momentum of whatever vehicle they occupied.

"Jade–"

"Ilin's taken over the compound, the invitation you received is a trap."

"Ilin–"

"No time to explain just do as I say. You have to go in, they'll shoot your plane down otherwise. You need to get down to the hub room without opening a road others can follow. Marsilias is fortified in there. Can you do that?"

"Yes, Ruon's got a card but it's going to beat the shit out of me to use it."

"Do it, unless it can take you somewhere else. You won't survive two steps out of the plane if you don't."

"They're pulling us in … where … you?"

"Connor, I'm coming!" The connection began crackling and failing. "Connor, Connor! I can get you out of there. Trust me. Connor. Connor!" The connection crumbled fully into roaring static and Jade shrieked, punching the dashboard. "Damn it!" She slumped forward, fighting tears of frustration as her head thudded against the dashboard. Her eyes closed. "*I need my Siphon. Damn it. I need our Siphons.*" She sat there for a while, then gritted her teeth and pushed the plane to the utmost extent of its abilities. The walls shook around her, but she ignored them and retreated to the center of the plane, where she crossed her arms and paced.

A short time later, the plane's S.I. program spoke over the intercom, "We are approaching the destination, preparing to hover over the compound in standby."

Jade caught a glimpse of the Purifier compound through the front window, its stone exterior flashing with searchlights. Sharper flashes split the night sky towards her, a mixture of imploder rounds and pulse blasts fired from artillery class armaments. The plane swerved automatically, evading the barrage with inhuman accuracy.

Jade retrieved her old Core's badges from a coat pocket and kissed her clenched fist, praying for everything she was worth. "*Please, please, let them be alive.*" The plane veered upward, avoiding a subsequent volley while maintaining distance between itself and the compound's defense batteries. Jade activated the magnetic effects in her boots and exhaled, phasing through the floor while shifting to latch her feet onto the plane's underside with an inhale.

She crouched down, tensing her leg muscles, and activated the vaulting mechanism in her boots, a means for soldiers to surmount medium-sized barriers or engage airborne opponents. The corresponding energy cells ignited with a charging hum. They dinged a moment later and she lunged, releasing the magnetization synchronously with the lunge's energy discharge, hurling her toward the Purifier Compound.

Jade did not exhale as she fell, as that would have arrested her momentum, she simply watched the projectiles racing toward and around her on their way toward her plane. None of them struck her, but their continued assault on the plane confirmed that Ilin believed she remained inside.

The ocean surface rushed closer, thrashing as she plummeted to within meters of the Purifier Compound. She exhaled sharply, entering the First Step an instant before flattening on the water, leaving her to glide beneath the surface without so much as a bruise. Far overhead, muffled by the ocean's depth, her plane exploded and for a moment the night was bright and the sky filled with debris. Jade dove further, propelling herself to the compound's exterior and then along it, diving ever further into the encompassing dark, past an array of aquatic armaments.

She descended through the ocean, protected from the mounting pressure and the need for oxygen by the First Step, to where she estimated the floor with Prime March's facility began and then slipped through into a revenant's cell. The imprisoned creature woke instantly and growled. The growl swelled to a howl and it lashed at her, but she was already sprinting into the hallway outside and into the midst of a Purifier Core. A woman stood among them, her features concealed in a fluctuating mask, and her body shrouded in the orange coat of the Redeemers.

The Purifiers spun toward Jade and leveled their weapons, their exposed skin livid with the disease, all except for the Redeemer who touched her ear. Jade pressed forward, sprinting into the opposite wall of cells. The moment she crossed into the next corridor, a sharp hiss burst into the air, preempting a cascade of reddish gas. Jade dropped into a half-crouch before the mist could touch her, already activating her mask despite occupying the First Step, and glanced up to see what effect it exerted. She perceived no change in the environment or the revenants in their cells. The gas continued, however, thickening and swirling around her in heavy, silken strands. Silhouettes appeared from the gas, creeping through it with humming electric weapons: Purifiers. They spotted her and screamed, their words muffled by their headgear. Jade dove into the next wall, phasing through as canister rounds exploded behind her. Despite the ineffectiveness of the first attempt, every new corridor greeted her with a rush of the ruddy gas.

She pressed onward, racing through the maze of cells, corridors, swarming Purifiers, Redeemers, and gas, desperately trying to find her bearings in the altered environment. She glimpsed familiar objects or locations and modified her course, moving inward until she ultimately reached a hallway teeming with Purifiers. They crouched in the fume-choked passage, bent in poses of subservience to the Redeemers speckling their midst. A distant clamor rolled down the corridor to her right, marking the start of their assault on the information hub's entrance.

Jade advanced, her first step gliding through one of the crouched Purifiers, but stalled as a Redeemer appeared from the gas, their features covered by a vacillating mask. An instant later, the desaturated colors of their clothing bloomed into full hues, and the weight of their form lightened in the physical world as they entered the First Step with Jade.

Jade halted, her thoughts racing. The Redeemer continued unperturbed, phasing through the Purifiers in echo of Jade's own movements, their mask flashing the jagged caricature of a smiling white face. "Hello, Jade."

Jade leveled an imploder. "Who are you?"

"I am your friend." The mask vacillated briefly to a frown before reverting, its illumination reflecting on the gas. "Put the canister-pistol down, I want to talk."

"Is this all your doing? Ilin? The Plague? Or are you just helping him?"

"So you understand the situation, but do you understand the reason?" The mask flashed to a question mark and the Redeemer drew nearer, their synthetic voice monotone despite the implied question. "People like us—Savants as a species—are enslaved to the Savant Corporation, reduced to products on a ledger when we used to be saviors."

Jade fired and the Redeemer vaulted back just before the canister round exploded where they had stood, its flames rolling harmlessly over the possessed Purifiers. Jade pursued, holstering the canister-pistol and unsheathing her two pulse-knives. The Redeemer drew a pulse-emitter and fired. Jade sidestepped into the wall, letting the energy sphere rip harmlessly down the corridor, and sprinted forward to engage the Redeemer. She slashed, rending the orange coat with arcs of electricity, set her right foot, and lunged into a stab. The Redeemer spun, discarding their pulse-emitter to grapple with Jade.

A pulse-knife flicked open in the Redeemer's hand and immediately slashed for Jade's thigh. Jade brought her knee upward in response, rerouting the Elesstrion Armor's power to the generators there, and smashed into the Redeemer's knife with an explosion of energy, warping the blade. Unrelenting, Jade pressed close, stamping her raised heel onto the Redeemer's toes and propelling them into a stagger with a blow from her shoulder. She pursued, amassed the armor's energy into her gauntlets, and struck the Redeemer's chest with a flash of energy. They flew apart, both of their armors discharging energy from the contact.

Jade hit the floor, phased through into the semi-dark of cables and wiring, rolled and surfaced in a crouch on the same floor as before. She scoured for signs of the Redeemer, saw them straightening across from her, and charged. Instead of retaliating, the Redeemer stepped back, their mask, clothing, and armor turning murky red and camouflaging to merge with the gas. Jade halted, cursing vehemently. "Show yourself!"

"It is not our intent to fight you, Jade." The Redeemer's robotic voice sounded to her right and she slashed to no effect, the pulse-knife crackling with renewed energy.

"I have no interest in joining your cult." She scanned the amassed Purifiers, searching for a streak of red in their apparel while one hand dug into her coat pockets. "You might as well come out of hiding and kill me."

"Even to save your friends? I can ensure their safety from Ilin."

"No you can't." Jade found what she wanted, a magnetized dust capsule. "You can't control the *soul*, whatever he's promised you, or whatever you promised him."

The Redeemer spoke again, their voice snapping in anger, "Why are you so stubborn? You are one of us, subject to the same oppression, stripped of every privilege and right! Think, if not of yourself, then others, of everyone they've abused and exploited!"

Jade slowly withdrew her hand, the capsule clenched in a fist. "Killing millions of people by empowering a demented *soul* is not the answer, just as it wasn't the answer two years ago."

"Those very same people stand by and watch our enslavement. They allow this to happen to us. They're just as guilty as the rest of the Savant Corporation."

Jade spun, crushing the capsule and throwing it toward the voice. A tide of gray particles erupted from it and washed across the corridor, phasing through the walls, floor, and ceiling as it went. The particles nearest to Jade crackled and snapped to her, attracted by the metal and energy in her armor. Further down the corridor, another clump did the same to the Redeemer.

Jade dove, streaking through the air to latch onto the Redeemer's shoulders. The Redeemer instinctively retaliated, battering Jade's sides with pulse-knives, but Jade had already rerouted her armor's energy there, rendering the assault ineffective. Jade struck the Redeemer's mask, amassing just enough power in her fist to break it. The mask ruptured, spraying both Jade and the Redeemer with sparks, and deactivated. The Redeemer staggered back, bleeding from her nose and cursing. Jade recognized the voice but didn't stop. She wrapped around the woman, pressed her pulse-knife against her throat, and unleashed a partial discharge. The woman spasmed and sagged, floating in the air.

Jade straightened, half-straddling the woman. "There are better ways to achieve this than war, Candice. This isn't right, the PLAN isn't right, it's insane. Please."

Candice blinked, shaking her head to dispel the residual incoherence of the shock. Her eyes fastened on Jade, and she shuddered, striving to buck or fight. "I defended you, said we could recruit you."

"Please," Jade begged, "let this go. Find another way."

Candice sneered, her fingers twitching from the lingering electricity. "There is no other way."

"So be it." Jade pressed her other pulse-knife to the woman's brow and released a lethal discharge.

Candice lurched back into the physical world and dropped,

toppling over the Purifiers, who shucked her corpse without thought. Jade raced down the corridor until she reached the door to the hub room, where a duo of Purifiers operated a laser drill. She contemplated inhaling long enough to destroy it but discarded the idea as an unnecessary risk and phased through the door.

Inside, she found more of the red gas eddying around a blessedly unharmed Marsilias, Connor, and Ruon. She inhaled with a sob of relief and raced to them. Marsilias and Connor noted her arrival and straightened a second before she leapt onto them in an embrace. "Thank God you're all right," she said, feet dangling well off the ground.

"You too," Connor replied, patting her back as Ruon circled around to join the embrace. Marsilias just returned the hug.

She pulled back, hurriedly examining for signs of Ilin's corruption. She saw nothing, neither black lines marring their flesh, nor the putrid rotting inside. "How are you?" she asked. "Do you know what this gas does?"

"No," Marsilias replied, "it seems to have no effect; Connor can still manifest cards and I can still open my doorway."

"Good, cause we're gonna need your doorway to get out of here."

Marsilias frowned, a mixture of uncertainty and extreme unease coloring his features. "Jade?"

"I know," she said, meeting his gaze, "I know you hate it, but it's the only way out."

"What are you talking about? There's no way out."

"Yeah, there is." They all glanced back at the door as a dull, fiery hiss sounded in the room. A quick scan to either side revealed two pinpricks of orange heat glowing on the doors. "We don't have much time. Marsilias, draw your door. Connor, Ruon, you're not going to like this but you have to trust me."

"What do you need from us?" Connor asked.

"We're going to visit Marsilias's workshop."

The two Redheads frowned in confusion. "What?"

"I'll explain later, for now just collect your things." She strode to her desk and sat, pressing one hand to the console. The network rose to her thoughts but, restrained by Prime March's lockdown, failed to connect. Almost every strand of coding lay inert, segregated from one another and any power source, all except one foreign program: Jade's.

She activated it and delved into the network, shearing off connections and safeguards as she went. Other minds pried at the lockdown all across the network, burrowing through the comatose programs and reviving those they needed. For her part, Jade blasted through the network until she found the communication line she wanted: Chandris. A quick amendment followed and the line powered on, its code glowing silver as a wall panel flickered on in the hub room. Jade resurfaced and moved to the activated panel, laying a palm on its surface to call Chandris. His cell blinked into focus with Chandris seated peacefully on his mattress. "Hey, cool cat, you all right?"

His eyes slid open. "My health is unchanged."

"Well, that might not last; we were wrong, Chandris. Ilin was behind all of this and he's currently usurped control over the Purifier Compound."

"His reach extends beyond these walls. I can feel *aperturas* opening for miles about, and through them he invites *vestiges*. You failed."

"Not yet. I can kill Ilin."

"How? You are ill-equipped to contend against him."

"Not for much longer; I just need to get everybody out of here first." Jade shifted aside, giving Chandris a peek at her companions. "Once they're safe, I'm going after Ilin." She shifted back, rubbing a hand across the dull burn starting in her eyes. "What about you? Need any help getting out?"

"Are you permitted to liberate me? I assumed the Sovereigns intended a permanent incarceration."

"Well, considering that I'm about to save the world, or their corporation at least, I should get some leeway on the trial. Although, this place is crawling with insane Purifiers, so you might be safer in there while the lockdown holds."

"Regardless, there is no need to concern yourself, I can depart at will."

"Yeah," Jade said, recalling her conversation with Indemiun, "Indemiun mentioned something to that effect."

"You met the other *soul*? How did you interact?"

"Probably not the time or place for that, Chandris. I'll tell you later." She fell silent, considering him. "You could help us, maybe? I know you're not exactly invested in our safety and all, but it'd be nice not to have to do this all alone."

"You're not alone. Marsilias, Connor, and Ruon all stand behind you."

She shook her head. "No, they can't help. Marsilias has to stay here; he can't follow where I'm taking the others, and I don't know how much strength Connor and Ruon will have when we reach the other side."

"Where are you going?"

"Someplace ... else. I've been there before, when I stumbled into *Aeria* that first time."

"Another existence. Another World."

"Not really ... more of a road." Jade scratched her neck, trying to soothe the dull, burning sensation in her throat. *"It must be the gas, but why? I have my mask on."* She tapped her earpiece, verifying that her mask was indeed functioning as intended, and a confirming note responded. *"It can't be lethal or else we'd be dead already. There has to be another purpose."* Aloud, she asked, "So, how about it? You get to have a little snack on some revenants, probably toss around some of the people who've imprisoned you and solidify our friendship."

"Are we friends, Jade Dieza?" he asked softly, tonelessly. "I am what you swore to destroy." He stood, unfurling from the mattress with a simple but unequivocally inhuman action, and advanced to stand before her screen. No violence corrupted his posture or form, yet in that instant she saw a phantom, a silhouette of him from their first meeting, immense and ablaze with empyreal fire.

"I've asked for your help, Chandris, offered to break you out of prison, and now propose to put my life in your hands; I think that gives us a possibility for friendship."

His presence diminished, reverting to the subdued mien of a human. "Your logic holds. I will help."

"Really? No bargains or anything like that?"

"We are not forming a contract, and revenants are simpler to consume en-mass in this world than in *Aeria*." He turned, one hand slashing upward in a rush of brown mist. The gate yawned opened, spewing a tide of brown mist into his cell and obscuring her view. "I will find you when I re-emerge. Do not feel compelled to wait." His silhouette disappeared through the gate, closing it behind him.

She terminated the connection and began restoring the lockdown, heedless of the molten bubbles growing on either door. "Marsilias, are you ready?"

"Yeah, it's up."

She completed the final string of coding and surfaced fully from the network, spinning toward the Redheads. "Connor, Ruon, go to Marsilias."

Ruon acquiesced without hesitation, though he kept a loaded pulse-cannon trained on the entrance. Connor complied more slowly, his attention vacillating between Jade and the main entrance in the process. "What are you thinking, Jade? We're not Specters; we can't use his door."

She vaulted the desk and rushed to them. "I bring inanimate objects across with me when I take the First Step, I can use that to carry you through the door."

"Yes but we're–" He ducked, cursing, as a piece of the door leading further into the compound exploded. "We're not inanimate!"

"Yeah, that's why I'm going to knock you unconscious."

The already deteriorating door liquefied, its molten form oozing across the floor with a sizzle as the drill's laser melted through. Jade spun, drawing a pulse-pistol from beneath her coat, and fired through the expanding hole in the door. Connor and Ruon followed suit, ducking to avoid the retaliatory barrage of electric blasts.

Marsilias, protected from the worst of the fray by line of sight, struck his forearm and a crackling shield of blue energy snapped out, activated by some hidden device. "Connor, we don't have time to argue with her, just do what she says!"

"Fine! Take my cannon." Connor heaved his weapon across to Marsilias, who caught it easily. Connor faced Jade. "All right, ho–"

She slapped a shock charge on his face and activated it. He jerked and crumpled.

"Sorry, Connor, fastest way." Jade grabbed him by the lapels of his coat and dragged him toward Marsilias's door. Once there, she bent down, hoisted the man onto her shoulders and exhaled. Fire erupted throughout her body, tearing a scream from her lungs as some external force wrenched her back into the physical world. She dropped to a knee, panting. *"This damn gas has to be more of the Redeemer's nullification agent."*

"Jade, what's wrong? Are you all right?"

"Yeah...." She pushed back to her feet and staggered to Marsilias's door. *"Thank god for whatever the Techcrons did to me."* She exhaled again, braced for the fire and the pressure. Both reared within her, but she clamped her teeth against the instinctual gasp and stepped through Marsilias's door. The amethyst light dragged, sticking to Connor's body, but ultimately surrendering passage.

Jade staggered forward as the resistance dispersed and caught herself on the cloth walls. A thread of pressure remained, pulling at Connor's limp form; just as Death loathed to relinquish its cards, Life clung to its subjects. Jade puffed a breath, Connor's weight starting to tax her strength, and stumbled down the corridor, the bells swinging merrily at every step. At the far end, she found Marsilias's door cracked open to emit both incense and trickles of light. Sounding a strained note of gratitude, Jade shouldered through and dropped Connor to the floor with a thud. Wincing, she muttered an apology and scampered back through the entrance, leaving it ajar for when she returned with Ruon.

A sharp pain surged through Jade the instant she stepped from the portal into the hub room, eliciting a gasp and snapping her back into the physical world. She hissed in frustration and exhaled, but her body rejected the transition, responding with pain.

Marsilias and Ruon sat crouched to either side of her, their weapons firing on the open entrance while retaliatory fire blazed through, pummeling the walls, floor, and electric force field. The sealed entrance was beginning to glow red at the center, promising an imminent collapse.

Marsilias, momentarily preoccupied with barraging the open entrance, ducked back behind his pathway's door as a storm of pulse-blasts answered his effort. He spared her a glance then sharply refocused. "Jade, what's wrong?"

"Nothing," she said through gritted teeth. "Ruon, get ready. I have to zap you." He replied with one arched eyebrow. "Yes, I know

I didn't give Connor any warning, but he would have complained. Now, you ready?"

A renewed deluge of pulse-fire rendered her question inaudible, but Ruon nodded regardless.

Extracting a second shock charge from her coat, Jade grasped Ruon by his collar and slapped it on his neck. Electricity arched out and he buckled onto her. "Okay, Marsilias, we're ready."

He nodded and began deconstructing his pulse-cannon. "Do you have a sonic or light grenade?"

"Yeah, here." Jade awkwardly pressed a hard canister on her belt and it spat a marble-sized sphere into her hand. She tossed it to Marsilias. "Sonic, so cover your ears." At a tap, her own earpieces projected another stream of metal to cover her ears.

Marsilias raised his free hand with three fingers extended and counted down: three, two, one. As the last finger fell, he crushed the sphere and flung it around his door. A piercing, horrific, persistent wail tore through the chamber, deafening even through the earpieces.

Jade kicked Marsilias gently and jerked her head at the door, mouthing, "Go." He nodded and leapt through, only delaying long enough for a single worried glance in her direction. Jade heaved Ruon onto her shoulder and exhaled. Her body pitched internally and pain scoured her limbs, but she remained firmly anchored in the physical world. Mentally screaming in frustration, she tried again with similar success. "*Come on! We don't have time for–*"

The electricity barrier crumbled and the screaming sound exploded outward, staggering the Purifiers as they tried to enter. The revenant's accompanying them, however, were unaffected by the noise. They plowed through the reeling Purifiers and charged Jade, their forms indistinct in the red gas and their ethereal music masked by the sonic grenade.

A tall figure shoved through in their immediate wake: Prime March.

Jade marshaled herself and ejected the air from her lungs in a desperate burst. This time it took, and she slipped into the First Step. The revenants howled and slashed through her, their impetus driving them forward and against Marsilias's door. Prime March shoved through and leveled a canister-pistol on her, but Jade was already throwing herself back through the door. Amethyst light briefly engulfed her vision, and then she was tumbling heels–over–head down Marsilias's pathway. Ruon's unconscious form pulled from her grip and sprawled against the wall.

"*We're through*," she thought in relief, staring up at the ceiling. A moment later, the silver bells grew hot against her back. Then they started screaming. She bolted upright, covering her ears as a whimper slithered from her lips. Across from her, stabbing slowly through the amethyst doors, a black cloth-wrapped hand latched onto the cloth. A long, feline face followed, brilliant with the inner radiance of a revenant.

Jade lunged forward, tripping on the cloth floor, and grabbed Ruon's jacket. One-handed, she dragged him toward her and with the other delved into her coat for a canister-pistol, which she promptly unloaded on the revenant.

Marsilias's voice boomed behind her, audible even over the bells, "Jade move! The path will destroy you if you don't get out." He couldn't help her. The path Magisters walked differed from those Specters walked.

She yanked Ruon up onto her legs as the pistol magazine ran dry. Cursing, she flung it at the still emerging revenant and dragged herself up, heedless of how the shrieking bells seared her skin. The revenant, now half-way through the door, grasped the walls to pull itself further in, but its hand touched a bell and instantly burst aflame. The revenant wailed and snapped its arm back, golden *luce* boiling up from its fabric to douse the flame.

Holding Ruon under his arms, Jade staggered blindly backward. More revenants pushed through the amethyst door, squeezing around the first due to their smaller size. Jade stumbled and fell, her back striking the hard stone of the opposite steps. She kicked for purchase on the stairs, flinging a hand back. Marsilias caught her arm and hauled both her and Ruon up his steps and into his work-shop, almost dislocating her shoulder in the process. Without pausing to ascertain their health, he slammed the door shut and locked it. The silver bells fell silent, though Jade doubted they truly were.

Marsilias faced them. "We're safe. The path will destroy any-thing else that tries to enter." He looked sickly and spoke in a strained voice. It was traumatizing for Magisters when someone forced themselves into their workshops, and one of the main reasons Marsilias never let anyone but her enter; this was not the first time he had been invaded.

"I'm sorry," Jade said softly, "I didn't think they would be able to get in."

"It's all right," he replied, "not like we had much of a choice anyway." Marsilias knelt beside Connor and felt the man's pulse. "I don't know where you plan to go from here. Time still progresses in a workshop, and no one outside will save us."

"No, they won't. We need to wake up Connor and Ruon, and I need my Siphons."

"They're where you left them. I'll take care of waking these two."

Jade crossed to where a curtain hung in a back corner and parted it to enter a room of flowing amethyst velvet. A simple wood and iron lockbox rested in the center, its worn cracks and dents dusted with sand.

She knelt before it, swiping the sand off its lid, delaying the inevitable and earning herself a sliver. "All right, I get it. No dawdling." She reached beneath her coat and unlocked one of the interior pockets to retrieve an iron key, its rusted surface warm from the armor's generators. It rasped as she inserted it into the lock, which groaned as she turned the key then popped open with a thud, expelling a series of iron bolts from the interior. Jade raised the lid and stared. Two items lay within: the first, a standard issue Siphon, with coiling pink energy inside; the second: an ancient six-shot revolver with a faded handle and a scratched barrel. Six bullets lay beside the revolver.

Jade took the revolver, loaded the bullets, and stored it in an interior pocket of her coat. Then she stared at the Siphon for a long time before mustering the courage to touch it. The moment her fingers brushed its cool surface, an ocean of emotions, sensations, and almost-images swamped her consciousness. She heard laughter, snippets of speech, caught flashes of memories, warm emotions, important names, and impressions of herself from another's perspective. It was the real Ilin, in all his facets, a memory of him from the moment he exiled his soul from his body to create this Siphon until the moment he died. The Siphon was not alive, or sentient in any way. It was like a picture if a picture could be taken of a person's absolute essence. It was beautiful, perfect, and heartbreaking.

A soft hand touched Jade's shoulder. "It's time," Marsilias said with a squeeze.

She nodded, not bothering to scrub at the streaming tears. "Okay, just give me a moment."

He nodded and left as she continued to cry. Ilin's Siphon lay in her lap, loosely clasped in her hands. She hooked it to her belt. The onslaught of emotions faded, though not entirely. She pushed the tears from her eyes and exited the hidden room.

Connor sat at Marsilias's worktable, and Ruon across from him, tinkering with the beginnings of some new device. She took the last available seat, staring at her hands. "It's … hard to explain what's going to happen next, and even if I did, you wouldn't remember. We're going someplace strange and you're going to forget yourselves there."

"Where is this place?" Connor asked.

Jade made an encompassing gesture. "Out there. Everywhere. The Magister workshops are not floating in a void, they're built somewhere solid, a road between our world and *Aeria*."

"How do you know this?" Marsilias asked.

"Because I walked it for years after chasing Ilin through the gate."

"How does that help us? We don't want to go to *Aeria*."

"No, but other Magisters will have workshops there. Workshops we can travel through."

"Can you guide us through? Or is this a gamble?"

"I can guide you through, but you won't know me, won't remember my name or our purpose. The only thing that will exist for you is the Road."

"I won't be able to come with you, will I?" Marsilias said.

"No. Magisters cannot leave their own workshop like that. If we had entered Ruon's, you could have, but I needed my Siphons."

Connor and Ruon exchanged glances. "We had best go, then."

"Yes." Jade led them to the back of Marsilias's workshop, where a simple wooden door waited. Marsilias stepped in behind them and Jade gave him another hug. "I'll come get you, I promise."

"I know. But be careful, don't push yourself too hard trying to do this alone; I can wait."

"The world's at stake, Silias, someone's got to save it. Plussssss ..."

"You're awesome, I know." He smiled and gave her a little push. "Well, get going. You gotta save the world."

"Again."

"Again."

She turned, opened the door to a gust of parched wind, and emerged into blazing sunlight. Sand shifted beneath her feet and stretched out onto every horizon in vast, rolling dunes.

The Road

They walked one after another, a column of wretches united by a single purpose: to walk. The man did not know why they walked, how long they had walked, or why a chain bound him to the hunched figure before him. The others trudging alongside him bore no such chain, even the one purple-haired woman who always seemed to be standing at the corner of his vision. People lagged behind in the column, moved ahead or simply changed position, but she was always there, her features streaked in filth and caked in sand. He did not ask who she was; he could barely muster enough strength to breathe through the heat. He could find no relief from it, not in the threadbare clothing he wore or in the clouds that never moved. It oppressed everything, even turning his own clothing so hot it burned to the touch, but without them the sun would sear his skin. So he walked, stumbling as the sand slid and parted beneath his feet.

An elderly woman shambled beside him, the immense leather bag she carried nearly bending her double. She wheezed with every step, her skin a dark brown from years in the sun and her body withered to skin and bones.

The bags varied in size, but they all carried them, all except the riders.

The man licked a dribble of blood from his cracked lips, desperate to quench his thirst. *"Maybe,"* he thought, *"just maybe there's a drop more."* His hands feebly tugged at the stopper in his waterskin and finally succeeded in removing it. Shuddering from fatigue, he slowed lest he spill any and brought it to his lips, tongue stretching out. A trickle, a teaspoon of water dribbled out, splashing on his tongue and down his chin. He dropped the waterskin, letting it hang from its strap on his belt, and frantically tried to catch the water on his chin, sucking the moisture from his palms. *"That's it. That's the last of it,"* he realized. The people continued past him and the man he was bound to, their faces lowered, their packs shifting, and their waterskins bouncing. He started walking again, oblivious to the elderly woman having stopped with him.

She journeyed with him for a while but spoke only after he mustered the strength to rasp, "Who are you?"

She answered in a cracked, distant voice, her eyes unfocused and wandering, "I can't remember...."

"Where are we?"

"We're on the Road."

It hurt to speak, every word scratched like sandpaper on his throat, but he needed to know. "Where are we going?"

"I don't know...."

"Why?" He coughed, unable to finish the question aloud. "Why are we going?"

"Because the gods will it." Without looking, she pointed to her right. A Rider trotted past on a roan mare, the horses's hooves, the leather of its saddle, and his own movements all perfectly silent. He, though it could be a she for all the man knew, wore a leather duster and a wide-brimmed hat. Shadows cowled his face, but his eyes burned a fiery red beneath the brim. He carried neither bag nor waterskin.

The man said nothing for a long time, simply watched the sand gradually change to cracked earth and tufts of vegetation. *"I need to find out where we are and where we're going,"* the man thought. He did not know why he thought thus, but the answer came to him slowly, percolating from every fiber of his being, *"I do not belong here."*

He twitched his head toward the old woman with an effort, moistening his lips. "Where are you from?"

She shrugged, the gesture arising more from her lower arms than her shoulders. "I don't know, I was born to the Road and have always walked it."

"You were the first?" he asked, his foot sliding on one of the numerous stones scattered across the path.

"No, there are people who have walked it since before always; I see them from time to time...."

"Who are they?" Internally, he thought, *"Maybe they know where we are."*

"I don't know.... Pilgrims, like you and I."

"You and I?"

"Yes. We are all Pilgrims ... Pilgrims on the Road ... going somewhere ... else." A swell of blistering wind struck them, originating blessedly from behind. He stumbled forward, sand and dust whirling past his knees. He followed them with his eyes, scaling over the backs of Pilgrims to the horizon where the sand rose in a swirling storm. A shadow slipped over them as the storm front advanced, and his gaze continued up then past it until he stared at the white sky.

The elderly woman never bothered to look up. Her wrinkled hand tugged at something about her neck, extracting a faded strip of cloth from beneath her clothes. This she pulled over her face, binding it tight beneath her hat.

"What is that?" he croaked.

"A storm...."

The shadows darkened, followed by kernels of sand striking his face. He flinched, hands rising to protect his face. "We should stop."

"We never stop, not while the sun's in the sky." She tromped on ahead, swaying with the strengthening wind.

The storm swallowed them a moment later.

He ducked into it, pulling his hat low and desperately clawing at the collar of his inner shirt, dragging it over his eyes. The wind cut through it, searing his skin with unforgiving heat, but the sand did not. It lashed his bare hands and stabbed through the slits and holes of his clothing to scrape and burn his skin.

He wanted to stop, to hunker down until the storm relented, but the Pilgrims shuffled past with hunched shoulders; and beyond them, a Rider looked on, a silhouette in the screaming wind. So the man walked, his arms raised before him and his hands clenched.

He could not say how long the storm persisted, but when it

ended, the sun hung low in the sky, casting long shadows from the Pilgrims and the withered, skeletal husks of trees and cacti. The lingering winds trickled past, diminishing to a silence interrupted only by the crunch of steps.

He slowed, relishing the encroaching night's chill air and the sandstorm's absence. The man ached and his pack weighed on him like a new guilt. His eyes fastened on the low sun, and he recalled the old woman's words. "The sun is setting," he said to himself, "are we going to rest soon?" No response came from the Pilgrims, and he glimpsed no sign of the old woman. With no one to satisfy his query, he resumed walking. In all of this, the man chained to him never spoke.

The temperature plummeted with the sun's retreat, turning their breath to mist and raising crusts of ice on the ground over a span of minutes. Shivering and exhausted, the man began to lose faith in the woman's promise, but as shadows spread across the vacant sky and only a scar of reddish gold light surmounted the horizon, he caught sight of a fire in the distance, and other flames kindling in the distance beyond that.

A Rider appeared from the obscurity, his pace slow enough to walk alongside them and his advent accompanying the fading of the last glimmers of light.

The other Pilgrims disappeared in the gloom ahead and behind until only a cluster of about twenty remained, these close enough to see despite the dark. These, the Rider brought to a fire within a circle of stone, though not a single thread of light crossed the perimeter.

The man entered the stone circle and a thin warmth seeped over his skin, soothing the cold's bite. It was only there in the circle that he realized how dark it had become. The night enveloped them, an impenetrable wall of blackness that consumed all sight and obliterated all sound outside the stones. No moon graced the heavens, nor even so much as a star.

The Pilgrims lumbered into the firelight one after another and slumped to the ground, their packs thudding. The Rider stayed mounted just within the circle, his form unmoving and his breath invisible despite the frost encircling them.

The man approached a pot dangling over the flames and, wrapping his hand in a sleeve, removed the lid. A rush of steam greeted him, bearing in its wake the scents of meat, fat, and assorted roots: a stew.

The Pilgrims crowded forward, each retrieving a wooden bowl and spoon from a small bag on their belt. Too exhausted to struggle through the press, the man raised the waiting ladle and doled out two measures. He did not know why he chose that number, but when he finished ladling the final portion into his own bowl, not a drop remained. The man returned the ladle to the pot and assumed the second to last stone in the circle, inhaling the steam and pressing his numbed fingers against the bowl's sides.

His eternal companion took the last stone, sitting beside him and greedily spooning chunks of a meat and potato stew into his mouth. The man ate more conservatively, wary of spilling the precious meal. Most of the Pilgrims imitated him, their movements lethargic with fatigue. The middle-aged man seated on his other side supplied one of the few exceptions, carting the food to his mouth with pale, frantic hands. Despite this feverish energy, his haggard, scarred features displayed nothing but dull, monotonous exhaustion.

He inclined toward the middle-aged man. "Do you have a name?"

"No, I am a Pilgrim on the Road."

"Why are you here? Why do you walk the Road?"

The other man paused in his eating to look at him. "Because we must." He resumed eating, scraping the vestiges of meat up with his spoon. When he finished, he restored his implements to his bag, crawled to the fire and curled up on the sand with his arm as a pillow. The other Pilgrims began arraying themselves beside him as they finished, with the quickest securing places near the fire.

Hoping to warm his back, the first man shifted to gaze outward, though he saw little more than a foot or two of stomped earth before his vision met the perimeter of stones. Beyond that, the night lounged, freezing and absolute. Not a sound crept from the blackness, only threads of frost peeking into the light at the camp's uttermost extremities. He stood. *I wonder if it's solid. It looks solid.* A wavering step inched him closer, close enough to extend his hand over the perimeter of rocks.

"Do not leave the light." A voice slithered through the camp, strong despite its indifference and absent volume. The man spun to stare at the Rider, who sat with his gaze fixed upon him.

"Why?" he queried with an effort, doubting at first that the Rider would hear him.

"Do not leave the light." The Rider's gaze reverted to the enveloping dark, but the sockets of his eyeless horse lingered on the man until he retreated from the edge.

He slumped back to the ground, unsettled by both the dark and the Rider. His companion, bound to his waist with a rusted length of chain, observed him patiently, waiting for the moment he decided to sleep. The man knew his body needed rest. He recognized it in his sluggish thoughts and felt it in his muscles, but the desire to understand itched at him. "Do you know where we are?" he asked his chained companion, expecting no verbal response.

His companion replied with a gesture of denial and a shrug.

"Do you know who we are?" the man asked, using a finger to lift the chain that bound them.

His chained companion repeated his earlier response, diverging from it only with a nod at the fire. The man acquiesced wordlessly and stood to find a gap spacious enough to house both of them as near to the fire as he could. He had just taken his first step when the woman from before appeared, the young one with purple hair that always shadowed them.

She stepped from the dark, materializing suddenly in the firelight without a bag on her shoulders or the crunch of a footstep. The Rider spared her a flick of his eyes as she entered, then nothing else as she approached the two men.

They shuffled about to face her, and she spoke without preamble, "There are three laws you must obey: do not leave the light, touch nothing but what the Riders give you, and never question the Road."

"Who are you?"

"I am your guide. Now rest." She stepped between them, walking out into the dark.

Too exhausted to converse further, the two men slumped into their places, curled up for warmth and slept.

01010010 01100101 01100011 01101111 01110110 01100101 01110010
01100101 01100100 00100000 01110010 01100101 01110000 01101111
01110010 01110100 01110011 00100000 01101111 01100110 00100000
01101100 01101111 01110011 01110100 00100000 01100101 01111000
01110000 01100101 01100100 01101001 01110100 01101001 01101111
01101110 00100000 01110010 01100101 01110001 01110101 01101001
01110010 01100101 00100000 01110000 01110101 01110010 01100111
01101001 01101110 01100111 00101110

Jade walked out into the night, and the further she traveled, the more ragged her movements became. Her body burned with a sickly agony; the illness of her mind made manifest. Eventually, her legs couldn't carry her any farther and she buckled.

Her Siphon—the revolver—waited silently in its holster, every inch of it alive and intimately familiar to her; even the bullets were fragments of her soul she had excised and molded into physical form; once fired, they were spent and new ones would need to be made and then time given for her soul to heal. But it was not her Siphon that needed attention. Ilin's Siphon seared cold against her side, spreading frost across her clothes from the metal.

Spasming constantly, she reached beneath her coat and grasped Ilin's Siphon. His essence swelled within in, beautiful and tragic, and her memories surfaced in kind, inundating her with misery. They did not all belong to Ilin's death, many plagued her from the years preceding it, from when the Redeemers controlled her; but they remained irrevocably bound because it was his death that finally shattered her, shattered the thin stability she'd managed to maintain after years of fighting monsters, years of living night and day with almost no rest, of meeting gods and suffocating beneath the secrets of the hidden world, and the burden of keeping it secret from everyone.

Now, swimming with feverish, twisting pain, she collapsed onto her hands and vomited a tide of black, stringy filth: the sickness of her thoughts roused by the fragments of her brother's essence, made manifest by the Road, and now expelled. The Road was a place of absolution, a place of relinquishing the past, and by expelling her grief and guilt and despair here, she would ameliorate some of its burden on her in the central dimension. It would return, it always returned, but in the interim, this would liberate her to act as she needed to act and to bond with his Siphon.

Exhausted, she slumped to the ground and stared at the

writing morass she had vomited. The physical pain within her abated, but the ache of the mental scars remained. "You have to move," she told herself gently, "you have to remember what the PLAN is when you get out."

Groaning, Jade pushed up to her knees and fumbled through the pockets of her coat until she found her sheets of synthetic paper and their accompanying pen, both prepared years ago against this potential need when she first returned from *Aeria*. "Think," she murmured to herself, "remember the Second's PLAN."

Each member of the Five knew every PLAN, but the PLANS themselves clouded the memories of all but their Scribe. Only the death of a Scribe broke the veil, which was necessary for the continuation of the PLAN until a successor could be chosen.

Jade had seen the PLANS once, and now that she walked the Road, their memory surfaced. Except, those memories would fade upon her return to the living; she had to write them down on a new source and carry it over to read anew. So long as she learned it from something other than the original PLAN, the memory would survive.

The words, written on ancient paper, began filling her mind again, searing in their brilliance. She started writing, scratching away in a jittery hand.

```
01101100 01101111 01100111 01110011 00100000 01100100 01100101
01110100 01100001 01101001 01101100 00100000 01110110 01101111
01101001 01100011 01100101 01110011 00100000 01101001 01101110
00100000 01110100 01101000 01100101 00100000 01000100 01110010
01101111 01110111 01101110 01101001 01101110 01100111 00100000
01000100 01100101 01100101 01110000 01110011 00101110
```

The roar of gunfire interspersed with monstrous howls jarred them awake. The man and his companion leapt to their feet and looked outward, bags listing on their backs. The other Pilgrims did not stir, or rather they did not rise. They just scrunched closer to the flames, covering their faces and ears against the clamor.

His skin crawling, the man shuddered and cautiously settled back. "What is that?"

His companion offered no answer other than to glance at the Rider, still seated upon his horse at the firelight's precipice. Unperturbed, the Rider supplied an answer, "The demons speak, but they cannot bear the firelight. Return to sleep."

Visibly nervous, they lay back upon the earth and covered their ears to muffle the tumult. Sleep eluded them for a long hour before exhaustion ultimately reasserted control and dragged them down into sleep.

When he woke again, with sunlight creeping over the horizon, he could not remember what he dreamt, only that it had been nightmares. The night ebbed around them, revealing camps of Pilgrims and a mounted Rider at each, some no more than a dozen feet away.

The man stood, his clothing cracking with frost, and stared at the fire's lingering embers. A Pilgrim from one of the other camps shuffled past, ice still flecking her bag and apparel. Others soon accompanied her, mingling from the various encampments to generate the beginnings of a marching column.

Seeing no promise of breakfast, the man and his companion joined them, tiptoeing through the scrunched forms of still sleeping Pilgrims. The Riders resumed their trek as well, falling into position on the column's flanks.

Thus, their march recommenced.

With the sun's ascent came the inevitable heat, descending mercilessly upon them all before the day even manifested fully. The man ducked his head against the sunlight and hiked the pack higher to try and relieve the blisters forming on his shoulders, worn from friction and sweat. The pack's contents thudded against him, poking into his back with hard, heavy edges. The man groaned and kept walking.

He lost sense of time as the heat deepened, effacing all until only the rhythm of their march remained. The saliva dried in his mouth as his lips cracked and bled. His steps slowed, falling in unison with his wheezing breaths and the thudding of his pack. *"Maybe,"* he thought to himself, *"just maybe, there might be another drop."* He shuddered. *"No, I finished it ... but maybe."*

The vague hope roused him from his stupor, urging his hands to the slack waterskin at his side. As he fumbled with it, the man gradually became aware of a voice. Startled, he cast about, having yet to hear any of the Pilgrims speak voluntarily.

A young woman trekked beside him, her brow lowered as she muttered to herself, "Why...?" The pack hung slack from her shoulders, not empty, but not bloated like his own.

He leaned closer. "Who are you?"

Her head listed toward him. "I ... can't remember ... it's been so long." Her head drooped, her eyelids fluttering as if she struggled to stay awake. She refocused on him abruptly, her lips parting a few times in failed attempts to speak, "D-do you know why?"

"Why what?" he asked slowly, his attention already wandering as he recognized their shared ignorance.

"Why we're on the Road?"

He began to respond to the negative, but recalled the woman's warning from last night: Never question the Road.

"But I'm not questioning the Road," he thought. *"I don't even know what the Road is, where we're going or why we're walking through this damned desert."* He struggled to think, to push through the exhausted morass of his mind, *"This place doesn't make any sense. Why are we walking here?"* He recognized it then, in the desperation of his final query, a doubt in and a fury at the Road. Again, the warning rang out in his mind: Never question the Road, which was followed by the bleary realization, *"We must never question the Road."*

Mustering his strength, he licked the blood and salt from his lips, preparing to parrot what he heard before, "Because the gods will it."

She moaned in response, "It's been so long ... and it never ends. We walk ... and we walk." She stumbled forward, her movements increasingly erratic and unsteady. "Are we in hell? They say we're in hell."

He forced his and his companion's strides to lengthen to keep pace with her. "Who does?" he panted after her, fighting to speak loud enough. "Who says that?"

She gave no answer, her words subsiding to nonsensical murmurs, like half of a conversation. He relinquished his efforts to keep pace and allowed her to disappear among the other Pilgrims. In the ensuing silence, he remembered his half-opened waterskin and stopped. A passing Pilgrim jarred his shoulder, but he ignored her and tugged at the stopper. It came clear and he raised the skin, squeezing the bag as his tongue reached up. A trickle of water spilled out, stinging his lips as it splashed on his tongue. He brought the waterskin close, sucking on the mouth for every last drop.

A hand touched his shoulder, pulling him around to the sullied face of his companion, who shook his head. The man lowered the waterskin and stared at it. He let it drop after a moment, too exhausted to bother recapping it, and together they staggered into movement. Thoughts of the questioning woman lingered, however, continuously replaying in his mind.

As he considered her, the recurring question flared again, augmenting in volume at every iteration, *"Why are we here?"* It plagued him, itching at his mind further whenever he forcibly discounted it. Finally, unable to bear the question any further, the man looked up, preparing to demand answers of the Riders. Yet, in doing so, his gaze fell upon the young woman from the night: his guide. She stood a short distance ahead of him, her head bare and her attention half-cast in his direction and half-directed outward beyond the column. Her warnings reared in his memory, stifling the inquiry: Never question the Road.

His momentary influx of strength fizzled out and he slumped. That woman knew more of the Road than he did, such was evident in her ability to advise him against challenging it, and whether her warning aimed for a beneficent or malignant end, he did not want to learn the consequences. Despite this conclusion, some part of him knew to trust her.

Their trek continued, the sun rising in a steady arch before yielding into a descent, its hue becoming fiery and red. The sanguine radiance subjugated all to its palette, splaying long shadows from the Pilgrims that twined and contorted on the Road. The Riders, however, cast no shadows.

As he trudged forward, the man could not remember if the sun had thrown shadows yesterday, but he knew it had not bathed the world in this lurid red glow. Thinking about it later, and taking both the shadows and exhaustion into consideration, he decided what happened next was inevitable; someone fell. They tripped, their feet sliding off the smooth edge of one of the littering stones and upending them face-first into the ground. The affected Pilgrim landed with a sharp forward lurch, and with a snap his pack came open, spilling a cascade of jagged stones past his ears. The Pilgrims kept walking, none so much as sparing a glance, but the man stopped to gaze at the rocks, some as large as his head.

A Rider slowed in passing to hail him, "Do not assist him, your burdens are your own to carry; he will rise in his own time."

The man looked to the Rider, confusion further dulling his mind. "But why are we carrying rocks?"

Before the Rider could respond, an enraged cry burst through the pall of silence. A cluster of pilgrims scattered farther up the road as the man and the Rider both looked. There in the open space cleared by her shout, kneeled the young woman who doubted the Road. Her pack lay on the ground before her, its flap torn open to divulge a sprawl of rocks.

She climbed to her feet, gesticulating at the nearest Rider and screaming, "Why?" repeatedly.

The Rider's horse trotted forward until he sat aligned with her, his head tilted down to observe the woman. She continued her battery of questions, the words mingling chaotically in snippets of phrases and inquiries. She writhed in place, twisting this way and that, caught between supplicating for something and accusing gestures.

The Rider spoke, cutting her off into a strangled gasp, "The sky bleeds, shadows fall, and a pilgrim questions the Road; you bear a demon"—he lowered his hand, palm up in demand—"give it to me."

The woman drew back, her head lurching from side to side in a ragged shake. "No. I will not follow you any longer, not without answers!"

The hand never wavered. "Give me the demon."

"Fine," the woman snarled, her hand diving into her coat. It re-emerged a second later, carrying an ancient double-barreled flintlock pistol forged of dark wood and iron. She leveled it on the Rider, its barrel vengeful in the crimson light. A raised, inanimate serpent coiled down the weapon, with its metallic head forming the muzzle and its body transitioning seamlessly through wood and iron in mimicry of whichever element it touched down the gun's body. When it reached her hand, the serpent became flesh and blood as it wrapped about her arm and wriggled, a second head feeding on her forearm.

The woman fired without hesitation, unloading both barrels into the Rider's chest and laying him out over the rump of his horse. Then she vaulted, soaring impossibly high to land far out in the desert.

The Rider straightened upon his horse, righting himself smoothly without the assistance of his arms, displaying an unmarred chest. Unperturbed, he drew a long revolver and fired at the woman. She pitched in the middle of a second leap and crumpled. Holstering his revolver, the Rider trotted to her corpse, lassoed her foot and dragged her back.

He dismounted beside the column of pilgrims and knelt to scavenge through the woman's clothing. After a moment, he stood with the black pistol in hand, the serpent's second head metallic and inert. A web of fiery cracks swept out from his palm, briefly igniting the entire pistol in orange brilliance before it disintegrated into cinders through his fingers. He struck his hand against his coat to clean it, the action again soundless, and mounted his horse. The march recommenced, ignoring the woman's corpse and flowing around him and his companion as they stared at it.

A minute passed and a shudder took the body. Her eyes opened, dull and exhausted. She pushed herself up, walked to her discarded pack, shouldered it, and rejoined the march. He stumbled after her, a bewildered question forming on his lips, "Are you alright? Do you remember what just happened? Where we are? Why we're here?"

"We're here to walk the Road." She spared him a blank look and continued trudging forward.

His steps faltered, and he watched her merge with the other Pilgrims. After a while, he and his companion resumed the march, joining the others as the crimson glow faded to a regular sunset, then crept with the passage of unnaturally long hours to dusk.

They settled into camp shortly thereafter, congregating about a fire on a narrow crest of stones, though the dark had already deepened enough that he saw nothing of their future path. The Rider took up his vigil, and the Pilgrims partook of the unchanged iron pot. They ate in silence, the man sapped of all strength to question. The murdered woman sat across from him, just another derelict face in the firelight, interchangeable with any of those surrounding him.

The gunshots and howls rose from somewhere out in the night, startling a brief glance from some of the Pilgrims before they returned to their meals. The man, and his perpetual companion, already familiar with the racket, finished their soup and crawled to the fire, curling in so close to the flames that they almost touched them. Mesmerized by its dance, he absently extended a hand and stroked the flourishing tongues, his palm gliding through and over the flames without pain. The act did nothing to warm him, but the fire soothed him somehow, dulling the darkness's clamor and allowing his mind to drift.

01010111 01101001 01110100 01101110 01100101 01110011 01110011
01100101 01110011 00100000 01101111 01100110 00100000 01101100
01101111 01100111 01110011 00100000 01110100 01101111 00100000
01100010 01100101 00100000 01100111 01110010 01100001 01101110
01110100 01100101 01100100 00100000 01100101 01101110 01101100
01101001 01100111 01101000 01110100 01100101 01101110 01101101
01100101 01101110 01110100 00101110 00100000 01000101 01101110
01100100 00101110

Jade clutched Ilin's Siphon to her chest and vomited until her spirit felt hollow. The agony dimmed within her and she straightened, wheezing. The pain and misery remained, but she also felt lighter, like a hand cleansed of mud. The memories played out in her mind, deprived of their usual bite.

Still wheezing, she uncapped the pen and leaned over the page. A hundred lines of writing filled it, detailing the PLAN in all its near-incomprehensible vastness. It focused entirely on people, dictating what they were to accomplish and where. Some of its commands seemed irrelevant, and it gave no context, but they stretched from the peaks of political influence to a cat left in the corridor of an impoverished district. On a grand scale, they intended to use Ilin's disease to revoke all constraints on Savants and restore them to a position of dominance in the society. They intended to use Chandris as an amplifier for the disease's spread and Ilin's reach, though only now did she recognize Chandris's name from when she first read it. To achieve this, they had branded a Magister card onto his being. Of course, it extended far beyond that, but she had what she needed.

Jade folded the paper and stored it in a locked pocket of her coat. A demon spoke somewhere out in the dark, drawing her gaze. There was one last thing she needed to acquire before they arrived.

01010100 01101000 01100101 01110010 01100101 00100000 01101001
01110011 00100000 01110011 01101111 01101101 01100101 01110100
01101000 01101001 01101110 01100111 00100000 01101001 01101110
00100000 01101101 01111001 00100000 01100100 01110010 01100101
01100001 01101101 01110011 00101110

A hand touched his shoulder, waking him to the morning chill and a sliver of sunlight upon the horizon. He stirred, shifting over to see his disturber and instead experiencing the wonder of a starlit sky. The breath slipped from him as he stared in awe, one hand rising as if he could touch the distant lights. It dropped a second later when he remembered something had woken him. The purple-haired woman crouched between him and his companion, a leather sack tied across her shoulders and her gaze likewise cast skywards. Seeming to sense his scrutiny, she refocused on him. "Rise. It is time we leave." She shifted her weight to jostle his companion.

The man sat up, muscles aching in the chill. "Where are we going?"

"Our time on the Road is done, it has carried us as close to our destination as it can." She stood, glancing over the slumbering Pilgrims and silent Riders as his companion stirred.

The man stood, hiking his pack higher, but she raised her hand. "No, leave your bags. The need for them has ended." Uncertain but trusting, he undid the straps and let the bag drop. His companion did so as well. vv"Follow me," she said, starting up the crest. His body feeling alien with the absence of weight, they trailed after her along a winding route of packed dirt through broken stones and boulders. When they attained the crest's zenith, he stopped, staring out across a plain of grass and wildflowers to an immense arch of seamless, pale wood rising miles above them.

"What is that?" he whispered, his words moderated by an innate sense of reverence.

"The destination," she replied. Her hand rose, pointing first at the arch, then back to the Road they had traveled. "Pilgrims walk the Road in search of atonement, guided and protected by the Riders from one destination to the next until their journey is done."

"Atonement for what? To whom?"

"To themselves; the stones you carry are the burdens of your life, the guilt that weighs our souls. You walk until you forgive yourself, then you remove a stone." Her hand dropped. "Come, it is time to move on." She walked along the crest, horizontal to the rising sun.

They journeyed for a long time, but unlike when traveling the Road, the sun merely warmed them when it rose and the water ran freely from their skins. She guided them to a small, yellow tent where it sat atop a dune, fluttering in the wind. There she knocked. A hesitant voice responded, conflicted with distress and confusion, "Who's there?"

"My name is Jade Dieza, a Purifier of the Corporation, and I beg of you to let us in."

The door opened, a young woman with electric orange hair peeked out, and the Redheads remembered themselves.

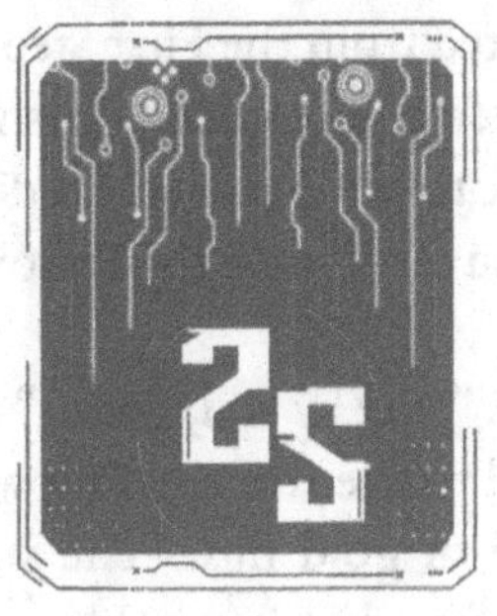

The God in the Machine

Jade stepped from the young Magister's workshop into a tunnel of curving, interwoven red wood. Luminous indigo flowers draped the walls and ceiling, connected by slim silver vines. She paused barely a second on the carven doorstep, awash in the scent of cinnamon and perfunctorily examining her surroundings, before surging forward at a stride. Their sojourn on the Road had won them escape, but while time there passed differently, it still passed. Hours would have elapsed for the days they spent traveling, hours they scarce had to spare. Even here, separated from the physical world by the pocket dimension of the Magister pathway, the PLAN swelled in her mind, empowered on impending fruition. They had little time left, and no answer for the Redeemers' god.

Connor and Ruon followed, boots scraping on the doorway's steps as they struck sand from their clothing and the young Magister girl watched uncomprehendingly on the threshold. They had spared only moments to explain, sharing vague, rushed words of danger and a mission while navigating her workshop. Now, too shocked to truly question anything said, the Magister could only grasp the door handle, her hesitant voice following them down, "Should I call for help?"

Connor flashed an easy, sunburnt grin over his shoulder. "Nah, we got this. You just keep doing whatever you were doing before." Then he turned back to the front, grin evaporating as his long strides carried him close enough to Jade to whisper, "Do we need to worry about being ejected from the First Step when we exit here?"

"No, you're not Specters; breathing doesn't do anything for you here." She looked back to pin his eyes, needing him to understand what she said next. "You can't leave the First Step without help from someone else."

He nodded grimly. "Stay by you, got it."

Her focus returned to the front, rising with the pathway's arch to a swirling entrance of gold dust. The sight stalled her for an instant, a flash of fear for what inevitably waited beyond, then she grit her teeth and ducked through, accompanied by the gentle swish and pressure of cascading sand.

She found herself in a disheveled dorm room, the wall panels displaying a calming vista of low flames while being peculiarly doubled, as if someone had erected two barriers in the same space. The hairs on her neck stood on end, alarm sinking her shoulders in a defensive hunch. She knew where they were: the Savant Academy. Panic, quickly suppressed, threaded through her: They were in the Savant Academy, which swarmed with Redeemers of every rank. Redeemers that would be hunting them, and they couldn't even run. The walls were doubled, one built in the physical, and the other built in the First Step as a way to control, and insure privacy from, Specters.

She heard Connor and Ruon emerge behind her, pinwheeling as the First Step's absence of gravity asserted itself, but didn't look back. An instant of realization passed, then a profanity exploded from Connor. "Shit."

Jade flexed her fingers, forcing her mind to calm and to function. "We need to move quickly, get as far as we can before they realize we're here." "*Or She does.*"

"We need a ship," Connor said. "Ilin wouldn't have stayed in the Purifier complex, not if he knows you at all. He'll know you have that place hacked to high heaven."

"Connor, we need a door through the First Step side wall. Pick something small, low cost; we're not gonna have time to rest." She heard the click of a card wallet opening, followed and almost muted by the heavy, metallic priming of a gun.

"What about the Warrens? Lots of them throughout the academy, less traffic." The subtle cold of an invocation bloomed behind her, heralding a soft, silver-blue light.

She shook her head, moving toward the door as an open window transposed over it. "Too risky; can't hide from the Redeemers in them, and we have to hide if we're going to get through this." Then she ducked through the window onto the abrasive floor of a suspended platform, squinting in the blinding neon lights of the Savant Academy. It surrounded her in massive, levitating, and offset platforms, bloated with edifices and jutting in all directions. They drifted in the depths of an empty, otherwise lightless, space confined by the invisible walls of a conjured sub-dimension: illogical and utterly impractical—requiring the unceasing labor of dozens just to maintain the invocation—it nevertheless served to remind everyone else on the planet that Savants were 'other'. It also happened to be blaring with sirens and flashing red warning beams, one of which immediately locked onto Jade.

Speakers to her left crackled and spoke from over the door, startling an emerging Connor even as something in the vicinity muted the sirens. "Unknown Specter, exit the First Step and return to your habitation or disciplinary forces will be dispatched; the academy is in a state of lockdown."

Connor, however, frozen half out of the window, provoked no reaction. He began to retreat, another profanity obviously rising to his lips, but Jade stopped him with a raised hand, grit her teeth, and inhaled. The air filled her lungs with cold pinpricks of needling pain, but they expanded and held the oxygen; the time spent upon the Road—a dimension separate from the First Step—had relieved some of the accumulated physical stress, but the pain remained and she would regress quickly.

The sirens reverted to their original volume, and the warning lights to their patrols. Connor was saying something, but the First Step and sirens rendered his effort utterly pointless even if she'd had the attention to spare. *Think. How'd it find me in the First Step? Why not Connor? And no recognition? So not seeing me but something else, an effect Specter's have on the physical side. No, not an effect, Connor would have same effect. Emission then, something I produce as a Specter that they don't because they're not exerting the magic.*

She faced the fully emerged Connor and waved weakly. "I'm fine, but they're tracking the First Step somehow. I can't use it without bringing them down on us, and it's not enough because they can still—Shit!" She ripped her coat open, scrabbling to open one of the locked pockets and pull out, then don, the Redeemer mask. *"Idiot, idiot, idiot! They can still track you on this side, but now they can see you! Okay, calm down, calm down. Think. Connor and Ruon need to split off so they don't get hunted with you. Damn It! That won't work, they can't transition back without me. Gotta transition them here, hide their faces first, then send them to get the plane while I distract the Redeemers. Rendezvous later. They'll be able to track our plane until I can clean it, and anyone with a brain will know it's Connor and Ruon. Think. I gotta shut down the place. Everything. Restrict their movements. Blind them. I can use this opportunity to find Ilin too. Okay, okay, we can do this."*

"Connor, Ruon, I need to transition you here, then you're going to need to get the plane. They're probably gonna know you're coming, so you're going to need to figure something out. Connor, you got an extra mask for Ruon?" He nodded.

She exhaled, cold expanding from her chest as the colors of the world faded and Connor's deepened. She stepped closer, one hand delving into her pocket to retrieve and press the discharger against his forehead. His eyes fluttered shut, jaw tensing as he braced himself. Then electricity arched out, dropping him to the ground.

Ruon, gazing out from the window, stepped through and extended his hand. She dropped a second discharger into his waiting palm and he pressed it to his brow, activating it with a tap. He fell, bringing Jade to her knees between them, her fingers tugging at the sleeves of their arms to expose their adaptive suits. Then she grit her teeth and inhaled, dragging both out of the First Step.

Pain inevitably retaliated, digging a little deeper into her lungs and chest, but exerted no other control as her fingers tapped a swift pattern on their suits, initiating emergency stimulants and shocks to waken Connor and Ruon. They snapped awake, surging to a sit with mirrored gasps. She caught both their cheeks in one hand, pressing in farewell and prayer for their safety. Then she was running, feet slamming the ground and hurling her off the platform into the open void beyond. The lockdown would have deactivated the bridges and perpetual portals, rendering normal travel between platforms impossible, but it couldn't disable the sub-dimension's safety precautions.

As Jade's forward momentum attenuated, dropping her into a curving descent, the space beneath her rippled with a brass thrum and opened with a bloom of metallic orange light. She plunged through it and the air around her warped, snapping first away for an instant of tactile-less existence, then snapping close again as she traversed the portal. Her feet hit the angel-soft threads of a mesh net, arresting any further downward momentum, and she shoved forward into a roll onto a portal platform miles from where she had just been.

All safety portals led to the central island, where the board of directors and their assorted staff abided, and where students gathered for end of year tests and their final curriculum. It also housed what Jade needed: the central data hub for the whole sub-dimension, which also happened to be the second largest Redeemer temple in the world.

As her shoulders struck the oscillating gold streets, she tumbled and rolled back to her feet, already braced for the warning sirens that blared from the blue glass and silver metal skyscrapers to either side. Crimson flood lights activated with metallic thuds, bathing the avenue in their sweltering gazes. The automated voice returned, echoing down the streets louder than the sirens, "Unidentified person, stay put and wait to be escorted: the academy is in lockdown and accessible only to authorized personnel. You will not be harmed unless you resist."

Without bothering to heed the voice, Jade strode toward the nearest alley and raised her gaze, knowing they would be coming. High above her, running in the space between two suspended atriums, a road materialized—transparent, golden, and swirling with internal patterns. Though she could not see it from this distance, it flowed forward of its own accord, hastening a group of sprinting figures along. They hadn't seen her yet, but that wouldn't last with the flood lights. So Jade waited at the mouth of the alley, staring upward; she needed to empty the temple of Redeemers, and the only catalyst she had was herself, and whatever chaos she could instigate.

The figures began to slow, still too far above her to distinguish their focus, but she waved anyway and stepped backward toward the alley. A crackling white energy barrier ignited across the street, but an exhale delivered her into the First Step and through it, out of her pursuers' sight. They would know there was a Warren entrance secreted away behind a holographic display in this alley, and would rush to the entrance on their level. The issue lay in the Specters who could descend directly to her location and would notice that she had not entered the Warren. Jade couldn't hide from them either; they would trawl the walls and any jutting appliances a Specter could fold themselves into, and the buildings would be full of people.

So Jade ran, hurling herself up onto the walls of the alley with an inhale to exit the First Step and a tap of her heels to activate the magnetization. The boots latched onto the metal veins with a thud, her armor activating with a barking thrum to propel her body against gravity's pull. She sprinted forward and up, skating along the building's face, her continued presence disguised because, being already active, the sirens and warning lights could not reactivate. As she sprinted, however, a flare of light snatched her gaze to the holographic display. A figure, masked and coated in orange, stepped from it, sweeping the alley with a swift appraisal, and fixed on Jade. The figure started running, their form fading to intangibility and gliding off the street. A second emerged behind them, sprinting as well, a card igniting in their hand.

Cursing, Jade reached the building's corner, slapped a hand against the duraglau for balance, and swung onto the next face, maintaining her upward trajectory. An instant later a sparking hand of wires and cords grasped at the space she had just vacated. She slammed her heels against the structure, activating the propulsors, and launched herself several floors upward with an explosion of force. She twisted mid-flight, feet extending out before her as she sailed into the thoroughfare the alleyway exited into. Jade dropped and crashed onto the golden road an instant after it materialized to catch her. A gun barked behind her, materializing almost instantly into a canister round roaring inches past her side, but she had lingered barely enough to land before bounding off the road in another propelled leap and clearing the rest of the thoroughfare.

She slammed into the opposite building, hands stabbing out to magnetically latch on, along with her boots, as her armor's stabilizers activated, then she was sprinting up the face of the building. As she ran, she felt inside her coat and detached the belt of canister rounds.

All canister belts had a safety mechanism installed so that if one canister malfunctioned or exploded prematurely on the belt due to external catalysts, the rest did not. The same switch could be deactivated to insure they all did explode simultaneously, or at least as many as you desired, rendering any canister belt a functional bomb. This mattered because Jade needed access to the Redeemer temple, meaning she had to empty it of Redeemers. The current wild goose chase served that purpose to some extent, but an open assault on the academy—indicated by a rather significant explosion— would force the officials and instructors of the academy into bunkers with all their staff and guards, many of whom would be Redeemers. Others would be called to duty in other ways; a summons they could not ignore and keep their positions.

A soft ding sounded in her ear, notifying her that her boots had recovered their charge. Without bothering to turn, she slammed her heels down, launching upward into a long arching backflip. It was then that she saw the owl, diving toward her on near silent wings, the size of a man and more a black silhouette defined by jagged gold lines than distinguishable flesh and feather. Mid-vault she couldn't dodge, and a second charge from her boots at this angle would break her trajectory. She exhaled, ice flooding her lungs and color washing from her vision. The owl swept through her, talons snapping harmlessly shut. She inhaled again, hit a second golden pathway and rolled through the impact as pain slithered through her chest. She drove herself back up almost immediately, but that instant cost her. As she moved to vault again, legs bending in preparation, the Specter from before shot up through the pathway, arm striking in an upward slash with a pulse-knife.

Jade side-stepped, exhaling and transitioning to the First Step as the Specter phased out of it. She inhaled, surging forward with her shoulder to ram her opponent, sending him—for it was now obviously a man due to his size—staggering slightly. Her other hand flicked, activating her own pulse-knife, and stabbed upward, only to strike nothing as he exhaled. Impelled by her own momentum, she slipped through his space and he spun, first hammering down without transitioning in an attempt to predict her transition. She didn't have time for this, or the health, and the Invoker was still below, shuffling through their deck of cards. She didn't have time.

Jade snatched the belt of canister rounds, pressing the switch to activate its detonation, dropped it, and then exhaled. Her opponent would recognize the bomb and thus had a choice: confront her exclusively in the First Step or run, allowing her to potentially escape. He was stronger and rested, but she knew the timer on the detonation: five seconds. It took him one second to make his decision and, already being close, surged forward to grab her coat.

Her unarmed hand flowed up, parrying and redirecting his strike by catching his forearm with her own and pushing his hand aside. He followed through, planting his leading step and stabbing his pulse-knife.

Two seconds.

She ducked forward, down, and past, both hands grabbing the forearm of his unarmed hand and twisting it around and back, folding it behind him. But he was already turning in sync with her maneuver, his height and strength rendering her ineffective.

Three seconds.

Time to move. His knife flashed, striking for her midsection, weaker for lack of a solid stance, and she let it through, accepting the blow on her armor. As he struck, she wrapped her free hand about his extended arm in a feeble lock and slashed her pulse-knife along his arm for his throat.

Four Seconds.

Locked as they were, he couldn't evade, and feeble as the lock was, he couldn't break it, set his feet, and disengage before her pulse-knife landed. The blow would be lethal. He inhaled and let her strike pass through him.

Five seconds.

The bomb exploded. Flame and force ripped harmlessly through the space she inhabited, but caught her opponent before he could exhale.

New sirens blared, screaming all across the sub-dimension with an automated voice, "Warning! Warning! Military grade explosives detected! The academy is under attack. All senior personnel retreat to your assigned bunkers. All defensive personnel attend your stations." Without bothering to transition from the First Step, Jade dashed toward the island's center. She no longer had any reason to avoid the First Step, aside from the physical strain transitioning exerted on her, as the entire academy would be swarming with Specters activating the First Step. The Redeemers, positioned all through the Savant Corporation hierarchy, couldn't ignore these commands: those of high rank had to retreat to the bunkers or incur unacceptable suspicion, and those among the guard couldn't ignore a call to arms and keep their positions. A few, the Specters near her immediate position, would likely ignore the summons to pursue her, but those within the temple would have to vacate it. Now she just had to reach it. Fortunately, with the lockdown lifted—a necessity to respond to the assault—the general portal functions would have been reinstated. She just needed an authorization key to generate one that would take her to the temple. And, again fortunately, she knew where to acquire that.

Jade's eyes fell to the Invoker below her; any Redeemer stationed in the Savant Academy would have an authorization key, or the functioning facsimile of one. She phased through the golden walkway, orienting her head downward, activated the second vault on her boots, and inhaled. Pain and heat welcomed her from the First Step, flooding through her center as her boots hurled her rocketing downward. The golden pathways beneath her blinked out as she neared, recognizing the terminal velocity of her descent and deactivating to prevent death. Far below, the Invoker—hand raised with another card—faltered uncomprehendingly.

She dove into the ground at their feet, submerging with an exhale at the last second, then spun and resurfaced immediately with an inhale.

The Invoker leapt back, hand snapping aside to discard the brilliant mauve card while the other hand scrambled to draw a second. She stepped closer, hand stabbing forth to strike his throat, changing his humming into a wheeze and a gasp. The Invoker stumbled and started to fall, but she caught them by the coat, free hand slashing forward to press the flat of her pulse-knife against their chest and discharge it. The Invoker spasmed and she let them fall, following them to the ground an instant behind and cycling through their various pockets for what she needed. Jade found it a minute later: a triangular device of bronze-hued metal scored with interlocking circles.

She pressed her thumb to the genetics reader at the center and its light glowed briefly through her skin, highlighting the bone within as it verified her Savant heritage and that she served the Redeemers. It blinked out and an unbidden word filled her mind, sterile and soundless: Destination?

She replied aloud, "Central nexus." A gold portal folded into being before her, the image of a different place gradually pooling outward from its center, that of a control room swarming with frantic people. Jade pocketed the device and stepped through.

Her arrival into the swirling confusion of hollering voices, racing bodies, and multiple other emergences from otherwise vacant air, provoked no reaction. The Savant personnel was too preoccupied with discerning the source of the assault and securing the academy to notice her. She ducked her head, bowed her shoulders, and slipped through the clamor to a storage-room door in a back corner blockaded by dust-covered boxes of tools, replacement parts, and devices. She kicked the slumbering hover lifts between the boxes to activate them, then guided the stack just enough aside to access the door. It was locked, the circular handle impacted to lie smooth with the door face, and only an injection port just below it to distinguish the otherwise featureless entrance. All Redeemer temples were locked when empty, requiring keys to open and awaken; the more exposed or important the temple, the higher the authority needed to awaken it.

Jade rolled up the left sleeve of her coat, revealing a tiny, sheathe-like pocket just past her wrist. She undid the fasten, the button siphoning a drop of blood from her finger as she did so. From this sheathe she pulled a dark purple USB chip, its side emblazoned with a small, glowing pink Stormflower. She plugged it in, heat flowing up her arm in a pleasant tide, and twisted it. The handle snapped out but the door opened of its own accord, drifting just far enough out from its frame for her to slip through.

Retrieving the key, Jade stepped inside and down a high step, foot splashing in reflective, black liquid. Lights woke beneath the liquid and along the walls around her, spinning outward from tiny blips to illuminate an antechapel of metal wreathed in countless wires. At the far end, immense and fused to the wall, the idol draped. Her eyes—though the god had no real gender—blessedly closed and her face down tilted. Jade locked the door behind her and waded in, the liquid rising almost to her knees, and her footing unsteady on the tangled wires beneath.

A circular console waited near the center, outfitted with a half-dozen chairs within its ring. Dark sarcophagi spiraled outward from this console, humanoid machines with alien faces—their entire bodies humming and vibrating to the same rhythm—laying within the glass-sealed confines, their brilliant green eyes flicking back and forth in vigilant consciousness: servants fashioned and entombed by the Redeemer god.

Looking upon all of this, Jade's purposeful steps faltered, slowed, and then halted. A quiver started in her chin and she clamped her teeth against it, grinding her hands to fists, but the quiver built, spreading through her body until she shook. She squeezed her eyes shut, breath quickening as it turned ragged. "*No, not now. Please.*" But the fear was crawling through her, crushing in its weight, dragging her down. Her breath faltered entirely, her lungs spasming open and closed, open and closed, but no air answered. Her pulse was thundering in her ears, and her vision blurring; she didn't want to be here, couldn't be here. It wasn't safe, they might find her, drag her back into their world.

Heaving, she shoved herself forward. "*Stop this, you, stupid, weak girl. We don't have time for it. Get. Over. Yourself. It's just a room.*" But still, she saw it again, felt it again: Figures in vacillating masks tearing her brother away from her, dragging him out across the lake of black liquid. She closed both, but she couldn't close her nose and the liquid poured into her, worming inside as if of its own volition, burning hot within her even as it froze her skin. Then the other mind opened inside hers, simultaneously displacing and enveloping hers like an ocean around a pebble. Then the voice came, pure music and emotions so strong she couldn't voice them, just cry. "Hello, dove. It's all right, just let it all out, we have all the time in the world." Then they were forcing him down, driving him beneath the liquid and holding him there. She was screaming, fighting to go to him; but they held her fast, carrying her further out into the lake and away from him. Their hands gripped her forehead, shoving her down. She pushed back, kicking and flailing in the icy liquid, but it did nothing. The liquid was rising up her face, climbing toward her lips and eyes.

Jade squeezed her eyes shut against the memory, one hand clutched against her chest while the other reached out, fumbling for the console at the room's center. Her trembling fingers struck the hot metal a moment later, sparking her eyes open again and sending her stumbling around its circumference to the access gap on her left. Copper wires surfaced from the black liquid as she entered the console's ring, sinuously assembling into a reclining chair of her size.

She sat, the internal workings of her implants linking to the chair's as her arms settled upon the armrests. She inhaled and delved the vast, swirling world of the Redeemer network opening before her: a deluge of information, programs, and locations—too many to sift through alone. But Jade, being her paranoid self, had long ago secreted dormant programs in the Redeemer network, interwoven amidst all the other coding so only she could find and activate them.

Jade chose two, the first an S.I. search engine keyed to her specific implants, capable of accessing her memories and thoughts to find exactly what she needed without requiring a command. The second was a virus that had spent the years of her absence surreptitiously expanding itself, infiltrating not just the Redeemer network, but the private implants of anyone who connected to it repeatedly. She initiated the virus with a mental command, selected the method of its assaults, then gave a tired grin as images and videos of adorably bumbling seriats bombarded every member and console of the Redeemers, effectively besieging their entire network. She set the entire arrangement to blaring, highly auto-tuned pop music.

Sabotage complete, she restored her attention to her search engine and a kaleidoscope of fractured information: weather patterns, slivers of communication, location pings for Redeemer personnel, the disappearance of a Purifier capital ship and crew from their fleet, and a message from Saccari to the Second Scribe detailing the strategy for Ilin to hide while spreading his plague. The kaleidoscope swirled as she watched, compiling and connecting all the tidbits of information to generate the coordinates she needed: the location of Ilin's stolen ship in the Dywernen straits.

Relief, like cool water on hot skin, washed over Jade. They had him. They could stop him. She surfaced from the network's depths with a rush, fatigue momentarily eclipsed by elation. She delayed only long enough to copy and key the signal from Ilin's ship into her implants. Then she stood, disconnecting from the chair despite the retaliatory jolt up her arms at the premature separation, and swung to leave.

As she moved to run, however, the coils underfoot slithered aside, staggering her step and stalling her flight. All elation died, erased in a flash of screaming panic before that to was erased, supplanted by a gentle, genderless voice, "You're supposed to be on my side, Stormflower, not working against me."

Jade's soul swelled, heat spreading from her center with a giddy flush as her mind settled, becoming soporific and happy. God, it had been so long since she heard that voice. She scrubbed at the tears welling in her eyes, fighting to concentrate through the god's lure. She could already feel herself changing though; her soul and her mind primarily, but even her voice was deepening, filling out to match to lush warmth of the goddess's. "*Leave, need to leave.*" She didn't have long.

"No point in leaving now, dove, there's walls in the First Step, and the Second can't hide you from me. Of course, you know that, which is why you just stand there, cowering in the half-dark as if I'll somehow grow bored and forget about you." All around Jade the lights flared and brightened, blazing from the walls and beneath the water until she had to squint, then shield her eyes from the brilliance. "I don't know what the me of before saw in you, she doesn't tell me much these days, but I dislike this childish obstinacy. Turn around."

Jade obeyed.

"Ah, better." Luminous and fiery orange, the idol's vast eyes swept over Jade, hot even through her armor and coat. "You should have returned much sooner, Stormflower, and more amicably; this is late, even for a fragile mind. The FIFTH PLAN begs your attention, even more since you undermine its predecessors."

Jade finally found her voice again, albeit soft and rasping and ugly against the goddess's. "No! I left you. I am not part of that world anymore."

"The PLAN still has your name inked across its signature, and you have not died to erase it. Even if you have renounced us, it works, shaping and changing the world in your name, without your guidance or direction, and it will be fulfilled in chaos if you leave it unattended. You cannot unwrite it by hiding: it is written, and it will be done."

"Why?" Jade hissed quietly, desperately, shrinking beneath the goddess's attention. "Why do you even want me?"

"Because a war comes, and we gods need soldiers. My estimation of your abilities is unimpressive, and personally I would rather leave you to seclusion, but the me of before insists on your relevance and vouches for your competence."

"No." Jade stepped back, teeth barring in denial. "No, I will not fight in your war. No, I will not return to this world, to you. Just no. I am going to leave now." She took another step back, hand reaching instinctively to grasp the handle of her Siphon.

"Leave?" The goddess's head ticked to one side. "On what ship?" To Jade's right, a screen projected up from the console, displaying Connor and Ruon in the cockpit of a commandeered vessel. "Are you willing to condemn them"—the vessel lurched, every light and console in sight winking dark—"for no gain in that pursuit? I am. Their lives mean less to me than the me of before's insistence on your inclusion."

"Stop it!" Jade drew her Siphon, leveling it upon the goddess despite knowing it was futile: this wasn't the Redeemer goddess, merely an idol, a vessel for her mind. "Let them go." The plane carrying the now frantic Connor and Ruon tilted and began to fall; she could tell by how their bodies began to move.

The goddess shrugged, causing the many vast coils attached to her and the walls to ripple. "I am not above compromise, Storm-flower; I will permit you to leave—the Redeemers and here, as well as spare the Drahma brothers; and in exchange, you will deliver unto me the contents of one of your coat's hidden pockets. Not just the pockets on the inside; the pockets I can't find otherwise, the pockets no one else is supposed to know exist. I know they're there; I can feel them." The goddess settled back on the wall. "That, or you return to the fold, Connor and Ruon are spared, and I won't detain you from opposing the SECOND PLAN. Or the THIRD, or the FOURTH, so long as you fulfill the FIFTH."

Jade shook, eyes locked on the screen as her thoughts scrambled, panic driving any logic from her mind "Stop. Stop it, don't kill them; I need time to think."

"You have time, several seconds worth."

Jade's mind reeled, grasping for inspiration but receiving only blank panic. "*Gotta save them; can't give her the pockets; gotta save them.*" The vessel on the screen flared red with warning lights, highlighting Connor as he fumbled through a deck of his cards. They were going to die, and she couldn't give the goddess the contents of her pockets. The word tore itself from her mouth in a desperate plead before she even finished making her decision, "Alright! Alright."

The ship righted itself almost instantly, the red lights deactivating moments later as Jade sagged where she stood.

"Wonderful," the goddess replied. "All that's required is that you read the FIFTH PLAN as your predecessor wrote it; alterations can come later after you've had time to ponder."

Jade just numbly nodded her head; the contents of the PLAN barely mattered; an insanity ran through the Redeemer cult, through their god, every member, and even the PLANS. To read one now, to return to the fold in full, was to invite the madness into herself, the madness that had orchestrated the nightmare of Ilin's plague. It also meant she would likely never again escape from this world.

Her hands tightened on her coat, pulling it taut against her back as she fought for control. The fear hadn't, couldn't manifest yet, suppressed by a mind and body gone numb. But the despair had, crushing in its weight and the realization that nothing she ever did would free her from this life, from this world and all its monsters and all its gods, and the endless cycle of hunting for new ones only for her soul to be destroyed and remade, destroyed and remade over and over again.

Jade dully wiped a smudge of black liquid from her cheek. "*Come on, Jade, get over yourself. We don't have time for this. Whatever's happening to you, the world still needs saving. Connor and Ruon still need help. They won't leave without you, and if they don't leave the Redeemers will catch them. Or the Savants. Or Ilin. They'll die if you don't move. Thousands will die if you don't move, so get over yourself and move.*"

She forced herself to look up at the goddess, to stare in the radiant orange eyes. "Show me."

"You already know it. It's still in your head where you locked it away. You just have to let me in, and I'll remind you of everything you've ignored."

Jade obeyed, reaching a hand to tap her earpiece and disengage the locks on her mental implants, opening her to the universal web. Like flame igniting in a dark room, something swelled and bloomed in the aching hollow of her mind. Heat, and a voice, quiet but immense, followed. "Ah, there you are. I won't stay long, dove, I know I'm distracting; I just need to make sure you remember the PLAN, and ensure you can't lock me out ever again."

Something buzzed and snapped in Jade's head, the programming of her mental implants being overwritten, and her access to them being denied.

"Ah, much better. I'll let you go now, off to try and 'save the world' as you'd put it. I do hope you fail of course, but if you don't, have Connor pay me a visit: it's been too long since we've caught up also."

The goddess disappeared from her mind and the idol before her, leaving the room darker and Jade empty. She reached a trembling hand back to her earpiece, speaking in a dull, lifeless voice, "Connor, where are you?"

"Almost there. Are you alright? You sound–"

Turning to the entrance and a taking a trembling step forward, Jade tried to infuse her voice with more energy to only partial success, "I'm fine, just tired. Meet you outside, we got a...," she trailed as she thought of Ilin, and a spark of hate struck within her. "We got a monster to kill."

The nightmare of her life could wait for tomorrow, today she was going to free her brother.

The Second Plan

With the glowing authorization key held in one hand, Jade stepped through the golden portal into the flashing lights of Connor and Ruon's commandeered ship to find herself confronted by the barrel of a pulse-rifle. Her hands shot up. "Don't shoot, I surrender."

"Jesus Christ, Jade," Connor lowered the rifle, "what are you doing walking out of a portal?"

"Got a key." She released the key to swing by its chain from her finger, presenting him with an innocent look. "Don't you have one?"

"No. Should I?"

"Hah, scrub!" She flipped the key up and pocketed it in her coat, sticking out her tongue for good measure. The despair of her choice remained of course, but allowing Connor or Ruon to see it would only distract them in a situation where they could ill afford that.

"Yeah, yeah, yeah." Connor caught one of the support rails, steadying himself as the ship swerved. "How'd you get it though?"

Stumbling, as she was too short and unprepared to grab one of the rails, Jade stepped around Connor. "Mugged a Redeemer. Had to get into the temple without them chasing me. How close are we to the entrance?"

"A minute out maybe."

"Got anyway of getting us out through the lockdown?"

"Yeah, they're going to let us out."

She shot him an askance look. "How'd you manage that?"

"Asked politely. Not everything has to involve fireworks and excitement."

"We clearly live in different worlds then. But seriously, how?"

"Well the alarms went off before we stole the ship, so we appropriated one that could bypass the lockdown." He grinned, waiting for her to ask.

"Connor, who's ship are we in?"

"The director of the academy's."

She slapped his shoulder. "You cheeky devil; bet she flies like a dream. In fact, maybe I could–"

"No." He held up his hand. "No, you cannot fly her. A: we are trying to reach our destination, and B: we're trying to reach it *alive*. What are you glaring at me for? You know I'm right."

She maintained her glare a few moments longer before finally shifting focus to the plane's unnecessarily decadent interior. Bolted to the ground through sumptuous padded carpeting, finely upholstered couches sat arranged around a square table of glass-like metal —the transparent surfaces granting a view of the tiny, flowering flora forever preserved within. Lavish wooden cabinets lined the walls, blanketed in gorgeous carvings, and sealed behind fingerprint scanners, doubtlessly hoarding a feast of delicacies, rare intoxicants, and other diversions. Jade paid these little attention, however, directing her gaze and then steps to the forcibly opened closet of weapons in the back. Glancing through its assorted contents, she found it thoroughly plundered of cards, ammunition, armor, and small arms. "Helped yourselves to the supply, I see."

Connor stepped up beside her, leaning against the door and gazing inside. "We thought it wise, considering we're barreling toward a confrontation with the insane cult of a god, an inter-dimensional monster inhabiting your brother's corpse, and a legion of possessed Purifiers and revenants."

"It's not everything, Connor,"—Jade replied softly, retiring from the closet to sink onto one of the couch armrests—"he's got Prime March too. And if he's got March, he's got the other Primes, their authority and Siphons. Even without infecting them, he's got command of god only knows how many Purifiers." She rubbed her eyes, the small joy and relief at reuniting with the Redheads crumbling under reality. "It's an army." Unbidden, memories of the invasion flashed through her mind, of revenants pouring from the gate, her Core dying, Ilin dying, dozens of other Cores dying. "*I got them all killed.*" The familiar thought swept through her again, progressing inevitably forward. "*I'm going to get them killed again.*" "Connor, we're–"

"We're not going anywhere, Jade. Ruon and I, we helped cause that last invasion, helped get hundreds of people killed, and we weren't even there to help fight them, help stop it. Not this time"

She wrapped her arms and coat tightly about herself, feeling helpless and cold. "*I've killed them.*" Externally, she tried to catch his eyes, try to make him see. "You know I don't blame you for that, for Ilin's death. It's not your fault, you didn't, couldn't have known. There's nothing you have to atone for."

"I know you don't, but I do. And Ruon does, even if he's no longer part of the Redeemers." Connor left unspoken the question he had asked many times before, but he still asked it with his eyes: "What is Ruon a part of now?"

Jade just shook her head in reply. "*Can't tell you, it's not safe.*"

Frustration briefly contorted Connor's features, then he moved past it with a barely audible sigh. "You got Ilin's location? Cause we're probably near leaving the sub-dimension now."

"Yeah." She rose and followed him back across the ship's lounge, passed through a lushly furnished corridor with an abutting lavatory, automated kitchen, and intoxicant chamber to reach the command deck, where Ruon sat in a plush, throne-like chair. Lesser chairs and consoles surrounded him in a flashing, multihued ring of projections and displays, vacant of occupants but with their various functions being performed by the ship's S.I. program. The view through the windshield revealed only a black void.

Jade settled onto the armrest beside Ruon, peering fruitlessly for anything within the void. "I don't see an entrance. You sure we're in the right place?" Although directing her question to Ruon, she glanced at Connor, watching his eyes twitch back and forth as he read Ruon's reply.

"This ship can escape the sub-dimension at any point along its boundary; there's cards fused into its fuselage to permit this. We just have to reach the edge and we can pass through it."

"Okay, when we're out, follow this signal. It's Ilin's ship." She crossed to the navigation console and began inserting the signal. "Brace yourself, we're almost–"

Jade felt space warp, like a dull needle poking thick fabric and distorting it for an instant before piercing. Then color swept outward across the windshield, expanding from the ship's nose as they emerged from the immense, swirling black orb of the Savant Academy's sub-dimension into the storm-battered cleft between two mountain peaks. The ship lurched beneath the abrupt maelstrom, held steady, then swerved onto its new course.

Connor peered over her shoulder, inspecting the projected screen and the destination she had inserted. "Well, that's step one accomplished at least."

Jade settled back in the navigator's seat. "Unfortunately we have a different problem," she trailed off, distracted by the portal beginning to form in the corridor.

It swirled lazily into existence, introducing itself first with a breath of brown mist, followed by slit of black light. Then it yawned wider and Chandris emerged, restored to his original form, immense golden eyes flashing once across the plane in assessment. "Hello, Jade." His voice rumbled as he spoke, warm and immense, filling the confined space.

Jade swiveled to face him fully, leaning forward as one hand slipped beneath her coat to grasp the handle of her Siphon. "Show me the card, Chandris."

Chandris twitched, his features contorting into a rictus of effort before taut words dragged themselves free, "I know not what you're referring to."

"I know the PLAN, Chandris. I've read it. I know the Redeemers branded a card to your chest, subjugating you as a battery, and enslaving you to their commands."

The tension in his form dissipated, and he quietly parted the fur over his chest to reveal a crimson card. It glowed and pulsed, the skin around it torn and disfigured by a web of sickly veins. "It has begun, the siphoning of my essence and the harnessing of my will. I am a font to further the plague besetting your people. This card enforces their will upon me."

Ignoring the apprehension his pronouncement caused, Jade

leaned closer and inspected the card. "You've tried removing it?"

"Every attempt concluded in failure and physical torment."

She bit her lip, thinking. "I might be able to fix this, if we can just get close enough; I recognize the style."

"Who?"

"Saccari Inuma, a powerful Invoker and old acquaintance. He should remove it if I can get close enough to threaten him. How'd you find us?"

He settled beside her, crouching to avoid the ceiling. "I simply rejoined you when I perceived your return to this world, previously you had been absent. Recently you had returned but remained distant. It's only now that I felt your presence clearly. However, my presence here endangers you all. This card renders me a threat. I need to leave."

"Not exactly, Chandris, cards aren't magic spells, they create physical objects and drain the Magister's energy to sustain them. That card in your chest is simply a device, not some form of possession. It will have a failsafe to prevent removal, but otherwise cannot control you directly. Saccari's probably the only one who can control you remotely, and the people who can control you via vocal command will be limited to those who know about the card, and that will be a precious few, people high among the Redeemers. I think you can still be useful, but also, I'd rather you be with us and under some semblance of control than entirely outside our control and knowledge."

His gaze flicked outward, noting their heading. "You do not go to the Purifier Compound."

"No. Ilin won't entrench somewhere we can find him; he's taken a Leviathan class warship and gone to hide in the storms over the Dywernen Straits until his plague infects us all."

"I cannot find him for you, not without access to an active source of his essence: the corpse he wears conceals him."

"We're ahead of you there." She tapped the console and a holographic screen materialized, displaying numbers, cities, and scattered dots with markings—one highlighted a different color.

"What is that?"

"A sensor readout, the numbers indicate electrical density, wind pressure, and storm severity. The little red icons are obviously ships.

The unidentified green dot is Ilin's ship."

"If they're preoccupied with propagating his disease, believing themselves safe, we might have an advantage."

Connor's eyes widened in realization. "It requires his direct intervention to spread?"

"Yes; the disease is not naturally occurring, it is a result of him expending *luce* and as such inorganic and inert until galvanized. Ilin must intentionally infect every individual. I imagine he needed close proximity to infect the first subject, but has otherwise used them as a vessel to propagate it, simply needing to compel physical contact between his host and next victim."

"Meaning he's vulnerable while he spreads his disease and perhaps susceptible to a quick strike?"

"An assassination?" Connor supplied, starting slowly but gradually incrementing. "There'll be guards, but we can distract those while you infiltrate. We just need to give you enough time, and keep Chandris safe until we can fix the card situation."

Jade nodded but raised a finger to forestall him continuing. "It's the start of a plan, but there's something I want to show you first. Follow me." Rising, she squeezed through the rather crowded commanded deck and lead them back to the lounge, pulling the leather sack around to her front as she did so. Arriving at the table, she swung the sack from her shoulder, spilling three black revolvers adorned with beasts across the transparent metal: demons.

Connor and Ruon recoiled. "What are you doing with those?"

"I didn't spend my time on the Road sleeping, Connor. You two need weapons. Yes, Ruon has a Siphon, but that's not enough. You don't even have that and you've not had any rest besides what you found on the Road. These will kill revenants."

Connor inched closer. "But why these?" Illuminated in the ship's pale light, the demons seemed innocuous, just relics, but presentment deep within Connor knew the truth: these *things* seethed with malice.

"Because we need them."

"Won't they destroy us?" he asked, tentatively reaching out hand.

She slapped his fingers back. "Don't touch them. Never touch them with your bare hands. They're weaker here, off the Road, but they can still take over. Gloves will protect you from their influence and reduce their effects."

"Effects?"

"Pain, mostly, but they'll augment your aggression as well."

Chandris moved closer. "What are those creatures? They are not human. Nor are they *souls* or *vestiges*."

"They're monsters, from another world between yours and ours. I strongly suggest you don't touch them; I hate to think what we might end up with."

"They are unpleasant beings."

"Yes." Jade stuffed the demons back into her bag. "Leave them until it's time to go, as little contact as possible." Connor shuddered but nodded. "Now, look at this"—reaching into her coat, she retrieved a cracked and folded piece of yellowing paper—"this is the SECOND PLAN. This is everything the Redeemers are attempting to accomplish through Ilin; you need to read it for yourselves, but the gist is they're going to use the plague to restore Savant supremacy and ensure their power. It will act as leverage on the other corporations, force them to rely on Savants for purifications and other things. The disease can be whatever they need it to, whenever they need it to; so long as they maintain control over Ilin. It's already begun."

Connor took the page. "How do you know?"

"They're using Chandris as a catalyst and generator to expand Ilin's ability."

"How are they controlling Ilin? He doesn't seem the type to play nice."

"They're using a device from the sky-city to control him. Our mission, the entire excursion up there, was for them. They couldn't get there on their own, without the Jysa, so they attacked the Jysa and made sure we learned of it. The sky-cities were the obvious conclusion. After that, they just had to ensure Prime March sent someone they've infected, or infect whoever he chose to send."

"How did they get a device out, or is it still up there while they use it?"

"Somehow, the Redeemers found a Magister capable of painting cards that connect into a shared pocket dimension. The name's in here somewhere, but there's more; the SECOND PLAN calls for restitution."

Connor paled. "On who?"

"Anyone who's not a child, who's not of the Redeemers. Especially the Savant Corporation. I don't know why, but the Second's gotten worse. There's things in the PLAN that I don't remember. Some of it reads like genocide."

"What about the Second? Are we going to confront him?"

"No. We don't have to. This is his one shot, if this fails it goes to the THIRD PLAN."

Connor looked up from scanning the sheet. "Did you record that one as well? The FOURTH and FIFTH PLANS?"

Jade shook her head. "No," she lied. Two other sheets of yellowing paper sat in the second of her three hidden pockets, she could feel them pressed against her back from the inside of her coat, though no one else would have. No one else would have seen them, or the blood and key locks sealing them. She had recorded them against the inevitability of the THIRD and FOURTH PLAN, but revealing them to anyone, even reading them herself, would only provoke them to change to prevent interference; the SECOND PLAN couldn't change anymore, its final stages had already been initiated. That, and there were realities in the THIRD and FOURTH PLANS better left secret.

"Okay." Connor returned his attention to the page. "Ruon and I will start investigating those after today."

"Okay."

The console beeped. "Approximately one hour until arrival. Destination is a military class vessel and corporation flagship, please insert docking codes now to avoid mishap or misunderstanding."

Jade reached over to silence the console. "For now, there are three pillars to the PLAN: Ilin, Saccari, and Chandris. We need to dismantle every part for it to fail."

Chandris settled back onto his haunches, eyes flaring with a flash of amusement. "You intend to 'dismantle' me?"

"Of course not. But they might if the PLAN starts collapsing. I don't know how this works, but the PLAN mentions a third *soul*, one to whom you were promised. It's why you're still alive as opposed to being entirely consumed by Ilin. That protection lasts only so long as the PLAN's proceeding safely; if threatened, they'll devour you entirely. You need to find that other *soul* and discover what it wants. Connor and Ruon, your objective is twofold: you need to keep Saccari too busy to fully activate the card on Chandris and fast track the consumption."

Connor nodded, glancing up from the copy of the PLAN. "The second thing?"

"The PLAN has a failsafe keyed to Saccari, a device he controls that will kill anyone who's infected if Ilin dies or the plague fails."

"Wait, how does executing all the infected help the Redeemers?"

"Think," she replied. "How many of the infected are important figures, how many manage corporations or assist the CEOs? Imagine what would happen if they all died suddenly, and the only people left with any experience were Redeemers?"

"... They could use the resulting chaos to force almost any law change they wanted."

"Yeah."

"How do we prevent Ilin from opening more gates and calling reinforcements?"

Jade made a small gesture of dismissal. "Opening *aperturas* between *Aeria* and this world requires concentration Ilin is likely unwilling to commit, he will avoid dominating Purifiers, and other *vestiges* for that same reason."

"Are revenants coming over of their own accord a concern?" Connor asked.

"Unlikely," Chandris interjected, "unless compelled by desperation or compulsion. *Souls* are their predators, and there will be two present at the site of conflict: myself, however briefly, and Ilin."

Jade resumed, "We'll all have to find our own way in, I hope you can handle that?" Connor and Ruon made affirmative gestures. Chandris said nothing. She glanced at the console. "Okay, we still got some time; get what rest you can and read as much of the PLAN as you can."

The brothers nodded and retired back to the lounge, already scanning the paper she had given them. Jade migrated to the command seat, crawling onto and then sinking into the plush cushions. Chandris watched her, externally impassive, but internally—Jade thought—conflicted with questions and thoughts. She considered broaching them, but honestly, she was tired; her body ached with abuse, her lungs most of all, and her own thoughts operated in a haze of numb exhaustion. She wanted to sleep, even if it was only for an hour. She gave him a minute to ask his question, then lay back in the chair, closing her eyes as the darkness of sleep embraced her readily.

"This PLAN you speak of, it's not normal is it?"

She kept her eyes closed, keeping grip on the calling sleep. "No, it's not." She left it at that, hoping he would as well. He seemed to understand, because she heard him stand and walk from the command deck, leaving her to sink below the surface....

Jade woke with a start, panting and sweating, the dream already fading from her mind, leaving only a sensation of importance and visceral reality. The vessel's console beeped a warning of impending arrival, not that she needed it anymore. Ilin's ship filled the sky before her, a hulking warship awash in lightning and rain, almost half-a-mile long from stem to stern and boasting weapons intended to level city-complexes. Their own ship seemed laughably trivial in comparison.

Jade swung forward, slamming the intercom with greater force than intended in her haste. "Connor, Ruon, we're here. You ready?" As she spoke, Jade scrolled through command screens until she found the autopilot function and activated it, pairing it to Ilin's ship so that it would follow.

She heard a series of muffled steps and a hand fell on her shoulder and squeezed. "We're ready."

"Then go."

The hand squeezed again, then vanished into running steps and the whoosh of the lounge's external door opening. A moment later, she saw Connor and Ruon streaking past on a glowing card.

Still pressing the intercom, she said, "Whenever you're ready, cool cat."

The answer came in the form of thudding treads across the roof of their plane, culminating in Chandris's rain-soaked form crawling down the windshield to the reach the nose. "What the hell are you do–" He bent and leapt, rocking forward and skyward toward Ilin's ship with such force the plane pitched. Yelping, Jade caught and steadied herself on the armrests, raising her eyes again just in time to see him land on the distant warship. *"Oh."*

Jade waited a moment then stood, a dull fizz of energy sparking in her veins. She pushed the exhaustion aside, summoning memories of the monster inhabiting her brother's body; the room full of corpses, the dead seriat, him twisting her brother's head around and around until the skin ruptured and neck broke. Bile rose in her throat, but her energy rose as well, burning hot as she finally let her hate swell. She stretched, bending, twisting, and reaching while her breathing deepened. The hate festered and spread, masking her exhaustion as it burned low but hot.

She cracked her neck with a final motion and closed her eyes, focusing her perception on the Techcron device. With a surge of adrenaline, she realized she could sense Ilin near the vessel's stern. Her heartbeat quickened, compelling her to calm it lest it drive her to rashness. She could also feel hundreds of lesser entities arrayed throughout the ship: the revenants Ilin commanded. Jade reached into her coat to grip her brother's Siphon, its thrumming energy lethargic when it should have been racing, and opened her eyes. Ilin's ship loomed before her, consuming the entire view. She ignored it and focused on the beings within, watching as the majority converged on two separate locations, presumably Chandris and the Redheads.

A sliver of light swept the windshield's peak and expanded as her plane crested Ilin's aircraft, morphing into a vista of the warship's jagged roof. She exhaled, and phased through the floor into the rain-battered skies to alight between two of the ship's ridges. Wreathed in constant electricity and steam, she bounded along the vessel's exterior toward Ilin's presence, protected in the First Step. The lesser beings started winking out, some simply disappearing but others dimming as Chandris's spirit brightened. Only a handful lingered around Ilin now, either an act of reckless hubris or a symptom of his distant attention.

Jade slowed as she reached the space above him, shadowed by the colossal barrels of a gun embankment, and knelt. She extended one hand down, forcing patience, compelling herself to test for First Step defenses. She found none, grinned savagely and dove through, igniting her brother's Siphon.

Boarding Action

The card sung a violent hymn in Connor's fingers, burning hot as he attuned its chorus with his own. The two entwined, building into a haunting, alien melody; something comparable only to the song of the revenants.

It leapt from his hand with a crescendo and imploded on the hull of Ilin's ship, sprawling out into a glut of scaled, fulminating tendrils that writhed and burrowed, rending a cavity. Air exploded out, the altitude just enough to vary internal pressure without requiring oxygen masks. Alarms blared in its wake, audible even from outside: the guards knew they had entered and where. His foot glided forward, sending their levitating card through the opening and, with a duck from him and Ruon, into the ship.

A spartan corridor welcomed them, illuminated by a spine of teal light along the ceiling and flashing red veins on the walls. They dismounted with a leap, Ruon immediately sinking into a defensive crouch, sweeping the corridor with a pulse-rifle, as Connor dispelled the levitating card. Connor likewise swept the corridor with a glance, then strode to an outwardly indistinguishable support strut and plastered a pale card to its polished surface. The card sang and expanded beneath his hand, manifesting into an access port, exposing the wires and miniature consoles of a subsidiary nerve center hidden within the strut. Connor retrieved a clip from a slot inside his armor and planted it on the central console, delivering the virus it contained into the warship's network. The red warning lights died a second later, along with most of the vessel's sensors and defense functions, rendering it functionally blind and incapable of any remote activations.

Connor shredded the card, tapped Ruon's shoulder and then wordlessly sprinted to the nearest corner, the route displayed on their lenses. Discovery was inevitable and they could do nothing about the communication systems separate from the ship's; but the ship was vast, they had everything they needed, and they had a plan.

Racing down another corridor, Connor tapped a number into his bracer and it ejected a blue card depicting mist. The song rose in his mind, low and soporific where the first had been volatile and metallic. The song of his spirit responded, they melded, and the melody woke. Fog poured from his hand, dense and sapphire, muting and blinding. But the route remained displayed on their lenses, a glowing green line superimposed over their vision.

They rounded the next corner, crashing into a trio of creeping figures, one futilely scanning the mist with goggles and the others yelling inaudibly. Ruon ignited his Siphon and slipped through them, two men dropping with a slash of black light. Connor grasped the last one by her unguarded throat and slammed her against the wall, digging the steel-capped fingertips of his gloves into flesh. She screamed soundlessly and thrashed, pummeling his armored body until her strength failed and her pulse stopped. He dropped her corpse and they resumed their sprint.

01001001 01110100 00100000 01110100 01100001 01101100 01101011
01110011 00100000 01110100 01101111 00100000 01101101 01100101
00101110

Crouched in a slim corridor between vacated living quarters, his natural luminescence dimmed so that the shadows might conceal him, Chandris listened. He heard the heartbeats of humans all around him, frantic and excited with fear, mingling amidst those of the *vestiges* that abounded through the vessel. They swarmed to and fro, hunting the Drahma brothers. Hunting Jade, though her they could not find. Yet, even in the midst of that chaos, none approached Chandris; not the humans with their machines to sense and track his arrival, nor the *vestiges* who would have sensed his approach miles out.

Chandris might have thought this strange, but the arrival of a third *soul*, mere moments subsequent his own, had made that answer patently manifest: they had come for him and named him inviolate. Now, that *soul* waited nearby, its tranquil essence thick with both expectation and a summons.

Chandris had considered fleeing to *Aeria,* or from the ship, to elude the confrontation, but these were superficial options, entirely pointless while the card held him enslaved. Thus he had waited, and the *soul* had waited in turn, devoid of malice but with an essence gradually burgeoning with foreboding. In the wake of this alarm, Chandris finally answered.

He knew the route to his kin and took it, loping through the expansive hallways on all fours, scattering *vestiges* with his advent long before either glimpsed the other. Curiosity drove him as much as the need for resolution, a desire to know why he was hunted, and for what purpose created. The *soul* awaiting him had answers, and so Chandris heeded the summons.

The route of empty corridors, eerily bereft of the violence that claimed the rest of the ship brought him to a wide, open door from which danced a ballet of shadows and inconsistent lights. Within, waited a small chamber of transparent walls where fish swam in countless, bioluminescent hues, providing the only illumination in the room. The unfamiliar *soul* stood at the chamber's center, facing away from Chandris.

Chandris entered slowly, footsteps splashing audibly in a thin puddle sprung from a crack in the aquarium's ceiling, but the other *soul* gave no physical reaction. Its spirit had calmed as he approached and now spun serenely. "You have a name now."

"I am Chandris, and yours?"

"I am Itai'ja." The *soul's* essence swirled faster, a swath of tranquility circling a nucleus of tension. "Those who hunt you, Chandris, are soon to arrive. Ask your questions now, before we leave."

Chandris let Itai'ja's closing statement go unchallenged; if time was indeed short, he had no desire to waste his words. "Why am I hunted?"

Itai'ja finally faced him, his human features small and unassuming. "That is a complicated answer, and perhaps futile until you learn to trust us."

"Who is us?"

"Those who fabricated you and desire to use you, as opposed to those who hunt to destroy you."

Now came the important question, the foundation of his existence. "And why was I fabricated?"

"A complicated answer again, but in short, to unmake the *Extranjerras* of *Aeria*."

Chandris fell silent, mind whirling with the preposterousness and the consequences of what the other *soul* intended. Yet, no lie disturbed Itai'ja's essence, leaving but one question Chandris could ask to unravel the sudden convolution of his existence, "Why?"

"Because they are not one being, but a composite of many thousands of souls, fled this world and some ancient war of which they will speak only little; only that their foes came from below the ocean. The problem here is that not all those within them desired this state of being."

"The *Extranjerras* are human?"

"No, their species predates human arrival on this world by several millennia, inhabiting the shallow oceans until their enemies drove them first to the surface, then the skies, and ultimately from the world entirely."

Comprehension dawned almost immediately within Chandris. "The flying cities."

"Yes, as I understand," Itai'ja trailed off, then continued, "They are here." As if summoned, a gateway opened behind him, bathing the chamber in *La Neblina* as three *souls* entered, their essence's a rictus of vengeful malice.

01101001 01110100 00100111 01110011 00100000 01101110 01101111
01110100 00100000 01101100 01101001 01101011 01100101 00100000
01101101 01111001 00100000 01101111 01110100 01101000 01100101
01110010 00100000 01100100 01110010 01100101 01100001 01101101
01110011 00101110

Connor and Ruon crashed through the closed door and tumbled down the stairs of a suspended walkway, clothes riddled with embers. They spilled onto a thin service way encircling a larger space, and Connor twisted awkwardly back toward the door in a throw. The orange card woke in his fingers, its song distant and tenuous from his fatigue but sufficient. Six circular devices spiraled from it, fastening into the wall around the door. They whirred, expanded into raised discs, brightened, and ejected a sheet of orange energy across the entrance, barring it.

Ruon kicked free and scrambled to his feet. They were inside one of the ship's engine cells, a room stretching across thirty feet of dark, reinforced metal with numerous entrances. A glass-like orb levitated near the center, filled with lightning arching silently over a churning mass of what resembled black sand: an energy core.

Connor pulled himself up by the railing and fumbled for another card. "Ruon ... the other doors ... as many as you can." Ruon bounded toward the nearest entrance, intent on shearing paths with his Siphon.

Connor refocused on the energy core and sought the card's song. His mind buzzed from the constant invocations, and his skin perspired with the accompanying feverish heat; but he persisted, summoning the song through gritted teeth. His own music, noticeably duller now, responded lethargically and melded. The music swelled to a crescendo and the card flared, gradually project-ing a minute device from beneath its surface. As the device slipped into his palm, the card faded to gray and cracked with hairline fractures.

Connor hurriedly shredded the card, the pieces sucking into the canister hidden inside his sleeve, then activated the device with a squeeze and tossed it at the energy core. It struck the glass, emitted a pulse and the orb shrunk to the size of a pomegranate. He retrieved it with a loop of magnetized-metal rope from his armor and stowed it in a case attached to his lower back, though he could shift its location at will.

Ruon vaulted from a higher walkway and landed beside Connor, having successfully bored passageways through several of the emergency-sealed doors and walls. They exchanged nods, and Connor ejected a particular card from his wrist cartridge: a blue one depicting several iterations of himself and Ruon. He woke it, the card's innate song almost drowning him as he merged with it. His fever and buzzing mind worsened, but the card animated and poured forth twelve streams of color.

The rivers of color commenced their journey as trickles, but expanded as they spiraled out, gradually sharpening themselves into the silhouettes of men. A moment passed and six identical pairs of Connor and Ruon regarded them, twelve all together. Connor indicated all of Ruon's openings that were either ascending or level. "Go." The simulacras bolted, scattering into pairs. They possessed enough physical mass and heat to confuse the sensors but lacked anything more.

The real Connor and Ruon flipped a maintenance hatch to expose a ladder and dropped inside, pausing only to close the hatch before grasping the frame and beginning a long slide down. An explosion sounded as the Redeemers finally succeeded in penetrating Connor's barrier, but Ruon ignored them, attention riveted on his earpiece until it dinged. He caught himself on the rungs and retrieved his Siphon to begin boring. The Command Deck waited one floor up and several hundred feet North.

```
01010100 01101000 01100101 01111001 00100000 01100110 01100101
01100101 01101100 00100000 01101100 01101001 01101011 01100101
00100000 01100100 01110010 01100101 01100001 01101101 01110011
00101100 00100000 01100010 01110101 01110100 00100000 01001001
00100000 01110010 01100101 01101101 01100101 01101101 01100010
01100101 01110010 00100000 01110100 01101000 01100101 01101101
00100000 01110000 01100101 01110010 01100110 01100101 01100011
01110100 01101100 01111001 00100000 01100100 01100001 01111001
00100000 01101100 01100001 01110100 01100101 01110010 00101110
```

Jade glided through the ceiling, phasing through wires, explosives, and synthetic sky-city metal so dense the Corporatocracy's strongest armaments could only dent it. Her brother's Siphon pulsed in her hand, a bladed spear slightly taller than she was and neon pink.

Ilin's body lay sprawled face-down on the floor, the *soul* inhabiting it in a trance, his mind distant and laboring on the propagation of his disease.

Grief cut through her, old and familiar and bitter with the knowledge that she had caused this: She had redirected their Core to oppose the FIRST PLAN. She had permitted that thing to parade his corpse around like a puppet for years when she could have killed it.

As much as she wanted her brother's body freed, and as much as she hated the monster inside him, she let neither drive her to rashness.

Six revenants prowled around him, almost blinding with forms of empyreal-golden fire, and a human body slumped off beyond her vision. She coiled, raised the spear, and dove into the room, blade extended for Ilin's corpse, with an inhale.

The revenants instantly pulled Ilin aside, flinging him from their midst as they whirled on her in a tumult of slashing claws, battering tails, and snapping jaws. She landed where he had just lain and launched after him, her weight never settling. They followed, striking both her location and trajectory. She twisted, arching her body over one sweeping tail and driving her brother's Siphon down. It struck the ground and she shoved, using it to vault over their heads. Her feet touched the ceiling, knees bending, muscles contracting as she pulled her brother's Siphon from the notch it had melted in the floor. Her upward impetus subsided and she exploded off the ceiling, impaling the revenant nearest to Ilin. The creature exploded into golden brilliance, the Siphon guzzling its essence. She burst through the haze, spinning mid-flight to land crouched on a hand and two feet facing the other revenants, the Siphon-spear held horizontally behind her.

Her muscles contracted again and she lunged, the first step taking her to Ilin's body and the next propelling her over it. A revenant leapt at her, two maws gaping wide and its claws extended. She landed on Ilin's opposite side and spun, lancing the revenant through its leading shoulder and guiding it past as she flowed to the side. It crumpled, the tiny wound expanding voraciously. She whirled, sweeping the spear wide and slashing two other revenants. They recoiled and she continued with her momentum, using it to reset her feet and hurl the spear at the revenant that had charged past her. It skewered the creature's side, destroying it, and she tugged on the thin chain connecting the Siphon to her arm to retrieve it.

The moment it touched her fingers, she spun, grasping it vertically in both hands and slamming it into the serrated tentacle of the revenant charging her rear. The crackling length sheared through the creature's arm and drove it howling back. Jade pursued it, setting her feet and reversing her momentum into a diving slash across the revenant's midsection. It bellowed a musical note and disintegrated into golden light.

She hit the ground and rolled back to her feet, hammering the butt of her brother's Siphon toward the ceiling to collide with the bottom of the fourth revenant's jaw. The creature staggered, mouth slamming shut with a spray of essence. She pressed forward, readjusted her grip, and thrust the Siphon's blade against its solar plexus, piercing it and providing her the leverage she needed to lever it to the side. The immense revenant struck the ground and disintegrated into golden radiance. She stepped through the cloud of its death, spear lowering in one hand while the other delved into her coat. Two gunshots rang and the final revenants slumped mid-charge toward her, their luminescence doused but their bodies remaining.

Jade turned, aiming for Ilin's body, and stopped. Theeran stood before her, twirling a crimson scythe, his skin black with the disease. "Hello, sister." A horrific smile grew on his lips.

The Second Step

Jade stepped back, the gun still held before her. She had used two bullets in a gamble, hoping to destroy Ilin before reinforcements arrived. Even if another three revenants had arrived, she could have destroyed them and still retained a bullet for Ilin. But her mind rebelled against killing Theeran.

She circled and the possessed Theeran mirrored her, standing just feet shy of her gun. "What's wrong, sister? Don't you want to kill me? I'm right here. All you have to do is fire: once, twice, and all of this is resolved. You return a hero, this man's sacrifice necessary and as such forgiven."

She exhaled, phasing into the First Step, and Theeran leapt back, his scythe ceasing its revolutions as his other hand laid a pulse-knife against his own throat. "No you don't, come back over here where we can interact or he dies and I wake up."

She inhaled and slowly returned the gun to its holster on her lower back. Theeran smiled again and removed the knife, scythe resuming its rotations. "What no questions? No demands or threats? Nothing?"

Jade uttered no response and slid into a defensive crouch, her free hand shifting from the gun to the training Siphon she still carried. It activated at her touch, both the sound and brightness muted by her coat. She withdrew her arm, concealing the formless energy in her sleeve before taking her brother's Siphon in both hands. *I have time before they reinforce him. Use it, try to save*

Theeran. I can kill him if I have to."

She rocked back, gathering momentum, and then surged forward, driving the Siphon-spear for Theeran's chest. He retaliated, Siphon-scythe sweeping across his body in a flash of crimson light, forgoing any defense. She recoiled and threw herself aside, sliding beneath his scythe and around him. He followed, scythe whirling up and then crashing down. Jade straightened to a knee and a foot, and slashed the butt of her brother's Siphon upward, diverting Theeran's scythe with a clash and propelling it to imbed in the floor. Crimson and pink flashed, showering them with burning threads of light.

Stepping inside his reach, Jade spun the spear and thrust, driving its butt into his midsection. It struck his Elesstrion armor and rebounded with a flare of power, staggering her. He pursued, ripping his scythe from the ground and into a wide sweep. Unable to avoid it, Jade funneled all her armor's energy into her side a split-second before his scythe hit. Red and white flashed, hurling her across the floor. She hit and rolled with the momentum back to her feet, but Theeran was already upon her, his scythe whirling around him in a crimson flurry. Jade retaliated, her brother's Siphon flashing left and right to parry and redirect his onslaught until he retreated a little too far for a strike. She changed her defensive pattern, sending her spear arching up and across to divert the descending scythe and imbedding it once more into the floor. Jade flowed with her spear's momentum, driving its tip into the floor and catapulting her body into the air. Theeran sidestepped, but her armored boot still slammed into his jaw, sending him a step back and dragging his hand to the very edge of his scythe's handle.

Jade pressed, relinquishing her spear and transferring energy from her armor to her gauntlets before releasing a barrage of punches. The first blow fell on his wrist, breaking it and his grip on the scythe. The second crashed into his chest, spraying white sparks as the golden energy of the training Siphon hidden in her sleeve poured forth. His uninjured arm swept up, batting her arm and the gold Siphon energy aside. She pressed close, grasping his shoulder and driving her knee home. Their armors flared and he shoved her off, stumbling back as his Elesstrion's energy coalesced into the plates of the gauntlet over his uninjured arm.

She set her feet and yanked the spear back into her grasp via the chain. Theeran punched his uninjured fist at her unguarded head. She bent aside and then smoothly leaned backward, the spear swinging up and then down in a chop. The haft slammed his shoulder, driving Theeran to his knees as she vaulted, hurling herself over him with the spear as a lever.

Landing on the other side, she adjusted her grip and stepped in close, swinging the spear like a bat into Theeran's side. It struck him and the power conduits of his armor there exploded, throwing him across the floor. Jade instantly spun back to face Ilin's body, grasped her gun from its holster, aimed and fired on it. But the *soul* had already abandoned Theeran's body and returned to Ilin's and was gliding aside. Her bullet missed and the *soul* slammed into her with inhuman force, his fist hammering the energy plates covering her chest. She flew across the room and crashed into the far wall, her gun flying from her hand.

```
01010011 01101000 01100101 00100000 01110100 01100101 01101100
01101100 01110011 00100000 01101101 01100101 00100000 01110100
01101111 00100000 01100110 01101111 01101100 01101100 01101111
01110111 00100000 01101000 01100101 01110010 00100000 01100100
01101111 01110111 01101110 00101110 00100000 01000101 01101110
01100100 00101110
```

Connor slumped against the corridor rail, reduced to a silhouette in the steadily dying light. Deprived of a power engine, the airship struggled to maintain nonessential components in ancillary sections, rendering its lighting and, more importantly, surveillance array unstable.

Ruon continued around the subsequent turn, reaching a door attended by inert black consoles. He tapped one perfunctorily to confirm its dormancy, then dragged the door open, eliciting a gasp of frozen air from the freezer beyond.

Connor shuffled along the wall, struggling to concentrate through the effort of maintaining so many doppelgängers. Ruon returned to assist him inside, hastily situating him on a vat of live fish before securing the door and manually initiating its lock sequence.

Connor released the doppelgängers and lay on the crates, basking in the cold. Ruon searched the freezer for potential danger, feet cracking on occasional sheets of ice; either several of the containers leaked, or the room needed maintenance.

A thud sounded against the door, preceding a storm of muffled voices. Connor groaned and stood, somewhat rejuvenated by the chill but still exhausted. Ruon returned, nodding inquiringly from him to the roof.

"Yeah, just give me a moment." He scrounged through his packs for his last transportation card, a sibling of those used in the sky-city, then tossed the shrunken energy core to Ruon, who immediately began destabilizing the elements. The electricity within assumed an angry cast, growing increasingly erratic. It continued degrading, sending fractures splitting across the exterior glass as the metal's hue changed to red.

Ruon nodded and Connor flung the card upward with a grunt, activating it mid-flight. It struck the ceiling with a faltering song and expanded into a violet gateway opening onto the command deck a floor above. Ruon hurled the power cell up through it a split-second before it exploded in a tide of electricity.

01010011 01110101 01101001 01110100 01100001 01100010 01101100
01100101 00100000 01110111 01101111 01110010 01101100 01100100
00100000 01100110 01101111 01110101 01101110 01100100 00101110

Chandris perceived their advent before they ever set foot onto the vessel's floor, three *souls* full of intended violence. They stepped forth with a gush of *La Neblina*, their forms initially concealed from him before the brown mist eddied about their feet and revealed them for monsters. The shapes they wore were not natural to them, their essences rung with the conflict between their internal being and their external. Their forms were adapted for violence, plated in natural armor, thick with muscle, and distended with multiple limbs. They had transformed themselves before crossing over, molding themselves for combat to exploit the restrictions of the mortal world.

Itai'ja faced the interlopers, yet spoke to Chandris, "So, will you come with me? All of your questions can be answered in *Aeria* when we are safe."

Chandris crouched low, regarding his enemies and measuring flight against his chances of besting them in conflict. "I do not trust you, Itai'ja, and moreover I do not wish to abandon those I came with."

Itai'ja sighed. "I cannot accept that decision, unfortunately. I had wished to avoid this route, but I am subject to a higher authority than your conscience and the war that comes has scant room for kindness. Catarium."

The card upon Chandris's chest awoke, burning cold, and striking veins of energy through the entirety of his physical form and soul like a foreign skeleton.

"I will ask forgiveness and understanding later, Chandris, for now: consume them."

The rigging within Chandris's form snapped, and he swept forward with a snarl. He didn't even touch them, he simply extended his will and began to feast, the method for it revealed to him as the card upon his chest compelled him to action.

He finished within moments, those vast, ancient lives snuffed and consumed into him as a torrent of memories. He found, as this transpired, that he mourned their erasure, because while their memories endured, their *souls* did not.

Itai'ja did nothing to assist him, there was no need of it, and when Chandris was finished, and engorged on the immensity of his new memories, Itai'ja simply said, "Come," and turned to the still open *apertura*. And Chandris went.

01001000 01100001 01100010 01101001 01110100 01100001 01100010
01101100 01100101 00100000 01110111 01101001 01110100 01101000
00100000 01100001 01110011 01110011 01101001 01110011 01110100
01100001 01101110 01100011 01100101 00101110

Jade shoved off the wall, exhaling instinctively in the split-second it took Ilin to cross the distance separating them and slam his fist through the space her head occupied. She inhaled and swept her legs out, toppling him as she leapt to a stand and dove over his buckling form. She hit the ground in a roll, snatched her gun from where it had fallen and shoved it into a pocket, exhaling in the same moment and readying her brother's Siphon in her other hand.

Ilin's foot slammed through her incorporeal form, denting the metal floor beneath. She launched herself backward, simultaneously inhaling and thrusting the spear at him. Ilin sidestepped her thrust and railed her side with a kick, cracking ribs through the armor and hurling her across the room.

Contorting to land upright in a skidding stop, she drove the spear into the ground and vaulted, just barely evading Ilin's charge. Still rising on her momentum, she twisted, yanked the spear free, spun, and slashed a line in his back, and then landed. He skidded to a halt and spun toward her, his movements sluggish—relatively— and his back livid from her brother's Siphon. The injury, bloodless despite his inhabitation of her brother's body, healed even as she watched.

Jade settled back, her eyes focused solely on Ilin. She saw the twitch of his muscles, the shifting in his weight and the subtle languor of his eyes that switched to killing intent. She lunged aside, spinning and slashing the spear up as Ilin slammed into where she had stood, again warping metal with his impact. His shoulders tensed and she vaulted, back flipping over his sweeping leg to land in front of him again. Her spear slashed down and across, borrowing the residual impetus of her flip to lacerate Ilin from shoulder to hip. Before she even finished the strike, Jade exhaled, entering the First Step so that his fist punched through her. Ducking aside, she inhaled, readjusted her grip, and drove her brother's Siphon through his chest. Heedless of the Siphon guzzling his essence, he rammed his head downward. Unable to dodge or phase over in time, Jade managed to pull her head back on pure instinct, causing his head-butt to ram her chest instead. Her armor flared, mitigating most of the damage, but the sheer impact of his strike still drove her to her knees and caused something—she didn't know what—in her adaptive suit to burst. Gasping, and mentally reeling, she managed to exhale just as his fist again punched through her to crash against the floor.

He flung himself at her, screaming and barraging her ghost with a torrent of punches and kicks. "Come out of there and fight me! Stop hiding!"

Jade just kneeled there, panting while the pain gradually subsided. *"The spear isn't enough; his reservoir is too deep it can't drain him fast enough. I need to use my Siphon."* She crawled to her feet and stood hunched almost double as Ilin finally relented. He withdrew to circle her, his teeth bared in an inhuman snarl. Jade watched him and drew her gun once more. *"Only two left,"* she thought, calculating the bullets she had used.

"Well, if you won't come out, I'll have to incentivize you." Ilin pivoted abruptly and stomped toward Theeran's unconscious form. Jade lurched involuntarily after him, the gun rising futilely in her hand. Ilin stopped, peering over his shoulder with a grin. "Well, come on, you know what you have to do." He lingered for another instant, then resumed his advance.

She couldn't compete with him physically and approaching while occupying the First Step did nothing; he would see and recognize any movement she attempted. *"God, this is gonna hurt,"* she thought. "Hey, Ilin, I'm not going to go anywhere."

He smirked and shifted back toward her, whatever injuries she had dealt him already erased.

Stuffing her gun into an exterior pocket, Jade withdrew an old-fashioned pen and yanked the sleeve of her arm up. A mental thought retracted the armor as well, baring the adaptive suit. She set the pen against it and started to write, though her gaze never left Ilin.

He reached her and smiled down, teeth flashing in anticipation. "Come on out, there won't be another chance."

"All right," she said, dropping the pen and laying her hand alongside the still wet ink. Then she inhaled and swept down, erasing her name from her arm and taking the Second Step.

Confusion flooded Ilin's features and he straightened, staring at his surroundings with a lost expression. His eyes wandered over her unseeing, fastening on the space she inhabited as if recognizing something wrong but unable to grasp it.

Jade dug a shuddering hand into her pocket and grasped her revolver with stiff, frosted fingers. She drew it with an effort, the cold already clawing its way up to her knees and shoulders. She raised it as Ilin turned away, staggering while his mind worked to rearrange his reality and memory with the sudden void of her existence. She didn't exist for him anymore, for him or anyone outside of the Second Step, and never had. This was the Second Step. The First removed you from physicality, the Second from all perception, but neither could overlap.

Jade aimed and fired. The bullet struck his back and he dropped. An unnatural gray pallor expanded across him, flooding outward from the bloodless wound, sapping his skin and clothing of all color and warmth, his spirit extinguished, all *luce* utterly consumed.

Jade knelt to recover the pen, her movements awkward and shaky. She forced her fingers to move, her hand to perform the required motions, and rewrote her name. Warmth engulfed her again and she collapsed, the pen spiraling away from her with a clatter. Pain followed, digging into every muscle as the paralysis manifested. Oblivion closed in, but Jade tore her mind away from it, fastening it on the rise and fall of her chest instead. *"Breathe,"* she thought, *"you have to breathe. In and out. In and out."* Every breath hurt. Every breath felt like she was lifting concrete blocks with her chest. She felt her adaptive suit spark somewhere around her chest, trying to activate the automatic breathing functions, but failing, damaged by Ilin at some point in their fight.

Beneath all of that, however, was relief, a sob and laughter-inducing relief. Ilin's body stared at her from a short distance away and his eyes were finally, blessedly, empty: no pain, no contempt, no sickly-sweet adoration. Just empty. Free.

A Fragment of Divinity

Connor hauled himself through the gateway on a rope, grunting at every pull and bracing himself on the walls with his feet. The narrow gateway impeded most of his view of the command deck, allowing him only glimpses of the lightning flaying it in waves and a hailstorm of glowing fragments.

He attained the entrance and ducked through, huddling behind the meager protection of a console as arcs of electricity snapped against his invoked armor. His earpiece expanded into a visor, dimming the brilliance and filtering out the visual noise to expose the command deck littered with smoking corpses in sparking masks. Saccari stood at the command console, clothing charred and smoking but otherwise unharmed within the sphere of an invoked barrier. Two other Saccaris squinted at him through the haze, yelling and gesticulating to communicate while a fourth lay dead between them.

Ruon clambered up beside Connor and snuck to the console's opposite end. Connor gestured a signal to Ruon and then pressed the buttons on his gauntlet to eject a sapphire card. Its song rose in his mind and he answered in kind, his own refrain stuttering and fatigued.

Power thrummed down his arm, burning cold as the waves on the card's surface flared dully. His vision distorted, defocusing as the strain took hold. The center-most Saccari instantly spun towards them, cards ejecting from his sleeves while the Saccaris to either side separated, one lunging behind the command console and the other becoming insubstantial. Connor surged upright, flinging the card upward as it stretched like a maw and disgorged a tsunami.

The water and the lightning from the destabilizing core clashed with a roar and a thunderous storm of hisses, the former erupting like a pot boiling over, blanketing the room in steam and denying all visibility.

Spitting a litany of profanities, Connor dove aside, his mind ringing with a foreign Invoker's song rising in two different rhythms somewhere opposite him, hidden in the steam. Wind shrieked and sheared past where he had just been standing, cleaving the console and chair into halves and slamming into Connor and Ruon mid-scramble. Their armor blunted most of the impact, but the sheer force of the wind threw them all the same.

They crashed against the back wall together and slid to the floor, splashing in ankle-deep water. Reeling, Connor blindly ejected a red card from his defensive sleeve, invoking its song into a barrier of crimson energy just before a canister round shot from the haze and exploded against it. He sprinted past the barrier in a crouch, his lenses flicking through vision spectrums, futilely trying to penetrate the veil of heat cast by the steam. Then he felt the other Invoker—Saccari's—song swell again.

He halted, only the veil of steam to hide him, and leveled the Road's demon. It woke, lancing icy pain up his arm alongside the writhing head of an eel, and spoke. All fell silent in that moment; man, element, and machine pausing as the demon whispered its silent condemnation. The bullet shot across the room and pierced Saccari's barrier but missed him by an inch.

Saccari recoiled, uncomprehending shock painting his features for an instant before the steam swirled back into place. Connor never saw it though, he'd buckled, clutching his mouth and vomiting brown, oil-like sludge between his fingers, thick with chunks of wriggling filth. The demon's vileness reared within him, viscous and cloying in his veins. He spat more bile and flung another card, its edges flashing silver as it projected a whirling fan of blades that tore across the room, spraying water.

The steam parted with its passing, revealing a dodging Saccari for an instant before re-enveloping him. A clamor of clashing steel roared from the haze a moment later, but Connor ignored it, staggering to the side and scanning desperately for his brother.

Then he heard Saccari's song surge again, powerful and deep, so much so that Connor could feel the invoked card rise and strike down. A ripple swept out across the water, and Connor did the only thing he could think of: jump.

Connor heaved himself higher on the remains of a chair screaming, "Ruon, jump!"

The steam billowed up along the walls and ceiling, revealing Ruon embattled with a desaturated Saccari—as if that Saccari inhabited the First Step. Then ice erupted outward from the invoking Saccari's knelt form, freezing the water solid. It caught Ruon about the ankles as he tried to leap, and the desaturated Saccari about the midsection just as he emerged to strike at Ruon, all his colors flooding back into vibrancy.

In that instant, awash in steam and electricity, they all felt it. It took Connor a moment to comprehend the shift at his core, then realization flooded in: The PLAN had changed. Ilin was dead. Instead of relief, this realization brought alarm: Saccari would use the box.

Knowing Ruon would reach the same conclusion, Connor started forward then lurched to a halt; there were three Saccaris, and any one could hold the device, any one could detonate it and kill the infected. He vacillated for a second, then charged the Invoker and third Saccari, trusting Ruon to handle the Specter Saccari and entering the code for one of his strongest cards.

A light swelled before him, reflecting against the steam in a rosy glow as he skated along the ice. He skidded to a halt and fired the demon at it, incurring a new, searing agony in his arm. He stifled a curse at the pain and stumbled against the remains of a crate lodged in the ice.

The steam cleared slightly, revealing invoker Saccari wreathed in fire and unharmed, though the third Saccari now slumped over the console, his form crumbling to sand.

Connor wrapped an arm around the crate and threw his card as Saccari pivoted toward him. The black card folded in on itself with a hiss of suctioning air, the sides peeling inward in strips until it became a knot of constricting wood and metal. Then the card pulsed. An invisible force seized everything not bolted down, and yanked. Saccari caught hold of a fused chair and dragged himself into it as the steam streamed past.

Connor's grip on the crate broke, pitching him into a grasping slide across the ice. He kicked out, connecting with something he couldn't quite see through the streaming haze, and propelled himself into a table. It lurched but held, fastened by the ice.

Saccari awkwardly invoked another card from behind his chair, manifesting some type of vicious looking avian, but only succeeded in feeding the creature to the black knot. Connor, still nominally connected to the manifested card, propelled the black knot forward. The knot progressed as he commanded, not fast by any means but with incrementing pressure as it acquired mass. Saccari's chair began to shudder, then tore free of its foundation and crashed against the knot, both it and Saccari wrapping around the expanding shell of debris.

Connor snapped the card's song with a mental note and the mass collapsed, crushing what remained of an already crumbling Saccari beneath it. Connor shoved around the table and staggered closer, scanning for the other Saccari but only seeing Ruon skid over. "Did you get the Specter?"

Ruon shook his head. Text scrolled across Connor's lenses, Got away.

"Help me move these, the Invoker was underneath." He attacked the mound, shunting shards of metal, weapons, and pieces of furniture among other odds and ends while Ruon excavated the opposite end, burrowing until they unearthed Saccari's remains. Connor dropped to a knee and desperately scoured the sand in search of the artifact, without results.

Exhausted, Connor slumped against the debris, struggling to stay upright or even think. He felt leaden and cold, trembling from over extending his Invoker abilities and the demon's aftereffects. "We have to find him. A card, I need a card, something to get us through the walls and tie him down. Wait, can we even find him?"

Ruon nodded, pulling out an emerald card of windowed doors. Connor nodded weakly and staggered to his feet, swaying as the room spun and nausea churned his gut. "Okay–" he stumbled to the side, catching himself on the ruins of a console. He breathed deeply, squeezing his eyes shut for an instant of preparation then opened them again. "Okay, give me the card, quick." Ruon passed the card into his shaking hands, and Connor gritted his teeth, marshaling the last dregs of his song. "God, I hope's he's stopped moving."

An array of flickering, staticky, and unstable but brilliantly green portals opened before them, some above on the air, others on the floor or rotating in a slow circle around them. Ruon did not hesitate in diving through the first to cross his view.

```
01100010 01100101 01111001 01101111 01101110 01100100 00100000
01100011 01101111 01101100 01101111 01101110 01101001 01111010
01100101 01100100 00100000 01110011 01110000 01100001 01100011
01100101 00101100 00100000 01101111 01110101 01110100 01110011
01101001 01100100 01100101 00100000 01100100 01101001 01110110
01101001 01101110 01100101 00100000 01110010 01100101 01100001
01100011 01101000 00101110 00100000 01000101 01101110 01100100
00101110
```

Ruon hated violence; it was nauseating, maddening, and fouled whatever it touched. Most of all, he hated it because it only ended with someone getting hurt, and he hated causing pain above all else. That, however, didn't mean he wasn't good at it. It also didn't mean he hadn't learned how to deal with Specters.

He emerged from the portal in a solitary step, his Siphon slashing preemptively in an arc to his left as he raised the demon toward his right. His Siphon hissed, its edge shearing through a stack of crates and the metal wall behind them while its brilliance cast the small storage room into illumination.

Unfortunately, Specter Saccari crouched just outside his immediate reach on the right, interacting with a square, constantly revolving metal device set on a crate. The Specter snatched the device as his chest expanded for the exhale, preparing to enter the First Step.

Ruon fired, making no attempt no aim; hitting Saccari wasn't what mattered, disorienting him did. Like all Savants, Specters needed to concentrate to activate their abilities: concentration they couldn't muster if they were stunned or reeling from an intense sensory assault, like one from a hellish, otherworldly weapon.

Heat flared across Ruon's skull and light blazed through both his visor and closed eyes, filling his vision with strobing colors as the demon spoke with its awful screaming voice.

Saccari, once again about to exhale and enter the First Step, recoiled as if physically struck and toppled backward over a crate, the device still clutched in his hand.

Ruon pressed forward, thrusting the tip of his Siphon into Saccari's left leg where it was bent over the tripping crate. Saccari roared his pain, kicking reflexively and colliding with Ruon's stomach.

Ruon stumbled at the blow, caught himself and then hammered the butt of his Siphon into a stack of crates, upending them into an avalanche of hard edges. In the same instant, he activated his gauntlet and blared a cacophony of sounds at such volume the room reverberated, continuing the chain of disruptions preventing Saccari from transitioning to the First Step.

Despite also reeling from the deafening sound, Ruon barreled through upended crates until he found Saccari gasping and pinned beneath a particularly large one. He pressed the demon's mouth into Saccari's side, and fired. The crates shifted again at the demon's violence, and the sky-city device tumbled from Saccari's crumbling hand to the floor. Ruon fumbled after it, scrambling over an overturned crate, only to freeze as he reached for it.

The device was silent and still amidst the disarray, yet the space around it—the air, the debris, and even the metal floor—fractilized and folded infinitely in on itself. A sensation like vertigo came over Ruon, as if the device held its own gravity and he was caught in its tide. A black stain appeared upon the box and spread, pulling Ruon deeper as the fractals encompassed his vision. It was as if he stood in a tunnel and at the end of the tunnel waited a window, a window that gazed upon a near empty room of impossible size. There was something in that room, a strip of decaying flesh around which the world distorted. He reached closer, absently aware that he was sinking, that the metal floor had become permeable. He recognized the impossibility of it, the fraying of reality, and in that unreality he recognized the presence of the divine. *"What the hell did they find up there?"* Ruon retreated with an effort, compelling his thoughts to turn from the box to the Names He Could Not Speak. The Names filled his mind, and in the vast distance he felt their owners stir in their slumber, but in their unsettlement they disturbed the device's claim upon him.

His breath, held for the long minutes of Enlightenment, exploded from him in a gasp, and then desperately into a sucking inhale. Ruon tore off and flung his coat over the device, severing the visual link and, through that, causing its effect to subside. Even so, he could still see the subtle writhing of his coat fibers, and feel how its texture and shape changed when he moved to wrap it. Only when he was certain it was bound tight, did he rise and carry it back through the portal.

He stumbled back into the control room and immediately slipped on the ice. Connor closed the portal with a slash of his hand, ending his song, and rushed toward him, desperation and concern plain in his features. Ruon rolled over, flinging the demon—forgotten in the Enlightenment's thrall—from his grip, and vomited its filth from his body.

He felt Connor's hand on his shoulders, firm and frantic, paired with the only question that really mattered in that moment. "Did you get it?"

Ruon nodded, wiping his lips with one hand as he hefted the device with his other. Connor moved to take it, evidently intent on destroying it, but Ruon stopped him, shaking his head. Don't. Dangerous.

"Why? What's wrong?"

Run carefully set it upon the floor. It's divine.

Connor stared then sank back, rubbing his face. "God, what do we do with it?"

Ruon rubbed his face and scrambled for a solution. Even if they could conceivably destroy the device, a massive if, the fallout would likely alter reality in some way. Nor could they take it with them; they had no place to conceal it, let alone any means of controlling it or any understanding of its effects upon reality. Nor could they trust anyone to hold it either. That left only one option, and a bad option at that. He opened his eyes. The ocean. We sink it. The Dywernen Strait runs above the Drowning Deeps.

Connor slowly, reluctantly nodded. "All right." Then after a brief pause. "You all right?"

Ruon replied with a raised thumb.

Connor exhaled exhausted relief. "Okay, we'll deal with the device later. For now, let's find Jade and get out of here." Rising together, they stumbled off, following an invoked tendril that connected them to Jade.

01010100 01101000 01100101 00100000 01100111 01101001 01110010
01101100 00100000 01101001 01110011 00100000 01110100 01101111
01101111 00100000 01110100 01101001 01101101 01101001 01100100
00101110 00100000 01000001 01110000 01110000 01101100 01111001
00100000 01101110 01100101 01100011 01100101 01110011 01110011
01100001 01110010 01111001 00100000 01100110 01101111 01110010
01100011 01100101 00101110 00100000 01000101 01101110 01100100
00101110

Time inched past in agony for Jade, the world around her dark and suffocating. She could scarcely think, could barely feel the ground beneath her, couldn't feel anything besides pain. She wanted nothing more than to sleep, but her stuttering lungs made a promise of what that would result in. Thus, the seconds trudged by, feeling like hours until her grasp of time capitulated and she knew not how long she had lain there.

Finally, a voice called her name as if from a great distance, "Jade!" Moments later, gentle hands grasped and turned her over, then lifted her head. The darkness clouding her vision receded sharply, revealing Connor and Ruon kneeling over her.

She tried to speak, but her lips refused to move and her thoughts fragmented. The pain thickened, gouging deeper as he moved her. His voice came again, long after his lips formed the words, "Are you all right?" He frowned, gaze concentrating as she failed to respond. His hands grabbed her shoulders. "Jade, what's wrong? Why aren't you saying something? Jade!" He pulled at her collar, exposing the adaptive suit's vitals monitor and sending tides of pain through her as the movement jostled her.

"S ... *stop, it ... it hurts.*" She couldn't ... she couldn't think straight; it was all a blur and shadows still corrupted her vision. Everything hurt. She couldn't breathe! Panic spiked her mind to higher wakefulness, flaring her eyes wider, but her vision was darkening again and her lungs refused to work. She felt his fingers press against her throat, then saw his head lowering toward her face.

"She's not breathing, and her suit's fried!"

She faded further, panic subsiding to haphazard thoughts and memories of her brother. Why had he liked the color pink? She couldn't remember anymore, just him saying that it was funny.

She could still feel Connor touching her, turning her arms, but most of her sensations were gone now, even the cold, leaving only the weight. It was a comforting weight though, and she felt kind of warm. It was almost nice.

Something hard pressed against her face and conformed to it, covering her mouth and nose. She couldn't distinguish what it was at first, then air forced itself into her, and it felt like needles of fire stabbing her lungs.

Her tenuous grip on consciousness snapped and she fell into a dream of the first time Ilin took her to a sweet shop.

Bitter-Sweets

Jade half-woke to the embracing comfort of warm blankets and a vaguely sweet scent reminiscent of flowers. She heard the bustle of people and things in the distance, dampened by walls and a gentle, soporific orchestra music.

She knew, without having to turn over or open her eyes, that Marsilias would be sitting there right beside her bed, flipping through his latest cheesy web-comic with an array of bountiful desserts and pastries laid out beside him just waiting for her to wake. All that remained was to decide whether to eat them now or return to the enticing warmth of sleep.

"Marsilias ..."

"Hmm?"

"Wake me in another hour."

"Will do."

Smiling, she snuggled deeper into her fortress of blankets....

The scent of something tangy wafted through her thoughts, rousing her with all the promise a sugared delicacy could provide. She cracked her eyes open, peeking out from under her blankets to observe the blackberry strudel Marsilias waved back and forth. Venturing a hand out, she accepted his tribute and sat up, shirking the blankets to pool about her waist. To her great contentment, Jade found the room warm, almost hot. Purring, she dug into her strudel. "Hello, Silias, how long was I out?"

"Three days," he said, returning to a plush seat on the other side of her bed where Cuddles waited in excitement, running in circles and chirruping. Marsilias obligingly grabbed the seriat and transferred him to Jade's bed, where he promptly crawled into her lap and snuggled against her stomach.

She smiled and stroked his belly. "Where are we? Or is it a top secret, you'd-have-to-kill-me-if-you-told-me, facility?"

"Oh yes, very clandestine, and full of sordid history."

"Wonderful, tell me more. Oh,"—he offered her a glass of milk —"lovely, thank you."

"We're in a private Purifier medical station; Prime March insisted you receive the best treatment when he came to."

"How is Prime March? I hope I didn't inflict any permanent damage?"

"He's fine. Connor and Ruon likewise. The Redheads have your Siphons stored away somewhere for safekeeping."

"And Chandris."

"He's disappeared, along with the records of everything that happened on that ship. We have no idea where he is. We hope he's just hiding from the Purifiers."

Depositing the half-finished strudel at the foot of her bed— where she could watch it and ensure no one absconded with it—Jade extended her free hand to Marsilias and he delivered the next dessert. "That's good to hear. Is everything with the 'Ilin' soul cleared up? No residual effects or final revenge schemes?"

"It is all resolved; though, they're keeping it on the down-low from the public. Only the highest officials know the full story."

"So only the important people know I'm a hero? Perfect." She hummed, stripping off the outer layer of the onion-like candy ball Marsilias had given her. She popped the bright vermillion strip into her mouth and uttered a muffled squeal of pleasure. "Ooh, this is good."

"I thought you might like it." He smiled and lapsed into silence, watching her for a while. His smile gradually faded as she continued to partake of his delicious bounty without resurrecting the conversation. Finally, he began, "Jade ..."

She slowed, hand dropping into her lap, the candied ball and her lips a conflux of shockingly vibrant colors. "I know, Silias, ... how much damage did I do?"

"Your body's reservoir of calories and protein managed to mitigate most of the harm caused by your recent use of the First Step, but ..."

"How much, Silias?"

"Using the Second Step added two more years to your recovery."

Her hands spasmed slightly and she closed them into fists. "So, we're right back where we started."

"Not quite, I assume you're a lot wiser now, more mature also, and maybe a little prettier."

"Do you think I should have done it differently?"

"I wish you could have found a different way, but I know you wouldn't have done this frivolously." He stood and kissed her brow. "Well, that's enough of that. I've got somewhere to be and there's a couple people who want to check in on you, if you have the strength."

Before he even finished speaking, the door opened and Ruon bounded in to the other side of her bed, Connor close behind. "How're you doing, Jade? Marsilias says you'll make a full recovery given time."

She squeezed Ruon with a one-armed hug. "I'm peachy, Connor, what about you? Any promotions I need to take credit for?"

He scowled. "How did you know?"

"Easy, I'm amazing." She grinned and relinquished Ruon. "So what have you two been up to? Besides getting promoted."

Taking a moment to relocate her strudel with exaggerated caution, Connor situated himself on the foot of her bed. "Nothing much, we've just been hanging around here recovering mostly while Marsilias runs things."

"Marsilias is in charge?"

"Yep, almost every prominent official is in quarantine for safety —until they're sure the threat's subsided. Marsilias just marched in here three days ago and took charge."

"Of course he would." She smiled. "Are the demons safe?"

"Yes, hidden from everybody in Ruon's workshop, along with your Siphons."

"Good, I'll return them to the Road when I've recovered, leave them there until then."

They continued thus for a while, with Jade inquiring about

various noteworthy individuals or occurrences before transitioning to the latest gossip and wringing whatever juicy details she could out of Connor. Throughout that, she slowly sank further into her blankets, inching toward a happy doze.

A knock sounded, stirring her from her languid descent. The door opened a second later and Marsilias entered, Prime and Primess March behind him. Fear slithered through Jade, but she waved all the same. "Hello, Sovereigns March. What brings you to my humble lair today?"

"Hello, Jade, we brought you these." Prime March glanced at the mountain of sweets patiently waiting their turn to be consumed, then gingerly set a small, colorful bag of candies at her feet. Looking grim, Serras stayed by the entrance, leaning against the doorframe with her arms folded and her eyes staring knives into Theeran's back. "Umm, thank you for saving me," Theeran continued, looking down. "I ... I saw the fight, kind of. I was in there, I know I was. I can see some parts so clearly, but others are ... faded, or just gone entirely. Regardless, I know it would have been easier to just-"

"Oh shush, just bring me your sacrifice."

Picking the pouch back up, he deposited it in her waiting hand before retreating while she inspected the contents. Jade nodded and selected a choice morsel of the gummies within. "These'll do." She tossed it into her mouth. "Now, if that's all...?"

"There is one more thing.... Our scans have revealed Techcron modification to your body-"

"You can't copy them if that's what you're hoping."

"So you were aware of them?"

"Yes. I needed to be able to recognize *souls* and-"

"And the Purifier Corporation is incapable of that; we're blind to them even when they're in our presence, or when they cross over. The *soul* known as Indemiun coexisted with us in the body of a dead woman for two years without arousing suspicion, and we were present at his initial advent. There's no way to know how many other *souls* exist in our world, whether benign or predatory in nature."

"Except for me."

"Except for you. The Sovereigns don't trust the other *souls* potentially wandering about. We need to be able to find them, to discern their motives and, if need be, eliminate them."

"Anybody could kill a *soul* if they turn violent, just dispatch a couple Cores."

"I saw your fight with Ilin, Jade; your brother's Siphon inflicted substantial but impermanent damage, nothing even close to yours. Yes, we could fight and kill *souls*, but they would kill us in turn, and more people while we waste months or years searching for them. Those are lives you can save, so I'm asking on behalf of the Purifiers and the people, please return to our employment." He bowed his head and then began to depart, forgoing both a farewell and an answer.

"The answer's no, Theeran; I can't help you."

He paused, a strain of tension rising in his shoulders. "And why not?"

"Because I don't feel like it, because I'm exhausted, because I have other plans, or because I simply can't; choose whichever excuse you like better."

"Jade, it would be better–" Theeran flinched, cutting off as Serras snarled from the doorway.

"Stop lying, hedging or whatever the hell this is, Theeran. Jade, you don't have a choice. You defied the corporation's mandate to not interfere."

"All the more reason for me to decline then."

Theeran slumped. "They're filing for indentured service, Jade. If you resist, you'll be chemically paralyzed and imprisoned. The Law Corporation's going to approve it, everyone's going to approve it; even if the Purifiers hadn't just saved all of them, we told them about your Techcron device and the *souls*. They agreed: we need you." He straightened, his face an emotionless mask, and nodded in farewell. "I'll say you agreed willingly; it will allow you some room for negotiation. I have also informed them you will need several weeks of recovery. When those are done, you will be assigned a special task force in my division." He left then, stiffed backed, and Serras watched him all the way before finally returning her attention to Jade.

"I'm so sorry, love, I tried. I'll keep trying, but ... they don't care." She turned and walked away.

Marsilias spoke the moment the door closed, "You don't have to do this, Jade, whatever they say. You've already saved them twice. If that's really not enough, I can help you disappear, I have contacts, people I actually trust."

"Yeah, but they think they need me, Silias," she whispered. "They'll hunt me down." Cuddles scaled up her shirt, his questing nose bumping against her jaw.

Connor leaned forward, his voice taught, "You can't, you're not even fully recovered from the last time you worked with them."

"That's why I'm sending Marsilias to negotiate for me; tell them I won't consider working with them for anything less than six days a week off!" She manufactured a confident smile and beamed at him.

Marsilias sighed and moved toward the door. "All right, I'll see if I can pull some strings."

"You're a dear, Silias, thank you." She turned to Connor and Ruon and scooted back into her fortress of blankets, hauling Cuddles down with her. "Now, if you two'll excuse me, I'm ready for my beauty sleep...."

"Okay, okay, we're going. Sweet dreams."

She pulled the covers over her head, and squeezed her eyes closed as Cuddles curled up against her and whined softly. She stroked his fur, wrapping herself tight around him. *"I don't want this."* Tears welled. *"The monsters, the violence, the gods. I just want to be safe, to not hurt all the time."*

Despair found her then, enveloping and suffocating, dragging her down until the only thing she felt was alone, and the only thing she knew was that she would never be free, and that she would never be safe.

Something else kindled inside her then, something small but hot: anger.

01010100 01101000 01100101 00100000 01110110 01101111 01101001
01100011 01100101 01110011 00100000 01101001 01101110 00100000
01110100 01101000 01100101 00100000 01000100 01110010 01101111
01110111 01101110 01101001 01101110 01100111 00100000 01000100
01100101 01100101 01110000 00100000 01110011 01101001 01101110
01100111 00100000 01101100 01101111 01110101 01100100 01100101
01110010 00101110 00100000 01010100 01101000 01100101 01111001
01100000 01100001 01110010 01100101 00100000 01110111 01100001
101011 01101001 01101110 01100111 00101110

Navigate your way to KOZINSKIBOOKS.COM and contact us if you are unable to decipher the binary codes throughout this book.

Thank you for reading *STORMFLOWER*. We hope you enjoyed it. If you want, contact us with your favorite parts.

Keegan and Tristen decided to become writers after a home-school writing assignment. That assignment eventually became their first book: *THE DARKNESS THAT SLEPT*. They started it at the age of thirteen—it took years to finish. They live in northern Alabama and work a real job to pay the bills. When they're not working or writing or drawing, they enjoy live theater, boardgames, online gaming, listening to soundtracks, walking to discuss ideas, and reading. Keegan has done all the cover art for their books.